ABOUT SVEN HASSEL

Born in 1917 in Fredensborg, Denmark, Sven Hassel joined the merchant navy at the age of fourteen. He did his compulsory year's military service in the Danish forces in 1936 and then, facing unemployment, joined the German army. He served throughout World War II on all fronts except North Africa. His fourteen World War II books, which draw on his own encounters and experiences as a soldier, have sold over 53 million copies worldwide and have been published in more than 50 countries. He peacefully passed away in Barcelona in 2012, where he had resided since 1964.

T0054260

BY SVEN HASSEL

SVEN HASSEL

THE BLOODY ROAD TO DEATH

Translated from the Danish by Tim Bowie

WEIDENFELD & NICOLSON

A W&N PAPERBACK

First published in Great Britain in 1977
by Corgi Books
This paperback edition published in 2014
by Weidenfeld & Nicolson,
an imprint of the Orion Publishing Group Ltd,
Carmelite House, 50 Victoria Embankment,
London EC4Y 0DZ

An Hachette UK company

3 5 7 9 10 8 6 4 2

British Library Cataloguing-in-Publication Data.
A catalogue record for this book
is available from the British Library.

ISBN 978-1-780-22810-5

Printed and bound in Great Britain by Clays Ltd, St Ives plc

www.orionbooks.co.uk

'Because of the magnitude of our losses at Stalingrad and the catastrophic shortage of reserve troops, our Führer has decreed that the period of pregnancy shall with immediate effect be reduced from nine to six months.'

Obergefreiter Joseph Porta speaking to Obergefreiter Wolfgang Creutzfeldt, Salonica, spring 1943.

Dedicated to my battalion commander and friend, now a General in the West German Armoured Corps, Horst Scheibert.

CONTENTS

CONTENTS

If I am not very careful, that damned man Himmler will soon have all my friends inside his concentration camps.

Göring to Generalfeldmarschall Milch,
22nd September, 1943.

Singing at the top of his voice Torpedomaat Claus Pohl leaves the brothel 'The Sign of the Shaking Bed' in Pyrgos. In the distance can be heard the noise of a free-for-all between a group of German sailors and some Italian Alpine troops.

Claus Pohl grins happily and decides to take a hand, but changes his mind quickly as his eye falls on a pretty girl whom he has noticed earlier that evening.

'Hey, Liebling!' he shouts, his voice echoing in the night quiet of the street. 'Wait for the Navy! It's dangerous to drop out of convoy!' He puts his fingers to his mouth and lets out a piercing whistle, putting the local cats to flight.

The girl looks back and smiles provocatively.

Claus increases his pace. He has been disappointed at the brothel. There were more customers than the ladies could cope with. He whistles again, and is so engrossed in the girl, that he does not notice the figures of men who have emerged from a side-street and are following him.

The girl turns down a little alley. When he reaches it she seems to have vanished into thin air.

Four men make a ring around him.

'What the hell!' he shouts, snatching for his P-38.

A noose, thrown expertly from behind, loops tightly around his throat. He chokes and falls to his knees, his arms thrashing wildly. His round sailor's hat rolls down the street like a runaway wheel.

A boot sinks into his crotch, a pistol butt crashes down on the back of his neck.

Next day Torpedomaat Claus Pohl is found by some Greek civilians, who alert the police. His naked body is lying in the gutter, only a few yards from German HQ. Identification is very difficult, and the identity of the corpse is first revealed when his flotilla reports Claus Pohl missing.

The case is treated as an unimportant routine investigation. Naked corpses of German soldiers are turning up in Greek gutters every day.

Two hours later three Greek prisoners are hanged publicly as a reprisal.

THE CACTUS FOREST

THE section stands looking at the corpses, which have bloated grotesquely in the hot sun. The body of a Leutnant sprawls across the stonework of the well. His tongue has been torn out and his mouth is one great clot of blood.

'Must've hurt like hell, that,' nods Porta, pointing at the dead officer. 'Been a quiet chap – if he'd lived through it,' says Buffalo, passing his tongue over his sun-cracked lips.

'Over in the bleedin' orchard, they've tied some on 'em to a coupla pulled-down trees an' let the trees go. *Rippin*' idea ain't it?' says Tiny, slapping at the flies with the sleeve of a Greek uniform.

'I'll cut their fucking joy-sticks off,' promises Skull and draws a parachute knife from his boot-top.

'And you a bloody NCO,' jeers Porta. 'Trouble with you is you haven't seen enough dead uns yet.'

'The bleedin' partisans've got to be let 'ave their bit o' fun,' considers Tiny. 'Us bleedin' Germans could've stayed at 'ome, couldn' we?'

Porta prizes the dead Stabszahlmeister's rigid jaws apart. His forceps glitter in the sun and Porta is two gold teeth richer.

Tiny acquires a full cigar-case. With a heavily put-on city director air he lights a fat Brazilian cigar, and moves into the shade cast by an overturned Kübel,[1] first pushing the bloody corpse of the driver to one side.

'Even the dead have a use during a war,' says Porta. 'They take up the attention of the flies and keep 'em away from us who're still alive.'

'So *many* flies,' says Gregor wonderingly, as a heavy swarm rises buzzing from the body of the dead driver.

Porta opens a tin of tuna and shovels the contents into his

1. Kübel: Heavy-duty, rough country troop transporter.

11

mouth with a bayonet. 'Tuna is *good* for you!' It says on the outside of the tin.

Behind the long building we find ten *Blitzmädel*[2]. They are dead, and laid out neatly in a row. They have not been dead for more than one or two days. The smell isn't very bad yet, and the birds have only pecked out the eyes of two of them.

'They've 'ad some fun with 'em first,' says Tiny lecherously, lifting up a blue-grey military skirt. 'This tart 'as lost 'er frillies!'

'Shut it, pig!' the Old Man rages at him. 'Haven't you any pity at all for these poor bitches?'

'Jesus wept, *I* don't *know* any of 'em,' protests Tiny. 'Want me to cry me rotten eyeballs out for every dead 'ore I runs across when there's a bleedin' war on? *Do* you?'

'If *I'd* been with them partisan boys,' laughs Buffalo, his whole fat body wobbling, 'I'd've took the arse with me an' fixed up some real *Kraft durch Freude*[3] a couple of times a day. Sex is healthy, they say in the States.'

A shrill scream makes us jump and grab for our weapons. Down the hill a woman comes racing, stumbling, followed by a fat little man waving an axe above his head.

The Legionnaire's Moorish knife flashes like lightning through the air and sinks into the man's chest. He continues running for a few strides then falls like a log.

To our amazement the woman throws herself sobbing across his body, and screams Bulgarian oaths at the Legionnaire.

'She says you're a goddam murderer,' explains Buffalo, who understands a little Bulgarian. 'They were just havin' their daily bit of fuss, and the axe was part of it.'

'Holy Allah!' groans the Legionnaire wiping his Moorish knife on his sleeve. 'Who in the world could have guessed it?'

A chattering Krupp-Diesel rumbles into the sun-baked village. A party of excited '500's'[4] jump down from it.

'They've slaughtered the whole bloody battalion. We're all that's left,' shouts a feldwebel, sweating with dirt all over his face.

2. *Blitzmädel:* Telephone girls.
3. *Kraft durch Freude:* Nazi holiday organization.
4. *500's:* Penal troops.

12

'Who has?' asks the Old Man expressionlessly.

'These bloody heathens,' the feldwebel screams, raging. 'Our battalion got here from Heuberg only a few days ago, and in the very first engagement we fell into an ambush. I dropped behind with my section and got away.'

'You ran for it, in other words,' grins Porta, sarcastically. 'Our Adolf wouldn't like that. *If* he was to hear of it, that is.'

'Can we join you lot?' asks the feldwebel, ignoring the jibe.

'Have you got weapons?' asks the Old Man, brusquely.

'Only carbines with twenty rounds a man,' answers the feldwebel. 'The Prussians aren't too generous with 500's.'

'Juice in it?' asks the Old Man, nodding his head at the Diesel.

'No, it'll only go downhill.'

'Then we're all right,' laughs Porta happily. 'The Greater German *Wehrmacht* is used to things movin' in *that* direction.'

'Stay if you like,' shrugs the Old Man, 'but remember *I'm* in charge!'

'Shall we turn in our pay-books?' asks a young 500, offering his.

'Wipe your bleedin' arse on it, son,' suggests Tiny, assuming a lofty air.

'We're hung up by the balls,' the Old Man tells the feldwebel. 'Our battlewagon's a burnt-out wreck, so it's foot-slogging for us, and a walk over the mountains.'

'Know 'em?' asks the feldwebel, with a sour smile.

'No!' the Old Man is laconic.

'They say it's the arsehole of the universe up there, and two days is a long lifetime,' says the feldwebel, looking worriedly at the black mass of the mountains. 'Snakes, scorpions, giant ants and God knows what else. Cactus with enough poison in 'em to stock a chemist's bloody shop!'

'Got a better idea?' asks the Old Man, biting off a chunk of chewing tobacco.

'No, I'm workin' for you now!'

'All your lot got battle experience?'

'Only a few,' the feldwebel laughs tiredly. 'The rest of 'em are swindlers an' thieves. There's a cunt-stealer among 'em, even!'

The Old Man sighs and sends a brown stream of tobacco juice at the well. He shrugs his Mpi[5] to a more comfortable position on his shoulder.

'Tell your coolies, we're on drumhead!'

'Drumhead court-martial, eh?' the feldwebel rolls it round his tongue.

'No misunderstandings?' asks the Old Man, sneeringly.

'You wouldn't think it,' laughs the feldwebel, wickedly.

'Glad we understand one another.'

'What about a couple of Mpi's or an LMG[6]?' asks the feldwebel, offering a packet of Junos[7].

'Think you're in a damned arsenal?' growls the Old Man, turning on his heel and kicking at a helmet which flies through the air and drops on a corpse. 'You drop your equipment anywhere,' he scolds. 'No *discipline* any more! How the hell can an army fight a war with its bloody equipment spread all over the map of sodding Europe?'

'God, but you're in a bad mood today,' remarks Porta, opening his third tin of tuna.

The Old Man does not answer, but swings his Mpi over his shoulder, lights his old silver-lidded pipe and wheels over to the ammunition-trailer where the feldwebel has seated himself, together with some of his unit.

'What's your name?' asks the Old Man, grumpily.

'Schmidt,' a short pause, and, 'line regiment,' he adds.

The Old Man takes his pipe slowly out of his mouth, and spurts a tobacco-darkened stream of spittle to one side.

'What's that mean?'

'I thought you'd be interested.'

'I don't give a sod if you're a feldmarschall!'

The Old Man stalks over and sits down with the rest of us, demanding his share of Porta's tin of tuna.

'Hell I'm *tired*,' groans Gregor despairingly, wiping his sleeve across his dust-masked face. 'Here we go, the flower of Germany, lettin' the *untermensch* piss all over us. My general

5. Mpi: Maschinen-pistole (German): Submachine-gun.
6. LMG: Leichtes Maschinengewehr (German): Light machine-gun.
7. Junos: A popular cigarette.

and me, we wouldn't ever have let that come about. If we'd had him an' our monocle with us the missing links'd really have had something to worry about!'

'If things go on as they are Greater Goddam Germany's gonna get wiped off the map,' says Buffalo, darkly, 'an' us Germans 're gonna drop back into bein' *the* background characters in Grimm's Fairy Tales.'

'We'll be the wicked ogres they frighten the nippers with after dark,' nods Porta.

'Pissy bleedin' outlook, ain't it?' sighs Tiny despondently, packing banderoles of cartridges glumly into the ammunition boxes.

From the mountains to the north artillery fire is audible.

'The neighbours are a'knockin',' sings Porta, turning a body over on its back to look for gold fillings.

'You take the heavy mortar,' roars Barcelona to one of the 500's. Barcelona is a feldwebel but doesn't get much of a chance to pull rank when he's with us.

'What about the blackbird there?' asks Heine, pointing with his Mpi at the padre who is sitting drawing circles in the dust of the road.

'He can go when we go, or he can stay where he is,' says the Old Man indifferently.

'Chase the black bastard out of it,' suggests Tango, a Rumanian-born German, who has been a teacher of dancing in Bucharest. Whenever he gets a break he dances tango steps to an internal orchestra of his own.

'Let's liquidate the bleeder,' shouts Tiny. 'The 'eavenly bleedin' reps down 'ere on earth always bring bad luck!'

'Yeah, let's turn him off. I never see a blackbird get a ticket for the one-way trip,' chuckles Buffalo, his rolls of fat wobbling in wicked glee.

'*I'll* tell *you* when I want anybody liquidated,' the Old Man decides, coldly.

'I'm going to keep an eye on him anyway. Soul and body don't always keep in step,' says Tango, circling in a few dance steps. 'The 44th sorted out a sky-pilot once who had no more connection with the heavenly host than the devil himself has!'

Everybody stares at the padre.

'Let me open the bleeder's throttle for 'im!' says Tiny, touching the edge of his combat knife.

A squadron of He 111's roars over us. One of them circles and returns.

'That's all we need, for them to take us for some of the heathen,' says the Old Man, looking nervously up at the fighters.

'Jesus, they're droppin' their shit!' howls Buffalo, dashing between the houses.

'Shrink!' warns the Old Man, creeping into shelter behind the coping of the well.

I follow Porta down into the well itself. The water is icy. I almost drown before he gets hold of me. We hang on to the bucket.

There is a crashing and rumbling above our heads. Machine-guns chatter. The whole squadron is attacking us. It seems like the end of the world.

The planes do not leave until the entire village is gone.

Strangely, not one of us is even wounded. Air attacks are nerve-racking but not really effective. Imprecise.

'Long as you're not where the bombs drop, there's no worry,' grins Porta, sitting down on the sand in the very same place he sat before the attack started.

'What about stopping here?' suggests feldwebel Schmidt. 'The Division'll pick us up.'

'Will the Division fuck?' cries Porta scoffingly.

'*Merde alors!* They have more than enough to do,' sighs the Legionnaire. 'What is a section to them?'

'We ain't worth as much as a lump o' dried cat-shit,' states Tiny, throwing a stone at a cat which is sitting, washing itself, on the corpse of a German soldier.

'Jesus!' shouts Porta angrily. 'Even the cats down here round the Black Sea have lost all respect for the German Army! Where's it all going to end?'

'In Kolyma!' grins Gregor, hitting the cat squarely with a well-aimed steel helmet.

'That bleedin' cat's a bleedin' Yid cat,' considers Tiny. 'It *might* even 've been thinkin' of 'avin' a shit on that poor German body.'

'What we have to go through,' sniffs Heide, angrily.

'The army's finished,' says Tiny, lighting a cigar. 'Even the Göring fly-boys shit on us!'

'Grab it an' get moving,' orders the Old Man, rising to his feet.

'The human body was not created to march with,' protests Porta, working his stiff muscles and shouting at the pain.

The mountains are depressing. Each time we reach the top of what we think is the last rise, we find another one, even higher, awaiting us.

The section has not gone far when the Old Man remembers that water-bottles have not been filled. Without water the Cactus Forest is certain death.

'Back to the well!' he orders roughly.

'Have I ever told you of the time my general an' me marched across the Danube?' asks Gregor.

'Can it, we've heard that one at least twenty times,' Barcelona cuts him off irritably.

'Did you eat with your general?' asks Tango, interestedly. He has a decided weakness for higher ranks.

'Of course,' says Gregor, condescendingly. 'Sometimes we even slept in the same bed with our monocle between us.'

'Was your general a fairy?' asks Porta, disrespectfully.

'A question like that could put you in front of a field-court of honour,' mumbles Gregor, insulted.

'Bloody 'ell,' shouts Tiny, in surprise. 'Is there *really* such a bleedin' court?'

'Did you sometimes *touch* your general?' asks Tango, with awe.

'I had to undress him every bloody evening, when he rested up to be ready for the next day's war,' answers Gregor, proudly.

' 'Bout time we shifted our baggy bleedin' arses under cover, ain't it?' asks Tiny, looking towards the mountains, from which machine-gun fire can be heard.

'How many jerricans have we got?' asks the Old Man, cocking his *grease-gun*[8].

'Only five,' laughs Barcelona, mirthlessly.

8. *Grease-gun:* slang for the German submachine-gun Model 40.

'They'll soon be finished,' grins Skull. It sounds like a bag of dried bones rattling.

'Water'd bleedin' run out o' you, fast as it went in,' says Tiny. ' 'Ow the bleedin' 'ell can a man *be* that bleedin' thin? I can't under*stand* it.'

'Skull ought to go to America. He'd make a fortune showin' himself as a victim of the horrors of the concentration camps,' suggests Porta.

'Cut the talk a minute,' snarls the Old Man, 'and listen. We've got to go over the mountains with or without water. It's our only chance.'

'Holy Christ!' breaks out Unteroffizier Krüger from the DR's. 'You don't know what you're saying! There's a forest of cactus with prickles the size of bayonets. We'll have to chop our way through with machetes and we've only got two. *They* won't last long. And there's not a drop of water *anywhere* up there.'

'What the hell do *you* suggest, then?' shouts the Old Man, desperately.

'The tracks and out on the road,' answers Krüger, looking around him for support.

'Mad as a bloody hatter,' the Old Man dismisses his suggestion contemptuously.

'The rightful owners of the country are lined up along the roads with the firm intention of knocking us off.'

'Let's kick 'em in the balls,' suggests Tiny, turning his cigar butt between his lips and champing on it. 'It's about time this Black Sea shower found out who it is as is visitin' 'em.'

'Brave little man, ain't you?' grins Porta, holding out his hand for a cigar. Tiny hands one over without a murmur.

Heide has to supply him with a chunk of liver sausage. Nobody dares to refuse Porta when he asks for something. If you want to stay alive the wisest thing is to keep friendly with him. He has that strange sort of sixth sense, otherwise only found amongst Jews, of being able to sniff out supplies at a distance of miles. Turn him out naked in the middle of the Gobi Desert and he'd find his way straight to something drinkable. Not an ice-cold beer perhaps, but at any rate water.

The Legionnaire kicks at the remnants of a bread-bag, and shouts bitterly:

'*On les emmerde!* The battalion must be somewhere behind those mountains!'

'Maybe,' answers the Old Man, laconically. 'That's the way *we're* going anyway. Now then. No firing at random. Fire only at proper targets. Don't forget shooting draws the enemy and we don't want that!'

'Plop, plop!' sounds from the north.

'80mm's,' decides Buffalo sagely, blowing his nose with his fingers.

'Crack, crack and crack again!'

'50mm's,' says Porta, hurling an empty bread-bag away disappointedly.

'Who *gives* 'em all that shit?' asks Gregor, worriedly.

'Italian and German traitors sell it to them,' answers Julius Heide coldly.

'They ought to be strung up. There ought to be only one form of punishment. Death! We're too soft. Womanish thinking.'

'You'n Adolf'd soon be the only two left in Germany,' Porta laughs noisily.

'God will help us,' mumbles the padre, looking over at us.

'Listen to the prayer-wheel goin',' jeers Skull, throwing a stick at the padre. 'God don't help us coolies. Kick us in the bleedin' arse more like!'

'Christ helps all who pray to Him,' answers the padre, quietly, and stares over the sun-blistered desert, where ruined buildings still smoke after the air attack.

'You an' your 'eavenly bleedin' 'ost,' shouts Tiny furiously. 'Them as kicked it at the bleedin' Morellenschlucht[9] babbled bleedin' prayers till they got it an' God didn' bleedin' 'elp the poor bastards!'

'I'm in touch,' screams Heide, spinning feverishly at the dials of the pack radio.

'Who the hell *are* you, you crazy shit?' he howls into the set.

'Flattery will get you nowhere! This is the People's Army. We'll be scraping you German shit off the road pretty soon now.'

'Get fucked, apeman!' rages Heide.

9. Morellenschlucht: Military execution square in Berlin.

'You've had it, sausage-eater! Fifteen minutes from now *you'll* be ready for the grinder!'

'Bighead!' Heide spits furiously at the radio. 'You're nuts!'

'You've *had* it, Nazi porker!'

'What a bleedin' barmy bastard,' shouts Tiny, incensed. 'Let's get up there after 'im!'

A long howl shrills from the radio. Contact is broken.

'Think they can see us?' asks Skull, nervously.

' 'Course they can't,' says Tiny, scornfully. 'If they could they'd 've done us by now.'

'They aren't ordinary partisans,' says the Old Man thoughtfully.

'Communist bastards. Red as a monkey's arse'ole,' shouts Tiny angrily, shaking his fist at the mountain peaks.

'Would anyone think now might be a good time to point one's penis in the right direction and follow it?' says Porta, pulling his equipment together.

'Exercise is good for you,' laughs Tango, taking a few dance-steps across the open square.

Buffalo stretches himself in the warm sand, and unfolds a large document.

'Me 'n' all my family've got to appear before a racial purity commission,' he said. 'It's because I've become me own grandfather!'

'That's impossible,' says the Old Man in amazement, and puts down his Mpi.

'Nothin' ain't impossible in the Third Goddam Reich. Before I know what's goin' on, I'll be me own great-grandfather. Wait'll those racial purity boys get goin' with me. It's my wife's fault, the crazy bitch. She's got a grown-up daughter me daddy got hot pants for an' went an' got hitched up with.'

'Your wife's daughter's got to be *your* daughter,' says the Old Man with a no-nonsense look on his face.

'Sure, sure, but still not sure. She had this daughter before we tied the knot. An' that just means my daddy he's become my son-in-law and my daughter's my mammy!'

'Understandable enough,' laughs Porta. 'Your daughter is your father's wife.'

'What a *mess*,' says Gregor despairingly, 'just because a man marries a woman who brings a prefabricated kid with her.'

'That, son, is only the beginning,' sighs Buffalo. 'I understand the Jews better now, those clever bastards. They don't marry nothin' but virgins. Two of the Vice Squad've lost their marbles over this case so far, an' more probably to come. They jus' couldn't stand comin' to the conclusion that me an' my little ol' lady'd got a son who was my daddy's brother-in-law.'

'That's obvious,' says the Old Man. 'He's your father's wife's brother.'

'Yeah, an' he ain't only my son, he's my uncle too,' groans Buffalo sadly, 'cause he's my mother's brother.'

'Yes, because your father's wife is your wife's daughter,' grins Barcelona heartily.

'Things got real complicated,' moans Buffalo unhappily, 'when my daughter, my father's wife an' my mother, had a son. He's my brother, cause he's my daddy's son, but he's the son of me daughter too, which makes me his gran'daddy.'

'Then your wife has suddenly become your grandmother,' roars Porta joyfully.

'Yeah, crazy situation ain't it?' mumbles Buffalo with a lost look at the heavens. 'I'm my wife's husband, but I'm her grandson too 'cause I'm the brother of her daughter's son, an' since your grand'mammy's husband's got to be your gran'daddy,' he throws out his arms despairingly, 'then it's piss-plain logical I'm my own gran'daddy and that ol' racial purity commission can't make out how that can possibly be done legitimate. An' that's why I'm accused of miscegenation – which is a kind of incest.'

'They'll put you inside, son,' prophesies Tiny, threateningly. 'Just 'ope Adolf never gets to 'ear about you.'

A heavy burst of shelling breaks into this strange family history. Muzzle reports and bursts roll, echoing deeply, across the mountains.

We move. A nervous unease catches at us.

'Let's stay where we are,' urges feldwebel Schmidt. 'It's madness to go up into that cactus. Even animals keep away from it.'

'*C'est le bordel*,' snarls the Legionnaire, fierily. 'It's madness to stay here. They'll have cut our throats before we even know it. The cactus is our only chance!'

'I know way. Very *bad* way,' says Stojko from the Bulgarian Guards Regiment. He is the only man left alive from a Field Surgery taken by the partisans. He saved himself by hiding in a bin of amputated limbs until the guerillas had left.

'March time?' asks the Old Man hopefully.

'T'ree maybe four day,' answers Stojko uncertainly, 'but we go very quick. No think 'bout water.'

'Water's the biggest problem,' sighs the Old Man, lighting his silver-lidded pipe.

'I've heard tell camels eat cactus cos of the juice in 'em,' says Buffalo.

'*Impossible, mon ami*,' answers the Legionnaire, 'they taste worse than boiled monkey-piss.'

'Couldn't you get *used* to the taste?' asks Porta, interestedly. 'I'd rather drink monkey-piss than die of thirst!'

The entire day dribbles away, without our being able to arrive at a decision. The corpses emit a powerful stench. The Old Man has several times told us to bury them but we pretend not to have heard him.

He gives up temporarily and sits down on a stone between Barcelona and the Legionnaire.

'We must put our trust in Stojko,' he says quietly, eyeing the Bulgarian in his filthy, blue-grey Guards uniform with its red piping and patches.

'He knows the bush,' says the Legionnaire, lighting a Caporal thoughtfully. 'These mountain peasants are masters at forcing their way through a cactus forest. And where *they* can go *we* can go too. I would like to see the peasant who is better than we regular soldiers.'

'You ever been in this kind of bush?' asks Barcelona with a mocking smile.

'*Non, mon ami*,' answers the Legionnaire. 'But I have heard quite a lot about it, and I know that it is worse than a trip barefoot across the cauldron of hell.'

'*I've* been there,' answers Barcelona sombrely, rubbing away at his Mpi. 'It's hell upon hell. The devil himself wouldn't dare go in there. It's a place God's forgotten existed. After a few hours you feel convinced that life is over. The whole place breathes death. The only living things are poisonous reptiles, which attack you on sight. Scratch yourself on one of those wicked thorns and you're finished.'

'What a look-out. What a look-out!' shouts Porta, swallowing a sardine whole.

'We'll soon fix them bleedin' serpents *and* the bleedin' cactus,' growls Tiny, with conviction in his voice. 'We're Germans, ain't we? Conquerors, ain't we?'

Late in the afternoon a mud-spattered Kübel roars into the village. A major in camouflage dress with a sub-machinegun in the crook of his arm jumps down and starts shouting.

'It's about time you people pulled yourselves together and got a road-block set up, isn't it?' He stamps on the ground. 'Closing-time is it? Putting the shutters up, are you? Reinforcements will arrive from Division latest tomorrow morning. And you, feldwebel,' he turns towards the Old Man, 'will answer for it with your head if this village isn't held!'

'We've not much ammo', sir. Can't hold this hole more than an hour!'

'Don't try to teach your grandmother to suck eggs,' screams the major, going purple in the face. 'You'll hold it, or you'll swing for it!'

He spins on his heel and climbs back into the Kübel which disappears down the road at a terrific speed.

'Moves like a mule with a cactus up his jacksey,' grins Porta. 'Does he really think we're going to do battle with the neighbours for this place.'

'He was moving *fast*,' says Tango. 'Wouldn't have believed a Kübel could *make* that speed.'

'Babby-shitters with a bad bleedin' conscience,' declares Tiny angrily, and kicks viciously at a torn-off foot.

'Goddam typical! Them shined-up bastards. Don't they just *love* orderin' other people out where it stinks of Valhalla an' a hero's goddam death!' remarks Buffalo despondently.

We sit down again. Skull snatches at flies. He eats them. Says they taste like shrimps. He's even got us to try them. We don't agree with him. Was he a bird in a former incarnation?

'*Allons-y!*' says the Legionnaire. 'To stay here is camel-dung.'

'What *about* holding the village?' says the Old Man thoughtfully. 'You heard the major's orders!'

'*That* bleedin' mother-fucker,' shouts Tiny. ''E's no bleedin' idea who we bleedin' *are*, even! That's the only bleedin' good thing about this bleedin' army. We all look the bleedin' same in bleedin' uniform.'

In a welter of foam-flecks, dust and glittering sabres, a unit of Vlassov Cossacks trots into the village.

A wachtmeister reins his horse in. It rears and whinnies nervously.

'What unit, you?' asks the Russian in bad German.

'The 'Oly Trinity unit,' answers Tiny, grinning broadly.

'You no cheeky, you obergefreiter!' snarls the Cossack wachtmeister, slashing out wickedly with his sabre in Tiny's direction. 'You stand attention, you talk me!'

'Why, you son of a bleedin' Caucasian goat!' shouts Tiny contemptuously.

'Think a citizen of bleedin' 'Amburg's gonna click 'is 'eels for shit like you? Your own lot'll string you up one of these days. Count on it, son!'

'Feldwebel, you make charge-sheet that man,' screams the wachtmeister, raging.

'Shut it!' hisses the Old Man, turning on his heel. 'Find another playground!'

The wachtmeister reins his horse so that it rears up on to its hindlegs.

Tiny jumps to one side to avoid being struck by its forelegs. He draws a deep breath of astonishment.

'What the bleedin' 'ell? Why you son of a syphilitic sow an' a 'or's bleedin' cunt-barber! I'll bleedin' teach *you*,' he shouts, giving the horse a straight left to the muzzle. He catches it round the neck and attempts to throw it to the ground.

The horse goes to its knees and screams in fright.

The wachtmeister slashes out at Tiny with his sabre.

'Murderous bleedin' monkey,' roars Tiny plucking the Cossack from his horse and punching away at him. ''Oreson bastard!'

'Stop it, *now*!' shouts the Old Man, lifting his Mpi.

'D'you think I'm gonna let this shrivelled-up bit of renegade shit, do me bleedin' in?'

An obergefreiter on a heavy BMW motorcycle brakes in the square and skids sideways to a halt.

'God! I thought you lot was guerillas. Everything's gone for a burton. I'm 12 Grenadier staff-DR! They cut our bloody arses orf. The guerillas is on route 286, an' all 'ell's broke loose round Karnobat!'

'Where you making for, then?' asks Porta inquisitively.

'I'm pissin' orf to Malko Sarkovo,' he tells us secretively, 'and from there on to Vayasal.'

'That's in Turkey!' Heide breaks in astonishedly.

'Too bloody right, it is!' grins the obergefreiter, his face aglow. 'I've 'ad enough of this man's bloody war. In three days time I'll be 'avin' it orf with a 'arem on the beach at Tekirdag, an' you boys can conquer yourselves to fuckin' death, far as I'm concerned. But without me, see!'

'That's desertion. It'll cost you your nut!' shouts Heide, outraged.

'Too bloody true, mate!' laughs the DR. 'Extension of life's what *I* call it. I wants to die in me bed, like the fuckin' generals do. That's democracy.'

'You're a traitor!' confirms Heide. 'Don't you know that the Constitution states that it is every man's duty, and right, to defend the Fatherland with his life?'

'I ain't never signed me name under that law, son,' says the obergefreiter, grinning. 'Them as 'as, can do the bloody fightin'!'

'Aren't you grateful to your country?' asks Heide indignantly.

'Am I fuck? *I* never asked for no Fatherland, an' the *clothes* I've 'ad to wear since the Fatherland took over responsibility for my bloody wardrobe ain't what *I'm* accustomed to, by *no* manner o' means!' He kicks the BMW's heavy motor into life, adjusts himself in the saddle, positions his Mpi, and pulls the helmet down over his forehead.

'Want me to give your love to the Turkish bints, an' the rest o' the fuckin' Muslims, boys?'

25

'You do that,' laughs Porta joyfully. 'Tell 'em to leave the gates on the jar, I'm on my way.'

'What about if they send you back again?' asks Gregor sceptically. 'The Swedes do. What makes you think the Turks aren't the same kind of shits?'

'That'd be Allah's bloody will, as they say where I'm orf to, wouldn't it, now?' shrugs the obergefreiter. '*If* you come bearin' no gifts, that is. I'm with the G-staff, mate, and I got a bit of interestin' Gekados[10] readin' material for the followers of the Prophet. Any of you sons want to ride along? There's room on the 'ore's cushion behind yours truly?'

'Anybody who can't march?' asks the Old Man, looking around him.

'Sir, sir!' groans Porta, limping about using his LMG as a crutch. 'Sir, I've got no feet left at all. I'm having to roll along on my bollocks!'

'Piss off, Porta!' says the Old Man.

With a thunderous howl the BMW disappears down the dusty road.

'Think he'll make it?' Gregor is still sceptical.

'His kind of German obergefreiter *always* makes it,' states Porta categorically.

'Understand a compass?' the Old Man has turned back to Stojko. 'I suggest compass figure 46. That still the way you know?'

'Feldwebel I say yes. Compass good thing,' answers Stojko, examining the instrument with interest as it lies on the map. 'We go Stojko way *and* compass way. In front bad soldier no shoulderstrap. Them cut road, chase snake.'

'Mo-o-o-ve!' shouts the Old Man, swinging his grease gun up over his shoulder.

For a time we follow the road towards Gulumanovo. Then we swing up into the hills and the road becomes no more than a set of wheel-tracks.

A machine-gun barks close by. The column halts for a moment, listening. We peer up towards the bush in dismay. None of us likes the idea of having to march through that maze

10. Gekados (Geheime Kommandosachen): Secret command documents.

26

of thorns and dry, tightly intermeshed, ghost vegetation.

The moon looks sallow and throws long spectral shadows.

'Swish, swish!' The machetes sing their song as two *500's* cut a way through the cactus.

We are taut and expectant. We smell danger and death. We hold our weapons at the ready.

'Goddam wicked place,' whispers Buffalo, fearfully. 'Gimme Ivan. We know *him!*'

'*C'est un bordel!*' says the Legionnaire. 'But it will get worse!'

Tiny stops so suddenly that I run into him.

'There's somebody watchin' us,' he whispers, hoarsely. 'Some sons o' bitches. *Murderin'* bleeders.'

'Sure?' asks the Old Man, anxiously. He knows and respects Tiny's animal instincts.

'I'm never wrong,' rumbles Tiny. 'Let's find 'em an' tear their bleedin' balls off.'

'Count me out,' mumbles Porta, nervously. 'It's black as the inside of a nigger whore's cunt in there.'

'Nigger 'ore, eh,' says Tiny. 'I could find one o' them in a black-out.'

Silently they disappear between the shadowy stems of cactus.

'*Beseff,*' whispers the Legionnaire, pressing the butt of the LMG into his shoulder.

Time drags slowly by. Almost four hours have passed. A death-cry splits the stillness.

'What the hell was that?' whispers Gregor, frightenedly.

Just before dawn they return carrying a large wild pig between them.

'This bleeder's the only partisan we run into,' grins Tiny. ' 'E was nearly as piss-frightened as us.'

'It was love at first sight,' shouts Porta, patting the dead wild pig's buttocks.

'What was the scream?' asks the Old Man.

'Our friend here,' smiles Porta. 'He didn't fancy getting his throat cut.'

'What about the partisans?' asks the Old Man.

'They're in there somewhere,' confirms Porta, staring uneasily at the tight mass of cactus. 'I don't understand though, how they can move through that stuff without cutting a path.'

Artillery thunders in the distance. The air shivers at the explosions.

'They're knockin' on, all right!' says the Old Man, uneasily 'Fore we know where we are, they'll be blowing the lot of us to kingdom come.'

An ex-leutnant from the 500's spraddles in front of the Old Man.

'Well, feldwebel! What now? Giving up? Then *I'll* take command. Even though they *have* stripped me of rank, you'll agree I have more experience than you in leading troops.'

The Old Man lights his silver-lidded pipe slowly, and regards the ex-officer, standing bobbing in front of him and looking important, with a dangerous stare.

'Soldier! Anybody ever tell you, you put your heels together and stand straight when you're talking to a superior.'

The ex-leutnant becomes slightly nervous, but he is stubborn.

'Feldwebel, stop that nonsense. I'll take over command and lead this unit. That's enough!'

Tiny goes over to him.

'Listen 'ere; sonny,' he roars, catching him by the collar. 'You ain't takin' command o' fuck-all! Get in your bleedin' basket an' lie down till you're called for.'

'Crack his nut an' let the shit out,' suggests Buffalo, licking his lips.

Tiny knocks the ex-leutnant backwards on to the newly-flayed pig skin.

The padre kneels and prays in a thin, priestly whine. He swings a home-made crucifix of twigs in front of him.

'Jesus there's gone bonkers,' laughs Skull.

Tiny lifts himself on one elbow and stares into the cactus.

'Those bastards are watchin' us again!'

Buffalo jumps to his feet, and before anyone can stop him he empties a whole magazine into the bush in one long crackling roar.

'Are you mad, man?' scolds the Old Man, raging. 'You'll bring a whole battalion of 'em down on us.'

'They drive you mad, them goddam cactus plants. There was eyes watchin 'us,' whines Buffalo, the pouches of fat on his cheeks wobbling.

'Oberst "Wildboar" ought never to have posted me from that job as chauffeur to my general,' sighs Gregor disconsolately.

'He never would've got it through if my general and our monocle hadn't been on a duty trip to Berlin. It was a tactical error splitting us three up.'

'You might even've won the bloody war, eh?' grins the Old Man. 'You and your general and your monocle?'

'Not impossible. We *belonged* together. You should've seen it when our monocle winked out at a Chief-of-Staff and we snarled, "Come here, sir, and take a glance at the battle chart . . ." *That* was enough to start the shit trickling down their legs. When we took off our cap their teeth began to chatter. We hadn't a trace of fluff even on our cranium. A real Prussian general's nut, we had. The QM officer was a twit who never should've made oberstleutnant. To get the DAGMAR support point removed he had to drive through enemy artillery fire several times with his waggons, and how he didn't like it.

' "Herr General," he'd say, timidly. "How am I to get my motorized units through the enemy shelling? I can only use route 77." And the fool would point it out on the chart. As if we didn't all know where 77 bloody well was.

'My general'd run a finger round his high uniform collar, and draw a deep breath. With his eyebrows lifted almost right up on top of his head he would look at this supplies officer.

' "If you feel it best you can have your troops *carried* over the terrain in palanquins by Kaffir bearers, or do you perhaps wish *me* to solve *your* problems for you? If you are in doubt of what to do I suggest you ask your drivers for advice." Monocle out, monocle in again.

'That oberstleutnant sobbed something that sounded like: "Very good Herr General!" The angels sang that day. Half the staff'd found a hero's death by afternoon already.

' "Cattle!" said my general, as we banged the doors shut and shot off, knocking down a couple of innocent orderly officers.

' "It is good psychologically to go off in a cloud of dust," my general explained.

'And we'd put our hand into our uniform, for all the world like the pictures of Napoleon.

' "Now these fools will perhaps remember for a while who it is who makes the decisions," said my general, taking a good gulp from his glass. We always drank cognac out of beer glasses. The usual ones held too little for us.

' "Yes, sir, Herr General!" I'd scream.

'I'd get one glass, but no more. My general didn't like his driver getting too much to drink. It was a great responsibility driving a general around, but I usually managed to sink a couple or three when he'd gone to bed. A bit after this we got our fourth star and took over an Army Group, but wicked as they are in bloody Personnel HQ they sent oak-leaves and red tabs to Oberst "Wildboar". If he was a horror as an oberst he was worse'n you could imagine as general-major. I went around there a couple of days just hoping they'd give him a division he could lead to death and destruction. But they didn't. Instead they made him Chief-of-Staff in my division. That was *my* bad luck. My general flew to Berlin to thank them for his new star and get new uniforms made now he was a general-oberst. The "Boar" met me in the ops. room when I came back from the airfield without my general and our monocle. He was smiling like the devil watching parsons roasting on the coals of hell. He gives me the choice of leaving immediately for the other end of the front line, or taking a summary with him chairing the court. The sentence was decided in advance. I could see the bloody gallows there all right in his wicked yellow eyes.'

'Whatever had you done?' asks Barcelona, wonderingly.

'When you're driving for a general it's easy to get mixed up in things which can get you into trouble. I'd never dreamed the bloody "Boar" had been saving it up for me. He hits me across the face with the documents and, with a horrid smile, he adds in his most fatherly way:

' "Unteroffizier Martin, if you had been born twenty years earlier, and lived in Chicago, Al Capone would have found a good right hand man in you. Even now, any court in the world would, without hesitation, sentence you to life imprisonment for the things you have done."

'For the next fifteen minutes he slandered me shamelessly.

30

As an unteroffizier you have to take that sort of thing when it's the Chief-of-Staff who's dishing it out. All those primitive military feelings ran away with him. He walked up and down, and every time he stood still he'd go up and down at the knees and make his boots creak. He had the *creakiest* boots. Specially made for it, like as not. His nose was one of the kind that has trouble with swing-doors and reminds you of Rome's bloody history. His glasses were like the headlamps on a Horch. I took a deep breath and held onto my guts and asked if I might wait till my general and our monocle returned so that I could congratulate him on the fourth star. It's not every Prussian who makes that. Generaloberst rank is only for the créme de la créme. My general had often told me it was easier for a murderer to get into heaven than for man born of woman to become a Prussian general.

'I had to ask twice before the "Boar" seemed to realize what I was asking for. He pushed his chin down into his collar and blew through his nose like a rhinoceros getting ready to attack.

'"Do you think me to be an idiot?" he screamed, enraged.

'I did, but I thought it might lengthen my life a bit if I kept that to myself. He knew what he was doing all right, that bastard. If he'd let me wait to say goodbye to my general and our monocle, it'd never've come to anything. It'd've been the same as the time I laughed at the generals shooting across the ice on their backsides[11]. My general has tried to get me back several times, but the bloody "Boar" stops it every time through the old boy net in Berlin. Ain't life terrible?' He looks up at the heavens as if some help can be expected from there.

'Have you ever realized how seldom you ever get what you wish for? Just when you're having it good, suddenly down the kitchen stairs you go. Look at these hands.' He displays a pair of filthy, torn, calloused hands. 'Before they were white and soft as a nun's. Look at my boots. All the shit of the Balkans hanging on 'em. When I was with my general they were polished like mirrors.' He sighs and wipes away a quiet tear as he thinks of past grandeurs.

'I wasn't made for all this farting about with the infantry.' He sighs again. 'In the temple of my heart a great candle is

11. See: *SS General.*

31

burning for my general and our monocle, and I know he thinks of me when he kneels in his night uniform beside his hard cot and entrusts himself to the Supreme War Leader and prays Him to bless our war.'

We have been marching for perhaps an hour when a machine-gun rattles at us from the cactus.

'Run, run!' screams Skull, hysterically, running back along the narrow path.

'Shut up you silly bastard!' scolds Porta, irritatedly, throwing a hand-grenade in the direction of the machine-gun fire. A hard, flat explosion and the gun goes silent. Almost immediately another begins to hammer behind us.

Panic breaks out. A hand-grenade explodes in the middle of us, blowing off the legs of a 500.

Tiny holds on to a cactus. Bullets shred the fleshy leaves around him.

I am down, pressed flat behind an anthill. Buffalo, some three hundred pounds of flesh, a steel-helmet and an Mpi, comes thundering down the path. His Mpi spits fire. There is a hellish row from the cactus. Buffalo's wild roarings are part of it.

'He's gone off it,' decides Porta, pressing himself closer to the ground.

A little later Buffalo appears from the cactus, dragging two blood-soaked bodies behind him.

'What the hell set *you* off?' asks Porta, watching Buffalo in astonishment as he wipes his battle-knife on one of the bodies.

'I got mad. That mad I could've cracked coconuts with me goddam arse,' he shouts angrily. 'Those partisan bastards've pissed on us long enough. They needed a couple of good German clouts alongside the ear.'

We drink the coolant from one of the guns, a Maxim. It tastes terrible but it *is* water.

The sun appears from behind the mountains, as we continue our march. Everything takes on a beautiful rose-red tint. We shiver. The nights are cold, but we still enjoy them. In an hour's time it will be hot as an oven. We begin to snarl at one another. By noon we hate one another. The padre we hate most of all with his eternal telling of beads and praying:

'God is with us! God will help us!'

'Shut your face!' roars Heide, enraged. 'God has forgotten us!'

'God's with the goddam Reds,' puffs Buffalo, using a cactus leaf as a fan. He sweats twice as much as anybody else. Twice as much as anybody else. Twice he has tried to leave the grenade-thrower behind but the Old Man notices every time and sends him back for it.

Two 500's lead the way with machetes. They are relieved every half-hour. It is hard work cutting a path through the cactus.

At midday the Old Man orders a halt. The unit is completely worn out. One of the 500's dies in terrible convulsions. They find a tiny green snake in his boot. Porta kills it and throws it at Heide who is so shocked he falls in a faint. They think at first he has died of a heart attack but when he comes to himself there is more life in him than Porta fancies. Two men have to hold him whilst a third ties his hands.

After an hour the Old Man orders us up, but progress is slow now. We cover no more than a few miles before sundown. Without a thought of eating we throw ourselves to the ground and drop into unconsciousness. We stay where we are for the whole of the following day. Darkness has fallen before we awake.

'Let's have some coffee and try to sort ourselves out a bit,' suggests Porta, removing the top from one of his five canteens.

Tiny sits in the middle of the path with his ludicrous bowler on his head. He is rolling a big cigar from one side of his mouth to the other.

'Make the best of everythin',' he proclaims. 'This cactus shit we're pissin' around in ain't near as bad as bein' frizzled to death, like a piece o' bleedin' bacon, in some bleedin' fox'ole by one o' the soddin' 'eathen's flame-throwers. You scream at the 'eat 'ere, but 'ave you lot forgot when we was in Kilyma where if you went outside to 'ave a piss your bleedin' prick fell orf? An' what the bleedin' 'ell's ants compared to Siberian soddin' wolves what's favourite food is Germans? When I think o' that lot, this lot's a bleedin' picnic by the side of it.'

'You're too damn stupid to understand how godawful this

33

place *is*,' says Buffalo, who is sweating as if he were in a sauna.

Tiny continues smoking, with his nose in the air. He knocks the ash from his cigar with an elegant gesture he has seen American businessmen use on the films.

'Stupid? Maybe I am, maybe I ain't! Military service, my friend, 'as taught me that'a 'ealthy body is needed if you're gonna live through it. Brains grow on their own, son. If you've got too much of the old grey stuff when you go in at the start, you go bleedin' barmy 'fore you know where you are. The brainy bleeders can't *take* it.'

A scorpion runs across the path. Skull crushes it with his rifle-butt.

The heavy rumble of artillery continues ceaselessly.

A swarm of Ju 87's – Stukas – appears over the mountains. Their bombload is clearly visible under the wings of the planes.

'Wherever they drop that load it'll cause a bit of dedigitation,' says feldwebel Schmidt, filling up the magazine of his Mpi.

The Old Man bawls out an ex-leutnant who has thrown two spare gun-barrels away.

'The next man caught abandoning arms'll get shot,' shouts the Old Man, in a rage.

'Wonder if they'll ever invent a Germany that's a pleasant place to live in?' says Buffalo, thoughtfully, crushing a long green insect under the heel of his boot.

'*Everywhere's* fun,' says Porta to nobody in particular – and most of those around him don't catch it. 'I remember the time I was under arrest in garrison at Munich – just because I wanted to get confirmed in church. They thought they were punishing me when they locked me up, but they were quite wrong. Those were some of the most wonderful moments of my life. Moments I'll always remember with pleasure. A spell of jail's a necessity if you want to get something out of life.'

'*You've said it*,' says Tiny, revolving his cigar in his mouth. 'Even in this bleedin' war we've got into, a man ain't bored.'

'You ain't telling us you *like* it?' shouts Skull, scandalized.

'Why not?' asks Tiny, with a happy expression on his face. 'I haven't time to waste feeling sorry for myself. I *enjoy* the war. 'Ow do *I* know what the bleedin' peace 'll be like? There's some

34

as'll tell you it'll be a bleedin' sight worse'n the war. My old gran'dad, as did an eight-year stretch in Moabitt, for 'avin' threatened to cut the cheeks of the Kaiser's bleedin' arse off, told me that even in Moabitt you could 'ave a pleasant time of it.'

'Think ants enjoy themselves?' asks Barcelona, stirring an ant-heap with the barrel of his Mpi.

'No living creature can exist without having fun,' answers Porta. 'Even hummingbirds break out laughing sometimes.'

'I see Detective-Inspector bleedin' Nass smile once,' shouts Tiny, 'and that ought to've been next thing to impossible. Vinegar's sherbet compared to *that* sour bleeder.'

'Down!' howls Porta ducking like lightning behind the SMG[12].

There is a sound like thunder and tracer tracks bite their way through the wilderness of cactus. I throw grenades. An Mpi blazes from behind a cactus stem. Screams are heard cutting through the noise, then a deathly silence comes down on the sun-blistered brush. Crickets continue their long drawn-out music.

We stay down and wait.

Heide rests the flame-thrower on a stone and sends a jet of flame hissing between the cactus trunks. A stench of burning oil hangs sickeningly on the sunwarmed air. Two living torches stumble out of the cactus forest, and roll about in agony on the path. They char slowly.

'What in the name of the livin' God, was that?' asks Buffalo in astonishment.

'Partisans,' smiles Porta. 'Something metal glinted or we'd 've had it, son.' There's still some of the devil's luck sticking to us. There are three Bulgarian soldiers amongst the dead partisans.

'Seems as if our Balkan friends are dropping us,' says the Old Man, pushing the barrel of his Mpi at the bodies.

'I'll slash your bleedin' throat open soon. I will, you black bleedin' Bible-thumper,' roars Tiny, who has got into a row with the padre. He pushes him hard enough to make him fall over backwards and hit his head on a stump.

12. SMG: (Schweres Maschinengewehr): Heavy machine-gun.

'Do you *have* to rough up a defenceless man?' the Old Man upbraids him.

'An' why not?' answers Tiny, spitting on the padre. 'Who taught me it! I *ask* you! The bleedin' army did, didn' they? You ever see a bleedin' private let 'is anger get the better of 'im with a bleedin' officer? *Did* you now?'

'That's too cheap an excuse,' says Heide, didactically, suddenly taking the padre's side. 'Wolfgang Creutzfeldt, you are a nasty type. Always brutal, always coarse. You are not aligned with the spirit of our new Germany.'

'Look after number bleedin' one,' growls Tiny, kicking out after the padre. 'Think I want to end up a captain in the Salvation bleedin' Army?'

'What's the compass say?' the Old Man asks Stojko.

'Forty-six, like you say, feldwebel. You not be mad I say you pick up arsepart, run fast!'

'Let's get on,' decides the Old Man nervously. 'Stojko at point.'

'Jesus Christ, *turn your arse to the front, boy!*' shouts Tiny, who is following immediately behind Stojko.

They descend a long slope. Even the 500's do better now with their machetes. The slope is so steep that we have to dig in our heels hard.

We reach a stretch of shale and have to use Gregor's mountaineering rope. The Old Man gives us no rest until nightfall. Roll-call shows two men missing.

The Old Man rages, asks for volunteers to go back and search for them. Nobody steps forward. Far behind us we can see rocket flares, and between us and the flares there are certainly partisans.

The padre gets up and offers to go back alone after them.

'No!' the Old Man turns his offer down, brusquely. 'The partisans'd have got you before you'd gone far, and I don't have to tell you what they do to parsons.'

'God will help me. I am not afraid,' answers the padre quietly.

'God, God, God,' sneers Tiny. 'Better put your bleedin' trust in this little ol' lullaby girl 'ere.' He pats his weapon. 'Them partisans don't like *'er* a bit. A 42 in the 'and's better'n God in 'is 'eaven!'

'Shall I go and look for them?' asks the padre, ignoring Tiny.

'I said, *no!*' decides the Old Man. 'I don't wish to be responsible for *you* getting yourself chopped to pieces.' He points to Unteroffizier Krüger from the DR's. 'Take two *500's* with you. Make a search. Get back inside two hours with or without 'em.'

'What the hell do *we* care about those jailbirds?' shouts Krüger, fear spreading across his face. 'Why should we risk our lives for *them*? They might 've deserted to the partisans. Shits without shoulder-straps'd do anythin'.'

'Shut up,' the Old Man interrupts him, 'and get moving.'

Krüger selects two *500's*. He is snuffling with rage.

'Take the lead,' he orders wickedly. 'As former officers you're used to it. Now watch yourselves. I've got an itchy trigger finger, boys.'

'What'd we ever do to you?' protests one of them weakly.

'Just *try* to do somethin',' roars Krüger, in a rage.

Long after they are out of sight we can hear his blustering voice.

Tiny has taken a trip into the cactus and returns with three Bulgarian gaiters and a Russian *kalashnikov*.

'Where'd you find that lot?' asks the Old Man, wonderingly.

'Won it playin' bingo,' grins Tiny, throwing himself down on his stomach. He keeps on laughing, seemingly unable to stop himself. He seems to feel that he has been amazingly witty.

They light a fire. The wood is completely dried out so that there is no betraying smoke.

Porta wants to brew up coffee, but it is only after a long drawn-out argument that the Old Man gives him permission to use any of the precious water. The coffee smells wonderful. We sit listening to the noise of the crickets and the distant voice of the war.

'When you are thirsty, it helps to suck on a stone,' the Legionnaire tells us.

'It's bleedin' lovely sittin' 'ere lookin' out into the night,' says

37

Tiny dreamily. 'Like bein' a bleedin' boy scout. I always wanted to join that lot.'

'It's gonna get rough!' says Tango, prophetically, polishing away at his gun.

'The black bird of death is coming to get us,' whispers Gregor, ominously, as we listen to a long drum-roll of explosions, which make the mountains shake.

Porta plays a tune softly on his piccolo. Tiny knocks out his mouth-organ. Tango dances, using his carbine as a partner.

'Sleep with me tonight?' he whispers a smooth question to the weapon.

A swarm of strange insects attacks us. Our hands and arms swell up violently at every bite. Porta and Tiny cover head and neck with their flame-thrower helmets, but the rest of us have no protection. Our faces are soon unrecognizable.

The thirst grows worse.

'*Bon, mes amis!* As long as you can sweat you will not die of thirst,' says the Legionnaire, tonelessly. 'When you sweat no longer *then* you are in danger.'

There is only water enough for four days, even at the low ration level the Old Man has set. Tango thinks it will take us at least two weeks to get through. We move only slowly. Some try to suck water from the cactus plants, and become terribly ill. Their stomachs literally turn inside out in bursts of convulsive retching.

Krüger returns without having found the missing men.

'Have you *looked* for them?' questions the Old Man suspiciously.

'We have looked everywhere, Herr feldwebel,' answers the ex-leutnant angrily.

'You, Unteroffizier Krüger?' asks the Old Man sharply.

'We have left no stone unturned. Should we have interrogated the ants as to whether they had eaten the men!' shouts Krüger, flaring up.

'They've gone over to the enemy,' says the ex-leutnant of infantry.

'Button your lip till you're asked!' shouts the Old Man, fuming.

'Is it them cunt 'unters as 'ave fucked off?' asks Tiny, with a broad grin.

'If you mean me,' shouts a voice from the *500's* over in the shadows, 'I'm still here!'

We have only slept a few hours, when the sentries awaken us. A column of partisans has passed in the dark without seeing us.

We strain our ears fearfully at the darkness. Two shots smash out not very far away.

'Make ready to move off,' whispers the Old Man, swinging his equipment over his shoulders.

I watch the rear. It is so dark I can hardly see my hand in front of my face.

Suddenly I find myself alone. I use my field lamp cautiously. Only cactus and insects. I listen hard. Not a sound. The unit seems to have sunk into the ground.

They're playing a trick, I think. They're mad enough to, even in a situation like this.

I listen again. All is silence. Not even the noise of the crickets. I take a few cautious steps forward. They've hidden themselves. Purely to enjoy seeing me frightened.

'Hell, show yourselves!' I call in a half-shout. 'This isn't *funny*!' Nothing moves. *Have* I lost them?

'Old 'un!' I call softly. The sweat of fear runs down my face. Alone in partisan country in the middle of this horrible cactus forest.

'Porta! Come out damn you!'

No answer. And yet? Wasn't that a voice? I call out again and listen. Nothing. The wind? Now and then I feel a puff of air touch my cheek. I realize, suddenly with horror, that I am alone. All alone! I've lost the unit and they me. They haven't noticed me falling behind. Don't even know yet, maybe, that I've disappeared. They'll be back, though, when they find out. The Old Man won't leave stragglers. They'd even go back for Krüger.

I stand quite still, listening to the night. Only the odd breaths of wind, the rustling of the ants and the buzz of insects. I have often been alone before during this war but never like this. I always knew where the enemy was, and the direction of our own lines. In this dreadful cactus forest the enemy could be anywhere. A merciless enemy. Our own lines are far away. I don't even know where. They might even have been broken for all I know and the Southern Army be fleeing back to Germany. I *must* try to find the unit. At the worst to get through on my own. I ready my Mpi and arm a hand-grenade. Keep your head, I tell myself. *Don't bomb your own lot!*

They *can't* have disappeared. I've been with the Old Man's unit four years now, and what haven't we been through together? Four years, day out and day in, on all kinds of fronts. All right we've been separated in field hospitals sometimes, but not for long. The *unit's* my home! I feel safe there. Even when you're lying comfortably in a hospital bed, you can feel homesick. Homesick for the unit out there in HKL[18]. When you got out and were sent back with three red lines across your papers – light duties and change of dressings every day that means – all your aches and pains disappeared at the sight of the well-known faces. And out you'd march to HKL with your unit. Even the lung-wound, which often came close to choking you in hospital, didn't worry you any more. You were home again. Nothing else mattered. Your mates looked after you. Put you on the SMG or gave you the radio to look after. You could manage that with a lung-wound not quite healed yet.

I won't *let* these ties be broken just by getting lost in a blasted cactus forest! They'll look for me as soon as they see I'm missing. Tango'll turn round and see I'm gone and give the alarm. Tango was right in front of me.

It'd be mad to continue on the line of march. We could easily miss one another. I'd better sit down and wait for daybreak. In the sunlight things always look different.

I've not been sitting long when panic fear suddenly grips me. I get up and begin to walk forward slowly. All the time, it seems, I can hear voices. But it is only the wind. Battle instincts whisper warnings. I am not alone any more. Silently I take up position alongside a cactus. My Mpi is at the ready. Silence. Nothing but silence. And a crushing darkness which seems as if it is choking me.

How long I stand there ready for action I'll never know. I decide to move on. From the darkness comes a rattle of steel on

13. HKL: (Hauptkampflinie): Main front line.

steel. It grates on my tattered nerves like a gunshot. Silently I sink down and pull a grenade from my jackboot!

'Hush, you great shit-house!' whispers Porta's beautiful voice from the darkness.

'Didn't do it on purpose, bollock'ead!' Tiny's bass rumbles, echoing, through the forest.

Somebody laughs. Must be Barcelona.

I'm shouting with relief inside, but the lump in my throat stops any sound coming out.

I move forward carefully.

'Halt or I fire,' howls Porta from the darkness.

'It's me!' I scream.

I'm home again. The Old Man is with them.

'Where the hell you been?' asks Porta, with a reproachful air. 'Next time we won't come back for you.'

'Been chasin' cunt, 'ave you?' asks Tiny, chuckling. 'It's in short supply round 'ere. Might get a fuck at an ant'ill, p'r'aps! Tickle your old knob up a bit though!'

I explain to them what has happened.

'You'll live through it,' says Porta. 'I did think we'd finally got shut of you this time.'

'He'll be there when we get our papers,' grins Gregor.

Just before dawn we continue the march. One of the wounded dies. He goes quietly, as we are carrying him. The Old Man requests us to bury him.

'Lay 'im out on that, an' 'e'll be gone before you know it,' says Tiny, practically, pointing to a giant anthill. 'Them red bleeders could get rid of an elephant while I'm eatin' an 'ard-boiled egg.'

But the Old Man is stubborn. He wants the dead soldier buried.

The padre fashions a cross from two stems of cactus.

Wickedly angry we dig a hole and roll the body into it. The grave is not big enough and we have to bend him and tread on him to make him fit into it.

The padre makes a small speech and recites the burial service over him. Finally we tramp the earth flat over his grave.

Buffalo throws a helmet onto the grave. A battered, dented tin hat which has seen service right from the beginning.

'*La merde aux yeux*,' sneers the Legionnaire. 'It's not every *poilu* who is seen off so nicely, with prayers and the casting of earth over him.'

'Thanks is not a thing Barras excels in,' says Porta acidly.

'Keep the Army out of it!' shouts Heide, bitterly.

'I don't give a shit for your Army,' answers Porta, angered. 'It's done nothing but twist me since the first day we met!'

'*My* Army, as you call it, will get *you* yet,' promises Heide. He lifts his hand threateningly. 'Bigger pricks than you have thought they could piss on her and get away with it.'

A whole row of bodies – Bulgarian Army men – lie alongside the path. Skeletons and tattered uniforms. The ants have hauled away the rest.

Porta leans one of the skeletons up against a cactus with one arm pointing south.

'Frighten the shit outa the next lone 'ero as comes past 'ere, 'e will,' laughs Tiny. He places a cigar-butt between the grinning teeth.

We have only a few drops of water left. We struggle heavily on through this blistering hell.

The padre's mind begins to wander. He thinks he is a bishop and the cactus plants are his congregation. He shuffles along beside the column, singing psalms in a hoarse, cracked voice, frightening the black carrion birds.

The Old Man can't stand it any longer. He slaps him stingingly several times across the face.

The padre sits down and cries like a child.

'My God, my God, why hast thou forsaken me?' he cries to the staring sky.

'Liquidate him,' suggests Julius Heide, coldly. 'These black swine bring bad luck. The Führer has told us these holy servants on earth are unnecessary. God can look after us without them.'

' 'As Adolf said that, too?' asks Tiny, wonderingly. 'What *ain't* that pissy-arsed little bleeder said in 'is time?'

We drag the padre along with us. He blesses us and guarantees us eternal life.

'Balls to that, parson,' shouts Porta, swinging his Mpi above

42

his head. 'Help us hang on to the life we've got now as long as possible, instead.'

' 'Ow about a couple o' the Lord's lightning bolts dropped on the 'eads óf these partisan bleeders, as are behind us?' asks Tiny, ever the practical man.

We are all sucking on pebbles now. They rattle about against our teeth as we do our best to draw the last drop of saliva out of our dried-out glands. We are close to madness from thirst.

The Old Man vows to shoot the first man who takes a swig from his waterbottle.

At noon the next day Porta catches feldwebel Schmidt drinking on the sly and drags him to the Old Man. He is ordered to carry the heavy grenade-thrower. He loses his next four rations of water. Only a mouthful for each man, to be sure, but more valuable to us than pearls.

Schmidt manages to steal water yet again. First he is beaten up, and if the Old Man had not intervened they would have killed him. Now he is running in circles in the sun, while the remainder of us take a break.

After thirty minutes of it he starts screaming and throws himself down on the ground. He refuses to rise. The Legionnaire gets him to his feet with blows from a rifle-butt, and he starts off again in the burning sun. Soon Schmidt is creeping round on his hands and knees.

The Legionnaire kicks him in the ribs and bangs his face down into the dusty ground.

'He's going to die,' says Gregor.

'That's right,' answers Skull, uninterestedly. 'His own fault, ain't it?'

None of us pity him. The Old Man trusted him with the water supply and as a feldwebel he knew what it cost to steal water. The Old Man has no choice in the matter. If he lets Schmidt get away with it, the rest of us will be at one another's throats over the water before nightfall. It's not always fun to lead a unit, and it's not in the Old Man's line to watch a man run himself into the grave. But if he merely shoots Schmidt we'd hardly notice it. We've seen too many men shot. It's an everyday thing to us. The first time we saw a man neck-shot we were sick to the stomach. Every man of us. Neck-shooting is

43

probably the nastiest way of liquidating a man. The pistol muzzle is placed in the groove of the neck pointing upwards. There's a report and the head twists almost entirely round. The brains flow down over the face. The body stiffens and falls like a log. The face often turns completely backwards.

Now we can watch a man neck-shot without a qualm. We can even find it amusing. Not because we are particularly brutal. But because war has changed us. If it hadn't we'd long since have become inmates of one of the Army asylums. Many *have* ended there.

Schmidt collapses. The grenade-thrower cracks against the back of his neck. Both boxes of shells fall from his hands.

'*Bête!* Up with you!' shouts the Legionnaire, in a rage. He jabs Schmidt with his bayonet, but there is no reaction.

'Bastard! Shitty weak bastard!' shouts Tango, contemptuously.

'Stick a cactus up his arse,' suggests Buffalo. 'That ought to give 'im a thrill!'

The Legionnaire gets Schmidt on his feet again.

'The Legion's school,' he laughs triumphantly. Soon after Schmidt is dead. He falls like a piece of paper dropped by a stilled wind.

His body is left on an anthill. It is soon thickly covered with huge red ants.

The Old Man gives the order to resume the march immediately.

The next day we cross a plain of stones and shale. Not even cactus can grow here. Our tongues swell in our mouths like great pieces of dried-up leather. There is no more than a mouthful of water left for each man. Then the jerricans are empty.

Two 500's die without a sound. Not even the usual convulsive jerk. Death from thirst is a different kind of death.

'Why couldn't those bastards have kicked it *before* they'd hogged their water ration?' complains Tango.

'Oh God, do you remember the time we fucked those Mongol girls under the waterfall?' shouts Porta.

'I'll *shoot* the next man who talks about water,' screams Heide hoarsely.

44

Skull discovers that the padre has a goatskin filled with water hidden under his gown.

'Hand over that water, parson!' demands the Old Man, sharply, catching hold of him.

'It is *holy* water,' the padre smiles foolishly. 'We must lave our feet in it before we enter the Temple.'

With a comical hop he is up on a boulder. He holds the goatskin high above his head.

'He ain't washin' nobody's feet in that goddam water,' screams Buffalo madly.

We make a ring about the padre. A ring which closes in on him threateningly.

'It is *holy* water,' he howls, 'holy water from Dimitrovgrad!'

'We don't give a fuck if it's the 'igh priest o' Jerusalem's own piss!' roars Tiny. 'Give it 'ere you Easter bleedin' maniac.'

'He's bringing us *bad luck*,' shouts Barcelona furiously. 'When I was with the Mountain Brigade, we had to drag a bastard like him about with us. Mahogany trees fell on us. The troop-transporter broke down. We walked straight into a minefield that cut us to ribbons. At Drutus the mountain rolled down on us. A month of it, we had! A Russki deserter – a commissar – convinced us finally it was all that pissin' parson's fault. But you know the Mountain boys – missionaries to a blasted man. Singin' psalms over the poor dead 'uns and *nobody'd* do this parson in. The Russki did it for us. He was educated up to have no moral scruples about doin' a parson. He crept up behind 'im while he was gettin' round some Georgian clotted cream. Bang! And the parson's brains're mixed up with the cream. The very same evening, lads, our luck was back with us.

'Everythin' went like a dream till we got to Elbruz where there was a new parson waiting for us. Off pisses our luck again. Eight days after he arrived the whole bloody Brigade's sittin' up in Valhalla.'

Fast as a cat the Old Man is up by the side of the padre, tears the goatskin from his hands and throws it to Porta.

'You're responsible to me for the contents!'

'Well, *well*!' Porta bows deeply. 'You trust me *that* much?

45

Even my old dad wouldn't have. Least not since he caught me drinking from his private bottle of *Slivovitz*.'

We march steeply upwards and meet cactus again. Tiny's body towers like the side of a house in front of me. His language is almost turning the air blue about him. When he stops I bang into him. He has the SMG, with tripod and all, strapped to his back. He seems tireless. He takes one step to my three. His size is abnormal. Huge muscles swell the tight-fitting uniform. His strength is abnormal. He can shoulder-charge a wall and down it goes. Breaking bricks with a single chop of the edge of his hand is child's-play to him.

Porta is confident that Tiny's great-grandfather was a gorilla which had got loose from Hagenbeck and raped his great-grandmother. She was digging peat, says Porta, just outside the Zoological Gardens at the time. Tiny is quite proud of this anecdote.

I get myself tangled in a patch of thorn. I bend to free myself and a branch whips across my face, ripping it open. Blood pours down. I stumble, and the long thorns go through my uniform and bore into the flesh like bayonets.

Porta helps me out. The unit takes a break while the medical orderly extracts the poisonous thorns and treats the wounds. By afternoon I am swelling up and have a high fever. Luckily the orderly has a supply of serum. He bangs the needle into me straight through the uniform and camouflage jacket. It feels as if it goes straight into a lung. Raging I hit out at him with my Mpi. The needle snaps off as he jumps to safety.

'You wicked monkey,' he yells, pulling out his P-38. 'I'll teach you to lay your filthy hands on the Medical Corps!'

His pistol cracks twice before the others reach him and wrest it from him. It takes him a long time to simmer down and even then he won't touch me any more.

A 500 who has had medical training removes the broken needle from my back.

'Death by thirst is the worst death of all,' says the Legionnaire, staring out over the stony desert. The air shimmers in the heat.

We reach an impenetrable wall of scrub. The machetes cannot touch it.

'Back!' orders the Old Man, setting his teeth.

Despair and fear slowly take hold of us. It all seems hopeless.

We hear violent firing – which seems to come from the other side of the hills. A Maxim stammers furiously and an MG-42 replies. The path leads us back into the bush.

Porta recognizes a spot we have passed earlier. We halt, overcome by fatigue, and let ourselves drop to the ground.

The Old Man studies the map carefully, wrinkling his brows and clattering the lid of his pipe. Stojko sits down and hums a peasant song.

'Where the hell are you taking us?' shouts the Old Man, angrily, banging the map.

'Why you mad, Herr feldwebel?' asks Stojko, wonderingly. 'You crazy march compass 46. Needle run round and round all the time. But Bulgarian Guardsman always obey order. Only dumb soldier think self.'

The Old Man snatches the compass and map from him.

'There's nothing wrong with the compass!' he shouts, red in the face.

But when Stojko comes near it the compass needle whirls crazily.

The Old Man looks at Stojko.

'What've you got in your pockets, you Bulgarian assassin you?' shouts Porta.

'Only thing I take use on farm when war over.'

The Old Man searches him and turns up the better part of a dynamo.

The magnet has, of course, affected the compass needle.

The Old Man roars like a madman and throws the magnet far into the brush.

'Feldwebel take care,' Stojko warns him. 'No make big noise. Bad cactus devil come. Cut with sharp machete knife! Cactus spirit no care you German, you Russki. Cut off turnip before you say "Heil Hitler", they say "Red Front". Spirit no like crazy man make big noise. You take much care. Sun go, bad devil come from cactus!'

'Your bad devil can fuck me *crossways*,' roars the Old Man, beside himself with rage.

Stojko crosses himself three times and spins round in strange jerks. These are, apparently, protection against the cactus devil.

'I don't like this,' whispers Tiny to me, crossing himself. He has a great respect for everything supernatural.

'Why in the name of hell didn't you take the road you knew?' shouts the Old Man in a fury.

Stojko shakes his head despairingly and throws his hands wide. The sun glitters on his broad Royal Guards shoulder-straps.

'Feldwebel order follow compass 46. Stojko think crazy but Royal Bulgarian Guards no think self, so I not *care* you crazy. Order is order. You order compass 46. I see needle crazy too but me not leader. *You* leader. You *not* say go *short* way home. You say this we home long time.'

'Jesus wept!' groans the Old Man. 'Why did I ever have to meet up with you?'

' 'E's a right 'un, all-right,' says Tiny with a belly-chuckle. 'Few more like 'im 'an guns'd never be enough to finish the complicated bleedin' kind o' war '*e'd* set up.'

The Old Man shakes his head several times, then sits down and pulls Stojko down beside him.

'Listen Stojko! Forget all about the military. You are no longer a soldier.'

'Feldwebel!' Stokjo stands up and starts to brush the dust from his uniform. 'Stojko go farm now. Do all work not done since bad war start. You write me letter when home Germania.'

He goes round saying goodbye to all of us. It takes the Old Man several minutes to pull himself together. Then he explodes with the intensity of an artillery barrage.

'I'll give you farm, you mad, mad man. You'll not be maulin' those bloody cows of yours for hundreds of years yet. *Sit*, you sod, *sit!*' The Old Man bangs his Mpi butt on the ground beside him. 'Listen to *me*, and keep your bloody mouth *shut* until I'm finished. Anything you don't understand, say so. Do you understand me?'

'Feldwebel! No understand!'

'What? *What* don't you understand?' asks the Old Man, his jaw falling open.

'No understand what you want me understand,' says Stojko, with a friendly smile.

The Old Man throws his cap up the path, kicks an ammunition box violently, then fixes his gaze for a long while on Stojko's face. The patient face of a peasant.

'You are a soldier again. I order you to think for yourself. Now! If there is anything wrong then tell me what it is!'

'Feldwebel! War is wrong! All war! I not understand *war*!'

'Jesus wept, and well He might!' shouts the Old Man despairingly. '*I* know *that*! But we've *got* a war. And we're *in* it. Forget all that. We're in the middle of a lot of cactus. It's all we can manage to think about *now*. Don't *you* think about anything else. Just think how to get us out of it. Will you *do* that? You are our only leader. You alone. I, and the whole unit, will follow *you*. You are *the boss. Do you understand me?*'

'You give stars, I give order. Bulgarian Guard no dare give order no stars.'

The Old Man pulls the stars from his shoulder-straps and without hesitation names Stojko acting temporary feldwebel (unpaid).

The unit presents arms.

'*Now* I understand. We two feldwebel.' He laughs happily. 'You do first time, we home now, drink good cold water. You wait. I find way in cactus.'

We have almost given him up when he bursts out of the bush several hours later. He is filthy and scratched, but with a pleased expression on his weather-beaten peasant's face.

'Me find path,' he shouts happily. 'Hard path but good path. We no meet cactus spirit. Spirit no like blue cactus. Blue cactus send hell quick. Many scorpion live blue cactus. No touch blue cactus. Kill scorpion. Then path easy.'

'Shoulder arms! Move!' orders the Old Man, already off on Stojko's heels.

The entire spectrum of war noises can be heard in the distance.

'Sounds as if the whole bloody brothel's on its way up,' says Porta thoughtfully, listening carefully to the rumbling of the guns.

49

'Better get movin', as the wench said as she was on the verge o' gettin' raped for the fourth time,' grins Tiny.

'Jesus, boys, think if we could only run across some goddam transport we could commandeer,' says Buffalo, dreamily.

'Transport? Here?' says Porta. '*Horses* is what *we* could use. When they die of thirst you can at least drink their blood.'

'Soon as we're back with the regiment, I'm going sick. Think if part of the cure was drinking a whole barrel of icy-cold water,' sighs Gregor, licking his cracked lips.

'I'll be consulting the pavement artists first about the state of the little old man down below,' shouts Porta lecherously. 'Think if the poor little sod had got himself a permanent disability from all this shortage of water.'

We cross an interminable sequence of hills and then come to one which looks different from all the others. It is steeper, higher and completely flat on top. We stand and gaze for a few minutes. There is a threatening look about it which disturbs us.

Stojko finds a slope which is negotiable. Panting and blowing we crawl upwards. At the top a fantastic panorama spreads itself before us. We throw ourselves down for a short rest. We have been lying half-asleep for only about fifteen minutes when the padre begins to scream. We snatch at our weapons, partisans our first thought. In hysterics he points out over the great stony desert, which lies before us shimmering in the heat.

'Water!' he screams. 'See! see! A lake with swans!'

The Old Man gets up and snaps out his binoculars. There is no lake. Only rock and stone. Burning hot, glittering stone.

The padre runs lumberingly forward, holding his long staff out in front of him. He tumbles and rolls down the steep slope. At first we think he has broken his neck, but then he is up again and lolloping on in and out between the boulders. He throws himself down and rolls about, the dust rising in clouds around his threshing body.

'Water! water! My God Thou hast not forsaken me!'

But it's not water he is rolling in. It is dry, red dust.

'Up!' orders the Old Man harshly, and starts to move off himself.

We have to use our carbine-butts to get some of them moving. One of the wounded is dead, but we haven't the strength to bury him. We push his carbine into the ground and hang his helmet on the stock. The Old Man puts his identity discs in his pocket. His parents will be told, and spared the pain of endlessly hoping against hope that he will come home.

The Legionnaire begins to sing. Porta takes his piccolo from his boot-top. Tiny taps his mouth-organ on his palm. Hoarse-voiced, the rest of the unit join in. It sounds like a party of maniacs on the march.

> Es waren zwei Legionäre,
> Michael und Robert,
> sie hatten das Fort verlassen
> und suchten den Weg zum Meer.
> Sie wollten nie wieder Patrouille gehen,
> und nie wieder im Leben auf Posten stehen.
>
> Es waren zwei Legionäre,
> Michael und Robert,
> *Adieu, mon général,*
> *Adieu, Herr Leutnant*[14]

Dull-eyed we watch the padre, who is lying in the dust making swimming strokes. None of us has the strength to help him. Our whole attention is turned inwards into ourselves.

'Water!' he screams. He laughs insanely, throwing the red dust high above his head, as if he were splashing himself with water.

'Let's crack his skull,' suggests Heide hoarsely, lifting the stock of the MG like a club.

14. There were two legionnaires,
    Michel et Robert,
    who deserted the fort,
    made a break for *le mer*.
    No more on patrol will they strive,
    Nor stand guard at their post in this life.

    There were two legionnaires,
    Michel et Robert.
    Adieu, mon général,
    Adieu, Herr Leutnant . . .

'Leave him be!' thunders the Old Man, wiping his sunblistered face with the veil hanging from his tropical helmet.

The sun is merciless. It seems to boil the marrow of our bones. Two *500's* begin to fight. Before we can get between them one of them has ripped the other's stomach open with his bayonet. Entrails fall out and the blue-green flies swarm to a new feast.

The medical orderly puts the mortally wounded man out of his misery.

It is not, of course, permitted to administer a mercy bullet, but it is necessary here. The Old Man hardly knows what to do with the murderer. He is an ex-stabsfeldwebel. We pass a verdict of temporary insanity and forget the episode.

The padre has disappeared. We notice it only when the Old Man asks for him. Two men are sent back to pick him up. It takes threats of summary trial and the Old Man's Mpi to make them go.

Far into the night they return. Angrily they dump the padre's body on the ground at the Old Man's feet.

'Safe at last in Abraham's breast!' hums Tango, dancing round in the sand.

'Oh the poor dear man. How sad he had to die right in the middle of the testing God was giving him,' sighs Porta, with a simulated air of condolence.

The unit is on its way again. Stojko and the Old Man in the lead. Tiny's broad grey-green back is still in front of me. I cannot see past him. His shoulders sway in a rhythm like the gait of a camel. His back bends under the weight of the SMG. In the old days the only weapon a soldier had to carry was a rifle, but take a look at us, the soldiers of the current World War. Machine-guns, mountings, replacement barrels, doublebarrels, pistol, Mpi, range-finder, a damned lot of ammunition, signalling equipment, and then personal effects. All we have dumped is the gas-mask. Not because it's particularly heavy but because the container is handy to keep small things in: cigarettes, matches and the like. If they ever begin to use gas without warning, the war will end abruptly. Very few soldiers have a gas-mask left. Half Europe is littered with unwanted gas-masks.

The stone desert seems endless. Rocks on the left, rocks on the right. As far as we can see in front of us an endless sea of stone hot as the hob of hell. The sun bakes the stones, which give off heat like a breath from the mouth of a furnace. At night it is freezingly cold. Our teeth chatter. No birds fly here. We see their bodies lying spread-winged, dried out by the sun. Dead bodies of birds are everywhere.

'Wonder what it is kills 'em?' asks Porta, pushing cautiously at the body of a large black bird with the barrel of his Mpi.

'Plague! Bird pest,' says Heide, who, as always, is annoyingly well-informed. 'Keep your grabbers away from 'em. Humans can catch it!'

Hastily Porta rubs the barrel of his Mpi with the red dust.

'*Plague?* Jesus that's a wicked bleedin' thing!' says Tiny, hoarsely, looking around at the army of dead birds. 'War an' pestilence. That's what the biggest part of the 'uman race kicks off from.'

'You can live through both war and plague, if you can get a bit of the old lucky shit rubbed off on you,' laughs Porta wearily, fanning himself with his tall yellow hat.

We fall into a deathlike sleep. A 500 kills himself with a handgrenade. It is a terrible sight. Entrails splashed everywhere. It interests us. Gives us something to talk about for a while.

Tiny is sure we are going to find water. He swears he can smell it and rubs the air between thumb and forefinger.

'There's damp in the air!' he states with conviction.

We come close to fighting over his statement.

Porta finds a handful of half-dead, yellow-brown snails. They taste fairly good. You just have to get them down your throat quickly. The whole unit crawls round looking for snails, until Tiny ruins it by suddenly asking Heide if snails can carry bird-pest.

We throw up. Only Porta is indifferent.

He collects the snails from those who cannot eat them.

Throwing them into the air he catches them in his mouth and swallows them like a stork swallowing frogs. You can see them moving down his long thin neck.

I can only manage five. The sixth starts to move in my mouth and I have to spit it out.

Strangely the snails seem to assuage our thirst. We feel a little easier, as we march on.

Stojko leads us down through a passage between cliffs. The granite sides tower above us on both sides. The clear blue sky with its merciless blazing sun is no more than a slit high above our heads.

'God, we're marching into a grave,' groans Gregor in despair. He is in the depths of despondency.

It doesn't even help when Porta starts up a conversation on Ferrari cars.

'How was that long Mercedes Benz high-compression sports job?' I ask. 'Did you and your general have one of those to run round the front with?'

Gregor merely stares at me with dull eyes. He has completely lost interest in sports cars. Even when we ask him to describe his general's mobile thunder-box of Meissen porcelain, we can't get him to liven up, and that is usually the magic key.

In the course of the day we emerge from the cleft and are out on the stony plain again. We are happy to have left its grim shadow.

Heide sees them first. Skeletons. Hundreds of them. Bones gleam whitely amongst the green of the cactus. They are not all human bones. There are also the bones of mules. Equipment lies scattered all around. Some of the skeletons are still wearing steel helmets. Most of them are Bulgarian, but we see also a few Italian Bersaglieri. We can see it by the helmet channelled for plumes.

'Holy Mafia, what's happened?' asks Barcelona uneasily.

'God only knows,' answers the Old Man. 'Partisans probably, and it mayn't even have been very long ago. The sun, wind and drought soon make a skeleton of a dead 'un here.'

'And the ants,' adds Porta.

Our diet becomes strange and various. The Legionnaire finds some beetles running around on the skeletons. They are big and fat and taste wonderful.

'We used to eat them in the desert,' he explains, breaking one apart.

Late in the afternoon we drag ourselves into a village where there are also skeletons everywhere, but here there are signs of

54

fighting. On the square a whole row of skeletons hang. Their clothing keeps them whole.

Porta disappears with Tiny on a search of the ruins. We can hardly believe our own eyes when they come back with a goat-skin filled with water.

The Old Man has to hold us back with his Mpi. We are like wild animals, and only quiet down when he is forced to shoot an ex-leutnant who refuses to obey his orders.

The bloody corpse stops us dead. Has the Old Man gone mad? He can usually maintain discipline without having to resort to arms. He swings the Mpi in a semicircle.

'Get into line you lousy bastards. Anybody else looking for a ticket to heaven?'

Pushing and snarling like mad dogs we fall into line.

Porta hands the Old Man the goatskin. One by one we fill our canteens, and the goatskin is empty.

Despite the Old Man's warning we drink the whole of our ration immediately. It tastes terrible. Tiny thinks it is most probably donkey-piss, but we couldn't have cared less. It slakes our thirst for a while.

Porta is so happy he pulls his piccolo from his boot-top and plays.

In the shadow of the gallows with its swinging, rattling burden of skeletons we get together and sing:

> Germany you noble house
> Hang the bloodstained banners out.
> Let them ever wave and strain
> God is with us in storm and rain.

We all become very sick from the water. Men squat every-where with their trousers down around their heels.

'Dysentery,' comments the medic.

Six men die before it is over. We lie dozing for several days while fever rages in our bodies. The medic gives us what he has available. Slowly we recover.

Porta has found water again. This time the medic insists on it being boiled. There is not much of it but it helps.

'See! What did I say? Didn't we find water,' grins Tiny in triumph.

It is Buffalo who first sees the two men in front of us. We had almost caught up with them. Strangely enough they do not see us. Silently we follow them. They are moving fast. It is as if they had some important errand.

We march all night. The moon casts her pale light over the stony wasteland. A dog howls far away. Where there are dogs there is water and usually human beings.

The house is an adobe hut plastered up against a slope and looking as if it might at any moment disappear down into the depths below it. The two hurrying men disappear behind the house.

Porta and I steal after them. The unit fans out. The SMG is positioned behind a rock. The night quivers with tension. Not a sound can be heard. It is as if the cliffs had swallowed the two men up. Porta and I stop and take cover behind a stack of straw which should give some protection against bullets.

We hear heavy knocking on a door, and a harsh voice cuts through the night.

'Delco! Olja! You've got visitors! Come out and greet us!'

There is no reply. Only that night wind whistling faintly. There is the sound of wood splintering under the blow of a rifle-butt.

'Come out, you bitches' afterbirth! You cannot hide yourselves from our justice.'

'Justice by night!' whispers Porta half-laughingly.

The two men stamp into the hut. Nailed boots ring ominously. The tramp of executioners.

'Delco and Olja! Come out and defend yourselves, you filthy traitors! Your German friends can't protect you now!'

'How wrong can you get?' whispers Porta patting his Mpi tenderly. 'Death comes, more often than not, as the result of an error!'

Light flares behind the small windows. It flickers and throws long shadows. We see the man holding the light quite clearly.

'What a perfect target he *does* make,' says Porta lifting his Mpi.

'Think I can win the cigar?'

'Get him!' I whisper breathlessly.

Njet! grins Porta. 'Let's find out what these two highwaymen are up to before we let their brains out. Couple of limp pricks, that's what *they* are. Nothing else!'

A long thin candle has begun to burn sleepily. On a low bed in the corner sit three people pressed up against the wall. A young woman, a man, and a child about five years of age.

'There we have Olja and Delco,' whispers Porta. 'Traitors, but of course depending on which side you see their case from. I know a lot of quite nice traitors, who are far more honest than these "five minutes after midnight" nationalists.' He puts a cigarette in his mouth.

'You're not going to show a light?' I ask, terrified. Porta looks at me contemptuously, knocks a spark from the razor-blade, blows on the charred cloth and lights his cigarette from the glow. The Russian 'lighter' is made for night smoking in wartime. Primitive as the people who invented it, but there is no betraying flame.

He expels smoke, holding the cigarette in the cup of his hand so that the burning tip cannot be seen.

'A good play calls for a smoke,' he whispers.

The man inside the room laughs aloud with satisfaction.

'Why didn't you open the door? Why should we have to break it down? Come here Ljuco! All the family together and quite speechless with happiness at the sight of us.' He laughs long and loud.

Ljuco, the comrade who has been standing by a narrow door at the end of the hut, comes stamping in. A cigarette holder moves jerkily between his teeth. He laughs. A strange dry crackling noise. Executioners laugh like that when they tell the story of some interesting execution.

'Got any schnapps?' he asks, opening cupboard doors and throwing tins and bowls to the floor. Poorly-made kitchen utensils smash to pieces on the stones.

'Wh-what do you want?' asks the man on the bed in a trembling voice. The whole room smells of fear.

'To have a little talk with you, my dear Delco. Shall we speak in German, or would you prefer our own language? Let us speak German. You have surely forgotten your mother tongue after all the years you have spent with your German friends.'

'I have nothing to do with the Germans,' Delco defends himself. 'Do you think if I had I would be living here?'

'Delco, dear little Delco, what nonsense! We know *all* about you. Have you had a knock on the head for your memory to be affected so? Have you no memory of Peter? Of Pone? Of Illijeco? *Of my brother!*'

'I don't know what you're talking about. I know what happened to your brother but I had nothing to do with it!'

'Loss of memory! Remarkable case,' jerks out the man with the cigarette-holder and the strange desiccated laughter. He has found a bottle of *Slivovitz* and drinks almost half of it, before handing the bottle on to his comrade.

'It seems to be contagious. Nobody remembers anything any more. The disease seems to be particularly virulent in wartime. What about you, Olja, have you also become infected with this loss of memory?'

The woman does not answer him. Fear stares from her large terrified eyes. She hugs the boy tightly to her.

'The dry air out here makes thoughts so light, perhaps, that in the end they fly right away,' laughs the cigarette-holder man. He belches loudly.

'Why do you come here in the middle of the night and break your way in? Why do you not come in daylight like honest men?'

'Delco, Delco, we missed your company so much that we simply couldn't wait when we finally heard where you were. Your German friends were kind enough to help us with a lift. We do a little work for them ourselves, you know. Or perhaps you *don't* know? They are very pleased with you and Olja. SD-Obersturmführer Scharndt asked us specially to visit you and to look after you! And now we are here and we *do* intend really to look after you.' He looks round the poor room. 'Your place in Sofia was much nicer.' The cigarette-holder man laughs, a weird, toneless crackle. It reminds one of a gallows creaking in the wind.

His comrade sings softly:

Wenn was nicht klappt, dann sag ich unverhohlen,
wie man so sagt 'Die Heimat hat's befohlen!'

Es ist so schön, gar keine Schuld zu kennen
und sich nur einfach ein Soldat zu nennen.[15]

They hoist themselves noisily up onto the table. They swing their legs. Their highly-polished riding boots gleam in the candlelight. The boots seem somehow threatening. These two are soldiers though still seeming to be partly civilian.

'Do you find it boring here in the mountains?' asks the cigarette-holder man, mockingly. 'With only scorpions, snakes and the little red body-snatchers to keep you company?'

With shaking fingers the young woman buttons her nightdress up to the throat. The little boy presses himself closer to his mother. He cannot understand German, but can feel the dangerous tension in the air.

The cigarette-holder man takes down a guitar from the wall, climbs up on the table again, and begins to experiment with the instrument.

'You hold musical evenings here?' He strikes a few harsh, dissonant phrases from the strings.

The little family presses tighter against the wall as if hoping it will swallow them up. Their faces are pale blots. The crickets sing loudly, almost drowning out the sound of the wild, mad guitar.

I look uncertainly at Porta and lift my Mpi.

'Not yet,' he whispers, shaking his head. 'Not our business yet. This is between the Greeks and the Bulgars. If anything illegal happens, we interfere. We are taking care of things on behalf of the police, who are not with us at this time.'

I smile tiredly and wish myself anywhere but here.

The hunters are triumphant inside the hut. Their prey is cornered. The boy pushes his tousled head into his father's chest.

'Why *did* you go over to those brown devils?' asks the leader.

'Because they thought it was to their advantage, of course,' laughs the cigarette-holder man. He takes the carbine slowly

15. And if *I* do wrong why then I can say,
    As always ''twas the Fatherland's order today'.
    It is so good, and to soldiers appealing,
    For innocence is such a wonderful feeling.

from his shoulder, snaps the lock noisily and extracts a clip of bullets from his pocket. He holds it up to the light. The six bullets gleam like gold. 'Pretty, eh?' he almost whispers. 'German bullets!' He removes one from the clip and studies it carefully. 'Very new too. Made in Bamberg in 1943, and I do believe they have your numbers on them!'

Olja is weeping silently.

'We have been looking for you for a long time,' says the leader coldly. 'It was not until we asked your German friends about you that we got a lead. Now we are here!'

'And you certainly don't seem overjoyed to see us,' laughs the cigarette-holder man, pressing the clip into the magazine of his carbine.

'Delco and Olja,' says the leader, as if he were enjoying the very taste of the words. 'You have been sentenced to death! You have betrayed your people, and we have come to carry out the sentence passed upon you!'

'We've betrayed nobody,' shouts Delco wildly, putting his arm around his wife. 'Our country is allied to Germany. Our Army is fighting in the Soviet. I am a Bulgarian policeman.'

'Delco, you understand so *little*! You *were* a policeman, the poor tool of the Royalists. The Bulgarian people does not wish to fight for the King and his Fascist vassals against the great Soviet brotherland.'

'The King *ordered* us to fight the Soviets,' screams Delco, desperately. The two carbine muzzles move slowly until they are pointing directly at him.

The cigarette-holder man laughs a laugh without a trace of amusement in it.

'How stupid people are,' he sighs. 'They simply *will* not understand.'

Olja screams plangently, and hides her face in her hands.

Delco makes a movement to get to his feet, but slumps down again despairingly. He is facing the inevitable. The boy seems to make himself smaller, pressing in between his terrified parents. Wide-eyed he stares at these terrible guests who have appeared so suddenly from the night.

The stillness of death reigns in the humble room.

The cigarette-holder man strums dreamily on the guitar.

Suddenly he throws it from him. Strings jangle and snap. He laughs noisily.

Two shots crash out almost together.

Olja slides down from the bed. Her hands are still pressed to her face. Delco lifts himself half up, then falls sideways across the bed clutching at the pillow. His body jerks and is still.

Immediately after the shots there is a strange quiet in the room. The two executioners remain sitting stiffly on the table for several minutes.

A long, piercing bird call comes from the unit.

Porta answers with the call of a raven. This tells them that we are all right.

'Why didn't you call them up here?' I ask in a whisper.

'Njet, the Old Man'd ruin the last act, and I don't think our good German God would like that.' Porta laughs ominously.

'Shall we go in?' I ask.

'No, no. Let them enjoy themselves a little longer. *The pair of shits!*'

The two executioners are still sitting on the bed watching the little boy. He strokes his father's hair lovingly.

'Will you shoot me, too? I am all alone now.'

The executioners look questioningly at one another. The cigarette-holder man lifts his carbine.

'No!' snarls the leader, knocking it down.

'Why not?' asks the cigarette-holder man in surprise. 'Best thing to do with the little traitor.'

I arm a hand-grenade. If they kill the boy I'll throw it. I am so furious I am shaking all over.

'Daddy, mummy, I'm all alone! Where am I to go?' The boy's voice trembles. It is easy to hear that he is close to tears. This 'great' war has hardened children in an unnatural way. The brutal face of death has become an everyday sight to them.

The executioners jump lightly down from the table. The cigarette-holder man laughs and looks through the cupboards again, to see if there is anything he can use. He pokes at the bodies with the barrel of his carbine.

Olja is still breathing. He presses the muzzle of the carbine against her neck. A shot crashes. The skull splinters. Pieces of bone and brains spatter the room.

Porta looks at me. We say nothing but we are agreed on what is to be done.

Noisily they leave the hut.

A little white dog comes rushing around the corner. The cigarette-holder man kills it with a couple of blows from the butt of his carbine and kicks the body inside the hut.

'It would be best to kill the child,' he says when they have gone a little way. 'If the Germans come he could identify us, you know.'

'You are right,' says the leader. 'Do it then!'

The cigarette-holder man laughs his dry, rasping rattle of a laugh. It tails off in a gasp as he almost runs up against our Mpi muzzles.

'Hi, there!' says Porta, pleasantly, tipping his yellow hat to them.

'Ooh!' comes in astonishment from the cigarette-holder man.

'Booh!' laughs Porta.

'We have *Ausweis*[16],' says the leader, nervously. 'We are employed by the SD[17].'

'Like fuck you have,' answers Porta, brutally, splashing him without warning across the face with his Mpi. The sight tears his cheek open.

I press my weapon into the pit of the cigarette-holder man's belly, and snick the safety off.

'Take it easy now, chum, or I'll blow your guts out through your back for you.'

Like all killers he fears death greatly.

'What are you up to?' asks the leader, wiping the blood from his face.

'Guess!' laughs Porta roughly.

'Shall we tell him?' I ask.

Porta spits in the leader's face.

'You have *Ausweis*, you say! Employed by the SD, you say! You're our friends, you say!'

'Indeed we *are*,' says the cigarette-holder man fervently. Panic terror is in his eyes.

16. Ausweis: Identity cards.
17. SD (Sicherheitsdienst): Security Service.

'Good, *good*!' says Porta with a terrible grin. 'Were you also friends of the two dear departed inside there?'

'Traitors, they were,' says the leader. 'Communists, Soviet spies.'

Porta whistles in surprise.

'And you two fixed their waggon for them? Sorry, sonnies, it won't work. We've been following you boys all night. One thing, you two certainly know how to run a good exciting, dramatic liquidation-scene. Five stars you get from this reviewer.'

'We were only obeying orders,' stammers the cigarette-holder man, nervously.

'Orders?' sneers Porta. 'Get your kicks from obeying orders, do you? See here, kiddies, *we* get *paid* for murdering. Paid by the German state, see? They've given us stripes on our arms and tin on our chests for it. We're *good* at it, you understand! Now usually we only do it for money, but you boys you're SD and you're our friends. So for you we do it for nothing. Won't cost you a *penny* to get your guts shot out. And by *experts*, too!'

We hear marching boots and the rattle of equipment coming up the path. The unit is on the move with the Old Man in the lead. I look quickly at Porta. He nods slightly.

'On your way, friends,' he says to the two executioners. 'If you can really run you can save yourselves yet.'

They seem not to understand us for a moment. Our expressions are friendly. We seem to intend them well. Quickly, they turn on their heels and are off at full speed.

'So long, boys!' shouts Porta, tipping his cylindrical, yellow hat.

Our Mpi's rattle. The two men fall and roll down the path.

'What the devil's going on,' shouts the Old Man at our backs. He sees the bodies. 'What's all this?' he asks, threateningly.

'Couple of the heathen,' grins Porta. 'They'd just murdered a wife and husband. We ordered them to halt, but they wouldn't. They ran and we opened fire, according to the manual.'

The Old Man looks at us suspiciously.

'If you've fixed up a phony "attempted escape", I'll get you two a summary!'

63

Tiny gets up with a short laugh and shows us three gold teeth.

'You fixed them up proper, all right. Nearly cut 'em in two. They must've been bleedin' barmy to make a run for it!'

The boy is still sitting by his father's body running his hand over the dead man's hair. His hands are covered with blood.

'I'm all alone now. Where must I go?' he repeats the words automatically, stonily.

The Old Man picks him up and comforts him.

'You'll come with us!'

We bury the parents behind the house. We search the hut, but there is nothing worth liberating. There is not much water either. Two goatskins partly full.

'They must have got water from somewhere,' says the Legionnaire thoughtfully and continues the search.

We try to question the boy but he seems as if paralysed and will only repeat, 'I'm all alone now. Where must I go?'

We come up again on to the dreadful open stretches of rock and stones. In a kind of clearing we find the bodies of five Bulgarian soldiers. When we touch them they fall to dust.

'Thirst!' says the Old Man, laconically.

'Deserters, most likely. Tired of war and all that shit,' considers Porta.

Tiny looks for gold teeth. There are none.

'Let's get on!' screams Buffalo desperately. He has become strangely thin lately.

The medic is going round the bend.

'Finished! Finished!' he keeps mumbling.

We are worn-out from thirst, and can only march a few miles at a time. After every break it takes rifle-butts to get us moving again.

A 500 is bitten by a scorpion and dies in terrible convulsions. Fearfully we stand around and watch him die.

During a rest period on the fourth day we are shocked by a pistol shot. The medical orderly has shot himself. He lies with his head in a pool of blood. The blue flies have already accepted the invitation to dinner.

'That's *one* way,' says Gregor, in a death-rattle of a voice.

'No silliness, now,' whispers the Old Man, hoarsely.

We cannot summon up the strength to bury the medic. The red ants are quick on the job and will soon clear him away. In the course of a few days only a uniform and a skeleton will be left. We remove the bolt from his carbine, stick it muzzle down in the ground, and place his helmet on the stock.

'Let's get *on*,' slurs Barcelona. He is using a rifle for a crutch. One of his feet is terribly swollen and gives off a stench of rotting meat.

In the afternoon Tiny and the white-haired ex-oberst begin to quarrel. They look like a couple of birds getting ready to fight.

The oberst fires. The bullet burns across Tiny's throat.

The Legionnaire lifts his Mpi and shoots the oberst down. He lies back down again quietly as if nothing had happened.

The oberst falls to his knees, both hands pressed to his stomach. Blood pours over his hands.

'Murderers!' he groans and falls forward on his face.

The little boy laughs suddenly. High and shrill. For a moment we look at him in surprise. Then we begin to laugh too.

The oberst lifts his head. His face is twisted. He looks for all the world like the clown in a circus. We laugh croakingly, like a group of maniac crows. The Old Man is the only one not laughing. He is watching the dead oberst as if he cannot understand what is going on.

'The general died at goddam dawn!' Buffalo screams madly, and kicks at the oberst's head.

We never know who cuts the head off. Tango is about to kick at it when a burst from an Mpi smashes into the ground close to his feet.

'Enough o' that,' snarls the Old Man, pressing a new magazine into his Mpi.

We come to our senses, and drop down where we stand. When the Old Man moves us on again four of us have died in their sleep.

Our feet feel as if we were walking on broken glass. In the afternoon we find a cactus, the juice of which is drinkable. The Legionnaire knows it from his time in the desert. We feel so refreshed we march five miles more before having to rest again.

Porta marches in front of me, mumbling strangely to himself:

'Snipe should always be allowed to hang. Plucking of feathers must be carried out with great care. The skin must on no account be broken. Wings can be chopped off. Allow the head to remain. The stomach muscle must be removed. The little villains often fill themselves up with sand. This *does* grit between the teeth when they are eaten but the rest should still be left inside the bird. Now tie a thin slice of fat around each beast. A little salt and pepper, and into the hot oven with the whole flock. For the Holy Elizabeth's sake do not, whatever you do, allow them to remain there more than eight minutes. The sauce should be thinned carefully with just a smidgin of water. The rest is done at the table over a tiny spirit-burner. A pat of butter and two spoonfuls of cognac is not a bad thing. The cognac should be allowed to burn itself off. The burning cognac and butter give the little monster the true aroma.'

He marches along in silence for a while. Then he licks his lips and throws a glance upwards at the blazing sun.

He marches as if he were completely alone. Then: 'I hope the hare has been allowed to soak for at least two hours in brandy and red wine. The onions we put into the butter. Eight ounces of pork, cut into large strips, should then be lightly boiled. Up then comes our swift-footed beast. Turn him nicely so that he is properly browned all over. A small handful of flour is then cast lightly on to the body. The whole must then be allowed to roast for a short time. Three glasses of red wine, a little soup, one clove of crushed garlic, and if you do not wish to incur the wrath of the Holy Mother of Kazan, do *not* forget the salt and pepper. Now allow the great runner to roast in the oven for about an hour, while the greens are being prepared: Ten ounces of mushrooms must be chopped as finely as if they were to be strewn upon the delicate breasts of a young virgin. Add to this: Chives chopped small. Then we must prepare the browned chopped onions. We remove the skin from eight seedless tomatoes and press them well. A little rosemary on top, and we choose our wine. For dessert I would choose *Hamantaschen* which your Jew consumes with delight at the great feast of Purim.'

'What on earth are you drivelling about?' I ask in wonder.

'I was just fixing up a meal for myself in my well-appointed kitchen!'

'Shut up, will you,' says Gregor, with tears in his voice. 'I'm nearly dying of hunger!'

'*If* we ever get home again,' says Porta, stopping for a moment. 'I would recommend to your attention a dish of pike in butter-sauce, or perhaps blue trout, but you must make quite certain that the fish is served straight from the water in which it has been boiled and with the true Hollandaise sauce. For a second course you will not be disappointed if you decide on mutton ragoût prepared in the French style. This *must* however be served on earthenware.'

'Between these courses you could take some Burgundian snails, in their own natural juices. They sharpen the appetite. *If* you choose the mutton you must, of course, finish the meal with crêpes flambées.'

'One more word out of you and I'll blast your bloody chops off,' roars the Old Man, aiming his Mpi at Porta, who is just about to explain which wine he would choose for his recommended menu, and why.

A Fieseler Storch spots us. The pilot circles above us several times. We lie spread out on the top of a plateau, in a state of complete exhaustion.

The Old Man shoots off all our signals ammunition.

A couple of hours later the Storch is back. It drops skins of water to us.

The following day we have strength enough to continue our march.

An armoured column finds us. We can hardly manage to pull ourselves up on to the lorries which carry us to Corinth. We spend a few days in the infirmary. The little boy is taken over by the Greek authorities. We never know what becomes of him. The unit offered to adopt him, but the NSFO[18] turned the idea down with a sneer. Adopt an *untermensch*? Permission *not* granted.

18. NSFO (Nationalsozialistischer Führungsoffizier): Political (Nazi) officer.

Once you have carried out an order for the SD you are tied to us for ever. Have you understood me? For ever ... No one leaves the Security Services alive.'

SD-Obergruppenführer Heydrich to
SS-Hauptsturmführer Alfred Naujock,
April, 1936

The time is a little past eleven o'clock on the morning of a warm summer Sunday in 1944.

The streets of Essen are empty and deserted. An alert has been signalled. Everyone is in the cellars. No, not everyone! From Rottstrasse an SS-patrol emerges. Mouse-grey uniforms, and silvery death-heads shining in their caps. In front of them walk two thirteen-year-old boys with hands folded on the back of their necks.

The patrol turns down Kreuzekirch Strasse. A little way down the street they wheel in to a bombed yard.

'Stand over there!' commands the SD-underscharführer, jerking the muzzle of his Mpi towards a soot-blackened wall.

The boys go over to the wall and stand against it. They let their arms sink to their sides. Eyes, deeply sunk in skull-like faces, stare in terror. They are both quite small and terribly thin.

'Faces to the wall!' screams the unterscharführer in a shrill, penetrating voice. 'Hands on your necks!'

The SD-men take a few paces to the rear, and lift their Mpi's.

The boys begin to sob. They press themselves against the wall as if security were to be found there.

'Stop!' cries a voice, suddenly. A well-dressed civilian rushes across the yard.

'What do you want, here?' asks the scharführer, slowly lowering the muzzle of his Mpi.

'Are you mad? You cannot shoot children like this!'

'We can't eh? We can, and we can do more than that, too!'

'But they are only children!' says the civilian, in an urgent tone.

'Don't bother me,' answers the scharführer. 'Looting during an air-raid is punishable by death on the spot. I couldn't care less if they were babies in arms.'

'I am Professor Kuhlmann, Oberstabsarzt and Superintendent of Support Hospital No. 9 here in Essen.'

'Well now!' grins the scharführer, looking round at his men. 'None of us reporting sick just now, doctor.'

'I forbid you to shoot these children! Do you understand me, Herr Scharführer?'

'Forget the "Herr" part,' the scharführer replies, a dangerous glint appearing in his eyes. He lifts his Mpi and presses the muzzle of it into the professor's stomach. 'Now listen to me, you sad sack. To me you're just a dumb civvy, and I'm orderin' you to clear out of here, and quick!'

'I order you to let those children go,' shouts the professor, going red and white by turns.

'I'm counting to three,' snarls the scharführer. 'If you ain't gone by then you'll be keepin 'em company. One . . .'

The professor moves backwards, slowly, step by step.

The scharführer smiles with satisfaction, and brings his attention back to the two boys at the wall. Their thin bodies shake with convulsive sobs.

'Fire!' he shouts. The command echoes round the yard.

Five Mpi's bark!

The boys collapse to the ground. A great pool of blood forms under them, flooding over the concrete of the yard.

The professor runs from the place, his hands pressed tightly over his ears.

The SD–men swing their Mpi's carelessly back on to their shoulders, and march noisily out of the yard. They have done no more than carry out orders.

69

THE FLEAS

Two bodies swing gently to and fro in the warm breeze. Dry beams creak.

No. 2 section is sitting under the gallows throwing dice. Tiny throws a worried glance upwards.

' 'Ope them two dead bleeders don't fall down on our 'eads sudden-like!'

None of us knows who has strung up the German general and the Russian woman captain. Everyone and everything in this village has been killed. Even the cats and dogs. The company has been sent out on a mopping-up operation. This village was already a ghost-town when we arrived in it this morning.

The corpses have begun to smell in the heat.

There is a larger gallows set up behind the school building. Two partisans and an SS-man from the Mussulman Division swing from it. The Mussulman is still wearing his grey fez. A great number of civilians dangle from the branches of trees in the woods.

The general and the woman captain seem to have been made to stand on a wine butt which has then been kicked away from under their feet. A good part of the wine has run out, but there is still enough left in the butt for us to be able to fill our water-bottles.

'Where the devil's Porta got to?' asks the Old Man, throwing a six.

'Hunting,' says Gregor, flourishing the dice-box above his head flamboyantly.

'Never thinks of anything else,' grumbles the Old Man. 'Gold teeth's all he *thinks* about!'

' 'Old on, old 'un, 'old on,' says Tiny protestingly. ' 'Ow's a poor bleeder to get capital enough to keep up with that bleedin'

Chief Mechanic Wolf without 'is gettin' 'old of a bit o' bleedin' loot now an' again?'

'Sod *that*,' snarls the Old Man, lighting his silver-lidded pipe. 'I'm not standing for it much longer, I tell you. Looting the dead's what *that* is, and it costs you your nut in any man's army, sonnies.'

Porta turns the corner, whistling merrily. He has three white furs over his shoulder.

'Poverty-stricken hole,' he shouts to us. 'Nothing but these three skins.'

The Old Man buys one immediately. Porta keeps the other two for himself. The nights are cold and we envy him.

Tiny asks Porta to lend him one for half the night so that he too can try how it feels to lie in soft and warm for once.

'When I've enjoyed them myself for a few nights, I've decided to rent them out,' says Porta, from the heights of ownership. 'You'll be first man on the list, my son.'

We sleep in one of the peasant huts. The Old Man sighs happily from the depths of his fur.

In the middle of the night all hell breaks loose. The Old Man is running roaring round the hut scratching himself like a madman. His whole body is covered with flea bites. His face is thickly sown with red spots which soon turn to blisters.

Shortly after this the rest of us are up, dancing around scratching. Thousands of fleas have attacked our defenceless bodies. The furs are alive with them.

We rush out of the hut, away from the tiny vampires.

Only Porta sleeps on untroubled. He is still lying there rolled up in his two skins.

We cannot understand it. *We* have been bitten halfway to the bone. Tiny thinks it might be because Porta is red-headed.

'We 'ad a 'ore on the Reeperbahn as was red-'eaded an' 'ad a 'igh-class beat round the Café Keese,' he explains. ' 'Ot-arse we used to call 'er. An' she *never* got crabs. Even when we *all* 'ad 'em in Sct. Pauli *she* never did. All the bleedin' Scandinavians as come down to get a cheap drunk on, went back with a load o' German crabs.'

'You come any closer with those blasted flea incubators, and

I'll have those furs burnt,' rages the Old Man, scratching away madly.

'Oh, oh!' shouts Porta, insulted. 'There's no fleas in these furs. You must've brought 'em with you.'

The day after we get back to Corinth, Porta is walking along with the three furs over his shoulder. He hasn't got far before the CO's Kübel catches up with him.

'What are those furs you've got there, Porta?' asks Oberst Hinka, leaning out of the Kübel inquisitively.

'Herr Oberst, sir, present from my Swedish uncle, sir. Should of arrived for my birthday but there's postal delay from Sweden just now, sir. Swedish post goes by reindeer, sir.'

'Have you really an uncle in Sweden?' asks Oberst Hinka, in amazement. 'I wasn't aware of it.'

'Herr Oberst, sir, the Porta family is all over the world. Feldwebel Blom has met some of us in Spain, and when we were stationed in Italy we saw the name on many a facade, sir. We're a roving lot, sir, never stay long in the same place, sir.'

'Where are you going with those furs? Do you intend to sell them?'

'Herr Oberst, sir, my Swedish uncle wants me to be warm at night but the good German *ersatz* blanket our Führer provides us with is warm enough for me. Yes sir, I never *am* cold at night so I'm off to Corinth now to sell these furs.'

'What is the price?' asks Oberst Hinka, passing his hand over the furs.

'Herr Oberst, sir, to you sir I'll sell them cheap. Two pounds of coffee, a bottle of schnapps and a carton of cigarettes is the price.'

'All right,' smiles Oberst Hinka. 'You can pick up the goods at the officers' mess.'

Porta throws the smallest of the furs into the back of the Kübel and swings the two others over his shoulder again.

'What's this?' asks Oberst Hinka in surprise, holding up the small fur. 'I thought I was buying all three?'

'No sir, Herr Oberst. The Herr Oberst was buying only *one* fur.'

'You're not being a little too smart, do you think, Porta?'

'Herr Oberst, sir, that's a very cheap price to pay even for *one* fur.'

'I don't doubt it,' mumbles Oberst Hinka. 'Very well. Let me take all three. Even though they *are* expensive.'

'Herr Oberst, sir. The Swedish furs and everything to do with them are now the Herr Oberst's sole property,' cries Porta, putting the other two furs on the back seat behind the adjutant.

'Oberst Hinka'll have you in jail till you *rot*,' prophesies the Old Man when Porta tells him where the flea-skins are now.

'I didn't *make* him buy 'em,' grins Porta, carelessly. 'He was mad to get hold of them. I even told him it was more than furs he was buying so he's got nothing to complain about.'

'Selling a flea circus like that to your own CO's pure suicide,' cries Gregor, with a dry laugh.

Very early the next morning Porta receives orders to report to the CO's quarters.

Oberst Hinka meets him, naked to the waist and covered with the marks of a flea-bitten night.

He addresses Porta for twenty minutes without stopping.

'I am *aware*,' he screams finally, 'that you have a promising career of usury before you. But don't try anything like this again with *mo*, or – and this I promise you – your career will be cut short most abruptly. You have been to Germersheim. What do you think of it?'

'Herr Oberst, sir,' answers Porta, clicking his heels together with all his might, 'from the opposite bank of the Rhine Germersheim makes a pretty picture which reminds one strongly of our great Imperial past. I have not heard of anyone in his senses who finds it attractive when seen from the inside.'

'Get out of my sight!' roars Hinka, jabbing his finger madly at the door.

Outside Porta meets the Adjutant, to whom Oberst Hinka has been generous enough to lend one of the furs for the night.

'You seem to be of the opinion,' snarls the tortured officer, 'that my blood is good food for fleas?'

'Herr Adjutant, sir, I know nothing about fleas. Perhaps some lousy officer, sir, on the staff, sir, has come near the Swedish furs?'

73

A few minutes later Porta is out on the village street with his furs and his fleas.

On his way up the sleepy street he meets the padre, who stares enviously at the white furs slung nonchalantly over Porta's shoulder.

'Are those furs yours?' he asks carefully.

'Yes, Herr Uberfeltkappellan,' answers Porta, saluting stiffly.

The padre passes his long, thin fingers gently over the furs and thinks what a beautiful saddle cloth they would make.

His horse stares at Porta, who stares back at it with the calculating mien of a born horse-dealer.

'You'd cut up into some lovely steaks,' he thinks, and works out in his head how much the horse would bring in, properly butchered, at Corinth meat-market.

'Those are very beautiful furs,' the padre praises them devoutly. 'I have never seen their like!'

'Yes, they're *Swedish*,' says Porta with emphasis.

'Swedish goods are quality goods,' smiles the military spiritual adviser, bending forward over his horse's neck. 'Where did our good obergefreiter obtain these lovely furs.'

'My Herr Oberst gave them to me. He got them from a fur farm in Finland,' explains Porta, with wide, innocent eyes.

'So your oberst has a fur farm in Finland?' The Padre's native suspicions seem to have been awakened. For a moment he looks inquisitively at the tall, thin obergefreiter in front of him. 'I thought you said the furs were Swedish?'

'Beg pardon, sir, these furs are from the Swedish-speaking part of Finland, which they call Nyeland up there.'

'But how has your oberst come to own a fur farm in Finland?'

'Begging your pardon, sir, my oberst's mother is one of the great daughters of Finland,' Porta looks up at the padre with an expression of such foolish good-will on his face that it would be enough to make even the most hardboiled NKVD prison guard break into tears.

'She is 6 feet 2 inches tall,' he adds, after a short pause, sighing audibly.

74

'My oberst's mother inherited a farm with all sorts of animals that have fur, like polar bears and sable and all the kinds that they have in the Swedish-speaking part of Finland. Please sir, do you know Finland, sir?'

The military parson had to admit that he did not.

'Our regiment was up there in the war one time,' Porta confides, scratching the priestly horse behind the ear. 'We were volunteer partisans under a Captain Guri[1] who was also a partisan. Believe it or not, sir, nearly all the neighbours we met died of heart attacks, sir. It was almost like an epidemic we carried round with us. 'Course, sir, this Captain Guri we had wasn't a German but a kind of Laplander, *and* a very religious officer, sir. Never see him kill a neighbour without first saying a prayer for his soul.'

'Yes, yes indeed,' answers the padre, thoughtfully, passing his fingers once more over the skins. 'For sale, obergefreiter?'

'What sir, me sir?' asks Porta stupidly. Experience has taught him that stupidity gets one furthest with military parsons. Holy people are most often stupid people.

'*No*, man, the furs, of course,' hisses the padre, irritated. It is a long time since he has met such an idiot as this red-haired obergefreiter. 'What are you asking for them?'

'Well sir, Herr überfeldkappelan, sir, I was thinking of: five bottles of schnapps and six pounds of coffee. Also I *was* thinking of five cartons of cigarettes, but if the furs are going to serve the good cause I'll only be asking for three.'

'One should not drink alcohol,' the padre warns him severely.

'No, sir, no! Never a drop passes my lips. I rub my knees with it, sir. It's such a help against the Greek rheumatism.'

'I regret I have no schnapps. Cigarettes and coffee are also out of the question. I will, however, give you 500 marks for them.'

'No sir, sorry sir! But I couldn't think of taking less than 2,000,' sighs Porta, sadly. 'A poor German soldier, sir, I am with nothing but my life and my Swedish furs in this world to give for my country. And my life, sir, isn't really to be called my own now is it? The Führer and the Army decide about that, sir. The last of my poor old mother's sixteen sons, I am,

1. See *March Battalion*.

sir. All fifteen of the others have been given to the Fatherland, sir.'

'That is very hard on your mother,' says the padre gently, thinking of the horrors of war.

'She takes it, sir, like a real German mother,' says Porta, proudly. 'She feels fifteen sons is the least she can give for Führer and Fatherland, when it means a thousand years of peace and freedom in the future. My mother says it's not every country whose Führer has come to it from God via Austria!'

The padre leaves Porta in confusion, with the furs hanging over his saddle-bow and his purse 1000 marks lighter.

Porta has suddenly discovered there is a goldmine in these furs if he only handles them properly. It can go on forever.

'What did Oberst Hinka have to say?' asks the Old Man with interest, as Porta enters the hut.

'Nothing much. He'd had an uneasy night with the fleas. He gave me the furs back and now they've entered the service of the priesthood. It's not every flea-bag that gets a chance like that.'

Tiny grins so much he chokes on his coffee.

'Bet you ten to one the parson'll be cursing you all night and the skins come back to you without a blessing tomorrow,' prophesies Gregor, rubbing his hands in anticipation.

The following morning the padre comes galloping up on a foam-flecked horse.

'You'll suffer for this,' he snarls, throwing the furs in Porta's face.

Porta lifts his arm as if to salute, but bends it instead and slaps the inside of his elbow with his left hand. The classic international sign for 'up my arse!'

'You'll hear from me, obergefreiter!' screams the padre, livid with rage. 'Don't think I'm done with you, yet!'

'Back to daddy, me little beauties,' laughs Porta to the fleas as he brushes the dust of the road from the furs.

The very sight of the furs makes us itch, but between Porta and the fleas there seems to be an armistice. They are friends and do not attack one another.

A BMW motorcycle and sidecar comes noisily down the hill. In the sidecar sits Chief Mechanic Wolf with the air of a general. On the motorcycle sit his two Chinese bodyguards, both armed with *kalashnikovs*[2].

Wolf stops in a cloud of dust when his eye falls on the furs.

'Whatcha got there?' he asks arrogantly, slashing at the furs with his *nagajka*[3], an heirloom from the NKVD.

'What's up? Those dogs of yours shit in your eyes? Can't you tell furs when you see 'em?' asks Porta, superciliously.

'Where'd you nick 'em?' asks Wolf, insultingly.

'Think we're all like you?' Porta turns the insult away, loftily.

'They're confiscated,' declares Wolf, categorically. 'Accordin' to HDV[4] anything found in the field is to be turned in to the nearest Army Stores. That's *me*, my lad! Understood, dogsbody?'

'Get stuffed! Crawl smartly up your own central orifice,' says Porta, contemptuously. 'The German armed forces and me've got different ideas on the subject of what's private property and what belongs to the arse-lickin' German people.'

'Your tongue'll get your neck stretched some day,' shouts Heide warningly from inside the hut, where he sits deep in *Mein Kampf.*

'What d'you want for 'em?' Wolf breaks in sharply. He jumps from the BMW sidecar, unbuttoning his holster flap as he comes. Experience has taught him to take no chances when bargaining with Porta. Anything can happen.

'Not for sale!' Porta turns the question away coldly and lights a big cigar. He hates cigars really, but thinks it a help to be able to veil himself in a cloud of cigar smoke at a critical moment, and to be able to blow smoke into an opponent's face. Al Capone, from Chicago, always had a cigar in his mouth when he was out on business. He is the only one out of sixty-two million Italian Porta looks up to and wishes to imitate.

'*Not for sale?*' Wolf cannot believe his own ears. Even his two wolfhounds look bewildered. Porta to own something which was not for sale? Impossible. He'd be ready to sell *himself* to Arabian slave-traders if the price was high enough.

2. Kalashnikov: Russian Mpi.
3. Nagajka: Russian whip.
4. HDV: Army Service Regulations.

Wolf plays idly with the LMG[5] mounted on the sidecar and, as if accidentally, the muzzle lines up on Porta.

'Cut that shit, you ginger bloody Yid!' hisses Wolf, irritably, swinging the machine-gun round as if ready to mow down the whole of No. 2 Section in one long roaring burst.

'I'm ready to buy them furs and when I'm ready to buy, I buy! Understand me? What I say *goes*! If you won't sell I'll take 'em without payin' see? Am I gettin' through to the shit between your ears? Throw 'em into the sidecar and you can pick up a pound of apples for 'em next payday. Make yourself an apple pie. Think yourself lucky I don't report you to GEFEPO[6] for stealin' 'em.'

'You ought to join a travellin' circus, Wolfie boy!' Porta laughs, jeeringly. 'You'd do all right falling on your arse between the turns.'

'I *want* those *furs*,' snarls Wolf, making his *nagajka* hiss through the air.

'Wish in one hand and shit in the other,' grins Porta, cocking his nose in the air. Swinging the furs over his shoulder, as a sign that he regards the subject as closed, he begins to go off up the road

'Here now, me old joker,' shouts Wolf, running after him, 'don't piss against the wind, you'll only get wet. We're a couple that can fix a deal good as any parson's daughters.'

Porta ignores him and increases his pace. He has noticed his friend the Greek village priest up by the bell-tower and waves pleasantly to him.

The priest waves smilingly back and begins to pull on the rope. The air fills with the tolling of the church bell. The villagers leave their houses on their way to Mass.

Wolf slaps his forehead in an attempt to start his brain working. He is almost choking with rage over Porta's stubbornness.

Porta turns into the packed bar, run illicitly by the roadmender, at the moment a dead-drunk infantryman gets thrown out with threats of a quick death if he tries to come back.

'Tonsil acid,' orders Porta knocking on the bar with his Mpi. A large tankard of poor man's champagne sails down the bar to

5. LMG: Light Machine-gun.
6. GEFEPO: (Geheime Feldpolizei) Secret Field Police.

78

him and with a well-co-ordinated movement of arm and neck he knocks it back in one go.

Tango pushes his way over to him with Buffalo close at his heels.

'We know where there's a load o' wine,' whispers Buffalo, secretively. 'The Greco's can deliver it tonight, and it can go back to Germany in empty ammo-baskets.'

'We've got something else, too,' grins Tango, cunningly, executing a few dance steps. 'And we can send it to Bielefeld marked GEKADOS in sealed zinc cases. Even the SS-Heini's wouldn't dare touch them!'

'Meet me at the parson's at eleven o'clock tonight!' says Porta, swallowing another glass, 'and beat it, my sons, and leave me in peace. I've got some thinking to do.'

'There's more'n *you*'ll buy it,' snarls Tango, looking meaningly at Chief Mechanic Wolf who at this very moment bangs in through the door.

Porta blows cigar-smoke gently into Tango's face.

'Look now, Tango my young son, you exist only because I am a good kind man. Your time in the Greater German Wehrmacht ends just as soon as I feel I do not want you to breathe the same air as I do any longer. Sons like you, who can't count to twenty without taking their boots off'd better be glad for every minute we let you walk about upright on the face of the earth.'

Wolf laughs loudly with satisfaction. He appreciates a joke, always excepting when it is against himself.

'Did you know you look silly when you laugh?' asks Porta, contemptuously.

Wolf swallows hard, and is about to say something coarse, when he remembers the attractive furs. He slaps Porta on the shoulder with affected comradeliness.

'When there's a war on then's the time for far-sighted people to do business. I know them zinc cases well. They're almost mine, but I will naturally withdraw and leave them to you, *if* you will sell me the furs.'

'You'd be a hit in the comics,' grins Porta, calling to a pretty, long-haired girl who is sitting on the lap of a wachtmeister of artillery.

79

'What do you want?' asks the girl with a cold look on her pretty Slav features.

Porta lifts up her dress.

'I'll show you mine if you'll show me yours!'

'Pig!' snarls the girl.

'Obergefreiter,' replies Porta, bowing from the waist.

'Cultivated lot, these Grecos,' grins Wolf. 'State their name, soon as you meet 'em. Jokin' apart, Porta my lad, what'd you say to six pounds of caviare, five cartons of Camels and a whole case of *Slivovitz* for your worn-out furs, and that's top price.'

'Six pounds of caviare! I'd have fins back of my ears and gills up my arsehole before I'd finished eating that lot,' grins Porta, sarcastically. 'Start talking about Scotch whisky and coffee and we might have at least a starting point.'

They start with a bottle of schnapps and after three hours of heated discussion, liberally sprinkled with threats, the deal is on. They have a drink on it and with uncertain steps go about their individual affairs, Wolf with the furs under his arm. He decides to go to bed early with a *Blitzmädel* to celebrate them.

'It'll be the most lively bang those two've ever had in their lives,' grins Porta expectantly.

'He'll let your guts out for you,' prophesies the Old Man, darkly.

Porta nearly strangles on his food at the thought of Wolf and the Blitzmädel's night with the fleas.

'Wish 'e'd lend them Chinese bleeders one of 'em,' says Tiny. 'What I wouldn't give for that pair to get to know them bleedin' fleas!'

Next day Wolf is back with his whole gang. The Blitzmädel is sitting between him and one of the Chinese in the armoured Kübel. The fleas have left her looking like a boiled lobster.

'What the devil's the matter with your face?' shouts Porta, with pretended surprise, viewing Wolf's swollen features with interest.

'You don't think, do you, you twistin' Yid bastard, that you're going to get away with doing *me*?' screams Wolf, grinding his teeth and hurling the furs at Porta's head.

'Shut your ugly great trap, Wolf. You make more noise'n a

pig with his bollocks caught in a meatgrinder,' answers Porta, with a condescending air. 'Didn't you go on your knees to me to let you buy those lovely furs? *I* didn't want to sell them.'

'You'll pay for this!' roars Wolf, aiming his Mpi at Porta. Raging, he kicks one of his Chinese.

'Relax, relax,' Porta reproves him in a fatherly way. 'People can die of high blood pressure!'

'Let's have my goods again,' shouts Wolf, beside himself with rage. 'You've got your bloody fleabags back!'

'Think you're talking to an idiot?' laughs Porta, shaking his head. 'If you return the furs that's your business, but repayment for them! Not here, my old son! Didn't you know we're in Greece now?'

'You *knew* there was fleas in those furs!' rages Wolf, scratching himself desperately.

'True,' admits Porta nonchalantly.

'Why didn't you say so?' snuffles Wolf.

'Didn't ask, did you?' smiles Porta. Wolf explodes in a long animal howl, and throws out bloody threats of strange and unusual revenges.

'You make a bad impression soon as you open your mouth,' says Porta. 'Even a starving Italian would be scared of accepting a free box of spaghetti from you!'

'I'll pull your bloody arsehole up over your ears,' promises Wolf, gnashing his teeth.

'We'll spit on your grave,' promises Tiny, from the darkness of the hut.

'You're a cheap skate, Wolf,' sneers Porta, 'and cheap skates get caught.'

'Quiet boys,' says Wolf, patting his slavering wolfhounds. 'You two are gonna get a nice little present. You're gonna get a wicked bastard's head in a nice pink box all tied up with a pretty blue ribbon.'

'You wouldn't believe what *we're* goin' to think up for bleedin' *you*,' shouts Tiny from the window of the hut.

'Think of that, now!' Wolf laughs jeeringly, and spits in Tiny's direction. '*You? Think?* I've seen your fuckin' papers, son. You had 39 at trainin' school for intelligence and to get even that they had to knock that headful of shit you've got up against a concrete wall for ten days. Since then your IQ's been *droppin'*, slow but sure. You're the boy they have to write his boot-size on his forehead for, when he's pickin' up new 'uns at the stores. Adolf's soddin' scientists at Buchenwald are beginnin' to wonder. If they can teach a nuthead like you to shoot off a gun, maybe they ought to be gettin' started on the apes!'

'Talk, talk, talk! You spew shit like a underground paper spews bleedin' lies,' shouts Tiny from the hut. 'I'm a bleedin' sight better off'n you are, Wolf! I got papers say I'm *barmy*, but I ain't bleedin' *silly*, me old son, an' don't you forget it. I'm *crafty*, I am, an' it's the crafty bleeders like me as'll come out of this war alive. The clever bleeders gets an 'ero's bleedin' death, am I right?'

'Chief Mechanic Wolf, you are the long-lost son of a five mark whore, and as such we'll push your nipples out through your back with bullets first chance we get,' promises Porta, solemnly.

'There'll be one for your bleedin' 'ead, too, you dirty dog,' echoes Tiny, happily.

'We'll upt a charge from a sawn-off shotgun straight up your arse, Wolf,' howls Gregor, excitedly.

'*All right* you shiteatin' shower! The real war starts *now* for you lot,' roars Wolf, slapping his Mpi. 'I'm gonna take you one by one!'

'If your mother was an invalid then you're a motherfucker, Wolf!' shouts Porta, spitting out of the window.

'Everybody knows why you never get leave,' shouts Gregor triumphantly. 'You've worn your five sisters' cunts out!'

Wolf's threats begin to take form the very same day.

It is sheer luck that Porta does not die of poisoning. He picks up two black puddings from the cook-waggon and is persuaded to give one of them to an importunate dog. Two seconds later the dog falls dead. Pale and shaking he throws the rest of the food to a pig which goes off to eternity as quickly as the dog.

The next day they find scorpions in their boots, and in Porta's greatcoat pocket the Old Man finds a tiny poisonous snake whose bite kills instantly.

Tiny gets thrown through the roof of the latrines when an S-mine goes off just as he has sat himself down to run through a new batch of filthy pictures.

It gets so bad we do not dare to move outside alone. We don't even eat from a Red Cross parcel without trying it out on somebody else first.

Late one night we are sitting in the hut making plans to kill Wolf. Porta cannot accept any of the suggestions.

Tiny grinds his forehead up and down the wall. He has heard that this helps when one has to think deeply about some problem.

'If we was to meet 'im accidental-like up on the mountain road,' he says, cunningly, 'some ill as the 'uman flesh is heir too, might overtake 'im?'

'Yes, he might, for example, accidentally get himself strangled,' sighs Porta, taking a swig of vodka.

'A fellow I knew in Hamburg once, died of heart-failure when some friends came to visit him with knives,' says Gregor, swishing a well-honed battle knife through the air.

'Wolf's not that nervous. And it'd be hard to get near enough with a knife,' mumbles Porta, sadly. 'I'd pay money to get the chance.'

'*Pas question!* We must discover some particularly refined method of doing it,' says the Legionnaire.

Porta goes to the doorway and stares out. The big electric globes swing in the breeze. He thinks of how Wolf would look swinging there head downwards with a broken neck.

'That dirty ol' bleeder,' shouts Tiny, banging his head against the wall. 'I'll blind 'is bleedin' mother I will!'

'What the hell to do?' sighs Porta dropping down on the doorstep. 'We can't winkle him out. He's fortified himself in there like Adolf in the Wolf's Lair.'

'Every Wednesday he goes up into the mountains to meet somebody,' says Barcelona, suddenly. 'I heard it, by accident, from a German nigger who's a regimental musician in the infantry.'

Tiny sends out a long, shrill whistle.

'An' if 'is bleedin' motor was to break down up by the bleedin' pass an' the bleeder was to get out to 'ave a look what was up with it?'

'With a little help from somebody, he might fall and hurt himself badly,' says the Old Man, after a few moments of thought.

'Per'aps a long knife might be somewhere in the bushes even, an' 'e'd cut 'is guts out on it, eh?' grins Tiny, happy at the thought.

'Not in the guts,' Porta rejects the idea. 'A bullet in the forehead! The way they do it to the cattle in the slaughter-house.'

'An' then we'll sling 'is poxed-up brain over to Crete an' let the wild dogs 'ave a feed on it,' shouts Tiny, jubilantly.

'What a lot of lovely blood'd pour out of that bastard,' Gregor roars with laughter.

'We'll give it 'im right straight between 'is little ratty eyes!' shouts Tiny, drawing his *Nagan* and sighting out of the window.

'They'll cut your heads off for murder!' prophesies Heide, blackly.

'Only people who get caught get executed,' says Porta, confidently. 'Boys who know how to shoot can bring off a bit of dirty work like this with no trouble at all. They're the kind who get the rewards *and* a pat on the back afterwards.'

'That's the way society wants it to be,' sighs Gregor. 'It's the dumb boys who get buried with their heads between their knees and called criminals. The wide boys do the same and get praised for not getting caught.'

'That Wolf, 'e's the cowardliest German pig I ever did meet,' shouts Tiny indignantly. 'I'm shadowin' 'im yesterday in Athens, an' all the time 'e's takin' cover be'ind women an' children. 'E knows bleedin' well as none of us'd kill *them* just to get *'im*. Any rate I only know of one on us as'd do it.'

'Who's that?' asks Gregor.

'Me,' says Tiny, laughing noisily.

'What about this?' shouts Tango. 'We could send him the Chinamen's heads in hatboxes.'

'His five sisters and the dogs'd be better,' suggests Porta. 'He doesn't give a fuck for the Chinks!'

'It might shake 'is nerve,' considers Tiny. 'So much, maybe, that 'e'll ask our pardon an' call off this private bleedin' war.'

'We'll find out how good he really is before very long,' says Porta, biting into a large piece of pork.

The same evening a Molotov cocktail is thrown at us, as we are on our way to the Greek priest's gambling joint. Tiny gets his uniform burnt off and only saves his life by jumping into the river.

A few days later Porta gets leave to visit a feldwebel of Pioneers, an acquaintance from the explosives school at Bamberg.

He watches, with interest, preparations for a major test of Russian toluol. The charges are in sticks and are placed by the Pioneers around a huge block of stone. Porta states later that it was three times the size of the Rock of Gibraltar.

The feldwebel explains the technique to Porta as proudly as if he himself were the inventor of toluol.

'Does it work every time?' asks Porta inquisitively. 'Aren't there ever any duds?'

'Bang every time,' guarantees the feldwebel.

When everything is ready, the squad takes cover. The feldwebel attaches two wires to a small black box.

'Now you'll see something,' he says to Porta, making some small adjustments to the box. He presses a button and the huge rock becomes a great cloud of dust.

'Well I'll be . . .' cries Porta, admiringly, and is allowed to hold the apparatus in his hands. 'Looks a bit like these new push-button radio controls. Push a button and some nancy-boy in Paris starts whiffling, push another and you get a shower fiddling on cat-gut in Vienna!'

'You *could* say that,' laughs the feldwebel, 'but the result's a bit different.'

After they have blown up a couple of wrecked tanks, Porta helps the Pioneers to pack up the explosives and take private note of where his friend the feldwebel packs the electronic detonator.

He is in fine fettle when he stops an SS amphibian, a few hours later, for a lift. He leans back happily in his seat and puts his feet up on the turned-down windshield. His pack is on the back seat, bulging with enough explosives to clear the streets of Tokyo in the rush hour.

'It's bleedin' surprisin',' admits Tiny, as he looks wide-eyed at the colourful leads, batteries and sticks of explosive Porta is shaking out of his pack. 'What a nice little pocket-radio you've got there,' he says, passing his hand lovingly over the electric detonator.

'You've said it, my son. It's that lovely you can hardly stand it. We're going to tune it to Station SD – Sudden Death,' and Porta laughs until he gives himself hiccups.

Tiny hits the table a blow which sends one of its planks flying up to hit him under his chin, but he is so pleased at the thought of Wolf's impending demise that he doesn't even notice the violent blow.

'That's bleedin' wonderful,' he shouts, juggling carelessly with a stick of explosive. 'These things ought to be able to give us a lovely big bang!'

'Knock the devil off his throne,' grins Porta, maliciously, 'and they're going to send Wolf, his Chinese and his dogs off on the world's longest day trip. When we see them go down over the horizon, we'll have us a *mik* you've never seen the like of.'

'Don't make a balls of it!' warns the Old Man, darkly.

'It is worrying,' says Heide, looking doubtfully at all the explosives.

'Mad lot, you are,' Gregor laughs heartily. 'There's enough there to free the entire Kingdom of the Hellenes from the un-wanted presence of Germans in their country.'

'If we're going to fix Wolf right, and I intend to do just that,' says Porta, decisively, 'a dozen sticks is minimum. I *know* that bastard. *I* think he's the Mafia's agent in the German Army! When he was called as a witness at a court-martial in Biele-feldt, the defending officer said:

' "Oberfeldwebel Wolf, if you had been born in Sicily you would have been one of the big three in the Mafia!" '

'I would recommend you to ensure that the detonator is set for the proper wavelength,' smiles Heide, thinly. 'It would be annoying for you if the charges were to explode under your-selves!'

'Holy Mary! Jesus forbid!' mumbles Porta, shocked, and crosses himself.

'It's bleedin' surprisin', as I 'ave said before,' says Tiny,

86

standing with the detonator in his hand and turning the dial. 'It's bleedin surprisin' what we 'uman bein's can invent. It's only a matter of knockin' your 'ead against the wall long enough. A little tiny box like this an', just think, it can blow the life out of a real wicked bleeder!'

'Hell's bells, man!' shouts Porta, terrified, snatching the detonator from him. 'You can send us all to hell turning that thing. What the devil was it turned to, now? Keep away from technical things you don't understand. This is only for people like me who've been to the powder-monkey school at Bamberg.'

'Now we're in trouble with that damned detonator,' sighs Gregor resignedly. 'Get all that shit outside in the fields quick before it goes up.'

'Nothing'll 'appen to *me*,' says Tiny, making an elegant gesture with his hand. 'I've 'ad me fortune told an' I'm goin' to die a quiet an' lovely death.'

'What the devil shall I turn it to?' asks Porta, uncertainly, twisting the dial.

'Put 'er on thirteen,' suggests Tiny, optimistically. 'Thirteen's my lucky number!'

Barcelona backs thirteen up and the dial is turned to that number.

They pack everything in two long cigar boxes, and put the finishing touch to it with a blue silk ribbon. They tie it with a large bow on one side.

'Here you are, then,' says Porta, handing the parcel to Tiny. 'Off you go, my lad, and deliver his present to Frankenstein's grandson!'

'*What!*' screams Tiny, in horror. 'Think I was born last week?' He pushes the parcel away from him gingerly. ' 'Specially now when we don't even know whether the bleedin' little radio 'as been dialled right or not!'

'You *said* thirteen was your lucky number!' shouts Porta, staring at him blankly. '*And* you said the gypsies had promised you'd die quietly! What are you *worrying* about, then?'

'You can't believe *everythin*' you 'ear, can you now?' says Tiny cautiously. 'That kind o' thing's for *sick* people.'

We sit down and think about it. The two dangerous cigar boxes lie on the table before us.

'I know!' shouts Tiny, his face lighting up.

'Last night I met an Italian copper they calls "Apeface". 'E used to be a nice feller, I 'ear, but that was before the Army fucked the poor bleeder up an' give 'im a bad reputation. 'E's been sent 'ere to the Grecos as a punishment for torturing blokes in some prison up north o' Naples. 'E boasts about it. Somethin' about 'ow 'e used to smash their toes one at a time, or somethin' like that. 'Is name's Mario Frodone an' 'e's ready to do business. They say 'e digs up the bodies after they've executed 'em, an' sells 'em to a sausage factory but I don't know if it's right or not. Still an' all, 'e looks like one o' them as can look after number bleedin' one all right!'

'Not bad, not bad,' answers Porta. 'Wolf's got a few numbers going, I know, with the spaghetti boys, so it wouldn't look funny if a macaroni-eater turns up with a little present for him.'

'I'd rather serve life in a Chinese prison 'n open *that* little present,' shouts Barcelona, slapping his hands delightedly on his thighs.

A little later Tiny comes back with the Italian corporal of police. His nickname of 'Apeface' fits him well. None of us has ever seen so brutal and untrustworthy a set of features before. We cannot doubt that he has been sent on a punishment posting to Greece for brutality.

Porta presses his hand with pretended heartiness.

'When you have delivered these two boxes of cigars, there's five cartons of cigarettes and three bottles of schnapps waiting for you here.'

Corporal Mario Frodone shows them a set of gleamingly white teeth in a smile. He feels certain this is the easiest piece of business that has ever come his way.

'Don't let him turn you away,' warns Porta. 'The gentleman who is to receive the gift is a very suspicious man!'

Whistling happily, Mario goes off with the package under his arm.

Porta stands at the window with his finger resting lightly on the firing button of the detonator.

'Let me push it!' begs Tiny. 'You know 'ow I love anythin' as makes a bang!'

'NO!' Porta cuts him off, brusquely. 'I want to have the

88

pleasure of doing this myself. You go out and keep an eye on the spaghetti-eater, and give the signal when he's handed over the cigars.'

Tiny rushes off and moving from house-corner to house-corner follows the happily whistling assassin.

Mario walks smartly across the wide square, at the far end of which Wolf's transport company is housed. Every way in to it is tightly closed, bolted and barred, and the guard lurking behind the sandbags has been doubled.

'Halt, who goes there?' roars Wolf from behind a steel sheet, when he catches sight of the whistling Italian.

'Royal Italian Corporal of Police, Mario Frodone. Good friend bearing gift from other good friends!' He holds the two cigar boxes up above his head.

'What kind of gift?' asks Wolf, pushing his head up inquisitively over the steel sheet.

'Cigar,' Mario roars back. 'Cigar from Brazil!'

'Who the hell'd be sendin' *me* cigars?' asks Wolf, suspiciously.

'Royal Italian Captain of Bersaglieri,' lies Mario.

'Approach slowly,' orders Wolf, sharply. 'Keep my present in front of you. No tricks, now, or you'll get your spaghetti-eatin' head blown off!'

Mario can clearly see five or six 'grease-guns' trained on him.

'*Gesu, Gesu,* kill these wicked people with slow cancer if anything bad should happen to Corporal Mario Frodone,' he prays silently, with his eyes turned upwards.

Tiny shivers in delighted expectation and moves closer so as not to miss anything.

A short way away one of the company Pumas is testing its signalling apparatus.

Corporal Mario Frodone is half-way across the square when Gefreiter Schmidt presses his sending button. There is a scream in his radio, followed by a long rolling explosion.

'What the hell was that?' asks Gefreiter Schmidt, putting his head out of the open turret cover.

A column of flame shoots up towards the sky and the entire square appears to sink into the ground. The houses round it crumble. Hundreds of white hens flap out of the poultry farm, which is pulverized into a cloud of mortar and brick dust.

Royal Italian Corporal Mario Frodone, disappears without trace in a colossal black mushroom of smoke which rises like an umbrella above the village.

Chief Mechanic Wolf, his gang, the wolfdogs, the two Chinese guards and five tractors are blown through the opposite wall of the house and land in the ruins of the market-gardener's establishment, five hundred yards away.

Wolf is weeping and the Chinese bodyguards swear to desert back to a quieter life with the NKVD liquidation squads. They both agree that the Germans have strange ways of sending presents.

'Jesus, what a bang!' gasps Tiny. Then he is lifted and carried up and away in a gigantic dust cloud, and flies, lying horizontally in the air, together with two lorries and an anti-tank gun, past the hut where Porta is still standing, staring wonderingly at the button of the electric detonator which he still has not managed to press.

Then the blast wave reaches the hut and it is whirled away up into the air together with the rest of the street.

Rescue squads are rushed from Athens. The partisans get the blame, as always when nobody knows what has really happened.

We are admitted to No. 9 Support Hospital in Athens. Wolf with both legs in traction. Tiny bandaged until he looks like an Egyptian mummy. The rest of us with more or less serious wounds.

A month later the following appears in the 'Deaths' section of the Italian newspaper *IL GIORNO*, Naples edition.

> Our dearly beloved son, brother, brother-in-law,
> cousin, uncle and friend
> Corporal in the Royal Italian Corps of
> Military Police, attached to the
> 4th Alpine Regiment
>
> Mario Guiseppe Frodone
>
> decorated with the *Ordine militare d'Italia*
> and with the *Croce di guerra al valore militaria*

for services, beyond the call of duty,
in the war which has been forced upon our
beloved Fatherland, has been called very,
very suddenly from us, murdered in frightful
fashion by wicked and evil persons.
May sickness and death strike them down!
The murdered soldier was the son of
Guiseppe and Catarina, the beloved brother of
Vittoria Maria, Fabio and Roberto.
The family will receive mourners on Sunday
at 12 o'clock at *Bombolini's* on the *Corso
Mussolini*.

Shortly before we are discharged, two Russian infantrymen are the cause of a terrific fight at the hospital. They state that the 250,000 Vlassiv Cossacks in German service are worth twice as much as the rest of the German Army, who only know how to goose-step, put together. That, they say, is why Germany loses all her wars.

'Hip, Hip!' howls a Bulgarian corporal of Jaegers throwing a full urine glass at the ward nurse who comes in to see what all the noise is about.

The nurse, who has officer rank, grabs him by the ears and bangs his head against the wall. He kicks her between the legs and she rolls screaming under the bed.

Porta hammers away at Wolf's leg in its plaster cast. The two Chinese rush to his help with raised truncheons, but Porta ducks and the blows fall instead on their plaster-encased boss.

Tiny roars like a wild bull and, swinging his arms like windmill sails, hits out at anything within reach, friend or enemy. He gets hold of two Russians and throws them out into the corridor, down which Buffalo is chasing a bald-headed Italian lance-corporal who is wearing nothing but his mountaineering boots. Screaming and yelling they fall over the two Russians and slide straight along the highly-polished corridor and into the operation room where a Leutnant is being prepared for an appendectomy.

The operating table with the leutnant on it disappears out on to the terrace leading to the gardens.

The leutnant scrambles away, as fast as he can on all fours, thinking the Russians have reached Athens.

A Rumanian sergeant with a face which looks like a cartoon of suppressed rage, throws his lighted pipe into the air and spreads both arms out, as if drowning in a turbulent current, before collapsing with a gurgle on the staircase.

An old supplies soldier, who has been out buying things on the black market, comes limping on crutches with a large shopping bag hanging around his neck. The orderly sergeant comes thundering up the stairs, with his pistol in his hand, at the same moment, and the old soldier, thinking he is for it, swings the packed shopping-bag round his head and lets the orderly sergeant have it straight in the face. Eggs, sausage, jam, hot macaroni, mustard and an enormous amount of tomato ketchup, spray to all sides, as the bag breaks open on the NCO's head.

A tall thin Italian comes hopping with a folding chair in one outstretched hand and a sausage, with ketchup dripping from it, in his mouth. He sees one of the Vlassovs, believes the Russians have arrived, and bangs down the chair on the Cossack's head. He goes down as if he had been hit by a bomb.

Doctors, nurses, orderlies and patients come streaming down the stairs and along the corridors. Chairs, tables, crutches and medicine bottles fly through the air.

In the twinkling of an eye the hospital looks as if it has been on the receiving end of a massive artillery bombardment. All the windows are out and not a piece of furniture is left whole. Even the two most stubborn malingerers in Ward 19 can now be counted with the seriously wounded cases.

Tiny runs for his life with Wolf's Chinese at his heels. One of them is swinging a short-handled chopper and there is no doubt what he will use it for if he ever catches Tiny. Everything in their path is ruthlessly smashed aside.

They turn in to the great covered bicycle track which the local inhabitants claim to be the largest in the world. It is certainly large, at any rate.

With a roar like a gorilla Tiny swings himself onto a brand new bicycle and charges at his pursuers. They jump for safety, over the barrier and into the spectators' seats.

Tiny pushes the pedals down with all his might and spurts

92

towards the big curve. His feet are going like the pistons of an engine at full speed.

'Great Buddha!' cries Wu, admiringly. 'That man and bike, they good together!'

At a dizzying speed Tiny goes into the curve and out again on to the straight with the rush and rumble of an express train.

His pursuers forget their anger at the sight of Tiny's spurt. Tiny, himself, is in ecstasy. He has always longed to be one of the great track cyclists with his name and picture in all the papers. That is why, when he started in the Army, he chose to join a cyclist unit, become a pedal dragoon.

He treads even more powerfully on the pedals, lying well over the handlebars and takes, at full speed, the curve just before the figure eight, which he enters at a pace which no professional could emulate.

As he swings into the straight on the far side, he sees, with a shock, that the track is blocked by a large barrel-shaped construction of planking. Repairs are in progress. He fumbles for the brakes, but there are no brakes on a racing bike. He pushes backwards on the pedals but they turn freely without reducing his headlong pace.

At breakneck speed he shoots up over the rounded barricade and hangs momentarily in the air. Then he seems to fly up and on towards the joists of the roof, turns a somersault in the air and falls to the track, striking it with a splintering crash.

'By Holy temples of China!' cries Wang, in admiration, 'that gorilla waste time in Army!'

The day after we leave hospital Porta runs into a staff quartermaster who is looking for a birthday present for his general. Through Wolf the QM officer has heard of Porta's three furs and is anxious to get hold of them, convinced that they would be the perfect gift for his general's birthday. Wolf has got it all worked out. This way he gets Porta a long term in military prison. What general is going to stand for getting bitten nearly to death by fleas? And on his birthday too!

They soon agree a price and the QM goes off beaming happily with the three furs.

Two days later the furs and the fleas are back with Porta as usual.

The general telephones Oberst Hinka and demands that Porta be severely punished.

Porta is again on orders, and this time Oberst Hinka orders him to remove the furs from the regimental area.

Sorrowfully he goes down to the naval base, where he meets an old friend, an Oberbootsmann, who is not himself particularly interested in the furs. He always sleeps by the boilers on board the cruiser. A Kapitänleutnant from the minelayer flotilla buys them, however, immediately, without much haggling over price.

An hour later his minelayer and all the fleas leave the Piraeus.

'Hope the poor little fellows don't get seasick,' says Porta, worriedly, waving after them with a miniature Greek flag.

Several days later he hears, from the Oberbootsmann, that the minelayer has been captured by the British and the entire crew are prisoners in England.

Porta can hardly hold back a tear to think he has lost the furs and the happy little fleas for ever. There is no doubt that the first British officer who sees them will confiscate them.

When Hinka asks him, some time later, what has happened to the furs and the fleas, Porta can answer truthfully.

'Herr Oberst, sir, regret to state, sir, the fleas have gone over to the British, sir!'

*Hitler has proclaimed himself the supreme judicial authority
of the Reich. From this moment he alone decides what is right
and what is wrong. And none may dispute his decision.*

Dr Goebbels, 30th January, 1934

Fortress Germersheim, 24th December 1944

*On the 25th of December, 1944, Major Bruno Schau, who
was sentenced to death on the 2nd of July, 1944, in Paris, will
be executed by a firing squad.*

*The execution will take place at Fortress Germersheim on
25.12.44, at 11.00 hours:*

> *Officer in command: Major Klein*
> *Commander firing squad: Leutnant Schwarz*
> *Legal officer: Auditör Brandt*
> *Medical officer: Stabsarzt Dr. Koch*
> *Padre: Oberfeldkapelan Almann*

*The firing squad will consist of ten men, good marksmen
only, detailed from No. 2 Company.*

*A deterrent company consisting of fifty prisoners. Ten men
detailed from each company.*

*A party to tie the condemned man to the post. One feldwebel
and two unteroffiziers to be detailed.*
Dress:

*Other Ranks: Service uniform, infantry boots, steel helmet,
leather equipment, two cartridge pouches, bayonet, carbine
K.98.*

Officers: Sabre, service pistol, and steel helmet.

*Other personnel on duties connected with the execution:
Service uniform and field service cap, belt and bayonet.*

*Unteroffizier Faber will be responsible for the erection of the
execution post. This will be collected from the Quartermaster's
Store at 09.00 hours.*

Major Schau will be informed of the time of execution at 09.00 hours. His wishes as to form of burial and advice to next-of-kin will be requested. He will then be taken, manacled hand and foot, to the padre for spiritual solace. The manacles must not be slackened or removed either during spiritual solace or during medical examination. The condemned will be at all times strictly guarded by two unteroffiziers armed with machine pistols.

The Adjutant will give the order to tie the condemned man to the post. Stabsfeldwebel Albert will be responsible for six pieces of rope of length five feet being fastened to the rings of the post. He will also provide a sighting cloth.

The firing squad will parade in front of No. 2 Company cell block at 10.30 hours.

The commander of the firing squad, Leutnant Schwarz, is responsible for movement to the execution square being carried out with strictest military order and discipline. Any kind of demonstration whatsoever will be suppressed immediately by the most severe means. Firearms may be used if the first warning is not obeyed.

Whistling, mumbling and ocular signals are to be regarded as demonstrations.

After the execution four men will remove the body, strip it, and place it unclothed in the coffin. The equipment of the executed man will be handed in to the Quartermaster, who will be responsible for repair of the uniform.

Unteroffizier Buchner will be responsible for placing the coffin behind the protective wall at 10.45 hours. He will also be responsible for delivery of the coffin, after the execution, to the burial authorities at the cemetery, and will obtain a receipt. The necessary documents will be obtained from the adjutant.

Major Schau will be tied to the post by two ropes crossing the chest, two around the waist and two just below the knees. The ropes will be pulled taut.

The padre will accompany the prisoner to the execution post and will recite an Our Father. He will then move four paces to the side and the commander of the firing squad will give the order:

'Take aim!'

The command: 'Stand at ease!' will not be given until the Medical Officer has declared the executed man dead. The firing squad will not march away until the body has been untied from the execution post and laid in the coffin. Two men from No. 1 Company will be detailed to remove all bloodstains. They will be equipped with cloths and shovels for this purpose.

Feldwebel Reincke will be responsible for the cleaning of the execution post, and for returning it to store.

From one hour before the time of execution and until the coffin has been removed and cleaning operations are completed, the execution square will be out of bounds to all personnel not employed on duties connected with the execution.

Signed: Heinicke
Oberst and Commandant
Fortress Germersheim

ESCORT DUTY

' 'Ow d'you feel without the bleedin' stars?' Tiny asks feld-webel Schmidt as they slant across the flat, marshy artichoke fields.

'All right, all right, bighead,' growls Schmidt surlily. 'Mightn't be all that long before you're on the way to the jug yourself with no stripes up.'

'So what?' says Tiny carelessly, spitting into the wind. 'Life with Barras[1] is bleedin' uncertain.'

'Too right it is,' sighs Carl moodily. 'A week ago a feldwebel an' today lower'n shit, an' all for refusing to fire on a flock o' soddin' Greeks.'

'Who was the twatt who made *you* a feldwebel?' asks Porta, shaking his head and handing Carl a piece of mutton sausage. 'Refuse to shoot a civilian, indeed!'

' 'E'll learn to obey orders in Germersheim,' grins Tiny maliciously.

'I don' believe it's as bad as they say,' mumbles Carl.

'Been there?' asks Porta looking at him out of the corners of his eyes.

'No, I've got a clean sheet.'

'You've shit on it now all right, my son!' says Porta.

'Ten years in the bleedin' nick,' shouts Tiny, joyfully.

Unimpressed, Porta cuts another slice from the long mutton sausage.

'I can tell you a lot about Germersheim, that they don't teach the kids in school.'

'We've got some nice little stories about Torgau, Glatz an' Fort Zittau, too,' grins Tiny, taking a piece of sausage.

'Bullshit the lot!' Carl brushes it off, stubbornly.

'You'll be surprised,' smiles Porta. 'I've seen the toughest

1. Barras: Slang term for the Army.

98

nuts break like eggshells five minutes after they've clicked their heels in front of Hellhound Heinrich.'

'You're off to where the devil roasts chestnuts,' shouts Tiny loudly, dropping an encouraging hand on Carl's shoulder. 'You barmy bleeder, you're goin' to be sorry you didn' knock them Greeks off, son.'

They regain the Corinth road and try to hitch a ride on a convoy but nobody stops for them.

Tiny chatters on about his experiences at Germersheim.

'I've drilled five bleedin' hours on end, in water up to me bleedin' neck, an' that was under the personal command of Iron Gustav[2]. All I'd done was drop a full piss-pot on 'is 'ead, but 'e ain't a bad bleeder really. 'E can crush your bleedin' ribs in that fast it don't even 'urt you while 'e's doin' it.'

'Watch out for Hellhound Heinrich,' says Porta with a quiet smile. 'If he throws you in Cell 42. You go in goosestepping and come out mincemeat!'

'Get into No. 3 Ausbildungskompagni[3]' Tiny advises. 'The Flea's got that – Rittmeister Lapp. 'E 'ops round on tin legs what squeaks that much, you can 'ear 'im comin' a bleedin' mile orf. 'E's stone bleedin' blind, too, nearly, an' that's a good thing 'cos 'e 'ardly can tell who 'e's talkin' to 'arf the time.'

They reach Corinth late in the afternoon, and catch a goods train.

It's raining in Athens when they arrive next morning, and the express to Salonica has just left. They get their orders stamped at the RTO and agree to take a look at the historic city now that they are there.

'We've got three weeks,' shouts Porta ecstatically. 'Three bloody weeks with travel money and rations! Do you realize what intelligent men can do with all that?'

They look into every bar they come to.

Carl worries about missing the train.

'Choke it orf, son!' says Tiny. 'We, your superiors, take full responsibility. You're our prisoner an' you'll be in chokey soon-a-bleedin'-nough. Don't forget that travellin' time is part of your sentence and whatever 'appens to you with us is better'n

2. Iron Gustav: See *March Battalion*.
3. Ausbildungskompagni: Instruction company.

what 'Ell'ound 'Einrich'll be dishin' out to you when 'e gets 'is 'ands on you.'

'He can't forget he used to be a feldwebel and that two obergefreiters are now telling him what to do,' says Porta understandingly.

'It's difficult after ten years in the rank,' sighs Carl apathetically.

'Well, you'll 'ave ten years in the nick to get used to it,' grins Tiny.

'You'll learn there what obergefreiter stripes mean. It's them 'as keeps the keys to the blocks!'

They go along Ermou Epmoy and reach Syntagma Place, the rendezvous of the Athenian upper class.

In a pavement restaurant outside the Hotel Grand Bretagne Tiny's eye falls on an overfat gentleman balancing on a white iron chair.

'Look at bleedin' fatguts there,' his shout echoes round the square. He inspects the fat man with interest. His buttocks hang down on both sides of the small chair seat.

'He must weigh at least twenty stone.' Porta thinks aloud, sucking his lower lip in between his teeth.

'Thirty,' guesses Tiny. 'Put 'im up on a elephant an' it'd go bleedin' swaybacked.'

'In the middle of a war with rationing and hunger everywhere,' shouts Porta indignantly. 'It makes me mad when I see things like that.'

'He very much money. Many ship in Piraeus, many villa on islands,' whispers a shoe-cleaner warningly.

A servile waiter spoons stewed bilberries on to the fat man's plate. Another sprinkles sugar, and a third pours cream. They do not conceal the fact that they expect large tips.

'Shit, see him *eat*,' says Porta hungrily.

'It's i-bleedin'-moral,' says Tiny, and grasping a spoon he smashes it down into the plate three or four times. Bilberries fly to all sides.

The fat millionaire falls over backwards, making noises like a railway-engine giving off steam.

All is confusion. Police-dog tags glitter from the other side of the square. From the Ministry of War a combined German-Greek police patrol comes sprinting with drawn truncheons.

' 'Ell, no peace for the wicked!' shouts Tiny, irritatedly, placing a boot on the fat man's stomach and letting his weight come on to it.

'You come,' shouts the shoe-cleaner running in front of them down Miltropo Street. They cross a backyard and crawl through an open window into a room where some ladies are trying on dresses.

'Gas inspection,' says Porta helping the shoe-cleaner through the window.

When Tiny follows him the ladies begin to scream.

'Take it easy,' grins Tiny. 'We'll put off readin' the meter till next time!'

'Rotten whores!' screams the shoe-cleaner, spitting on a picture of the King.

'You *are* a nice girl,' says Porta, pinching one of the girls' behinds.

She screams sulphurous curses at him. A piece of firewood flies past his head.

'Women as swears an' talks dirty, they're the best,' states Tiny with a knowledgeable air. 'We 'ad one o' them in Sanct Pauli. When she opened 'er mouth the shit flew. Everybody thought she was a real bitch because of that, but they was wrong. Cinderarse knew what she was doin'. She wound up marryin' a baron an' drivin' to the church behind milk-white 'orses. We never see 'er on the Reeperbahn again, but the luxury pimps used to meet 'er in the top joints along the Alster an' raise their 'ats to 'er though she never condescended to reply. She'd got *that* upper-bleedin'-class she couldn't even take a deep breath an' shout arsehole after 'em. Just sniffed real loud, like a cow sniffin' a bull in the arse. Them tough nuts from Sanct Pauli got that worked up they threw all their bleedin' lids away so's not to keep gettin' shat on by 'er.'

They stood outside a travel bureau where *Kraft durch Freude* is advertising trips to Venice.

'Hey, what about taking a trip to Venice and having a ride in a gondola?' asks Porta, pointing at a colourful poster.

'You out of your mind, or something?' protests Carl, nervously. 'We can't go to Venice when we're supposed to go via Vienna.'

'An' you been feldwebel in a 500-battalion!' sighs Tiny, shaking his head despairingly. 'Do as we order, man, for Jesus Christ's sake! Nobody can blame the bleedin' prisoner for the bleedin' escorts' travel arrangements. Who the 'ell can prove we don't think Venice is a short-bleedin'-cut to the pokey? We didn't get top marks in geography, did we now?'

They drive to the Acropolis in a horse-drawn cab.

'Now we *are* here, we might just as well see the sights,' considers Porta. 'Here, where we are driving at this very moment, the legions of Rome once trotted along,' he explains with pathos in his voice.

'They still bleedin' are,' says Tiny unimpressed, pointing to two Bersaglieri laboriously ascending the hill with three girls.

'Whoa mares, like a trip?' cries Porta pointing invitingly at his flies.

The girls laugh and climb up into the waggon. The Bersaglieri snarl like hungry tigers whose meat has been taken from them.

'Anything to see up there?' asks Porta pointing to the Acropolis.

'No much. Stones and broken steps you can break a leg on.'

'Turn back,' Porta orders the cabman. '*You* can tell us what *you've* seen, that way we won't waste time.'

'Do you fuck?' asks Tiny. The girls prefer not to reply.

They stop at a tumbledown restaurant owned by the cabman's brother. After the third bottle of wine, Tiny and the cab-driver dance the *tjaka* till the house shakes.

'My 'usband ees at the front,' says Sula, a dark-haired, very pretty girl.

'Which one?' asks Porta practically.

'I do not know,' she confesses.

' 'E ees an officer. Greek 'ero.'

'May I touch you?' asks Porta, apparently overwhelmed. 'I've never met a hero's wife before.'

They walk through the royal park, pausing by the temple of Zeus, where they eat birds from the Seich-Sou woods. It is nearly light when they tip-toe up the stairs to Katina's flat.

'Please go quiet,' she whispers. 'There would be trouble eef anyone found we 'ad Germans here. They all Communists in thees quarter.'

'Ought to be bleedin' shot!' shouts Tiny, spitting on a crudely drawn hammer and sickle.

'Red Front!' shouts Porta to an old woman, peering inquisitively through the crack of a door.

She snarls at him and bangs the door.

'The Party is always right,' grins Carl, kicking at the door.

The flat smells of cheap perfume. Sula throws herself on her back on a broad bed and kicks her feet in the air, exposing a stretch of bare thigh above her stocking-tops.

Tiny rolls his eyes and pushes Katina on to a large sheepskin lying on the floor.

She screams indignantly, presses her legs tightly together, pulls down her skirt around them and hangs on to it with both arms.

'That's right,' whoops Tiny with satisfaction. '*Nice* girls 'ave their drawers *took* off!' He finds a goosefeather and tickles her under the arms to make her let go of her skirt, but she is not ticklish.

'What ees thees theeng you do?' she asks in wonder. 'Ees thees some new German perversion? I 'ave a captain one time, 'oo scratch me weeth a nail. When thee nail make marks on my legs 'ee shoot 'ees load!'

'I'll fix you up with some marks, my girl,' promises Tiny solemnly, 'but not with no bleedin' Greek nail I won't!' He catches her by the ankles and holds her up as if she were a hen hanging for sale in a Sicilian market.

Katina turns her body in the air like an acrobat and sinks her teeth in his crotch. With a howl of pain he drops her and presses both hands between his legs.

'I need to pee,' she giggles and runs out to the unbelievably tiny toilet, use of which makes pins-and-needles an occupational disease.

Tiny bulls after her. From his experience he expects her to make a run for it. His huge body blocks the door opening.

She hums happily. Water tinkles into water.

Tiny thrusts a cigar between his lips and expels a cloud of smoke.

'That's enough pissin' for a kid of your size,' he shouts impatiently and grabbing her by the hair he drags her back into the room.

She lets out a piercing scream, kicks him in the shins and bites one of his ears almost off.

'Jesus Christ, she loves me!' he howls in his cracked bass.

'I 'ate you, bastard!' she snarls, struggling wildly to free herself.

'You love me, you bitch!' Tiny shouts with pleasure. 'Give us a kiss!' He tears at her clothing, but it is made of stout material not easily ripped. She is wearing a knitted skirt which gets longer and longer the more he pulls at it.

She rolls over and over until she resembles a roll of carpeting. They battle fiercely over the skirt. Coat, blouse and brassière have long since been torn to bits. He seems to be trying to tie her into knots. His sighs of passion alternate with roars of pain. At one moment he is on his knees on the bed, the next his head is hanging over the edge of the table.

Somehow they arrive up on top of the enormous wardrobe. It topples and falls with an ear-splitting crash.

Suddenly they are out in the kitchen drinking water. There is a scream of terror to alarm the whole house.

Tiny is hanging out of the window head downwards, while she smashes away at his crotch with a rolling-pin.

'Feelthy peeg, enemy of my country,' she screams and pours a can of petroleum over him.

Porta and Carl get there in time to stop her setting fire to him.

In two giant jumps they are back in the living-room and continue their battle for the remains of her clothing.

'Jesus Christ you're the best bleedin' tart I ever did meet,' gasps Tiny, biting her in the thigh, 'but now you're goin' to get the lot!'

Before she knows where she is she has only one stocking and a shoe left.

A tangled ball of jackboots, leather belts, stockings, shoes and suspender belts rolls across the floor and under the bed.

There is a second of silence. Then a piercing howl is heard and the wide bed is lifted on end so that Porta and Sula are thrown out of it.

Tiny rushes round the room, out of the kitchen and up the narrow staircase, with Katina riding him like a jockey.

A little later they come crawling down again. Tiny with a split upper lip and with a bunch of black hair gripped in his hand. They roll across the table, fall to the floor with a crash, but no matter what Tiny does Katina always turns the wrong way. With a wrestling grip he immobilizes her arms and legs but somehow, suddenly, she is free again. Over by the window, still grappling, they come close to falling down the fire escape.

'If they fall out,' whispers Porta fascinatedly, 'we'll be going to a funeral tomorrow!'

Mysteriously they regain their balance and fall back into the room. Katina jumps up and down on his stomach and hits him in the face with a high-heeled shoe. He spins her like a top, attempting to make her dizzy.

With a shattering noise they fall over the wardrobe and go through the thin backing in a shower of wood and splinters. The wardrobe turns over, the doors fly open and out comes Katina. Tiny is after her with blood in his eye.

Carl and Thea manage to duck just in time as the two fly over their heads.

Then Tiny is on top. She kicks her feet up towards the ceiling.

There is a sound like a baker kneading dough. Sucking, slapping, panting, gasping.

'Maybe we'll get some peace now,' sighs Porta wrapping his arms round Sula. They go at it energetically in the big bed.

When they get hungry they toast sausages out on the tiny balcony. Then they change partners. Katina climbs into bed with Carl and tells him he is the man she has been waiting for all her life.

Tiny throws himself flat on the floor and says he is dead, but Sula pulls him on to the bed and sits herself across him.

Thea and Porta join them. Soon satisfied sighs and gasps are heard.

In the middle of it all an eiderdown splits and the air is filled with tiny, spinning feathers like snowflakes.

Sula gets cramp in her belly from laughing so much.

Suddenly the door slams open with a crash and a huge man, completely bald, with a dried fish swinging in his hand, rolls into the room.

Katina, who is hanging round Carl's neck, tears herself away and begins screaming at the top of her voice.

'The German peeg 'as raped me!'

'*Did* he?' roars the bald man. Catching her by the hair he pulls her down over an old-fashioned box-sofa and beats her viciously with the dried fish.

Then he opens the box-seat and throws her into it, grabs Carl and throws him in on top of her, and sits on it to make it close properly.

'Fuck!' he roars wildly. 'Fuck till your fuckin' hair falls off an you're bald as me! Fuck! Then *I'll* fuck you both till your arseholes are spread all over Athens!' He falls down heavily at the table.

'My wife's a whore,' he addresses the air. 'She's fucking the enemy, the sow! I'll kill 'em both! Fucked if I won't!'

'That's the way,' says Porta in a friendly voice, pushing a bottle of beer within reach of the cuckolded husband who is lying sobbing across the table.

'Old Greece is goin' under,' he sobs, 'our women've got their noses up the enemy's arsehole.'

'True, true!' Porta heaves a deep sigh. 'People have no moral backbone anymore. It is because your king has left you.'

Sula dresses herself slowly. First she pulls her stockings up over her outstretched legs, and wriggles into a black and red striped suspender belt. She plays with her brassière before fastening it in front and cupping it to her breasts. A short black underskirt is draped over the table.

Tiny kneels on the bed and watches her interestedly. He is still wearing his jackboots.

Over at the table the bald man sobs even more loudly.

'Striptease arse-about-face,' mumbles Tiny delightedly.

'It's enough to make all ten toes on a castrated Arab stand on end,' says Porta.

'An' turn 'im into a bleedin' rapist,' whispers Tiny.

Sula smiles, and wriggles her bottom inside the tight black panties. She has everything a man wants a girl to have and she knows it.

Tiny takes the electric light bulb out and throws it into the street. It gets no darker. He hasn't noticed that it is now daylight again.

A tram rattles through the streets. Two Messerschmitts whine overhead.

Sula wobbles towards the door, throwing a jug of water over the sobbing cuckold in passing. At the door she turns and throws half a sausage to Tiny on the bed.

' 'Ere Fido!' she says condescendingly.

Before she can turn the doorknob they have reached her and thrown her back on to the bed. Her clothes come off faster than she'd ever have thought possible.

It is almost dark again before they leave. The bald man and all three girls wave to them from the balcony.

They walk backwards down the street waving for as long as they can see them.

'It will be boring when the Germans leave Greece,' says Sula with a deep sigh.

'Then the English come,' smiles Thea. 'They can also be fun. The uniform is different, the rest the same.'

For the sake of appearances they put the handcuffs on Carl as they approach the station. He is, after all, a prisoner on his way to jail.

'It makes a better impression,' says Porta apologetically as he snaps the cuffs together. 'Here's the extra key,' he adds putting it in Carl's pocket. 'Then you can always get 'em off if we escorts get knocked off or the war's suddenly over and we forget to release you in our rejoicing.'

'Couldn't you put something over 'em so everybody can't see I've been pinched?' grumbles Carl, holding the shiny handcuffs up in front of him.

'No, no, man!' declares Porta. 'If people can't *see* them you might as well not have them *on*. Liven up now and look downhearted. Somebody might give you something we could split afterwards out of pity.'

'If we're asked, we'll say you've knocked an oberst's 'ead in,' says Tiny craftily. 'People like that, they do!'

'Oh Lord!' sighs Carl sadly.

'Now don't get angry with us when we hit you across the back with our truncheons,' continues Porta. 'We have to show people what socialistic discipline is in the Prussian Army. Get that *gruff* look on your face,' he says, nudging Tiny as they tramp into the station building with plenty of heel-banging.

The escort and prisoner arouse satisfactory notice. Most send Carl pitying looks whilst the two cigar-smoking escorts are regarded with hate-filled eyes.

'They'd bleedin' *kill* us, if they dared,' whispers Tiny happily, blowing a cloud of smoke into the face of a little man in a bowler hat.

An old woman with pigs on a lead-rope pats Carl on the cheek and runs her hand pityingly over the handcuffs.

'He's in for a rough time, the poor little soldier!'

Carl gives her a nod of agreement.

'Don't worry my lad. Life down here's not worth much anyway, and if you've shot an officer or robbed the rich there'll be a place in heaven for you.'

She digs Porta angrily in the ribs.

'But your kind'll end up in hell! Running the big men's errands for them and taking poor boys to the gallows!' She pats Carl again on the cheek.

'Go with God, little soldier. They can't hang you but once. Here's a piece of cheese for your long trip.' She pushes a large round goatsmilk cheese under Carl's arm.

'Cocksuckers!' snarl two gefreiters, sitting on a bench and rolling dice.

'Obergefreiter Joseph Porta,' Porta bows in acknowledgement.

'The train, the train!' people scream and rush like an avalanche along the platform.

Civil and military police try to maintain order but it is hopeless.

The pig woman comes rushing along the train like a battering-ram. The pigs are squealing like mad things.

'Think this is one o' them trips they calls *Kraft durch*

Freude?' asks Tiny wonderingly, and swings his arms like a windmill to make room in the crowd.

Sweating conductors run along the train banging doors shut. Baggage is thrown through windows. The owners crawl after it.

The train is off. Everyone caught it but the buffers are packed. Everybody but two fat MP's, that is.

'We've *got* to get on board!' they shout. They try to jump on but nobody will make room for them. One of them falls on his face on the platform, his steel helmet rattling in under the train.

At Lamia the Red Cross bring round pork and beans and Turkish coffee. Porta, of course, gets three helpings.

A prison car is coupled on to the train. A long goods waggon with heavily-barred doors and ventilation openings.

'Dachau, Buchenwald,' says Porta, licking his mess-tin clean. 'Wonder if *they* get beans, too?'

'A kick in the arse is what *they* get,' growls an infantryman, sourly. A Red Cross sister has reported him for trying to get an extra helping. It will cost him a year without leave and three times three days confinement.

'Sister o' fuckin' mercy. She's one all right,' sighs a Pioneer. 'Make you die o' laughin' wouldn't it?'

At Salonica the train has to wait for hours and is checked continuously. Late in the afternoon they announce that it will not leave until the following day. The line has been blown up. Troops can go to the barracks for meals. The civilians light fires on the platform to prepare their food.

After a pleasant night in the town the three arrive at the station only to be told that it will be three days before the line can be repaired.

A sour-looking freckled MP stamps their papers.

'Escort and prisoner,' he reads out, and stares happily at Carl's handcuffs. 'What's *this* monkey been up to?'

Porta feels that the real crime – refusal to obey orders – will not make enough of an impression on the freckled MP and launches into a gory story in his best style.

'Monster – a *real* monster – that's what this one is,' he says pushing at Carl. 'This boy shot his oberst, slashed his Company Commander's gut open and ate his liver and lights. He'd got on to his hauptfeldwebel when they caught him with the man's prick and balls in his hand. A religious maniac!' Porta turns his eyes upwards and twiddles his finger at his temple. 'The madman thought he could save the world by stopping the German people from reproducing.'

'Madness,' says the headhunter in wonder. 'It's not that easy to stop us Germans.'

'No,' Porta nods, 'but he was an honorary member of the society "No More War" so for him perhaps it was logical to try.'

'Where you escorting him to?' asks the MP, who seems unable to take his eyes off Carl.

'Germersheim,' smiles Porta friendly. 'They'll blow the life out of him, there.'

'He bloody deserves it,' decides the MP hoarsely. 'My father's a hauptfeldwebel in an infantry mob.'

'Ain't lost *'is* prick yet, 'as 'e?' grins Tiny, smashing his fist down on the table gleefully and making all the rubber stamps dance.

A little way into the town they are stopped by a leutnant for not saluting properly. They have to manacle Carl to a lamppost while they march past the leutnant four times saluting correctly. After this they salute everyone in uniform they meet, even postmen and park-keepers.

They have to go into the 'Proud Eagle' after a while to rest their arms – and to drink beer.

'Now you won't run away and get us into trouble with the military prison service, will you?' remarks Porta, as he removes Carl's handcuffs.

' 'E'd be off like a shot *if* 'e got the chance,' states Tiny, banging his tankard on the counter.

'Stop that bloody noise,' snarls the proprietor, a *Volksdeutscher* with the party emblem in his buttonhole.

Tiny's giant fist catches him by the tie.

'What gives a wizened-up prick of a *Volksdeutscher* the right to give *us* orders?'

'Piss an' wind!' shouts the publican angrily, tearing himself loose. 'I can soon 'ave the MPs here!'

'MPs?' cackles Porta banging his Mpi on the counter and slapping an MP arm-brassard down alongside it. 'MPs! Who the hell do you think you're talking to? *We're* the bloody MP's, man! Shut your flapping face, or *you'll* be the one arrested *and* it'll be for the first and last time. Want to get executed in your own shithouse, do you?'

'Let's get out of 'ere,' says Tiny spitting in the host's face, ''onest bleedin' coppers can't drink beer in this 'ole.'

'Thanks for the drinks,' nods Porta, as he leaves without paying.

They go into the 'Welcoming Breast', a little further down the street, where women do the serving.

'We are the police,' boasts Tiny, leaning over the counter so that everyone can see his MP-brassard.

'What would the gentlemen like?' asks the barmaid, lifting Tiny's elbow to wipe the bar.

'Three mixed,' orders Porta, laying his Mpi on the bar.

'Shift that grease-gun!' snarls the barmaid.

'Don't you cotton to ironmongery?' asks Tiny. 'You can cancel debts with this kind, you know.'

Porta removes his Mpi without a word.

The girl fills three large tankards half-full of beer, mixes *Slivovitz* and tomato-juice into them and stirs with a glass rod.

They wish one another good health and empty the tankards in one long slobbering draught.

'It tastes like hell,' wheezes Carl, 'but it does the job fast.'

'Until this minute, I've 'ad me doubts as to whether the bleedin' world did really spin round an' round,' says Tiny in wonder, 'but now I can *feel* it bleedin' well doin' it. 'Old tight on to the bleedin' bar, boys or you'll bleedin' fall *off*!'

Die Zeit kennt keine Wiederkehr, they sing, as they reel along Metropolis Street towards the brothel the 'Green Turkey'. In some unexplainable way they land in the police station on Nicodemeus Street where they shake hands all round with the amazed Greek policemen and say that they have been asked to bring regards from mutual friends.

'When you're goin' to get 'ung you 'ave the *right* to spiritual solace,' says Tiny as they sit on the edge of a fountain around midnight catching goldfish which he swallows alive.

'The military manual covers all eventualities,' hiccups Porta in agreement.

Tiny falls into the fountain trying to prove that he can stand on one leg on the edge with his other leg straight up his back.

'Much ado about nothing,' Porta explains to an invisible audience.

'Now don't you think you can get away from *us*,' says Tiny threateningly, grabbing Carl by the collar and pulling him into the fountain. 'Don't get to thinkin' we're just a couple o' peasants with our brains in our bleedin' bollocks!'

'We, and the army with us, do not take escort duty lightly,' shouts Porta with lifted finger.

They wobble down the street, saluting a cat which they call 'Herr General!'

'Ha, there you are,' screams Porta, falling on the neck of a passing gentleman on his way home from his mistress. 'You'll have to take a turn at the infantry school at Hammelsburg and learn to eat old army boots for breakfast.'

'It is very 'elpful to everybody in later life,' hiccups Tiny.

'Cavalry's the thing,' drools Carl happily, trying to mount an iron fence and falling off repeatedly on the other side.

The civilian wrenches away and continues rapidly down the street.

'Give my love to our mother,' screams Porta after him, 'only you and I know she was German.'

'We must make an example of somebody,' says Tiny as they find themselves at dawn in the vegetable market. All the waggons are beginning to come in from the country. He presses his P-38 against the forehead of a street-cleaner who is leaning on his broom, fast asleep. 'What would you say if I was to shoot you? Do you think you would like it?'

'Heil Hitler! Heil Hitler!' shouts the sweeper. It is the only German he knows. He has discovered it to work well with most German soldiers.

Tiny drops his pistol as he embraces him, and falls into a man-hole from which it takes several people to extricate him.

'In Brussels we caught a group disguised in Salvation Army uniforms,' says Porta to a greengrocer.

'Salvationists!' cries Tiny. 'I love 'earin' about them. They're that *nice*. When you 'ang 'em they go to the bleedin' gallows without a yip.'

The train stops at Stoby. Partisans have blown up the tracks. Croatian police units hang three civilians from telegraph poles. Somebody has to take the rap for the partisans who got away.

Machine-guns can be heard in the distance.

'They're knocking off another train,' says the RTO, slapping the train commander on the shoulder. 'You were lucky, major, getting delayed at Salonica.'

A woman runs screaming from a waggon. At her heels is a drunken soldier, coatless and with his flies gaping.

An infantryman, leaning against a lamp-post chewing at a piece of bread, sticks out his foot casually. The soldier cartwheels along the platform.

Two men from the station guard throw themselves on him like hungry wolves.

'Would you let me have his papers, major, so that we can notify his unit when we hang him?' asks the RTO.

'*Will* you hang him?' asks the train commander in surprise.

'Yes, of course, we're in the field here. A quiet little summary court-martial. One officer and two soldiers to judge the case. The soldiers are told what the verdict is to be. We've knocked up a gallows over in the quarry. Nothing much, just a log over a couple of posts. We can hang ten men at a time. Our executioner, a civilian, gets 5 marks a man, and is quite satisfied with the rate.'

'Good Lord!' says the train commander, and wipes the sweat from his brow.

'Don't you expect trouble over this, someday?'

'Why ever should I?' asks the RTO wonderingly. 'Our courts-martial are all according to regulations and all judgements are recorded. The executed persons are buried in consecrated ground. All in good order. *We're* not like the SD. The worst of the worst get proper legal treatment here, *and*, I might add, spiritual solace.'

Towards evening goods waggons mounting automatic cannon are coupled on to the train.

Two flat-cars filled with sand are coupled on in front of the engine as protection against mines. The prisoners are placed on the flats. If the track is mined they will be killed.

Well into the night the train moves off. Speed is not

increased until it enters the Struma Valley. This is considered the most dangerous part of the route.

The prisoners in the open waggons are illuminated strongly, as a warning to the partisans. Slowly the passengers are rocked to sleep.

Porta and a marine-obermaat are shooting dice. He has two years arrears of pay to get through and he succeeds.

On the final throw the train is shaken by the roar of an explosion. There is a horrible sound of bucking metal and splintering wood. The synchronized quad-guns start up a raging return fire. Cascades of flares illuminate the mountain slopes. The heavy flicker of explosions lights up the terrain right over to the cliffs on the far side of the Struma. Machine-guns bark irritably, sending strings of phosphorescent tracer towards a wave of dark figures which pours down the slopes and out into the foaming river.

'See you in the community grave!' shouts Porta, jumping through the smashed window followed by Tiny and Carl.

A scimitar-like shard of glass has nearly removed the head of the marine-obermaat.

The whole compartment is dripping with blood.

Porta and Tiny crawl in under the half-overturned waggon. Carl runs forward to a mound where a discarded LMG is lying. He loads quickly and fires short bursts at the partisans. They are now over on the near side of the river.

A couple of mortars spit out grenades. For a moment the attack is held up, but new waves come flocking from the ravines and slopes of the mountains. They seem inexhaustible. Incessantly, dark figures storm forward.

The mortar section gets the range and stops the attack. Shrill screams hang in the night, which shields the bloody business along the railway track from sight.

The attackers withdraw as suddenly as they came; tracer streams glittering after them. Hand-grenades fly through the air, and the blue glare of explosions light up cliffs and earthworks. There is a photographic glimpse of a human body suspended in the air. Then a falling death-scream.

Close to the track is an old fortification where a group of partisans have taken cover. A bundle of hand-grenades tears the steel door from its hinges. A couple of Molotov cocktails disappear into the dark. A hollow muffled explosion follows and flame flashes from the firing slits. The survivors stagger out with clothes on fire. The machine-guns take care of them.

Porta wipes the sweat from his face and crawls from under the waggon together with Tiny. Carl's cheek has been torn open by a piece of shrapnel. A medical orderly fixes it up with two large pieces of tape.

'Shit!' he cries. 'Here we are on escort duty and according to the manual the prisoner must arrive at destination unhurt. These partisans don't seem to have read the manual though.'

A deafening explosion shatters the silence and blue flame fountains upwards. It seems as if the whole mountain has gone up. Great rocks come tumbling down the slope carrying partisans and German soldiers with them into the depths. With a long rolling roar the avalanche rolls over the train taking several carriages with it into the river.

'Gawd Almighty!' gasps Tiny, 'if we 'adn't the luck of the bleedin' devil 'imself we wouldn't 'ave lived to be this old.'

In the course of an hour it is all over. The partisans disappear into the darkness. Only the dead are left.

The heavy engine is unharmed. Its pumps tick away quietly. A thin plume of steam jets from the side.

The engine-driver and his mate are dead. The body of one hangs in the door opening. The head dangles loosely downwards. The other is lying across the coal with his throat slashed open. They were Serbians, killed by Serbians. They were aiding the enemy.

The civilian personnel of the train are gone without trace. The partisans have taken them with them. Before evening their mutilated bodies will be found in the streets of the nearest town. A warning.

The Vlassov Cossacks arrive on sweating horses. They slash at the bodies with their long sabres. A German rittmeister in Cossack uniform receives instructions from the train commander. 'Squadro-o-o-n, form line abreast! Forward!' he screams in a shrill voice. And long after they have disappeared from sight the thunder of their hoofbeats can be heard.

A flare rises in the distance and angry machine-guns make themselves heard.

'Now they're slaughtering 'em,' says a feldwebel of Pioneers gleefully, and continues stripping his Mpi.

'Who's slaughtering who?' asks Porta contemptuously.

'The Cossacks are the partisans,' grins the feldwebel with satisfaction.

The wind plays around the shattered waggons, with a sound like ill-adjusted mandolin strings. Far away, dogs have begun to bark. The sun rises over the mountains and sends its hot rays down over the smashed train. The corpses on the slope begin to swell. Millions of flies swarm, glittering blue-black in the sun and feeding on great open wounds.

'War's a good time for flies,' says Porta disturbing a swarm. They are crawling on a torn-off arm. The hand has lost three fingers.

'Wonder where the bleedin' rest of 'im is?' Tiny asks, interestedly.

'The devil knows,' says Carl, 'but he must've been a seaman. See all the tattoos.'

Porta picks up the arm and examines the tatooing more closely.

'He's been in Bangkok. This is Chinese here. Pity a nice artistic arm like this has to be eaten by a swarm of Yugoslavian shit-flies.'

Tiny rolls over comfortably on to his back, puts his hand into his dirty grey shirt and pulls out a flattened packet of cigarettes. He shakes it impatiently until a cigarette comes up, and takes it with a pair of bloody lips which have been in recent contact with a rifle butt. Silently he offers the packet to the two others. The cigarettes are English navy cut; he has taken them from a partisan body.

'Lying here with a good cigarette, you could almost forget there's a war on,' says Carl dreamily, putting his feet up on a torn-off door. 'Noticed how pretty it is here?'

'Bloody beautiful,' says Porta with satisfaction, pushing his gas-mask container under his head for a pillow.

'Maybe the bleedin' war's ended while we've been lyin' 'ere,' dreams Tiny. 'Takes time to get news out to places like this.'

'I could do with a fat nigger bint,' laughs Porta, lecherously, blowing smoke through his nose.

'All the cunt there is in the world an' the women've got the lot,' says Tiny, emitting a long-drawn-out fart.

'Cunt ought to be supplied from the Army canteens,' considers Porta.

'You'd better get all of it *you* can while we're on this bleedin' escort trip,' says Tiny to Carl. 'Once you're inside, mate, you've 'ad it, far as *that's* concerned, for ever.'

'What do you mean, for ever?' asks Carl, taking the cigarette from his mouth. 'I'll be out again in ten years' time.'

'They'll kill you, son,' prophesies Tiny, ' 'eed the gypsy's warnin'. They finish *all* the long-timers off. They'll put you in a minefield clearance unit, and that gives you five days, *if* you're very lucky.'

'Why should they kill me, if I keep me nose clean?'

'Anybody who's been in pokey more'n a year 'as seen too much,' states Tiny firmly. 'Officially there ain't any prisons in Germany. Don't forget we're a socialist state with a leanin' to the right!'

'Lot o' swine!' sighs Carl.

'Now you're talking sense!' laughs Porta. '*We* found *that* out long ago.'

'When you're workin' in the common graves, you really 'ave to watch it,' Tiny explains. 'Can 'appen they buries *you* along with the real bleedin' dead 'uns.'

'Have you seen that happen?' asks Carl, doubtfully.

'I ain't seen sod-all,' grins Tiny. 'I read about it in Grimm's Fairy Tales.'

'I won't get amongst the mines nor in no mass graves neither,' says Carl. 'I don't volunteer for anything, if they put me in solitary for the whole ten years for it.'

'*You* don't know what *you* are talking about,' laughs Porta jeeringly. 'You'll be willing to eat shit to get out of *that* cell.'

'It's only half ten years anyway,' says Carl. 'The war'll be over in five years time, an' I'll be marching home a hero.'

'Perhaps,' answers Porta doubtfully, and shrugs his shoulders.

' 'Ow'd she 'ave to look, this piece o' nigger cunt you was

talkin' about?' asks Tiny, coming back to matters of more interest.

'Not *too* fat and long black hair,' says Carl. 'I can't stand these frizzy Lizzies.'

'To hell with the hair,' grins Porta. 'That's not what you're after. Mine'll be fat and with muscles in her titties strong enough to break your jaw if she swings 'em in your face.'

'Gimme a long thin 'un with music in 'er arsepart,' shouts Tiny joyfully. 'I 'ave 'eard as nigger wenches are the best in the bleedin' world. When they spins their 'ips you wind up with a prick you can use to pull corks with, for ever an' ever, amen!'

A signal rocket explodes far on the other side of the mountains, but the noise does not reach the train.

'Them bandits are up to somethin' again,' reckons Tiny. 'It ain't just to see the pretty colours they shoot bleedin' rockets orf.'

'Think they'll be back?' asks Carl, nervously.

'They won't let up, until this bleedin' train's spread all over the Struma bleedin' valley,' says Tiny, weightily.

'I'd suggest we move off sharply before that happens,' says Porta. 'We have, after all, no real meeting point of minds with those fellows.'

'Are you mad? That's deserting the colours,' whispers Carl, terrified. 'I couldn't do that. I've always done my duty as a soldier.'

'That's probably why they give you ten years,' grins Tiny. 'You was born in too clean a bed. Do as we do an' you'll manage all right.'

'Pack your shit and let's move,' decides Porta resolutely, getting to his feet. 'There's a couple of boxes of flares over by that smashed waggon. I'll lay an egg in one of 'em and as soon as they start going off we make tracks. They'll all look that way and not notice we're making a tactical withdrawal.'

'This could shorten us by a head,' sighs Carl resignedly.

'Or lengthen our lives by a lot,' says Porta, with a short laugh.

'Wise boys always leaves the ship in the first lifeboat,' philosophizes Tiny, picking up a hand-grenade. 'The captain's the idiot as leaves last.'

Carl looks at him in horror as he screws the blue cap off the grenade.

''Old on to your knackers!' grins Tiny happily. 'Thunderstorm blowin' up!' He swings his arm and the grenade drops neatly between the boxes of flares.

He laughs until he almost chokes when signal rockets and flares fly up into the air, and fizz in and out between the waggons and carriages.

'Ta-ta, love. The key's on the window-ledge,' shouts Porta, taking to his heels.

An Mpi barks viciously and the bullets plough up the ground just behind Tiny, who has got himself hung up in some barbed-wire.

'*Job tvojemadj!*'[4] he screams, and pulling round his Mpi sends a whole magazine at the train, where everybody takes cover. He loosens himself from the wire and races headlong after the others.

Breathless, he lands in a narrow crevice in the ground.

'Bleedin' shower o' shit'awks!' he curses. 'They bleedin' *shot* at me! One of their own bleedin' countrymen!'

'All Germans are bastards,' says Porta, 'but don't let these considerations hold us back. They'll all be here soon. At the moment I feel we'd be safer with the partisans than with our own lot.'

'What a load of shit you sods've got me into,' rages Carl. 'Be shot as a soddin' deserter more'n likely, before I even *get* into the jug.'

Breathlessly they push through heavy brush and enter a long valley. As they turn round a rock bullets whine past their heads. High on the hill-top stands the train commander threatening them with an Mpi.

'Going for assistance, sir!' shouts Porta encouragingly, waving his tall yellow hat.

'Come back, you swine!' screams the major hoarsely.

'East, west, 'ome is best!' shouts Tiny happily, and disappears around a cliff abutment, taking time to wave to the train commander as he goes.

They keep moving all day, avoiding villages and roads.

4. *Job tvojemadj* (Russian oath): Go fuck your mother.

Towards midnight the sky lights up brilliantly and a long rolling explosion makes the earth shake.

'That was the train,' says Tiny, looking back.

'We can forget about getting assistance, then,' says Porta.

'That's that, then,' laughs Tiny.

'Hard luck on the bods,' says Carl quietly.

'It's always hard luck on the bods,' says Porta throwing his arms wide, 'but great eras crave great sacrifices. We belong to an unlucky generation.'

After a short rest they move on and by the following morning reach a wide road. They are about to move onto it when Tiny puts up a hand and drops down into the ditch.

A black three-axled Mercedes passes them at top speed and stops a mile further on at a farm. Five men in mouse-grey uniforms jump out.

A short burst of Mpi fire is heard. Then everything is quiet again.

'SD-ghosts,' whispers Tiny. 'I ain't a Greater-bleedin'-German obergefreiter if they ain't 'ead-'untin'.'

'Let's get out of here,' stammers Carl unhappily.

'We're doing nothing but,' grins Porta unworriedly.

'What about 'arf-inchin' their bleedin' gondola, eh?' asks Tiny, smacking his lips thoughtfully.

'It is less tiring to drive than to walk,' says Porta.

'Don't think I'm going to get mixed up in stealing a waggon right out from under the soddin' Gestapo,' shouts Carl, aroused.

'Nobody asked you,' decides Porta brusquely. 'You're a prisoner under escort. Whatever kind of song and dance you make about it, you still do as the escort says or get executed on the spot.'

'An' now we're orderin' you to drive in a black Mercedes!' says Tiny with severity. 'Prisoners must obey orders! Or what will things be coming to?'

'You pair o' crazy bastards!' Carl shouts, stamping on the ground with rage. 'I'll write a report about everything when we get to Germersheim.'

'Report?' Porta laughs aloud. 'It'll be a novel! *And* nobody'll believe it.'

'They'll send 'im to the nut'ouse at Gressen,' considers Tiny.

Carefully they approach the big Mercedes which is standing under a large tree practically shouting 'police-car!'

Carl lags behind, cursing and almost in tears from sheer fright.

Porta tiptoes around the car a couple of times. He is wearing an MP brassard and badge.

'I won't do it,' whispers Carl, stubbornly, shoving at Tiny.

'You just stay 'ere then an' explain to the Gestapo who it was as run away with their bleedin' gondola,' grins Tiny. 'They'll be that pleased, they'll bore their Mpi barrels straight up your poor bleedin' arsehole! An' then they'll 'ave you for breakfast, mate. They do that with prisoners y'know.'

Porta waves at them.

'There are four full reserve jerricans,' he whispers. 'We can drive straight to the gates of hell in this bucket.'

'It probably knows the way too,' says Carl. 'Steal from the soddin' Gestapo! Jesus Lord Christ! I'll be white-headed by the time we reach Germersheim.'

'God 'elp us if they ain't left the bleedin' keys 'angin' in 'er,' grins Tiny in delight. 'You'd think they wanted to get shut of it. Wonder if they stole it themselves.'

'We won't get far with SS number plates,' pipes Carl despondently. 'And *black* too. It stinks of Gestapo a mile off.'

'Who's to say *we* ain't Gestapo?' asks Tiny. 'Them bastards use real army uniforms too, y'know.'

'We'd better push it down the road a bit,' says Porta, releasing the handbrake.

Gravel squeaks under the wide tyres.

'She's bleedin' '*eavy*,' groans Tiny, getting his shoulder behind the car.

Porta edges himself in behind the wheel. Tiny springs athletically over him and takes the front seat by his side. He polishes the half-moon MP badge carefully with his sleeve.

Carl crawls into the back seat and makes himself as small as possible.

'Jesus if this comes *off*!' he mumbles nervously.

'And now we must start quietly,' says Porta, groping around the dashboard.

'Ain't she a beauty!' says Tiny admiringly, running his hand over the polished instrument panel. 'Wouldn't I like to roll down the Reeperbahn in this baby. Old bleedin' Nass'd lose 'is leather coat an' is turned-down 'at-brim at the sight of it.'

The motor gives out a sucking sound as Porta turns the starting-key. It sounds like a roar to them, but not even the feeding hens react to it.

Porta tries with a little more choke but the motor merely sighs and gives off a strong smell of petrol.

'If them SS bleeders come out I'm cuttin' loose,' snarls Tiny, positioning his Mpi.

Carl bites nervously at his hand and sends a silent prayer to heaven, although he is not a believer.

'What the hell's wrong?' asks Porta, wiping sweat from his face. 'These high-compression jobs start off if you just look at 'em, as a rule.'

'Might be an idea to get a move on,' says Tiny, blowing his nose on his fingers. 'Even if we *are* a kind of MP it'd be a bit difficult, maybe, to explain to them SS fellows what we're doin' sittin' in their bleedin' car.'

'I can't understand it,' sighs Porta, shaking his head. 'Can it have flooded? Stinks like a blasted Arabian oil-field.'

'Try to give it the lot,' suggests Tiny, always an advocate of violence.

Porta pumps desperately at the choke and treads on the self-starter. The motor sighs gently.

'Hell!' he shouts, pushing the choke in irritably.

The engine starts with a roar and the exhaust bangs like a gun-shot.

'Jesus!' gasps Porta. 'There must be a bundle of dynamite under that bonnet!'

An SD man comes rushing out to the gate just as the car begins to roll away.

'Stop!' he shouts. 'That's our car. Stop you bastards!'

Stopping is the last thing in the world Porta is thinking of doing.

The car shudders and shoots forward like a shell from a gun as Porta treads heavily on the accelerator.

An Mpi burst whines above their heads.

'No peace for the bleedin' wicked,' growls Tiny, turning round angrily. He lifts his Mpi and sends two short bursts at the SD man who sinks to the ground.

The heavy Mercedes roars along the road, taking the curves with a long rising whine. The exhaust is backfiring continuously.

'Holy Mother of Kazan!' groans Porta. 'I've met a lot of queer vehicles during my time in this blasted army, but this one has 'em all beat. We'll have to exchange it, somehow, before it turns my stones to bloody gravel.'

Tiny sets the siren going and looks importantly to all sides.

'You crazy bastards,' rages Carl from the back seat. 'You'll have the Gestapo on our tails in a minute.'

They roll into Brod at a more than respectable speed. Porta stops outside a large army workshop with long rows of wrecked cars lined up outside. He wrestles two WH[5] numberplates from an Opel and hands them to Tiny.

'Put these on instead of those bloody SS plates. I'll take a look round while you're at it.'

'This is forgery, fraud with Army property,' protests Carl. 'A court-martial board of deaf, dumb and blind Kaffirs'd hang us for what we've done, only up to now, even.'

'Shut it!' orders Tiny. 'You're shakin' like a bleedin' jelly, man!'

Porta disappears, whistling happily, into the large workshop, and runs straight into the arms of a mechanic with obergefreiter stripes.

A carton of cigarettes disappears into the workshop man's boiler-suit. Porta accepts three tins of paint and a triangular command flag from the wreck of a Horch.

'All right for movement orders?' asks the obergefreiter mechanic. He seems to have a sense for the practical.

'Yes,' says Porta, thoughtfully, 'you've got something there. May I invite you to partake of a little something in the canteen?'

'Never been known to say no,' answers his colleague. 'See that glassed-in office over there? When you enter the door to the left you'll find a bookcase behind a blue curtain. In this are kept

5. WH (Wehrmacht-Heer): Army (WD).

123

open movement orders. Take a bundle. There's enough in one to take you to America, at least.'

'Rubber stamps?' asks Porta, with a cheeky grin, as the third glass follows the first two. 'Where the Prussians are concerned, orders which haven't been stamped aren't worth as much as shithouse paper.'

'When you have the movement orders,' explains his colleague, pushing forward his glass for the fourth time, 'go up the stairs to the gallery, second door on the left. There you'll find all the rubber stamps you'll ever need. Take one with an FPO number. They are in the yellow rack. Copies are in the black rack. Look out for Pigface. He'll shoot you on the spot if he catches you.'

'How'll I know Pigface?' asks Porta, practically.

'You'd expect him to grunt at you,' answers his colleague.

'Live till you die, and make a handsome corpse!' grins Porta, encouragingly, and stamps up the stairs to the gallery, having removed a whole bundle of movement orders. He looks carefully into the office, and finding it empty walks nonchalantly in and removes two rubber stamps.

'What are you doing here?' comes a falsetto voice from behind him.

Porta draws a deep breath, whirls round, and clicks his heels together.

A major of Engineers with a face which bears a remarkable resemblance to that of a pig is standing before him.

'Sir,' screams Porta, 'wish to state, sir, I am looking for Workshops Chief Mechanic Lammert, sir!' Porta had seen the name of the glassed-in office below.

'What do you want with the Chief?'

'Sir, I have a message for him from a friend, sir!'

'He has no time to waste on friendly messages. He is engaged in winning the war,' grunts Pigface crossly. 'What are you doing in my office?' He makes a lightning inventory of loose items.

'Sir, I would like permission to use the telephone, sir!'

'What do you think this is? A telephone booth?' screams Pigface. 'Get out of here, you idle man, and quickly! If I see you here again in my workshops I'll have you arrested!'

Behind a wall they paint the black Mercedes with Army camouflage paint. For verisimilitude Porta gives it a couple of dents with a sledgehammer. The Eastern front finish, he calls it.

'It's a pity. It was such a *nice* car,' says Tiny.

They drive slowly through the town.

'Let's have a cup of coffee,' says Porta, pointing at a large pompous building which resembles a luxury hotel. All it needs is the pavement tables and sun-shades.

He swings elegantly in to the entrance.

'Don't stop!' shouts Carl. *'Look at those sentries!'*

'Jesus,' mumbles Porta. 'This doesn't look like our kind of place at all.'

'SD!' moans Tiny fearfully. 'If anybody asks I'm not with you.'

Porta guns the motor and the car shoots forward, letting off a couple of colossal backfires which cause the SD sentries to duck and take cover.

They pass several police patrols and road blocks, but as soon as the police catch sight of the triangular command flag they wave the car on through and soon they are out of town.

The following day they swing into Kukes where they meet an Italian *Ajutante di Battaglia*[6] who is chief cook to a high-ranking staff unit.

To their surprise they discover from him that they are in Albania.

'We are on our way to Germersheim via Vienna,' says Carl sadly.

'So you are a leettle off your road,' smiles the Italian. 'But now you here you take a leettle food wiz me?'

Two kitchen orderlies lay a table on the pavement under a large sunshade in Italy's green, red, and white colours.

The first course is turkey with a green sauce.

'Thees was for my divisional commander,' says the Italian whose name, he tells them, is Luigi Trantino. 'I geev heem other food. Luigi's guests have right to good food.'

They wash the turkey down with mountain wine served in an enormous jug.

6. Ajutante di Battaglia: WO.1.

125

'I am brave soldier,' states Luigi, pointing at a row of brilliantly-coloured ribbons on his chest. 'These I get in Abyssinia.'

'What, were you down there teachin' the blacks the true Roman faith?' asks Tiny. Luigi nods, his mouth stuffed to speechlessness with turkey.

'They understand quick. Only one God!'

'Of course,' Porta agrees, leaning back and dropping a piece of turkey into his wide-open mouth.

'What're they like there?' asks Tiny inquisitively. 'Do they bite?'

'They nice people,' says Luigi waving his fork about. 'They not smell, like American say. This with race big nonsense.'

'Doesn't worry me, either,' shouts Porta, dipping his bread in the green sauce.

'Before war I have first-class hotel,' boasts Luigi. 'All big men they come eat wiz me. Musso eat two times. Big 'arem! All kind of cunt. *All*! Then Fascist pigs make peaceful Italian go fight war!' he sighs. 'Soldiers take my hotel. Make me wear uniform. All sheet-bad! Africa terreeble! For many month no see *zuppa de calamaro*. No culture there. Bad as German. Italian die body and soul if there long time.'

The orderlies bring in the next course.

'*Pasta con le sarde*,' proclaims Luigi, proudly. 'This *Mafia* eat when big man plan big job.'

Porta clicks his tongue.

'You Romans certainly know how to enjoy life.'

'We no do bad,' admits Luigi.

'Have you got spaghetti?' asks Porta. 'You know with brown sauce and cheese over it.'

'We 'ave, of course!' The order is passed on to the kitchen immediately.

'I start bordello I never take girl who not brought up on *Spaghetti alla Carbonara*,' shouts Luigi, delightedly. 'It grease works good inside.'

Tiny takes a huge helping of spaghetti from the dish in the middle of the table. He chews, swallows and battles with it bravely. It seems as if the spaghetti will never disappear down his throat. Slowly his face begins to turn blue.

'You must 'ave cheese wiz this,' says Luigi, with a professional air.

Tiny nods, his mouth stuffed full. He shakes cheese on to what seems to be mile-long strips of spaghetti.

'He's going to die,' says Porta, watching Tiny's purpling face with interest.

In desperation Tiny grips the spaghetti in both hands and rips it apart.

'Jesus Christ, 'ow do you Italians *live* through a meal of spaghetti?' he groans.

'You must learn eat,' explains Luigi. 'See like so!' Like lightning he rolls the spaghetti around his fork. 'See now,' he says again with self-assurance, and repeats the trick several times.

Porta and Carl give it up immediately. But Tiny in his stubbornness gets himself tied up in it. At last he gives up and eats the remnants with his fingers.

'Thees place a real *sheet* place,' declares Luigi darkly, when they have gorged in silence for a while. 'The officer ees a lot of *sheet*. I get pain soon in belly. They greedy all time. The wine she ees too cold or she ees too young. Roast duck they weel 'ave, venison, lobster. They no seem know they in middle of thirty-year-long war, with 'unger and misery everywhere. Me I get angry so could *peess*.'

'You eat and drink well,' says a voice suddenly to one side of the table.

'What een 'ell?' cries Luigi, and can hardly believe his own eyes.

A coal-black Negro with a red fez on his head, wearing a double-breasted greyblue Jugoslavian uniform coat, stands in the gutter grinning broadly. On his left foot he is wearing an Italian mountaineering boot. On the right foot a German officer's long riding boot.

'You eat well,' he repeats, pointing at the food on the table. 'Give me!'

'Manners maketh man, me old black son,' says Porta with dignity. 'You are in white company.'

'Get stuffed, German. Want your teeth knocked out?'

'Well blow me bleedin' brainless,' shouts Tiny, indignantly.

127

'The bleedin' Colonials've learned to talk! On your way 'ome to the bleedin' Reich are you, mate?'

'If he is he'll get a shock,' sighs Porta. 'Socialism isn't what they say it is!'

'Where you come from, neegger?' asks Luigi inquisitively.

'Fuck you too, *spaghetti*. I didn't ask *you* where *you* crawled in from, did I? Let's have some food!' He pulls out a chair and sits down at the table without waiting for an invitation, pushing Carl's plate to one side to make room.

'Beppo!' shouts Luigi to the kitchen. 'Breeng a lobster. You like strong sauce?' he addresses the Negro with a sly grin.

'I can eat fire if I want to.'

'Christ I'd like to see *that*,' shouts Tiny. 'I've seen one on the Reeperbahn but she was a 'ore.'

'Red devil extra No. 1!' orders Luigi, with an expectant look on his face.

Porta gets up and goes out into the kitchen to help Beppo.

'Chili,' he orders, emptying a whole tin of powder into the sauce. A spoonful or two of Cayenne pepper and a dash of black curry. He remembers red peppers just in time.

'Paprika she *full* of vitamin C,' says Beppo, handing him a large tin of the condiment.

'Lovely grub,' grins Porta winding up with a big helping of powdered garlic.

Beppo is laughing so much he almost drops the five lobsters on the way to the table.

'Slow service!' shouts the Albanian Negro.

'Here is the special sauce,' says Porta, 'but I feel sure it will be far too strong for *you*. Only white men can stand it.'

'Nothing is too strong for me,' barks the Negro, conceitedly, and catching hold of a lobster he tears the meat from it, cracks the claws with his teeth and drops the contents into the Red Devil Sauce.

Porta watches him with wide eyes like a man watching an attempt at suicide.

'We reeng for fire-engines, no?' asks Beppo staring hard at their victim.

The Negro pushes the lobster into his mouth and swallows.

His face turns suddenly grey, stiffens, his mouth falls open and terrible grimaces move across his features. For a moment he appears as if already dead. He tries to speak. Not a word passes his lips.

Politely Porta offers him some wine.

He grabs it and swallows half the contents of the jug. Now the sauce really begins to work. Like a rocket he flies into the air panting for breath, runs in circles, then out through the kitchen where he jumps through an open window. He emits a long shrill howl and stops for a moment by the table.

Automatically Porta offers him the wine jug. Down goes the rest of the wine and the sauce burns a thousand times worse than before.

'A-a-a-a-a-ah!' he screams like a gut-shot wolf. One hand grips his stomach and the other his throat. He rolls over onto his back and kicks his legs in the air. The Italian mountaineering boot flies off. He arches his body and moves down the road wriggling like a snake on his back. Then he is on his feet again. He springs into the river and drinks as if he were trying to empty it.

Shortly after he comes out of the water and goes up an almost vertical cliff wall like a mountain goat.

''Mazin' what these bleedin' cannibals can do when they want to, ain't it?' cries Tiny.

'What devil you put in devil sauce?' asks Luigi.

'Some tranquillizers that'll make a good boy of *him*,' grins Porta.

Shortly after, the Negro comes back. He looks like a man who has crossed the Gobi Desert on foot. He offers them his hand politely.

'You're leaving already?' asks Porta.

'I am going back to Libya!'

'Whatever for?' asks Tiny.

'The food here does not agree with me!'

Beppo's lobsters exceed their wildest expectations. Porta praises them lavishly.

Luigi holds up a claw as if it were a marshal's baton.

'They soon shut up shop here. I am pack and weel *not* go back to Italy a poor man!' he whispers confidentially.

'True for you,' Porta smacks his lips. 'Only fools leave a war poorer than they got into it.'

'The most are eediots,' states Luigi, dipping a piece of lobster into the garlic mayonnaise.

'God be praised,' smiles Porta happily. 'It is His work.'

'It weel be good to again be in Italy,' says Luigi. 'War I not interest in. I 'ave what I need for me in Italy.'

'That's the way I see it, too,' agrees Porta. 'All they get out of it is us Germans and you Italians getting the shit knocked out of us.'

'Give 'em our love in Italy,' says Tiny, through a mouthful of lobster. 'Maybe we won't be far be'ind you.'

'*Gesú, Gesú,*' cries Luigi in horror, almost choking on his own lobster. '*Madre di Christi* forbid thees!' He crosses himself and rolls his eyes heavenwards.

'I hope and I pray that the last of the Germans 'as left Italy before I come 'ome to 'er!'

'What, don't you *like* us then?' asks Porta in surprise. 'We're allies and are fighting shoulder to shoulder in a war which has been forced on us.'

'I no say Italian love German,' says Luigi, shaking his head. 'When like now very nice fellows, but when many together make too much noise, take up much room.'

'Somethin' in that,' admits Tiny, licking the bowl of garlic mayonnaise clean.

'You allatime shoot,' insists Luigi, 'no understand thees dangerous. You shoot at man, he shoot back most time.'

'True enough,' sighs Porta.

'We take coffee, cognac, 'ere?' asks Luigi, standing up.

'I've eaten that much I *can't* move,' laughs Porta, unbuttoning his trousers. 'I love food. I could live merely to eat!'

'You've fixed yourself up here very nicely,' Carl praises Luigi, as he tastes his cognac with the air of a connoisseur.

' 'Ere ees good,' Luigi admits, stretching his legs comfortably. 'I want only freedom. Maybe Tommy come soon and 'it us so 'ard we no want shoot back.'

'Any left?' asks Porta, pushing his empty cognac glass towards Luigi. 'God only knows when we'll see this stuff again.'

Smiling, Luigi fills his glass to the brim so that Porta has to bend down to it to drink. He sucks it up like a cow drinking water.

'They're gettin' a bleedin' beltin' just now,' says Tiny, spitting in the direction of an idealized SS-man on a recruiting poster.

'A general I see go through, with much leeberated loot in truck following, only yesterday,' says Luigi. 'That good sign.'

'There's summary court-martials on everywhere,' says Porta, slipping a cracking fart. 'There'll soon be more watchdogs out here than soldiers. Even the ammunition shortage doesn't stop 'em. There's always a beam and a rope. Spare the rope, spoil the child as the pedagogues say.'

'The Greater German Wehrmacht is on its bleedin' arse, as *you* might say,' sighs Tiny, throwing a piece of apple-pie over his head to the great happiness of a dog behind him which wolfs it down.

'I'll wind up this famous campaign in Germersheim, and make hay when I get home as a politically persecuted person,' laughs Carl with satisfaction. 'That could lead to a lot. Yesterday's villains are tomorrow's heroes.'

'Don't laugh too soon,' warns Porta ominously. 'It won't be long before the dopes get over the shock of having lost a war.'

'They say the 'ole of the 9th bleedin' Army's deserted to the enemy,' confides Tiny secretively.

'9th Army? That was wiped out long ago,' Carl says wonderingly.

'Generalfeldmarschall von Mannstein's sitting on a rock in Poland crying his eyes out,' says Porta confidentially.

' 'E ain't no von Mannstein,' shouts Tiny, the all-knowing. ''E was born Levinski, a name Adolf ain't too 'appy about. Say what you bleedin' like, but it's a very surprisin' thing!'

'Eet funny theeng. Good news never come in army newssheet,' philosophizes Luigi.

'The Führer has said that there is no more need for tactical operational geniuses,' explains Porta. 'Now we are to have army commanders of the boneheaded type who will lead us with a happy shout into battle, and stand on the line.'

'Then that *is* the bleedin' end,' confirms Tiny importantly. 'An army o' bleedin' cattle as just stands still our good neighbour's armour'll fix up in two shakes of a 'ore's arsehole.'

'What a shower of soddin' *lies* they've filled us up with the last few years,' says Carl despondently.

'Apart from a few of us everybody believed 'em,' Porta smiles a superior smile.

'And eet ees the worst that many steel believe them,' whispers Luigi.

'Ought to be bleedin' shot,' says Tiny.

'Our war leaders have lost their grip on the reins,' decides Porta. 'Bottoms up, mates!'

'They once *'ave* grip?' asks Luigi in surprise. 'I think always Germans fonny people. Square een head!'

'Gröfaz⁷ 'll soon be frizzlin' in 'is own fat,' says Tiny, optimistically.

'We are moving towards difficult times,' says Porta. 'We won't be able to turn round soon without being called deserters.'

'They must all be mad at the Führer's HQ,' considers Carl.

'Who God will let get fucked, he first strikes with blindness,' explains Porta, with pathos in his voice.

A company of recruits comes singing down the winding mountain path. Their boots and equipment are clean and polished and their helmets shiny and new with the eagle on the side.

Porta scratches his back with his bayonet, and looks at the singing recruits thoughtfully.

'When you see a bunch of well-groomed German heroes like that, all spit and polish, you could almost begin to think the myth of German heroism still existed.'

'Three day from now partisans weel 'ave wiped these boys out,' states Luigi shortly.

'Thank God we were in at the start,' says Porta. 'Otherwise we wouldn't be alive now.'

'Old soldiers never die,' exhales Carl, stretching so that the wicker chair he is sitting in comes close to breaking apart.

Tiny lets out a long rolling belch, which stops the company feldwebel in his tracks.

7. Gröfaz (Grösster Feldherr aller Zeiten): The greatest military leader of all times (cant name for Hitler).

'Are you able to salute?' he asks angrily.

All four salute silently, but without rising from their wicker chairs.

A thunderous noise starts up away to the east and rolls nearer like a rapidly approaching storm. A salvo of shells falls with a roar into the town. Earth and fire cascade skywards. A long row of houses disappears in a great chalky cloud. The school across the road is lifted into the air and collapses into pieces quite slowly. The roof falls down intact on top of the pulverized walls.

The company feldwebel is cut in two and the pieces thrown high up on to the mountain side. The company of recruits melts away in a sea of flame.

Luigi disappears with amazing celerity into a slit-trench, closely followed by Porta and Tiny. Carl picks up a wicker chair and holds it above his head in the weird hope of protecting himself from the shrapnel which is raining down all around him.

The blast from an exploding shell throws him into a depression in the ground.

A shell scores a direct hit on the house in which the divisional kitchen has established itself. Black clouds of smoke rise as the house falls slowly in upon itself. Only the chimney and a huge shining copper boiler are left undamaged.

The large green, red and white sunshade comes sailing through the air and settles gently down on the slit-trench.

'The colours of old Italy!' says Luigi proudly. 'They breeng luck!'

A new salvo falls. Their mouths are full of brick-dust. Trees on the slope snap like matchsticks and fly through the air. Broken bodies sail above the roof-tops. A pair of horses is thrown far up the slope. The street becomes a volcano of flying stones and splintered wood.

'Let's get out of here!' shouts Porta. 'Coming, Spaghetti? They don't need your culinary art here any more!'

Luigi stands thinking for a moment. Then he claps his plumed Bersaglieri on his head. He throws a last fond look at the colourful sunshade.

'Si! I go 'ome to Italy now!'

133

Carl comes rushing down the street, with the wicker chair still elevated precariously above his head.

'Who the hell's doing all the shooting?' he shouts excitedly.

'Ring up and ask Information,' suggests Porta.

To their amazement they find the Mercedes undamaged amongst a mass of wreckage.

'The devil looks after the Gestapo,' grins Porta, as they leave the town at top speed.

They ascend a narrow mountain road. Porta's instinct warns him not to use the broader metalled road.

'Where we go?' asks Luigi, preening his plumes.

'A far-off place,' murmurs Tiny mysteriously.

'Jesus but these new-fangled wars are *terrible*!' says Porta.

'Think they were more fun in olden times?' asks Carl.

'*Quite, quite* different,' answers Porta. 'A chap called Marius beat the Vercellae on the plains of Provence with the help of war dogs.'

'It's a bleedin' lie,' shouts Tiny, 'but it must've been more bleedin' fun then. War dogs! *We'd* soon fix them bleeders.'

A Jaeger major stops them and orders them to give him a lift.

Tiny takes the back seat between Carl and Luigi. They drive into Kralfero at the head of a battalion of Jaegers.

The major inspects the Mercedes with a doubtful eye.

'What are you men doing here?' he asks suspiciously.

Porta hands his forged documents over quietly.

'Oh-oh!' snarls the major, leafing thoughtfully through the movement and rail orders. 'Aren't you a little off the route to Vienna?'

'With all respect, sir, the partisans wouldn't permit us to take the direct route,' smiles Porta genially.

'What's that Italian doing with the German army?' growls the major sceptically, and demands Luigi's papers.

Luigi searches his pockets desperately.

The major waves to two MPs, but before they reach the car they are cut down by a burst of machine-gun fire. Hand-grenades rain into the street. From the roofs machine-guns open fire on the Jaeger battalion. Wounded soldiers crawl moaning to cover. Molotov cocktails explode with a hollow sucking whoosh. The burning liquid splatters men and material.

'Partisans!' gasps the major, jumping from the car.

Porta salutes and smiles idiotically.

'Yes, *sir*! They're going to do us, looks like.'

A burst from a machine-gun rakes the street and bullets shake the bodies of men already dead.

Porta backs the car close in to the house wall, from where they can watch the drama in comparative safety.

An armoured car mounted with an automatic cannon rattles round the corner, strafing house walls and roofs. Hand-grenades fly through windows into houses. A long white sheet unfurls from one window. Soldiers storm the street doors. Soon after the bodies of men and women whirl from the windows. They strike the roadway with a thick soggy sound.

Two Pumas thunder forward. Their machine-guns send bursts of tracer through windows.

The major is there again, suddenly.

'You are under arrest!' he shouts, aiming his pistol at Luigi. He falls forward with a gasp.

Tiny rolls to one side to avoid the falling body.

Carl's Mpi rattles. A figure falls from a roof. After him an Mpi comes whirling down.

An hour later it is all over. The prisoners are packed into a church. Enraged soldiers surround them.

'This bitch killed old Herbert from No. 4!' shouts a fat Artillery wachtmeister. He smashes his fist into the woman's face, splitting her lips, and then boots her between the legs.

'Bitch!' others scream. 'Finish 'er off!'

A leutnant works his way through the crowd.

'Pay attention!' he shouts, his voice cracking with rage.

Not until he fires his pistol in the air, do the enraged soldiers notice him.

'Prisoners are to be treated *correctly*,' he orders. 'We are not bandits like the enemy! Wc are getting a summary court together and they will all be shot but first they must be tried.'

'Just wait, you bastards. We'll pull your guts down through your arseholes!' an oberjaeger threatens three prisoners who are sitting against a wall with their hands folded behind their necks.

135

'Why waste time tryin 'em,' asks a gefreiter from a Pioneer Battalion. He points at a young woman standing in a corner. 'That bitch there is mine. By Jesus she's going to sing before she goes out!'

'You heard the Leutnant,' a cavalry wachtmeister warns some soldiers who are beginning to exhibit signs of doing more than threaten. 'We are the *Herrenvolk* but we are not brutes!'

'When Ivan the *untermensch* comes this way these bastards'll know the difference,' shouts a feldwebel, maliciously.

A tall, thin soldier jabs a young man with the barrel of his Mpi.

'This pig smashed up our kitchen waggon. He's the sod we've got to thank for no hot dinner today.'

'Smash his face in,' suggests an old infantry-man with a sausage under his arm.

A legal officer has established himself behind the altar, which with the help of a flag, has been turned into a judgement seat. His rimless spectacles reflect the light down on to the two rows of prisoners lined up in front of him. He clears his throat, takes up a long list and in a thin piping voice begins to recite their names. After each name he looks up and says solemnly:

'In the name of the Führer and of the German people I sentence you to death by shooting!'

He repeats this sixty-seven times.

The sentenced are taken outside the town. In a gravel pit a mile from Samaila the Pioneers hand each of them a spade. They are to dig one long communal grave. This is the most practical way of doing things.

When they are finished they wipe the spades before returning them to their captors. They are poor peasants and know the value of a spade.

A very young leutnant is in command of the execution squad. He is sweating and stammers nervously.

The prisoners are lined up along the edge of the grave so that they can fall backwards directly into it.

'Come on, come *on*!' shouts the leutnant. 'Next, next, let's see some movement here!'

The youth who smashed up the kitchen waggon is so frightened that he falls into the grave and has to be helped out again by his fellow prisoners.

Some of them break into the *Internationale* and shout 'Nazi murderers!'

The oberst, who has come to see the execution, expresses his admiration of the prisoners' conduct.

'Excellent, excellent!' he says. 'Many a German traitor could learn something from these people. It's a pleasure to see them!'

'God will no doubt take everything into account,' says the adjutant, swallowing with difficulty.

'They deserve it,' says the oberst, a deeply religious man.

When the last man has been executed, earth is shovelled over them and the Pioneers tread it down.

Porta swings the Mercedes up on to a primitive gravel side road. A bridge on the main road has been blown up.

Suddenly there is a thunderous explosion and the road splits open. A sheet of flame rises towards the sky. The Mercedes is lifted into the air and the four men thrown from it.

'What now?' pipes Luigi, unhappily, as they sit in the shelter of a haystack looking at the wrecked Mercedes. The only thing left untouched is the command flag.

Porta pushes it into his belt. It might come in useful some other time.

'What now?' asks Carl worriedly. 'Am I *ever* going to get to Germersheim and start working off my ten years?'

'Every day you're with us, is a day off your sentence,' Tiny comforts him.

'Why I no stay with my own people?' asks Luigi tearfully. 'I get new division kitchen. Never Italian Army make war without kitchen for *spaghetti carbonara.*'

Rain begins to fall as they tramp miserably down the road. The cold comes down from the mountains. Down in the valley the Danube winds grey and sad. In the distance machine-guns rattle.

Towards night they take up quarters in an uninviting chilly villa on the outskirts of a village, but they have hardly closed their eyes when they are awakened by a party of infantrymen who are also in search of quarters.

137

A leutnant fumes at them and orders them to show their documents. These have been burnt in the wreck of the Mercedes.

'Tomorrow you will be turned over to the MPs,' he barks brusquely.

'We *are* MPs!' says Tiny proudly, taking out his brassard.

As he does so, machine-guns begin to hammer and handgrenades tear up the road outside the house. Harsh voices are heard shouting orders in Serbian.

'Move!' screams the leutnant. 'Partisans!'

'Let's get *out* of here,' whispers Porta and moves smartly out of the back door with his three companions at his heels.

As they leave, a group of partisans enter the villa. Wild-looking figures emerge from side-streets. Molotov cocktails crash through the windows of houses.

'Going our way?' grins Porta, swinging himself up on to a truck in a convoy which is on its way to Belgrade.

Just before the convoy reaches Belgrade it is attacked from the air. The truck they have hitched a ride on is thrown into a field. Shrapnel hits Porta in the shoulder. Tiny's foot is crushed under a box of shells. Carl's arm is broken.

They drag themselves optimistically into Belgrade and report to a field hospital. Tiny is using a rifle as a crutch. Luigi is hopeful of a train to Italy from Belgrade.

'It would really be better if *you* were wounded too,' says Porta, looking hard at Luigi and fingering his Mpi. 'It would get you a new set of documents.'

They come under fire in Ubi. A grenade explodes in front of Luigi, blowing off half his face and an arm. He lies groaning and before they can give him first-aid he is dead from loss of blood.

They bury him in a railwayman's front garden and hang the plumed Bersaglieri helmet on a birchwood cross over the grave.

'Eight days should be enough,' says the sour-looking MO at Reserve-Kriegs-Lazarett 109 in Belgrade.

A flak[8] gunner tells them with a tastelessly gleeful air that the previous patient in Porta's bed died only an hour ago.

8. Flak: Anti-aircraft.

'That's *lucky*!' cries Porta, pleased. 'It's not often two people die one after the other in the same bed.'

'They've crossed my documents in red,' says an infantryman quietly, from a corner where he is sitting staring at a fly on the shade of the nightlight preening its wings. 'Think they're gonna shoot me when I get better?'

'O' *course* they'll shoot you,' says the artillery gefreiter who had been in the hospital a long time. '*You* are a self-inflicted wound. Most of the blokes here are batty,' he says, turning towards Porta. 'If the enemy was to put a spy in here he'd go back an' report that the whole German Army was made up of maniacs. We've got a fellow from the Engineer Corps (Buildings). He was supposed to build a chimney for the Catering Corps (Bakeries). In some weird way he wound up with the chimney built and himself *inside* it and unable to get out. This happened in a rarely used part of the building and he was posted as a deserter. If a baker hadn't happened to come into the room where he was inside the chimney they'd *never* have found him. They got this nutcase out with the help of a couple of pneumatic drills. He'd been in the chimney twelve days and was raving when they got him out. Now they want him to confess it was an attempt at desertion. *He* says he didn't think what he was doing and the mortar'd dried before he realized where he was.

'He couldn't go *up* because the chimney got narrower towards the top. Now they've got a commission coming from Berlin. They've photographed the chimney and made drawings of it. They've tried to climb up it to make sure he really *couldn't* get out that way. But they still insist on his having done it in an attempt at desertion.'

'Well, if he couldn't get *out* of the chimney,' says Porta seriously, 'it'd be difficult to *desert*!'

'Our opinion exactly,' laughs the artilleryman, 'but the red-tabs're of a *different* opinion. An MP officer visits him every day an' sits by his bed shouting: *Confess man,* or you will suffer for it. You were trying to desert!'

'Want some poor bleeder they can shoot at, I s'pose,' says Tiny, gloomily. 'A war without nobody to execute, ain't much of a bleedin' war.'

'There are a lot here who're seriously wounded. I've lost both legs and half my stomach myself.'

'*You* won't be hard on the rations then, will you?' says Porta, with a practical air. 'Got to *think* of that sort of thing in wartime, you know. How did it happen?'

'I was asleep in an orchard.'

'Doesn't sound dangerous.'

'It is when a self-propelled gun runs over you,' says the artilleryman, sadly.

'Aren't you in danger of a self-inflicted charge?' asks Carl.

'No, the SP commander's got to take the blame. The orchard was out of bounds for exercises. It'd been commandeered by Division and I was picketing it. I was asleep in my dinner break. The SP chief's crawlin' round the eastern front now pickin' up mines. The driver's got his for careless driving. Solitary in Torgau.

'In B-Block there's the blinded and the one's who've gone dumb,' says the artilleryman. 'They're readying a ward for the deaf, too. There's only one just now an' they'll be shooting him next week. Failure to obey orders. Forgot to put his ear-plugs in. Rail artillery he was. They held the court at his bedside and had to give him the sentence in writing as he couldn't hear it read out. He's been crying ever since and tryin' to volunteer for everything, but who wants a soldier who's got to have all his orders in writing?'

'No, there's not really time for it, is there?' agrees Porta, thoughtfully.

'In A-Block we got the malingerers. Lively over there, it is. They start 'em off every morning with No. 9's and a dose of emetics, no matter what it is they're sick with. Same again at the end of the day. A phony typhus case died of it day before yesterday. There's one fellow been playing barmy for a whole year. Soon as anybody comes near him, he growls like a dog and goes for their legs. Still an' all the most interestin' case of the lot's this boy in the next bed here. Broke his neck, *he* did, tryin' to show his mates how to dance the *prisjatska.* He went at it too hard an' when he came to the big jump into the air, missed his bearings like, an' flew straight out the window. Broke a flagpole off on his way down, spun over and *would've* landed on his feet if he hadn't got turned over again by the regimental notice board. As it was he landed on his napper and broke his neck. It's gonna cost him a packet, too. They've told him his injury can't be regarded as bein' in line o' duty an' he'll have to pay for all the damage he's done *and* for the treatment.'

'That'll teach him to keep away from those damned Russian dances,' philosophizes Porta. 'Give me something more smoochy. At least you've got a partner to hang on to when you're doing the waltz.'

'Ought really to get hold of the padre, and get our sins off our consciences,' says a dragoon.

'So we can start off again with a clean sheet, too right!' agrees Porta.

The door flies back with a crash against the wall and a little soldier in grey Finnish uniform stamps noisily into the ward. Over his shoulder he is carrying a brand-new captain's uniform. He bangs his heels together and salutes.

'Jaeger corporal Jussi Lamio from Taijala, here by mistake.' He hangs the captain's uniform on the lamp, crawls up on to the table, cuts himself a couple of slices from a long loaf and slaps a thick piece of sausage between them.

'Any of you been on Næsset?' he asks between mouthfuls.

'Get undressed now and into bed,' orders a nurse as she enters the ward. 'Down off that table and get that uniform off the lamp!'

'You German bitches good to give orders!' shouts Jussi, 'make no mistake. I am Corporal Lamio from the 3rd Sissi Battalion, and in Kariliuto they call me the scourge of God. In Karelia we don't stand for any German bitch to tell us when to go to bed. We want to sit on the table we sit on the table, by God. I hate women who try to give orders. Women's place is in the kitchen or else to give us a good time in the sauna!'

The nurse shakes her head, and leaves as soon as she has made up the bed.

'On Næsset we fixed a battalion of bitches from Leningrad, good! They were *real* daughters of Satan. Not like that piss-pot emptier there who thinks she can tell a Finnish corporal what to do. I *want* to sit on the table I *sit* on the table.'

'*Women* soldiers?' asks the flak gunner wonderingly.

'In Russia it is not necessary for you to have a prick dangling between your legs to do an infantryman's filthy job in the trenches. These Communist bitches gave us their machine-gun bullets for as long as they lasted. And then they come in with the butts. We had two companies of Jaeger troops from the Sissi Battalion and we were on their tails all the way from Suomisalmi. It was a tough trip. We are often over in the enemy territory. We are moving so quick it is hard to live a normal life. These Russians can feel us Finns breathing down their necks all the time. Our Company Commander, the son of heathens from Lahti, who had death and women and nothing else on his mind, had decided he was going to have some of these women from Leningrad. People who read more than the Bible, and know what they are talking about, say it is wonderful to get such an ideology bitch in the hay. Maybe we should have *read* some of those books in the libraries we burnt on our way. Then we should not have been so happy, perhaps. Twice we are close to getting them. Ahiii they were *bad* bitches! You can feel in the air this fanatic Communist fever. We promise them everything if they will only put their hands up and give in. Our captain had a machine to make his voice louder and could speak Russian so they knew what we were saying to them.'

'*Veruski roj!*'

'But they lay no weapons down. I do not know how many times he shouts '*Stoi!*' through his machine. I am not a book-keeper but it was many. No man in God's image can persuade these Communist bitches to lay down the guns and end the fighting.'

Jussi sends a long stream of spittle out through the window and takes a fresh piece of sausage. He is chewing tobacco at the same time.

'Does that taste all right?' asks Carl in wonder.

'Otherwise I would not do it, would I?' answers the little Finn carelessly, biting into the bread. 'In the end we get these bitches backed up against the sea where they could only have got home again by swimming,' he continues, 'but their politics had not made them *so* mad. Now we are Christians, most of us, and we feel it is wrong to shoot women dead, even when they are Communist bitches of soldiers. We do not go so hard at them at the start but soon have to change our minds. They sing heathen songs and go at us with infantry spades so we have to stitch them up back and front with our machine-gun bullets. Our Suomi's[9] were red-hot. But we have to go on until every one of them is dead as a herring on the square at Wiborg. Then we liberated what there was and there were many good things to take with us. Our captain, that son of a devil, took all their hair. Out of this he made fine brushes to hang on the walls of his house and remind him of these bitch soldiers from Leningrad.'

The nurse comes back with two Medical Corps feldwebels who are looking for some action, but before they can say a word Jussi gets down from the table, bangs the big Finnish ski-cap on his head, salutes, and breaks into a roaring song:

It was war that led our feet
through hail and snow and sleet.
We went where bullets whined
far from country, kith and kind.
Life in the trenches here
is not all skittles and beer,
and maybe in the end
we'll die for what we defend.

'Don't say any more,' he turns to the nurse. 'I have got down from the table, and I will take my officer's uniform from the lamp and I will go to bed. But make no mistake. This I do because *I* wish it, not because *you* say I must.' Without a glance at the nurse and the two feldwebels he hangs the Finnish captain's uniform on the rack behind the bed, brushes it off carefully with a small clothes-brush, polishes the Finnish lion on the lapels and salutes it.

Silently he undresses and rolls his own uniform up, as is the custom in the Finnish Army.

'What kind of a uniform is that you've got there?' asks Porta with interest.

'You can see it is the uniform of a Finnish Captain of Jaegers.'

9. Suomi: Slang for Finnish Mpi.

'What the 'ell do *you* go around with it for? *You* ain't a captain!' asks Tiny.

'Lord Jesus but these Germans are stupid people. I do not understand how you ever have dared to get into a war! You do not even know that the hen is bigger than the chicken. Who has said that *I* am a captain of Jaegers? If anyone has, then I say that he is a liar. *I* am a corporal in the Sissi Battalion, and the uniform I have fetched from the tailor at Kuusamo. Captain Rissanen should use it for a fine party, but Lord Jesus be praised we have not paid a mark for it yet. The captain will no doubt still be sitting waiting for me in his underpants. He had only his battledress which he had been chasing the enemy in for many months, so that it had become a little worn and stained. Nobody can go to a fine party with pretty women and smart staff officers in an old Finnish summer battle blouse, even if there are stars on the collar. Sooner or later I will get this uniform to him. I think I must ring to him before I get back. I must tell you that Captain Rissanen can get very angry indeed in the head. He was, for some time, at the Lapintahti Asylum near Helsinki because, in a rage, he had shot a Forest Ranger, but when this war came they are short of officers and declare him well again. The Colonel has orders not to excite him. When he is not angry he is a very nice man. If it had not been for you stupid Germans, Captain Rissanen would have had his uniform long ago and would have been able to go to many fine balls and parties.'

'Don't talk shit,' laughs the flak gunner. 'How could us Germans be responsible for your captain not getting his uniform?'

'If you had ever met your SS mountain artillery regiment *"Nord"* you would not be asking the question of a fool,' replies Jussi throwing his arms out helplessly. 'They commanded me to go with them, made a very great noise and said a lot of nonsense in German. As you can hear I am able to speak good German, but these peasants could not understand me. In Oulu I was suddenly, in some strange way, on board a large steamship which carried the name of S.S. *Niedeross*, and on this ship we travelled to many places which I would never have seen if these skull people had not made me accompany them. They then sent

144

me from regiment to regiment. It is not impossible they have wished me well and would relieve the monotony of this war for me. I was in Ssennosero, Kliimasware, Rovaniemi and Karunki, and then one day I was sent to Hammerfest with the 169th Thuringian Infantry Division. From there we continued by ship, an ugly piss-pot of a ship, and it seemed to me that everyone was in some way afraid. We moved as if Satan himself was behind us turning the screw. We would go ashore then quickly away again. We were many, many places in Norway. I do not know the names of all the towns. They were not specially noticeable, so there was no reason to remember them.

'One morning we come to a new country. Sweden. All the waggons were sealed and these Swedish men ran about with weapons and tried to look very terrible. They looked foolish instead. If the enemy had seen them he would have gone home comforted.

'In Engelholm twenty-three men disappeared. The Germans said that men always disappeared in Engelholm no matter how careful a watch was kept. It was as if Engelholm swallowed them up. That trip was very strange trip altogether. Everyone sang and was happy until we reached Engelholm but as soon as we left it you saw nothing but sad and disappointed faces.

'In Trelleborg I go for a walk, but this is something one should not do if one is not Swedish. Everything is idiotic and the other way round in that country. You wait quietly to cross the road looking to the left as you have been taught at home, and suddenly there is a truck which almost takes off your nose. You panic and begin to run, still looking to the left, but these devils keep coming at you from where you least expect them. When you come to the middle of the road and begin to look to the right, as sensible people do, they come racing at you from the left and hunt you like a rabbit. I became so angry that I pulled out my bayonet and began to shout the Finnish Army's ancient war-cry:

' "*Hug ind, nordens drenge!*" '[10]

'You can believe me when I say these Swedish men moved. Our Russian neighbours could not have been quicker. One of their police with a sabre at his side tried to stand in my way.

10. Hug ind, etc.: Strike hard, Northern boys!

' "Crawl back up where you came from! Up your mother's cunt!" I cried. "Make way for Finland's free sons!"

'More came and tried to arrest me, but they did not succeed. No long thin-legged Swede can stop a Finnish corporal of Jaegers who has blown more than a hundred of our godless neighbours to Satan. But then the German MP's arrived with victory helmets of iron and all the personal artillery they could carry hanging on them. They shouted all kinds of heathen words at me. It sounded like Russians having a party.

'We enjoyed ourselves for half-an-hour or so. Blood flowed freely and uniforms hung in ribbons. It was a lovely day.

' "God be thanked," I thought, when I was again on board my ship. "Now you are on your way to Finland again with Captain Rissanen's new uniform." But I was to be disappointed. I was landed in Germany! "Very well," I told myself, "now you will see Germany, Jussi. You will have some stories to tell when you get back to Karelia!" But they will think it all to be lies. Will you do me the favour of writing your names in my pay-book? Stamped all over it is. I would not be happy to think they might put me against the wall for a deserter when I get back home again.'

'You'll need a devil of a lot of stamps to get *that* tale believed,' chuckles Porta.

'Let them doubt me, then,' cries Jussi, banging his fist down on the blanket. 'Doubt does no harm. It is a healthy thing. What if we were to believe all the lies the politicians tell to the poor?

'In Berlin I met a Finnish major, a tall thin man with his cap pulled down over his eyes as if he was afraid of being recognized and taken before a court to answer for his crimes. He was a bad man, with spurs and black riding boots although he was not even a dragoon. I do not like these people who wear spurs but have not even been issued with a bicycle. He wore on his face the same look that all these high gentlemen have and militarism radiated from him. He boasted that he could have me sent back to Finland very quickly.

'Two men from the Finnish Military Mission took me to the train. On the way to the station we had a look at the town and we managed to get a good Finnish drunk on. After some discussion with the Germans at the station we were allowed to pass through the barriers. The Germans helped me into the train and off I went. My two Finnish friends waved and shouted hurra as long as they could see the train.

'What had happened in Berlin I do not know,' continues Jussi, 'but the train was going in the opposite direction. Instead of getting to Helsinki I am now in Belgrade and here I have been wounded. They are mad here. They shoot at people from all over the place. "Stop, you sons of Satan! I am no German! I am a Finnish corporal of the Jaegers, who has nothing to do with this war here!" I shout to them. But still they kept shooting at me and in the end they hit me, those devils!'

He pulls his blanket over his head, rolls himself into a ball like a dog, and falls straight asleep. The rest of his time at the hospital he does not speak a word to anyone.

Early one morning they are discharged and given new movement orders. They are, as Porta says, become as new men with all their old sins forgiven.

At the railway station they are told that their train will not leave until late at night, and they go over to *Tri Sesira* where Porta extravagantly orders *Bosansk cufe*. They eat the meatballs cold, but this does not make them taste less exquisite.

They run into three prostitutes and go home with them. 'Just,' as Carl says, 'to see how they live.'

All Porta remembers of this episode is naked girls and a kitchen chair which collapses.

'It's all right, Nico, all we want is a few titbits,' explains Porta pleasantly to the head waiter in evening dress at the high-class restaurant 'Zlatni Bokal'.

A string orchestra is playing Strauss and there is a scent of expensive perfume in the air.

Well-dressed people crowd the foyer.

'My name is not Nico!' says the head waiter, coldly.

'No? The resemblance is striking!' smiles Porta, swaying on his feet. 'Step aside, Nico, and let us at the trough!'

'My name is *not* Nico!' snarls the head waiter, his cheeks reddening. 'My name is Pometniks!'

Porta bows from the waist and raises his yellow hat.

'Obergefreiter Joseph Porta, and this is obergefreiter Creutz-feldt. Come here Tiny and pay your respects to Monsieur Nico!'

''Ello, mate,' grins Tiny foggily, grabbing the head waiter's tiny white hand and crushing it in his giant fist.

Pometniks draws a deep breath and straightens his white tie.

'I regret M. Porta. This is an exclusive restaurant. You would not feel comfortable here, and regrettably all tables are taken.'

Tiny breaks out into a meaningless roar of laughter and runs his hand through the head waiter's well-oiled hair, making it stand up in spikes.

'Nico, Nico, you're a bleedin' *card*! There's a table empty there with two chairs.' He lifts Pometniks up so that he can see over the heads of the crowd of guests.

'Great stuff!' shouts Porta. 'We'll take one of these chairs!' And with a chair under his arm he pushes his way through the thickly-carpeted restaurant.

Pometniks has to run to keep up with them. He is swearing softly, but viciously, in Serbian and German.

'The table is reserved,' he pants, 'you can have that one in the corner, but only for one hour. Then that too is reserved.'

'And when are *you* reserved for, Nico?' asks Porta, tickling him under the chin.

'*Pometniks*,' he wheezes.

'You mean to say you *aren't* Nico, the notorious sex crimi-nal? Unbelievable, the resemblance!'

'You're *all* right!' grins Porta pushing his hand through the head-waiter's hair again. He takes off his uniform jacket and hangs it on the back of the chair, pulls his tie and shirt open and scratches his hairy chest.

The guests gape over at their table. The orchestra misses a beat as the leader forgets to swing his baton.

A tiny waiter with a face like a mouse hands them the menu and waits with pencil poised.

'Mickey, remove the reading matter!' says Porta. 'We're not in a library, are we?'

'Is *'is* name Mickey?' asks Tiny, looking at the waiter with the expression of a hungry cat on his face.

148

'Isn't it obvious,' laughs Porta. 'He'd never get past a hospital. They'd have him inside in a cage with the rest of the experimental animals in a minute.'

'The messieurs wish?' asks the little waiter, unwillingly.

'*Prase,*' Porta demands arrogantly, leaning back and rocking his chair.

'Regret, monsieur, we have not sucking-pig roasted on the spit.'

'Mouse-arse, *can* you *perhaps* manage *Djuvic?*'

'With pleasure, monsieur. You wish it to be strong?'

'Of *course,* Mickey. You don't think we eat Serbian hash that's *not* strong? But let's have a good big dish of *Poddvarac* first to sharpen our appetite.'

'Chicken in sauerkraut *before the hash?*' gasps the waiter. 'I do not think the messieurs can manage . . .'

'Think, stink!' grins Tiny. 'Bring it on, mate!'

'Bring us first of all some plum tea to get the shit out of our teeth. Better make it two bottles immediately,' orders Porta.

The waiter has hardly opened the first bottle before it is empty.

'That's the best bleedin' tea I ever did taste in my life!' shouts Tiny excitedly.

'It hasn't got a fuck to do with tea,' answers Porta. 'It's spirits.'

'Why they call it tea then?' asks Carl in wonder.

'Then they don't have to lie to their wives when they say they've been out drinking tea,' explains Porta.

When they have finished the second bottle Tiny drops his arm over the shoulder of a lady at the next table who is wearing a low-cut dress and flips one of her breasts out.

Porta begins to sing an obscene song in a high piercing voice.

Carl grabs the cigarette girl and begins to dance the *spjetka* with her. They trip and cigarettes fly all over the floor.

The head waiter comes rushing over followed by two waiters and a doorman.

'This is enough,' he shouts, softly. 'This is not a brothel. Out with you!'

'We've not eaten yet,' protests Porta. 'Be a good boy, now, Nico. Mother *said* we could go in here on our own!'

'Out, or I call the MP's!'

'Don't bother, we're here already!' Porta holds up his invaluable brassard.

'Throw them out!' the head waiter orders the commissionaire.

The man puts out a respectably-sized hand towards Tiny.

'Come on, don't let's 'ave no trouble now!'

'Hit him in the teeth!' shouts Porta, catching up a plateful of sauerkraut rolls from the table next to him and dashing them into the head waiter's face. He throws a glass of red wine back at Porta. In a few seconds there is nothing left on the table to throw. Tiny swings back his iron-tipped boot, size 12, and lets it go. It contacts the doorman's instep. He lets out a scream and dances round on one foot.

Two waiters, in green hussar uniform jackets, grab at Carl, who cracks a chopping board down onto their heads.

The cigarette girl comes running and scratches Tiny's face. He throws her into the orchestra, which all the time continues playing the Blue Danube waltz.

Porta drives a fork into the head waiter's hand. A tureen flies through the air, lamb soup showering out in all directions.

The guests roar with laughter. They think it is an act. In 'Zlatni Bokal' there is always some kind of surprise act.

A Generalmajor laughs so heartily that his false teeth fall into his soup.

As they leave, Porta takes two bottles of Slivovitz from a shelf and declares them confiscated by the military police for analysis.

As Tiny passes the buffet a pot of Servian hash is pushed out from the serving-hatch. He regards it as a gift, but puts his head through the hatch first to say thank-you.

Nobody protests. The head waiter is glad to see the back of them. He could see his whole establishment on the way to being smashed to bits.

'I'll put a Molotov cocktail into that joint, sometime!' screams Porta, as they climb into a horse-cab and drive to the station. They go into the first class waiting-room, where the chairs are softer, place the Slivovitz and the pot of hash between them and go to work on them.

'We ought to go back and shoot that bleedin' Nico bastard's 'ead off!' shouts Tiny with his mouth full of food. 'Then we ought to set fire to that doorman bleeder, an' watch 'im cook. That's what *I* think. We've lost *face*, we 'ave! We've let 'em *piss* on us. We ain't represented the Fatherland as we ought to've done!'

A railway official, who is on his way over to them to throw them out of the first class waiting-room, changes his mind when he hears Tiny's remarks.

The train rocks through dark mountains, and crosses the border without stopping. It is already two days late. Outside Budapest there is a stop for the entry signal.

Carl's eye falls on some military graves with rusty helmets hanging on cheap crosses.

'Poor sods!' he says in a melancholy voice. 'The Fatherland doesn't give the dead heroes much, does it?'

'The Fatherland's a load of cunning Jewboys!' states Porta.

A large gull lands on one of the crosses. It screams a protest when a crow chases it off.

Inquisitively the crow sticks its beak under the helmet, stops to preen its feathers and then investigates again.

'See him looking,' says Porta. 'The black bastard hasn't forgotten the good times when they let the soldiers' bodies lie on the ground long enough for the crows to get their favourite delicacy, human eyes.'

A Rumanian soldier shows them his stump of an arm.

'Bang, crash, *Germanos*,' he explains in a strange homemade lingua franca, at the same time gesticulating fiercely with his good hand. '*Malo køszenep szepen*[11]. *Job tvojemadj! Nic hamm nesjov*[12].'

The train crawls into the Budapest main station. Three hours to wait. Troop transports have first priority.

In the dirty station restaurant, which stinks of unwashed soldiers, they try to get some food.

There is a very elegant menu. They choose chicken soup piquant. If the menu is to be believed it contains: chicken meat, celery, carrots, dried ginger, onions, bean shoots, eggs and

11. Malo, etc.: Many thanks.
12. Nic hamm, etc.: We have nothing to eat.

sliced lemons. It turns out to be yellow-white water in which the closest inspection shows no trace of even fat on the surface. The piquant chicken soup is also cold.

'This soup is cold!' says Porta, pointing to his plate.

The waiter, in his greasy dinner jacket, sticks a finger into the soup to test it, and shakes his head with a smile.

'Is warm, herr German soldier!'

'Is cold, herr Hungarian waiter!' replies Porta.

The waiter fetches the cook, a big, fat wicked-looking fellow, who, without a word, takes Porta's spoon and tastes the soup.

'Warm!' he grins, showing blackened teeth, and turns on his heel to go.

Tiny catches him by the back of his collar and pushes his face down into the soup.

'Get drinkin' then, you gypsy bastard!' he yells, raging.

The cook drinks like a thirsty horse to avoid drowning in the soup. They pour the two other plates of soup down inside his trousers, and followed by earnest threats to shoot his head off he bolts into his kitchen.

When they leave the restaurant with their hunger still unsatisfied, the Rumanian veteran comes running after them.

'Nicn ham[13]!' he shouts despairingly.

The train is more than crowded. There is only room in the first class. There they can put their feet up, whilst everywhere else passengers are packed like sardines. They even have to stand in the toilets, where they laugh at people who want to use them.

'Piss out the window,' they advise, 'not against the wind, please. Here's a lady wants to go. Anybody got a rubber pocket?'

Every Central European uniform is on display. MPs with shiny half-moon badges push their way roughly through the crush. They nod discreetly to leather-coated civilians with pulled-down hat brims. Gestapo. There is always a check on. Let your mouth flap too loosely and you'll feel a heavy hand on your shoulder as you leave the train:

'Geheime Staatspolizei!'

Without a ripple another person has disappeared.

13. Nicn ham: Nothing to eat.

There are three thousand people packed into the long express train, which thunders, without light, through the country on its way to Germany. Germany, lying like a tumour in the guts of Europe, with its barracks, prisons, concentration camps, hospitals, execution squares and cemeteries. A land where tortured millions spend most of their nights sheltering in cellars.

The engine-driver takes a swig from his thermos of coffee. He has been driving for eighteen hours without a break. Rules say, no more than eight hours, but there is a war on and engine-drivers are in short supply.

His mate shovels coal into the flaming maw beneath the boiler.

In the first class carriages people are getting ready for bed. An oberst in long underpants is listening to a major from the secret police.

'In Odessa we used to stand them up on a truck. When we drove away, they were left there hanging,' laughs the major. 'It was quite comical to see.'

The oberst nods silently, and continues to press carefully at a pimple, staring into the mirror.

Loud sighs can be heard from the next carriage where a Rumanian oil engineer is taking care of a German oberst's wife. She has been to Bukarest to visit her husband who is seriously wounded. The engineer kisses her and slides his hand over her rounded bottom. She giggles and pushes at him.

He bends her back on to the plush of the seat, lifts her grey pleated skirt so that a black suspender belt comes to view. He lifts her a little higher up.

She laughs excitedly as he pushes her legs apart.

'No!' she whispers. 'You mustn't!'

He catches her around the behind and pulls her towards him. To the rhythm of the train they enjoy the pleasures of love.

In a carriage a little further down the train a German nurse is lying with her dress up above her hips. An infantry leutnant has his face pushed down between her legs. She twines her legs round his neck and rolls her body, panting pleasurably.

On the seat across from them a naval officer is pulling a pair of red panties down over the hips of a well-known doctor's wife from Vienna. Her fingers are tearing at his trouser buttons. She stares in fascination at the couple on the opposite seat.

Porta has just completed a deal concerning a black pig which will walk on a leash like a dog. Carl and Tiny are shooting dice with two sailors. The boxes hang on the floor which they are using as a table. Between throws Tiny is stroking a Rumanian country girl along the thighs.

'When you get to 'Eyn 'Oyer Strasse, just ask for Crooked Albert. ' 'E'll 'elp you get a *proper* job. A bint like you 'adn't ought to 'ave to burn 'erself out in a bleedin' factory.'

'What will the Gestapo say?' asks the girl nervously.

'Keep away from 'em, an' what the 'ell do *you* care what they say?'

Howls and organ-like notes sound in the black night. The engine-driver drops his thermos flask, and springs at the brakes. His mate is at the door, ready to jump.

The oberst in underpants listens nervously, toothbrush in hand. The major jumps down from the upper berth and begins to hunt feverishly for his uniform.

'Planes!' he shouts. 'No peace for the wicked. If it's not one thing it's another. It's about time they discovered that bloody final weapon!'

'What is it?' asks the nurse who now has her head buried between the leutnant's legs.

'Listen!' says the oberst's wife to her oil engineer. Her naked behind is sticking straight up in the air.

'To hell with it!' gasps the engineer, who is almost finished. He intends to finish too, even if the entire American Air Force is going to attack the train all at once. He grabs her thighs and presses himself madly into her.

The naval officer and the doctor's wife are on the floor. She is on top. They are concentrating so hard on what they are doing that they do not hear the voice of war outside.

'What the 'ell?' roars Tiny who has just got the drawers off the country girl. 'Couldn't those flyin' bleeders've waited ten more bleedin' minutes?'

'We're leaving,' says Porta, tucking the black pig under one arm.

Carl throws himself on to the floor and holds his hands over his head as protection against what is coming.

A naked girl runs screaming down the corridor with her lover after her in socks and a brief shirt.

'The German soldier can be *made* filthy but never *is* filthy,' states a Generalmajor proudly. He is speaking to some Hungarian and Rumanian officers in an insulated carriage. They do not hear the Jabo's[14] which come screaming from the clouds, sending tracer tracking down at the railway line.

The following wave drops bombs. Earth lifts itself in fountains on both sides of the tracks. Stones, earth and mud cascade down over the train.

On the next sweep they hit the engine. The stoker saves himself by throwing himself off. Head over heels he goes, down the slope, is up like a shot and running towards the woods. It is not the first time he has saved his life like this. He throws himself down into a depression and stares towards the train which is slowly losing speed.

'Jesus Christ, Jesus Christ!' he gasps. 'They're cleanin' up all right!'

Automatic cannon hammer. Another carriage ploughs down the slope, rolls over on its side and disappears. A German and a Jugoslavian carriage steeple on end as if in a loving embrace. The bogies smash down on to the rails.

The oberst in long pants runs sobbing across the track. A tracer burst goes straight through him. Like a slaughtered pig his body rolls down the slope.

A pair of torn-off wheels run straight across him, cutting his body in two.

The major of police is running with his black GEKADOS folder under his arm: a folder which contains sentences of death. He falls into a hole but arrives in it together with an aerial bomb. There is nothing left of him or his GEKADOS folder.

The naked girl has taken cover under an overturned carriage. The blast of a bomb sends the carriage sliding further down the slope. The girl is plastered to its side like butter on to warm bread.

14. Jabo's: Fighter bombers.

The nurse and the leutnant come running along the side of the train. Nobody notices she has only stockings and a suspender belt on. They run straight into a burst from a Jabo and never even feel the kiss of death.

The doctor's wife from Vienna is thrown through a window. A long pointed piece of glass cuts her body open lengthwise. Her entrails hang in the splintered glass of the window.

The naval officer has disappeared completely. Only his cap remains lying on the floor of the compartment.

Most of the passengers are lying strewn about between the tall slender fir trees. Crows flap slowly over the smashed train.

The bombs have bored their way inside the train and blown the passengers out amongst the trees. Screams and cries arise from the mass of chopped meat, brains, bones and joints.

The Generalmajor is throwing up over a body. The screams of the injured drown out the sounds he is making. He is usually proud of his toughness. He has seen blood enough in his time, and is used to the sight of mangled bodies. But the sight of bluish-red entrails covered with masses of wet gorged flies has been too much for even a tough German Divisional Commander, who glories in the thought of a hero's death.

An SD officer is lying a little way inside the wood. Looking up through a lacework of fir needles and morning light, he sees the remains of a woman transfixed on the point of a tree. The arms are gone. The legs hang to one side like the wings of a bird gliding. A hat with a blue feather is still on her head.

She must have been hit by blast, he thinks, and cannot pull his eyes away from the grotesque corpse swaying in the treetops. He cannot move. A stake has gone straight through him and pinned him to the ground, but he feels no pain.

Several carriages remain on the track. Inside they are like slaughter-houses. Wounded and dead in a mash of crushed bones and shredded meat.

A soldier runs shouting down the track. Blood spurts from his shoulder.

'Bastards, bastards, look what they've done to me arm!' He stumbles, falls forward and dies.

A gefreiter, no more than seventeen, sits on a torn-off carriage door and stares at his legs. They are hanging by shreds of sinew. His face is bloody. Only his eyes are alive. He touches his Iron Cross 1st Class. A crumb of payment for lost youth. The Fatherland's dirty thanks to a betrayed generation.

A relief train arrives from the opposite direction. It stops just in front of the overturned engine.

An oberstabsarzt in long shiny riding boots examines the scene of butchery coldly. He barks some orders, and medical orderlies swarm out with tarpaulins under their arms. First wounded German soldiers, then dead German soldiers. Then German civilians, and last of all people from the occupied territories.

'Jesus,' cries Porta, who is sitting on a windshield between Tiny and Carl. 'Those bombs can really tidy up! Much more effective than shells!'

'What's that 'e's got in 'is 'and?' asks Tiny, pointing at the body of a dead cavalryman.

Carl bends over and opens the clenched hand. A hundred mark note and three dice appear.

'Looks as if he'd thrown a six,' says Carl.

'Holy Mother of Kazan!' bursts out Tiny, in astonishment.

'Won himself a spot in Heaven, then,' considers Porta.

'Poor sod. Died with three sixes and a hundred marks up on the game,' sighs Carl, pulling the cork from a bottle of schnapps. He caught it as it came flying through the air from the restaurant car.

'Your bleedin' pig's eatin' a body,' grins Tiny.

'Always hungry, that pig,' says Porta, shaking his head. 'Been too long with the Germans.'

Two medical orderlies come past with a dead leutnant on a stretcher. His leg has been blown off and they have laid it across the body. It falls off and rolls down the slope. The long shiny boot is still on it and completely undamaged. The spur winks in the sun.

Carl picks up the leg and puts it back on the leutnant's body.

'*Sag' zum Abschied, leise Servus*,' sings Porta after the stretcher with the dead leutnant.

'There's a few as 'as got it 'ere,' says Tiny. 'The Fatherland's a greedy bastard.'

'Makes you creep to think of all these people killed so quickly,' says Carl.

'A man who cries over this sort of happening is not a true German, he is *gutless*,' says Porta, picking the pig up and placing it under his arm.

'I'm that bleedin' 'ungry,' says Tiny. 'Wonder if they're goin' to give us some grub?'

They stop beside the bodies of two *Blitzmädel*[15].

'Shit!' cries Porta. 'What a pair of thighs. The devil knows what he's doing if that's what he wants.'

'Army field service mattress, model 39/40,' grins Tiny, lifting up a skirt inquisitively. 'There's them as does it with dead bodies,' he whispers confidentially.

'Are you mad?' says Porta. 'You'd go straight to hell.'

From a coppice they hear cursing and groans. They push the branches aside and find a dying unteroffizier with an unexploded 20mm shell projecting from his chest.

'Cursing like that and him a dying man,' says Carl in outrage.

'If God won't have him the Devil must!' says Porta the practical.

Medical orderlies carry him away. A workshops train removes the remains of the shattered express.

In Vienna their journey is broken for several days. Porta wants to go to Grinzing.

'You can always pick up something there,' he explains to the other two. 'You'd have to look like Frankenstein with a hangover to go home without getting it *there*.'

In Munich they meet an acquaintance of Porta's. A gefreiter from the Alpine Jaegers who is celebrating the day his mother almost died, twenty-five years ago. The black pig is invited. It learns how to drink beer at that party.

It is raining when they leave Munich, a miserable, wet day. The carriage smells of wet clothing and sour bodies.

Carl is out of humour. He is not in a hurry any more.

They stand close together in the corridor and stare out at the sad-looking country which rushes past them. Ruins everywhere.

15. Blitzmädel: Female telegraphists.

They have to wait several hours outside Stuttgart while an air attack is in progress.

''Ail the 'appy German warrior!' says Tiny.

Porta bites thoughtfully into a piece of bread.

'How lucky we were to be born in Germany,' sighs Carl despondently.

'Anybody here who thinks I love the Fatherland and the thought of letting myself be killed for it?' asks Porta, provokingly, in a general question to the other equally miserable-looking passengers.

Tiny shakes with laughter, and stares at a German peasant who is in the process of pouring a drink from a bottle of schnapps.

'If you was to offer me one, do you think I'd say no?'

The peasant passes him the bottle grudgingly.

Tiny takes a huge swig and passes it to Porta and Carl, who almost empty it.

The peasant looks sorrowfully at the remains, and decides to drink what is left while there is any.

On a cold rainy Sunday afternoon they arrive at Karlsruhe, where they change to a small local train.

A cross-looking RTO officer stops them and demands their papers. He looks Carl up and down, sneeringly. Then he points at the black pig which follows Porta on a lead.

'What you got there?' he hisses.

'My dog!' answers Porta, clicking his heels.

'That's a dirty pig,' protests the major.

'No, sir, it's clean!' answers Porta.

The major shakes his head and marches away with a jingle of spurs.

They travel only a short way with the local train. The track has been bombed. Fifteen miles or so from Germersheim they decide to walk the last stage. It is pouring with rain. The pig squeals. They cover it with ground-sheets.

' 'E's 'ungry!' says Tiny.

'If we had some flour we could make pancakes,' suggests Porta, licking his lips. 'Pigs like pancakes too.'

'Jesus an' Mary, *pancakes! Pancakes* with sugar an' jam,'

shouts Tiny, excitedly. 'Maybe there's rum somewhere about? It's that lovely it don't bear thinkin' about.'

'Be a nice farewell meal for Carl, too, before he moves into Purgatory,' says Porta. 'We are bloody well *going* to have pancakes and rum with sugar and jam. We bloody *are*!'

'Shut it!' snarls Carl. 'You lot make me sick!'

'You're going to have a tip-top meal before we turn you over to those bastards in the pokey!' promises Porta solemnly.

'We'll get it with our bleedin' grease-guns,' shouts Tiny. '*Then* they'll know – these bleedin' sausage-eatin' stay-at-'ome bastards there's visitors come in from the bleedin' east.'

After ten miles of it they take a rest, soaked to the skin and tired, in the ditch at the side of the road.

'Jesus, I'm *tired*,' groans Carl shaking water from his cap. 'If my legs wasn't plainly visible, I'd think I'd worn 'em off.'

'*You're* all right,' says Porta, pouring water from his boots. 'You've only got another ten miles to go, but *we've* got it to do all over again, and who's to say the regiment's still at Corfu? They might have moved. Might be up in the north of Finland. You've got to take all that sort of thing into account when you're travelling on Army business.'

'Holy Mother of Kazan!' shouts Tiny, in fright. 'From Corfu to the north o' bleedin' Finland. I don't think I'd make it.'

'Those whom God loves, he sends out into His world,' says Porta quietly.

' 'E must bleedin' love us lot,' considers Tiny.

'Let's get in the dry,' says Porta, getting on to his feet.

> 'Here He comes on heavenly wings
> A wondrous message to you brings . . .'

sings Tiny loudly. His voice rings out over the fields.

At Russheim they reach the Rhine. They seat themselves on the wet quay and watch the river boats.

'If we could snitch one o' them,' says Tiny, thoughtfully, 'we could sail to 'Olland with no sweat.'

'What would *you* do in Holland?' asks Porta in wonder. 'The German liberators are there too, you know.'

'You're bleedin' *silly*,' shouts Tiny, waving his arms in the air. 'Don't you know that when you're in 'Olland you're right up against the bleedin' sea? At the Munich station I see a map as shows as England ain't no farther from 'Olland than you can piss, with the wind behind you.'

'That'd be great,' sighs Carl. 'They say it's lovely in Scotland.'

'You'd have a good time there as an anti-German,' grins Porta.

'Look at that current!' says Carl, pointing at a river boat which sweeps past at speed with the strong current behind her.

'The Rhine runs fast,' says Tiny.

'Who wouldn't,' grins Porta. 'It's passing through Germany.'

At Sondenheim they go into an old inn, the host of which Porta knows from his time at Germersheim.

The inn-keeper, an old man, is overcome with joy when he sees Porta come through the doorway.

He makes pancakes when he hears where Carl is going.

'Heavenly Lord God!' sighs his wife. 'Is he for the fortress? Won't they ever stop putting people behind bars, the fine gentlemen?'

'A battalion left for the east yesterday,' declares the inn-keeper, as he brings in the pancakes.

'There was a former oberst from Karlsruhe with them,' says his wife, blowing her nose. 'Such a nice man. Always treated his soldiers well.'

'That's probably the reason they broke him,' considers Porta. 'The service of the Fatherland requires you to be hard as Krupp steel or you'd never be able to make anybody go to war and let themselves get killed.'

'Have you come a long way?' asks the inn-keeper's wife, smoothing her starched apron.

'You *could* say that,' says Porta. 'We come from the land of the gods.'

'Oh indeed?' says the woman smiling and not understanding a word of it. She shovels a large pile of pancakes on to each plate and pours a generous helping of jam over the food.

'What's happening out there?' asks the inn-keeper, lighting a long porcelain pipe.

'Ruins, bodies, trouble an' woe, but us Germans can still cross the frontiers without a passport,' says Tiny importantly.

'Yes, it'll be a serious hardship,' sighs Porta, 'when we can't get by with a gun in lieu of documents.'

'Been in the army long?' asks a guest from over in the corner.

'*Too* long!' confesses Porta. 'I was homesick after the first hour of it.'

'Aren't the NCO's nicer now?' asks the old woman. 'We've heard some of them have been shot in the back by their own soldiers.'

'Now and then one kicks the bucket like that,' Tiny admits. 'A nickel-jacketed bullet in the back of the neck makes some impression even on the most stupid.'

'The only *good* NCO's are dead NCO's,' says Porta with a curt laugh. 'At least they keep their mouths shut.'

'It must be terrible at the front,' says the woman, thoughtfully.

'Here on earth you can have it any way you want it,' says Porta. 'You just have to fit in.'

'Is it true what they say about the treatment they give the prisoners in the fortress?' asks the man in the corner.

'At Torgau they made us form a living bridge with planks on our backs, and then they drove lorries over it,' says Tiny seriously, and remembers, with a shut-off expression on his face, the hell of Torgau.

'Lord save us!' whispers the inn-keeper's wife, and heaps Carl's plate with fresh pancakes.

They spend the night at the inn.

'We've been so long on the road, a day more or less can't hurt,' says Porta.

The following morning they walk into the village of Germersheim with Carl between them. A cold wind is blowing from the river, and it is still raining. They have turned their greatcoat collars up around their ears, and shiver in their wet uniforms. They stop and look out over the Rhine, before proceeding down the steep road which leads to the military prison.

Outside a pub, the 'Hapsburg Court', Carl stops abruptly.

'Shall we take one last one for the road? *Your* road!'

'Why not?' says Porta.

They order sausage and potato salad. It's the only thing on the menu.

Porta orders beer and *Wildkatze*.

They make a leisurely meal before continuing on towards the prison. When they are almost at the gate they stop, hesitantly.

Porta looks at Carl with a little smile.

'Bad shit, mate. And just because you wouldn't kill a few people. It's more often for doing just the opposite people get sent to jail. Should we take a stroll in the park?'

They sit down on a mound between the trees. Porta pulls a recorder from his boot. Tiny knocks out his mouth-organ. They play together softly and look out at the rain:

'*So weit, so weit ist der Weg zurück ins Heimatland . . .*'

Porta drops a hand on Carl's shoulder.

'Run for it, if you want! We won't shoot, and we won't report for a couple of days that you've gone missing.'

'You'll be jailed yourselves,' says Carl.

'To 'ell with that,' says Tiny. 'We know what it's like.'

'I wouldn't get far. The headhunters'd get me,' considers Carl.

'Get to bleedin' 'Olland,' suggests Tiny. 'You could 'ide on a bleedin' river boat an' swim to England, mate.'

'You can't *swim* to England,' protests Carl.

'Some lucky bleeders've done it,' says Tiny, optimistically.

'With just a little bit of luck I'd've been born somewhere else than in Germany,' sighs Carl despairingly.

'Luck's everythin',' says Tiny, spitting into the wind.

'I want to thank you for looking after me the way you have,' says Carl. 'I didn't mean what I said when I bawled you out.'

' 'Ad a bit o' fun, didn't we?' asks Tiny.

'You're telling *me*!' says Carl with a quiet smile. 'But in one way I'd sooner have had a quicker trip here. Being with you two makes the jail seem worse somehow.'

'You'll soon get used to it,' Porta consoles him. 'But don't cross 'em. Whatever they say do it without question. You can get what you want from life long as you can fit in!'

'You can't beat *them* bastards,' says Tiny knowledgeably. 'I was the toughest bastard they've ever 'ad. They still boast about me. But they broke *me* inside two months.'

'They didn't make you soft!' says Carl with a crooked smile, eyeing Tiny's huge, muscular body.

'No, *nobody* can do that,' says Tiny with conviction. 'I'd let 'em kill me first! No, I saw the bleedin' light an' did what they told me. Then they left me alone.'

'Thanks for the advice,' nods Carl. 'I'll remember it.'

'I'm buying,' says Porta. '*Wildkatze!*'

They go back through the park to the 'Hapsburg Court'. They get down several *Wildkatze.*

'Let's get it over with,' says Carl decisively. 'I feel easier about it now.'

They pull their equipment into position, and check one another.

A former feldwebel, too old for Hitler's army, inspects them carefully. He nods, satisfied.

'Now you can go in there without a qualm. You're more correctly dressed than the drawings in the bloody manual.'

'Boot studs!' shouts their host, in fear.

The feldwebel looks their boots over. Tiny is short of three studs. One of the guests rushes out and procures them. They are ready to go.

They swing their Mpi's over their shoulders and place Carl between them.

'If I run into 'Ell'ound 'Einrich I'll let the shit out of 'is 'ead on the bleedin' spot,' promises Tiny, patting his Mpi.

'Don't,' says the old feldwebel from the Kaiser's army. 'Wait till the war's over. In the disturbances that will follow it you can fix him any way you want to.'

'Then I'll pull 'is bleedin' lights out through 'is arse'ole an' push 'em into 'is bleedin' ears!' shouts Tiny, enraged.

'Take it easy,' pleads Carl. 'Ten years is enough for me.'

The guests stand in the doorway to see them off.

The Guard Commander, a feldwebel, regards them suspiciously with ice-cold eyes. They have entered a different world. A cold, silent world. Here there are no people. Merely automatons.

'Take the prisoner to the office,' he snarls.

They march across the courtyard. The barred gate closes behind them. Prisoners are running in a circle. In the centre of the circle stands a feldwebel with polished boots and brilliant leather equipment. His holster-flap is unbuttoned. In his hand he swings a long rubber truncheon. With narrow eyes he watches for mistakes in the drill.

The sound of rattling keys comes from A-Block. Steel against steel and heavy doors closing. Whistles shriek and harsh commands are heard.

Outside B-Block they are drilling. At the double with packs filled with sand on their backs.

Three men lie slumped in the middle of the courtyard. One of them is a broken oberst. He coughs and is close to dying.

The oberfeldwebel kicks him in the ribs.

'Weak old bastard!' he snarls, contemptuously.

The oberst is dead.

In the office they meet Hellhound Heinrich, the notorious Stabsfeldwebel Heinrich Lochte.

Carl empties his pockets and hands in his equipment.

Trained hands search him. He signs some documents.

Two well-developed unteroffiziers stamp in.

Hellhound Heinrich points silently at Carl, and almost before Porta and Tiny realize it the prison has swallowed him up.

When they are a little way away, just before entering Fischerstrasse, they turn and look up at the fortress. Grey and gloomy it towers in the pouring rain.

'Good thing we're walkin' *away* from that bleedin' place,' says Tiny, turning up his coat collar.

'Poor Carl, poor bugger,' sighs Porta. 'Jailed for *not* murdering people! Bad show!'

'Yes, 'e can't even 'ave the pleasure of sittin' in there an' thinkin' 'e's done some bastard like 'Einrich,' says Tiny.

They catch a lift on a Pioneer battalion truck as far as Karlsruhe. In Munich they suddenly remember the black pig. They haven't seen it since the 'Hapsburg Court'. They talk about going back for it but decide, in the end, it is too risky.

In Budapest they are held back for three days because of a forgotten stamp on their movement orders.

In Belgrade they visit the hospital to crack a yarn but meet only strange faces.

Outside Niz they get in a fight with the partisans. Between Salonica and Athens their train is blown up.

At Athens the feldwebel in the RTO's office looks at them thoughtfully and leafs through their various movement orders.

'You've been around, eh? Looks like you've been exploring 'stead of escorting. Keep moving, laddies, you've got a long way to go yet.'

Grinning, he hands them their new orders.

'Brest-Litovsk!' cries Porta, looking at the documents.

'Your regiment's in Russia, boys, chuckles the feldwebel, 'and if you two are as long about getting back as you've been getting out, the Third World War'll be half over before you get there.'

So back they have to go through Prague, Berlin, Warsaw, where they get arrested when Tiny steals a hen which is the property of an oberst.

At Brest-Litovsk they are sent by mistake to Riga. Nobody will believe that they are there by mistake and they get arrested. Released after a few days they are sent in the direction of Minsk.

'If they send us back from there,' says Tiny tiredly, '*I* am goin' over to the bleedin' enemy. I've got to get back into the war an' get a bleedin' *rest*!'

One morning early, they are walking along a muddy road. Tanks and artillery rumble past, splashing them as they go.

In the distance they can hear the rumble of the front line. Thousands of explosions paint the sky a bloody red. The final part of the trip they make on motorcycles.

They're back at last.

'Still alive I see,' says Oberst Hinka, a trifle surprised, apparently. 'How are things at home?'

'Ploughed under, sir,' answers Porta. 'Our enemies are really going to town on the Fatherland. They've begun to take things far too seriously.'

'Herr Oberst, sir,' grins Tiny. 'Request to report the enemy 'ave finally learnt *real* German thoroughness!'

'Your task is to execute the orders I issue and not to discuss them.

'Go back to your work, gentlemen, and do not entangle your-selves in politics.'

Hitler to a group of generals,
October, 1937.

'*Without our oberst none of us would've got out. They shot at everything that moved, even our signal-dogs,*' explains an obergefreiter with bandaged eyes. '*Companies were down to fifteen or twenty men, and there were fires everywhere. More than five hundred wounded were laid out in the factory. A lot of them killed themselves by rolling over to the hoists and letting themselves drop. Nobody was in any doubt about what'd happen if they fell into the hands of the Russians . . .*'

'But how did you get out?' asks a gefreiter amongst the crowd standing around the bed.

'Well, see, that was a case apart. It was sabotage of orders, as they call it, or certain death, but our oberst made a firm de-cision and ordered us to retreat. That was after both his sons had fallen. They were both leutnants and had command of companies. Wounded were to go with us, ordered the oberst. They were loaded on sleds and off we went into the snowstorm. A lot died during the march. We marched through the Russian lines with our oberst in the lead with an Mpi under his arm. Ski-troops were bashing at us all the time. The oberst had all the guns spiked, so's we could use the horses to pull the sleds with the wounded.'

'What the devil are you saying, man?' shouts a feldwebel, indignantly. 'Ruin your own artillery? A fine leader, by God!'

'You weren't there, chum. You had to go through it to realize what it was like. Cossacks with drawn sabres, and ski-troops with flaming Mpi's. 45° Centigrade below and a snowstorm! You'd have loved it, wouldn't you, mate?'

'Who're you calling mate?' roars the feldwebel. 'Can't you see I'm an NCO?'

'I can't see anything at all nowadays, chum! I lost my eyes in the snowstorm. Ice, you understand. To me you're just a voice.'

'Blind or not you're still a soldier, obergefreiter!' roars the feldwebel, fiery red in the face. 'You can stand to attention still. Pull yourself together, now, or I'll have you on orders for refusing to obey an order. Let's see your paybook!'

The blind man turns his paybook over to the feldwebel, who prints name and unit down, conscientiously, in a notebook.

All round him wounded soldiers are growling under their breaths.

'Quiet!' roars the feldwebel, 'or I'll have the lot of you on orders.' He stamps out of the field hospital.

'What about this oberst of yours who blew up his guns?' asks a Pioneer who has had both legs amputated.

'An oberstleutnant from GEFEPO came and took him away the day after we broke through. Two days later he was in front of a board. All the witnesses were on his side and our divisional general spoke for him but they still shot him the day after. You know the charge. Sabotaging his orders.'

'Swine!' comes from over in the corner. Nobody takes the feldwebel's part.

168

DARJEELING TEA

As soon as we get the order to fall out, we drag ourselves into the huts and drop down half-dead. The company was supposed to have held Deadman's Heights for another three days, but the *company* has gone out of existence. The greater part of us lie in mass graves. The lucky ones are in the field hospital. Deadman's Heights are just what the name implies. A hell on earth for the living.

None of us has the energy to go for rations. One thought only possesses us. Sleep! Forget the ten days you have just been through. We stumble into the mouldering billet and fall at once into a deathlike sleep.

The Army's harsh demands pull us back to reality. Our new Spiess[1], Hauptfeldwebel Blatz, wants a roll-call. He still thinks he is at Neuruppin NCO's School, together with Hauptmann von Pader, our temporary OC.

Grumbling and with murder in our hearts we fall in on the square.

'Where are the rest of you?' shouts Blatz, irritably.

'They'll be a long time coming,' grins Oberfeldwebel Berner, disrespectfully. 'They're pushin' up the daisies!'

'Call the roll!' orders Blatz, sharply. He has it called several times over before he is satisfied.

'Tally the dead! Tally the wounded!'

'125 fallen, 19 missing, 42 wounded, sir!' barks the Old Man, stiffly to attention.

Blatz goes white, but quickly pulls himself together. Not for nothing was he recognized as the terror of the NCO's school. He doubles us across country; to get some life back into us, he says. He is not satisfied until two men drop unconscious.

1. Spiess: Slang for the German equivalent of a CSM.

169

'I'm gonna *get* that bastard!' promises Gregor, grinding his teeth.

'No, son, it'll be *my* pleasure,' laughs Porta, wickedly.

'I'll drive the bleeder mad first, the bleedin' psycho twatt,' says Tiny. He pulls himself up to his full height and screams, to everybody's surprise:

'C-o-o-ompany *halt*!'

'Who said *that*?' roars Blatz, his neck reddening.

'The fai-ai-ai-ries,' comes like an echo from Tiny's direction.

Blatz explodes in foaming rage and chases across the field after the company.

'You! What's your name?' snarls Blatz, sticking his face close to Tiny's.

'*Me?*' asks Tiny putting on an idiotic expression, and pointing a finger at his own chest.

'Are you crazy?' asks Blatz, softly.

'Sir, 'Err 'auptfeldwebel, sir, I be backward they do say them army doctors do, sir,' says Tiny, putting on a yokel's accent.

'I asked you your name!'

'I did think as 'ow the 'auptfeldwebel 'e wanted to know if I was a idiot like, now I did, sir.'

'You'll get to know me, man!' snarls Blatz, threateningly.

'An' 'appy to know the 'err 'auptfeldwebel I'll be. Them doctors do say as 'ow it be good for I to get to know many as I can.'

'To the woods! At the double, man!' roars Blatz, beside himself.

Tiny jogs off towards the woods with a broad, stupid grin on his face.

'*Run,* man, *run*!' screams Blatz desperately. Tiny stops and holds his hand to his ear, as if he were deaf.

'Run, man, run!' repeats Blatz.

Tiny trots back to the company.

'About-turn!' howls Blatz. 'Forward march! Into the woods!'

Tiny continues to approach the company.

'Halt!' orders Blatz. 'Down on your face! Twenty push-ups! 'Shun! Knees bend! Port arms!'

In the end he gets mixed up in his own orders. Sweat pours

down his face. He looks like a sandstone monument eroded by rain.

Tiny has stayed lying down as if that was the last order he has understood. He puts one hand under his chin and looks up good-naturedly at the desperate Hauptfeldwebel.

'I do reckon, 'err 'auptfeldwebel, sir, as 'ow I can't get all them orders like to go into my 'ead *quick* enough. They says to me now, when I was in trainin' like, as 'ow an order 'ad to be clear. That was in the *manual*, they said. Now I can't folly all them orders all at once, like, an' I must ask the 'auptfeldwebel as if 'e'll 'ave the goodness to say now what 'e wants me to do for 'im, like!'

Without a word Blatz turns on his heel and marches with assured steps into the Company Office. Shortly after, he returns in the wake of Hauptmann von Pader, who looks extremely energetic.

'What are you doing lying down there playing the fool?' he sniffs at Tiny.

' 'Err 'auptmann, sir, I be obeyin' orders like, I be,' answers Tiny.

'Get up, man!'

Tiny gets up like an old, old man, using his carbine to help him.

Hauptmann von Pader goes purple in the face.

'You're confined to quarters indefinitely!' he says, shortly.

'What's that for, now, sir?' asks Tiny, wonderingly.

'You swine!' shouts von Pader, losing control of himself. He regrets the outburst as soon as the word leaves his lips. A Prussian officer should be able to control his anger.

' 'Ow's this then, 'err 'auptman, sir, 'ow's this? Arrestin' a *swine* for bein' what 'e be? Why then the 'ole German army'll soon be in the 'ole then for there ain't none as ain't swine in 'er, now is there?'

'Have you lost your mind, man?' screams von Pader, his voice cracking. 'Are you saying that all German soldiers are swine?'

'Well sir the Quartermaster, 'Err Sauer 'e do say as 'ow we're all on us a lot o' Jew wart 'ogs 'e do, an' Doctor Müller 'e says as 'ow we're a lot o' malingerin' swine.'

171

'Attention!' whines Hauptmann von Pader, dark blue in the face. 'Forward march! At the double! To the woods!'

Tiny moves off like a man shot from a gun. Nobody can say he is not carrying out orders. Reaching the woods he runs into a tree and continues running on the spot up against it with high-lifted knees.

'Go round the tree!' screams von Pader, stamping the ground hysterically. 'Double march! Quick march! Go round all trees!'

The devil takes hold of Tiny. He runs straight up over the brow of a hill, disappears into the valley beyond, appears on top of another hill, zig-zags through the trees, whinnies happily and rears up like a horse.

'Halt, halt!' screams von Pader, his voice breaking several times over, but Tiny, who is a long way off, pretends not to hear him and continues to run, prance and whinny.

He disappears over a hill but long after he has gone from sight we can hear him whinnying.

'The moment that man returns,' pants von Pader, 'he is to be manacled and kept locked in a cellar until the military police can remove him!'

The company falls out. We see nothing of Tiny. The woods and hills have swallowed him up. Porta says he has deserted to Berlin and at the speed he is moving he'll have got there before long.

Hauptmann von Pader writes several pages of a report on No. 5 Company in general and Tiny in particular. Oberst Hinka is expecting it. He has heard about Tiny's one-man rodeo show from other sources.

The Hauptmann's monocle falls from his eye in astonishment when he hears the CO's snarl on the telephone.

'What the hell are you up to von Pader? Pack drill with your company during a special rest period which *I* ordered. When the men get back from the line they're to *rest*! *Rest*! D'you understand me?' The oberst bangs down the receiver so hard that von Pader is nearly deafened.

'They don't know me yet, those wicked men,' boasts von Pader, 'but they're *going* to!'

'Shall we send the charge sheet to regiment, sir?' asks Blatz, innocently.

'I never, ever again want to see a charge sheet concerning that horrible man,' screams von Pader furiously, tearing the charge sheet into a thousand pieces. 'He doesn't *exist* any more. Never speak his name in my presence again!'

Hauptfeldwebel Blatz steamrollers through the company, breaking up card games, confiscating supplies acquired illegally, demanding accounts of ammunition expended from section-leaders, and handing out fatigues right, left and centre. When, late in the afternoon, he has bawled himself into a state of exhaustion, he feels convinced that he has No. 5 Company by the short hairs.

'Soft as *shit*, they are!' he says to the company clerk. '*I'll* soon teach 'em who they've got for a Hauptfeldwebel now. Those check lists come from Chief Mechanic Wolf yet?'

The clerk swallows. He knows Wolf and can see trouble approaching.

'Check lists! Have they come yet?' repeats Blatz.

'No, Herr Hauptfeldwebel, and I'm afraid they won't! Wolf asked me to, – er! Well! To fuck him crossways, sir!'

'Is the man mad?' almost whispers Blatz. He cannot believe his own ears.

The clerk shrugs his shoulders. He does not want to make an enemy of Wolf.

Blatz goes to Wolf. This is a matter of discipline.

Wolf welcomes him sitting in his own personal rocking-chair with his feet on the desk. He lights a big cigar carelessly without offering one to Blatz.

White with rage Blatz advances on him, but stops short when both wolfhounds show their fangs and begin to growl ominously.

'What do you think you're up to?' he asks, trembling with indignation. 'Where are the check lists I ordered you to prepare? Don't you know who's Hauptfeldwebel in this company?'

Wolf laughs noisily, and points at Blatz with a cossack sabre.

'Fuck off and keep your nose out of my business!'

'You'll regret this!' hisses Blatz.

'Beat it, before I set the dogs on you,' grins Wolf, pointing to the door.

Blatz leaves him, cursing and swearing revenge. He marches

confidently down the dusty village road. Passing the CO's quarters he hears noisy singing from behind the house. Cautiously he looks round the corner and sees Tiny, lying alongside a turnip trench and singing with lusty voice:

> My darling, my sweet, my dove,
> I'm bleeding, I'm dying for love.
> Come here and we'll never more rove,
> From this silent and solitary cove.
> Where I lie in the cold and the snow . . .

Blatz is about to draw back round the corner and disappear, when Hauptmann von Pader knocks on the pane and waves to him.

No help for it, he'll have to go in however little he wishes it.

'Blatz, remove that singing idiot!' hisses the Hauptmann, furiously. 'Shoot him, if you like!'

Blatz shuffles his feet like a laying hen.

'Herr Hauptmann,' he stammers, confusedly.

'That's an order! Get that clown out of here!' screams von Pader, beside himself. Blatz sighs like a condemned man. With uncertain steps he goes out to move Tiny on.

From behind the curtain von Pader keeps an eye on developments, in company with a bottle of cognac. To break and crush a soldier has been as easy for him, up to now, as swatting a fly. He takes a long swig at the bottle. With any luck he'll soon be back in Berlin, and then these half-human front soldiers will really get to know him. He peers cautiously out of the window and sees to his satisfaction that Blatz is talking to Tiny. If anybody can break that yokel it will be Hauptfeldwebel Blatz, the terror of every NCO's school, Bonecrusher Blatz!

Von Pader laughs croakingly to himself, takes another swig at the cognac bottle, and starts to walk to and fro in the low-ceilinged cottage; he has quartered himself in the style to which a German officer with blue blood in his veins is entitled. The owner of the cottage has, of course, been ejected and has taken up residence in a hole in the ground. Baron von Pader would not condescend to live in the same house as a Russian *untermensch*. They might give him some filthy disease or other.

174

He had fired at the Russian woman when she had made trouble about some pots and pans she wanted to take with her. What the devil good were pots and pans to her? He was told one of the shots had hit her, but would not let the medical feldwebel look at her. German medics should not have to touch *untermensch*. They had not been given their expensive training to look after *them*. Never be nice to a Russian. It made them cheeky, like the niggers. The whip was what they needed. And an execution now and then wasn't a bad thing. Hauptmann von Pader liked hanging people. Oberst Hinka, now, was against that sort of thing. He required the *untermensch* to be treated like Germans. Well, that puffed-up oberst would soon get the wind taken out of his sails when they got him down to Admiral Schröder Strasse. Defeatist, racial saboteur!

Tiny is singing even more loudly from out by the turnip trench. Hauptfeldwebel Blatz has disappeared.

Baron von Pader tightens his lips, snatches up the Mpi from the table and pushes the curtains to one side. At the same moment a pane of glass splinters behind him. A hand-grenade rolls across the floor. He screams in fear and throws himself flat.

Tiny rushes in, with his Mpi at the ready, stops in the middle of the room, looks from the OC on the floor to the spluttering hand-grenade. He bends down, picks up the grenade and throws it neatly out through the open doorway.

Von Pader crawls to his feet, brushes off his slate-grey uniform and turns his back demonstratively on Tiny. Tiny does not, of course, exist.

Tiny couldn't care less. He chatters gaily about training grenades, partisans and many other things which are part of life behind the lines.

' 'Err 'auptmann, sir, I do be sure as 'ow it's some of these 'ere officers as are tryin' to make game o' 'ee! Now if *I* was to get 'old of a dead rat, as stinks a bit, like, then we could throw 'er into the middle of they. Why 'tain't no joke 'avin' trainin' grenades thrown at 'ee, now is it? An' you a new man at the job, as you might say!'

Hauptmann von Pader clenches and unclenches his hands in an effort to contain his rage. He fingers his holster. Should he shoot this man and say he had attacked him? He decides not to.

Porta is sitting across from Chief Mechanic Wolf, at Wolf's long, broad desk, discussing four lorries and several cases of canteen supplies. Wolf is working away at half a pig's head. Porta is building himself a sandwich in the way he feels a sandwich *should* be built. First a piece of coarse bread with a layer of goose fat. Thereafter a sizeable piece of smoked ham, covered with slices of hunt sausage and a little of anything else to hand. The whole finally covered with a layer of gooseberry jam!

He opens his jaws wide and manoeuvres the enormous sandwich into his mouth. He finds it difficult to get his teeth through it but finally manages to do so.

'I hope you choke!' says Wolf, cheerfully.

Porta gets the last bit down and picks up a chicken over which he pours a whole jar of jam.

'Don't hope too much, Wolf,' he says filling his mouth with chicken. 'I could swallow a fair-sized pig whole, listen to it grunt inside me all day, and wind up shitting it out again in the form of a whole litter of live sucking pigs!'

'I wouldn't wonder if you could,' mumbles Wolf, crossly, shovelling sauerkraut over pig's feet. 'Just remember, though, it's *my* grub you're surroundin' and to the best of my knowledge you weren't invited to either.'

Porta laughs noisily, resting his jaws.

'You're forgiven, son Wolf, but I ought to say I never *am* invited. It's unnecessary! I come *un*invited but am always dressed for dinner!'

They eat silently for a while, looking at one another calculatingly. The only sounds are of bones cracking and wine swilling food down.

Wolf, who has been well brought up, drinks from a glass, Porta takes it straight from the bottle. Wolf has his own private dinner service. Porta is willing to guzzle his food straight from the pot. The main thing, as far as he is concerned, is that there is enough of it.

'Shall we share the pig's head?' he asks, bringing a long kitchen knife down accurately between the animal's eyes as it dominates the table with a tomato in its mouth.

Wolf growls something unintelligible ending in 'shit'!

Porta cuts the pig's head in two, taking the larger part for himself. He empties it with a long slobbering, sucking sound unsuitable for queasy stomachs.

Wolf looks at him with loathing.

'Tell me, son! Don't you ever eat in the mess-hall?'

'Of course I do,' smiles Porta. 'There's *food* there isn't there?'

They lean back in their chairs. Two long, satisfied belches make themselves heard. Porta takes off his boots and socks and lays them on the table. An acrid aroma rises from them. He looks sharply at Wolf, who has started on a dish of steaming black pudding, and pushes one of the socks closer to him, with a big toe which is not notable for cleanliness. He wriggles his toes luxuriously.

Without turning a hair Wolf pours apple sauce over his black pudding.

Porta starts to cut his toenails. Slips of nail fly past Wolf's ears.

The wolf-hounds snuffle with displeasure and move further away from the desk. Porta's socks they find a bit too much for sensitive noses.

'What's that bloody stink?' asks Wolf, suddenly, looking up from his sausage.

'Stink?' asks Porta, innocently. 'To be expected isn't it, in your company?'

'Don't get familiar, son,' growls Wolf, warningly. 'Don't forget who's Chief Mechanic and Stabsfeldwebel here. And don't forget who's the holder of the German Cross in silver. Move those bloody socks, man! Who ever heard of socks on a dining-room table?' With his fork he flips them on to the floor. They land in front of the dogs which back off whining and howling.

'I know where there's three tractors,' says Porta, after an extended silence. 'Chain-drive, like the heavy artillery play about with.'

'What tractors?' asks Wolf, with apparent disinterest.

'First class jobs. Not ruined by bad oil and petrol. They've come straight from the States, addressed to Ivan.'

'What make?' asks Wolf, soaking up grease with a piece of Ukranian peasant bread. 'If they're Fords, I couldn't be less interested. Tito began to hate the capitalists in earnest when they sent him some of them. They're America's revenge on Europe for us sending them all our unwanted black sheep.'

Porta washes his mouth out with a half bottle of Crimean champagne, to which he helps himself without being asked.

'Who said anything about Fords? I'm talking about Caterpillars. What do you say to that?'

'You're lyin',' comes from Wolf before he remembers the first rule of buying: show no interest in what is being offered.

Porta opens a tin of beef, without asking permission, and shovels the contents down his throat with his bayonet.

'Where you keepin' these Caterpillars?'

Porta finishes off the tin before replying and is obviously enjoying Wolf's impatience.

'*I* haven't got 'em. I just happen to know where they're at just now.'

'We're wasting one another's time,' decides Wolf, brusquely. 'You can't sell something you haven't got.'

'*You* do it all the time, Wolf,' laughs Porta, craftily. 'Do we get coffee to fill up on after that modest lunch?'

'I'll move the bloody shithouse in here for you, if you like!' snarls Wolf. 'Get your stinking feet off the table, you bastard. You'll never learn culture, you! Stickin' your feet up alongside your host's plate ain't gonna make you popular. I did think of offerin' you a job when we finish the war, but it'd be like lettin' a ravening pig loose on the unfortunate rest of the world.'

'Mocca!' Wolf orders his servant, a former Russian sergeant, to bring coffee, but unwillingly.

'The man said *coffee*!' shouts Porta after the Russian.

'Since getting to know you I've been converted to the Tory party, an' boy how I do hate the socialist gutter proletariat,' rumbles Wolf, sourly.

'I drink only Java,' roars Porta, without feeling himself insulted in the slightest.

'Java? Where in the hell do you think I'd be able to get Java from?' lies Wolf.

'Get the shit out of your ears, Wolf,' laughs Porta, confidently. 'You picked up three sacks of Java a month ago. You can fool the entire German army all the time but me you can *never* fool, chum!'

'Ain't Santos good enough for you? The poor, persecuted German people'd give their *bollocks* for one cup of Santos. There's some of the *Herrenvolk* who ain't ever even *tasted* Santos.'

'You're a really wicked man, you *are*, Wolf!' Porta smiles winningly. 'In the first place I am *not* one of the poor, persecuted Germans you mentioned before. Between you, me and the gatepost they can all get fucked as far as I'm concerned. I'd sell them, the Fatherland and all it contains, *including* flags, to neighbour Ivan tomorrow. I don't *want* your bitter Santos shit. I want Java. And, friend, if *I* don't get it now, *you* won't have any left in stock tomorrow!'

Wolf turns his head and roars after the Russian sergeant.

'Igor, Java! Blend B!'

'Blend A, friend!' Porta corrects him.

A beautiful aroma fills the whole stores. They eat cheese tart with their coffee.

'I've got ten pounds of tea,' says Porta, after the fourth cup of coffee. 'Darjeeling with a little green in it,' he adds. 'Grand stuff, it is. Make a Chinese mandarin shoot up in the air with his bollock's rattlin' the Radetzsky March all the while he was on his way up!'

'Bullshit!' says Wolf. 'Tea's unobtainable today. I ought to know. I've tried. China's big enough and it's *covered* with tea. My China boys tell me there's enough for 'em to be able to drown themselves in it if they wanted. But we're not in China!'

'Connections,' boasts Porta, superciliously. 'I've got the lot. Fancy a camel train with a full harem *and* some Arabian bumboys, or an English submarine complete with shells an' torpedoes? Easy meat! Scotland Yard's breathin' down the neck of the engineer, so he goes with it. You can cruise to your heart's content, Wolf!'

'Piss!' growls Wolf unimpressed. 'Camels I've got. Who wants camels nowadays? It's *wheels* they're after! What you want for it?'

179

'What'll you pay?' asks Porta, picking his teeth with his combat knife.

'Ten thousand marks,' offers Wolf, with a covetous look in his eyes.

Porta throws himself back in his chair, roaring with laughter.

'I ain't short of shithouse paper, Wolf!'

Wolf rises without a word and goes into an adjoining room. He runs his fingers along the wall. It opens and a safe comes into view. He unclips several leads and opens the safe. Anyone else opening it would get himself blown to pieces.

When he gets back Porta is sitting on the table teasing the wolf-hounds which snarl and snap at him in rage. Wolf laughs heartily.

'Stop trying to feed my dogs, young son!' He kicks at a sausage, which is lying on the floor. 'I could make *you* eat it. How quick d'you think *you'd* kick the bucket?'

'I'm pretty resistant,' Porta smiles in friendly fashion. 'I'd give myself thirty seconds, I reckon.'

Wolf chases the vicious dogs into a corner. Snarling, they lie watching Porta, who comes down from the table.

'Here!' says Wolf, sliding a black box across to him. 'You can have those for your tea!'

Porta examines the three large diamonds with a jeweller's glass.

'You're *funny*! Top of the bill in the village circus, you'd be. *You* know, the boy who falls on his arse all the time. Show that shit to an Amsterdam Jew, Wolf, an' he'd have you under the doctor before you could turn round.'

'Hey?' said Wolf, insulted.

'You know what I'm talking about, all right. Christmas at Tiffany's. Shove that glass up your arse and save it till you have to deal with a Socialist, or some other kind of idiot.'

'I don't understand a word of it,' sighs Wolf, banging the lid of the black box shut.

'You look like a wet newspaper with the print all smeared out,' grins Porta, jeeringly.

'All right, forget it!' Wolf gives in. 'I admit they were paste, but how was I to know you hadn't got yourself a brain injury when you got blown up last week in your battle waggon? Times are hard. It was worth a try.'

'You're bringing tears to my eyes, Wolf!' says Porta.

'Wouldn't you like a month's leave?' Wolf smirks. 'Or, maybe, a duty trip up an' down Europe? How about, now, a hospitalization with a real ailment as no M.O. can cure? That is, not before you *want* to get cured.'

'Jesus, Wolf, you're full o' shit!' Porta shakes his head re- signedly. 'If I wanted leave I'd be out of here in ten minutes time. If I want to be sick I've got ten thousand diseases you've never even heard of, ranging from growing pains to plague and pestilence. God love us, any hospital'd roll out the red carpet for me if I really went to town on it. General Sauerbrauch, the top man'd be on his way by air to follow my complicated case as closely as possible. And duty trips! Duty trips *I*, Wolf, am the expert in arranging. Let's see what else you've got in that safe, now!'

'Porta, you just get *close* to that safe and you'll have more holes in your Yid body'n a colander has. It'd take all the bloody doctor-generals in the German *and* the Russian armies to plug 'em up again, son!'

'All right, Wolf, *I* don't need to take off my boots to count to twenty. We're not going to do a deal!' Porta gets up and moves towards the door. He tightens his pistol belt, releases the safety catch on his Mpi and walks backwards. 'Luckily I know a few other people who know what Darjeeling and green tea are worth. I made the offer for old time's sake, so don't break into tears when I come and tell you, in ten minute's time, that I've sold the lot.'

'Take it easy, now,' smiles Wolf, trying to look pleasant. 'Where'd you get that crazy idea that I didn't want to buy the tea?'

They seat themselves on Arabian cushions. Wolf's security chief serves them with more coffee. A bottle of Napoleon brandy appears. Cigars appear from a silver box which once belonged to a Rumanian prince.

After three hours of hard dealing the tea has changed hands. They go to pick it up. Smilingly they cover one another with Mpi's. They have known one another for a long, long time.

The tea is hidden behind some large bales of straw in a *kolchos*. Wolf tastes it sceptically. His tea experts, the two Chinese, examine it more scientifically and after a while declare it to be Darjeeling with an admixture of green tea.

'Where the devil'd you get it from?' he asks, suspiciously.

'From China,' answers Porta. 'Where else? That's where they fix this kind o' stuff.'

'You ain't been to China ever, Porta!'

'Look now! Did I ever ask you where you get the coppers to *buy* Darjeeling with green tea?'

'There's something fishy about this!' Wolf mumbles, darkly.

'Tea good, tea *very* good,' shouts Wung. 'I guarantee good tea. No better tea!'

'I believe it,' says Wolf, thoughtfully, 'but I got an instinct more certain 'n fifty Jews. There's somethin' wrong that ain't right. There's bells goin' off in my head.'

'Forget it then,' says Porta indifferently. 'I'll get rid of it easy enough. Then you can see where your fifty Jews've got you!'

Wolf tongues the tea again and looks up at the heavens as if expecting a sign from God. The tea is good. It is very high quality tea. He straightens up and looks wickedly at Porta.

'Joseph! If you're doin' me down with that tea, then Jesus Christ and the Holy Mother of Kazan be merciful to you! You'll need more. You'll need every single saint in the bloody calendar just to keep you alive, son!'

Wolf pays and goes off with the tea.

Porta makes to step up into Wolf's amphibian, but the bodyguards push him back down roughly with their Mpi's.

'Deal's closed! There's no room for you here, Porta! Walk like the rest of the clodhoppers. Only the military upper classes ride.'

'You might have kept a little of that tea back for us,' says the Old Man disappointedly, when Porta returns.

'This stuff is better'n tea!' grins Porta, holding a box of ancient gold coins up triumphantly. 'Tea's soon pissed up the wall, but this yellow stuff keeps its value.'

'Bleedin' 'ell,' cries Tiny in amazement. 'There's enough

there to buy one of' the gold-braided bleeders an' all 'is staff, lock, stock an' bleedin' barrel.'

'Maybe I'll do just that one of these days,' answers Porta, mysteriously. 'Those chaps go up in value when our neighbours the enemy start holding war criminal trials.'

'Would you *help* 'em?' asks the Old Man, disgustedly, lighting his silver-lidded pipe.

'I'll help anybody with anything as long as they pay me enough for it. The Fatherland and flag-waving aren't my cup of tea.'

'You'd sell your own mother if you got the chance,' says Heide, contemptuously.

'Why not, then?' answers Porta, smiling. 'Once they got to know her they'd be willing to pay me to take her back. Now you'll have to excuse me, I've got a couple of the Army's tractors to get rid of, pdq.'

Wolf has guests when Porta arrives. A QM officer from the 4th Panzer Army, who has actually come to buy perfumed soap and girls. His eye falls on a bag of tea, and he forgets what he came for.

'What's that you've got there, Wolf?' he asks, with a greedy look in his eye.

'Tea,' replies Wolf in a subdued voice, kicking himself for not having put the bag out of sight. There are limits to the price he can ask of the QM.

Porta grins openly when he sees the light of greed in the QM's eyes, and begins, without the least thought of comradeship, to extol the tea's high quality. Wolf is not going to make much of a profit on that tea, and Porta is openly happy about that.

'How much is there?' asks the fat QM officer, weighing the bag in his hand.

'Two pounds and a bit,' mumbles Wolf, wishing he were able to kick the QM in the balls.

'What kind of a price were you thinking of asking, Wolf? To *me* that is!'

'I'm afraid I'm not able to sell it, sir. It is not mine.' He pours out cognac and hopes the QM will lose interest in the tea. He begins to describe the charms of the Polish and Slav ladies he is in touch with. 'Real monkeys on a mattress they are, sir. They know how to wiggle more than their ears, they do!' he shouts enthusiastically.

'Let us get back to the question of who really owns the tea,' says the QM, with a cunning gleam in the eyes behind the pebble lenses of his spectacles. They make him look like a fat toad sitting on a sun-warmed rock.

'I'm *sorry*, sir. The tea belongs to a high-ranking officer.' Wolf pats his shoulder and runs a finger over his left breast several times to indicate just *how* high-ranking.

'I've heard of even high-ranking officers having things stolen from them, despite their rows of medals,' considers the QM officer, inflating his fat cheeks.

Internally Chief Mechanic Wolf has to agree with him.

'Sir, sir! No indeed. I'm an honest man. I could never do a thing like *that*.' For a moment Wolf looks like a saint in a stained-glass window.

Porta coughs discreetly in the background, and pours more cognac into his glass. Wolf has quite forgotten him. When he tilts the bottle over his glass again, Wolf tears it out of his hand and fills his own glass and the toad-like QM's. Quick as lightning Porta exchanges his empty glass for Wolf's full one.

Wolf sends him a wicked look. A long discussion, on the subject of the tea, follows between Wolf and QM Toad. The QM explains, pleasantly, the procedure by which he could if he wished commandeer it. He is, of course, Chief of the 4th Panzer Army's Quartermaster Branch.

Wolf replies with a beautifully oblique threat, which the QM allows to slide off without any visible reaction. He has too many irons in the fire with Wolf to be able to allow himself to feel insulted. Wolf has hold of the right end of the stick. If he goes, the 4th Panzer Army will go with him, and the tidal wave will take more than a few others with them. Even in Admiral Schröder Strasse this would be noticed.

After a long time, the QM officer leaves with his bag of tea. He is on top of the world. Partly from cognac, partly from having obtained the tea. He has completely forgotten the highly-praised ladies. He loves tea and has calculated on now having enough of it to last him for the rest of the war, even if it turns into a war of attrition with trenches and the milder forms of poison gas.

Wolf has become the happy owner of a large brown bear, which can drink beer and throw hand-grenades.

'What do you want with that horrible monster?' asks Porta, in amazement, as he stands with Wolf watching the bear, which has just arrived as passenger in a large Mercedes. The driver, an SS-oberscharfürer, salutes as he dismounts from the vehicle. The bear has a green NKVD officer's cap on its head and is immediately supplied with a crate of beer. Wolf knows how to make a high-ranking Russian officer welcome.

Porta laughs until he is on the verge of getting cramp in his stomach, and soon becomes good friends with the bear. They kiss in Russian style. Wolf looks thoughtfully from the bear to Porta.

'I'll sell him to you,' he decides. 'He'll be enormously useful to you at the front. Teach him to eat Reds, and when you're on a moppin'-up job he can sniff out their hiding-places for you.'

'That's not a bad idea you've got there,' considers Porta, looking at the bear with great interest. 'I've heard these bears are a lot easier to teach than dogs or horses. I could teach him to do the Red salute with a clenched paw. The gold-braided boys'd love it. Even they couldn't punish a Russian bear for being true to Moscow. What'd your conscience permit you to let him go for?'

'I don't know,' says Wolf, slowly. 'Bears are a bit outside my field. I've taken him over from a bankrupt Russian circus.'

'They're a drug on the market,' says Porta, knowledgeably. 'Siberia's swimming with 'em.'

'We ain't in Siberia though, Porta,' Wolf reminds him.

'You'll get there sooner or later,' Porta warns him, ominously.

'Yeah, the way the sun seems to be settin' over the German Reich, with the strong possibility of a new movement of the German peoples northwards, you may be right,' Wolf points at the bear. 'It's possible there's many like him in Siberia but they haven't all learnt to drink beer and swing a club.'

'You're wrong, man, wrong! Haven't you heard,' cries Porta. 'The Siberian bars are full of 'em till far into the night!'

They go over to discuss Caterpillars, and when they finally agree, and Wolf has seen them and found that they are so new that the protective grease has not yet been removed, he cries, in wonder:

'Hell, Porta. Did the Yanks consign these straight to you?'

'Not far wrong,' Porta boasts, gesturing broadly with his hands. 'They've come by rail direct from God's Own Country via the Arctic Circle. There's even a Bible installed just behind the carburettor!'

'Jesus, boy,' comes admiringly from Wolf. 'Keep on like this an' you'll soon be sunnin' yourself along with the big Greeks in Monaco!'

They drive home to Wolf to have a drink on the bargain. The bear rolls itself into a ball in the corner and eyes the wolf-hounds with contempt. They keep a respectful distance.

'To prove I am your true friend,' begins Wolf, solemnly, 'I will give you the bear as a present!'

'*That* is meant friendly?' asks Porta suspiciously. 'You *want* to get him out of your hair, Wolf! He's unsaleable, and those brown boys eat more than a hungry German who's lived through the last three wars. To be perfectly honest I don't care much for your present. It'll certainly bring me more problems than pleasure. Before you know where you are you get blistered on a monster like that. Remember that pig we had. The one we couldn't bring ourselves to slaughter. If the neighbours hadn't captured Sophie we'd've had her yet, and that brown boy there looks to have more charm than Sophie *ever* did! Pets don't belong in the Army. Look at his eyes! What he needs is a good home, to ensure him a happy old age. What's his name, by the way?'

'I've asked him, but he don't say! Want to see him drink beer?'

Without waiting for an answer Wolf places four bottles of *Schlosspilz* on the table and beckons to the bear.

'Aren't you going to open them first?' asks Porta, wonderingly.

'No, no, no, no! He does that himself!'

The bear waddles over to the table, takes a bottle and bites the cap off with his teeth. Then he empties the contents down his throat with the speed of a thirsty docker, throws the empty bottle at the wolfhounds and picks up the next.

'Holy Mother of Kazan!' cries Porta, in amazement. 'Well I'm *damned*! D'you think he could be taught to fire a *kalashnikov*?'

'Sure, *sure*!' says Wolf. 'Teach that bear anything, you can! A *very* clever animal. He was with a special unit in Moscow before he came to the circus.'

The bear waddles over to Porta, lays a huge paw on his shoulder, and gives him a great wet kiss in the middle of his face.

'He *likes* me!' shouts Porta enthusiastically. 'There ain't many who do, you know!'

Coffee is served to Porta and Wolf. They agree to pick up the tractors in the middle of the night. Preferably between 02.00 and 04.00 hrs. That is the time of night when the guards are at their sleepiest.

Wolf's big white tom-cat comes strolling arrogantly from the neighbouring storeroom.

Porta calls to it. He loves cats. He has never really got over the loss of Stalin[2]. Wolf's cat ignores him completely. It swishes its tail angrily when he calls to it again and offers it a piece of pâté.

'He's a French cat,' boasts Wolf, on behalf of his cat. 'From Paris!'

'That's obvious. A strong sense of patriotism.'

'Too right,' says Wolf. 'My French prisoners are the only ones he'll let touch him and give him food.'

'Won't he let *you* touch him?' asks Porta.

'*Non, monsieur*! Don't reckon he's ever got over us stealin' Alsace-Lorraine in 1870.'

'That *was* a typical German thing to do to good neighbours,' admits Porta, solemnly. He watches the cat admiringly, as it passes the wolf-hounds with tail up and an air of the deepest contempt for all dogs in general and those two in particular.

When Hauptmann von Pader hears about the bear, he gets straight on to Regimental HQ.

'Porta and a bear, eh!' laughs Oberst Hinka. 'Take it on

2. Stalin: See *Legion of the Damned*.

187

strength. There's nothing in the manual that forbids keeping bears.'

'Do you want it to parade?' asks von Pader, crestfallen.

'Your business! You're the OC!' Oberst Hinka cuts him off, uninterestedly.

The bear parades with the company. After a while everybody gets used to it. The only thing that enrages it is the sight of khaki uniforms. These change it from a good-natured giant to a snarling beast of prey. Its eyes get smaller and glint dangerously.

We hold a gigantic christening party for it and name it Rasputin. There is something about the bear which reminds us of the Russian monk. Especially when it drinks beer.

Wolf arrives at the party with his private choir.

Between the songs speeches are made. Heide becomes so drunk that he lets himself be converted to Communism. Later that night he gets qualms of conscience, becomes a Catholic and is given absolution by Porta who was once with the Padre Corps[3].

The Old Man rises with difficulty. Stubbornly he tries to seat himself in a wheelchair and finally succeeds. The result is wonderful. Off goes the chair across the storeroom. Tiny opens the double doors politely and he rolls swiftly down the narrow path and straight into the river. A rescue chain is quickly arranged.

'Honoured singers,' he babbles when they get him back on shore. 'That man there,' he hiccups and points waveringly at Gregor. 'That man ... That man there! He sings like a pig! Just like a pig!' He looks at Gregor again. 'And he has *three* heads!'

Gregor gets on his feet with great difficulty. Schnapps has reached the level of his tonsils. Uncertainly he supports himself against a 20mm cannon.

'I must tell you, *sir*!' he hiccups, and tries to spit in the Old Man's direction. 'I must tell you that you are the dumbest dummy I have ever met! You are a real shit, sir!'

The Old Man falls across the table face downwards into the floral decoration.

3. Padre Corps: See *Wheels of Terror*.

'German soldiers! Cannot sing! Be shot at dawn! Not worthy live!' he mumbles, his voice stifled by petals. He is eating the table decoration.

'Sing, you bastards!' screams Gregor. He has crawled up on to the little seat behind the 20mm. 'One, two, three, *sing*! No more o' this idlin',' he snuffles. 'If we can't sing there's nothin' left. Song is the, the, the bloody, bleedin' backbone of the Army!' He carries out the loading drill on the gun.

'Sh-sh-sh-sh-shoot me at last!' stutters Porta, sitting by the side of Rasputin and stinking drunk.

'I'll shoot who I like an' when I like I'll shoot who I like,' stammers Gregor, and suddenly throws up all over the gun.

'You'll clean that gun,' roars Heide in a rage. 'If you're a thousand times an unteroffizier, you'll *clean* it, boy!'

The gun goes off, sending a whole clip of 20mm shells through the roof. Luckily they are armour-piercing and not HE.

'Stop your nonsense, now,' Wolf admonishes them in a fatherly tone.

One of the shells took his cap off. 'We are a sober choir engaged in honouring a christening and not a war-mad shooting club on militia exercises in the local park on a Sunday morning.'

'Feldwebel Beier will sing the next song,' drools Gregor, in a thick voice, falling off the gun.

'I'll have *you* picked up by the MP's!' shouts the Old Man. He is trying to swallow the long stem of a carnation. He thinks he is eating asparagus.

'Unteroffizier Gregor Martin!' shouts Heide. 'You are a disgrace to the German unteroffizier corps. The men *laugh* at you! Unteroffizier Martin, you are a blot on the corps!'

'Members of the corps who do not understand that the troops must be kept down by the exercise of strict discipline should never have been made unteroffiziers,' roars Wolf, solemnly. He attempts to get up from his chair, but fails completely. Instead he falls under the table where the Legionnaire has arrived before him and is sitting giving orders to a camel squadron. He thinks he is somewhere in the Sahara.

'*Mille diables*, can you smell the date palms, *mon ami*? They are in bloom at this time of year. *Allah el Akbar*, on your knees in prayer!' he yells, knocking his forehead piously on the floor.

Wolf pulls himself up again into his chair, falls on Heide's neck and tells the world how happy he is to have found his eldest sister, whose husband has left her, again.

'We'll break those fuckin dogfaces!' roars Heide.

'It's us he means,' says Porta, insulted. He puts his arm in comradely fashion round Tiny's shoulders. 'He doesn't understand the true military rank classifications, the brown turd.'

The bear lifts its head and growls threateningly at the word 'brown'.

'Unteroffizier Julius Heide,' says Porta, condescendingly. 'You have shit where your brains ought to be. I came close to saying you were dumb as a German, but I rarely shit on my own doorstep.'

' 'E's a stupid quim,' drools Tiny. His eyes go glassy and he falls on to the dogs who bite him in the leg. Fortunately he is too drunk to feel it. 'Julius,' he hiccups, 'Don't you know that us obergefreiters in some ways rank equal to staff officers. You don't always find an unteroffizier or a feldwebel with the General Staff, maybe not even a leutnant. What you *do* find is 'alf a score o' us obergefreiters runnin' round keepin' the bleedin' morale o' the place 'igh.'

'Tiny knows what he's talking about,' Porta praises him. 'We carry with dignity and pride the two tapes that are only handed out to soldiers with grey matter inside their skulls. Listen you shits of unteroffiziers,' he continues in a voice which cuts through the hellish din. 'In some beds obergefreiters outrank bloody generals!'

'Just you lot don't forget as the German Supreme Commander ain't no more'n a gefreiter,' grins Tiny, glassily. 'An' 'e never did get the other bleedin' tape!'

'As I say,' drawls Porta, 'it takes grey cells to get to be obergefreiter.'

'Let 'im watch 'imself,' warns Tiny, belching resoundingly.

'Brüder, zur Freiheit, zur Sonne ...' sings Porta in a shrill voice.

'High treason!' howls Heide, enraged. 'I ought to have you arrested.'

'Die Strasse frei. SA marchiert ...' he screams, trying to drown out Porta's Communist hymn.

'Arrest 'em,' grins Wolf foolishly, scrabbling on the floor for his belt and holster.

His wolfhound, Satan, brings it to him in its mouth.

Wolf salutes the dog and thanks it. With difficulty he draws the 08 from its holster. He holds the pistol in front of him with both hands and attempts to take aim at Heide. The muzzle swings to and fro, covering first one then another.

'Unteroffizier Julius Heide, you drunken twit, you are under arrest. If you attempt to escape I shall fire on you.' He falls over the table, and his gun goes off. A bullet whines past Heide's face and bores itself into the wall behind him.

Heide looks about him in terror.

'Partisans,' he whispers, rigid and shaking with fear.

'*Nix partisanski*,' grins Porta, and sings:

> 'Heute sind wir roten
> Morgen sind sir toten.'

'What the hell?' babbles Wolf, swaying dangerously, and describing circles in the air with the muzzle of his pistol. 'Didn't I get you, Julius? Let's have another go! If at first you don't succeed . . .'

'*Fire!*' commands the Old Man, who is by now half-asleep.

Heide emits a shrill scream of terror, and dives under the table. Two shots whine past him.

'I'm wounded, I'm dead, orderlies!'

'Are you balls!' chatters Wolf, leaning on his Russian bodyguard. 'Just you wait though, Julius, we'll get you. If we're allowed to liquidate Communists then why not bloody Nazis?'

'Prove you're Chief Mechanic and also responsible for ordnance,' Barcelona encourages him in happy drunkenness.

'Straight in front, brown target, fire!' roars the Old Man energetically.

Wolf picks up an Mpi turns it at the table and lets off a burst. Glass, wine and beer rain about our ears.

'I'll shoot your prick off,' promises Wolf, changing clips. 'You're as hard to hit as that bloody Russian chum's cat[4].'

'I'm dying,' howls Heide from under the table, waving a white flag of truce.

4. See: *Legion of the Damned.*

191

Wolf pulls himself up and salutes the Russian bodyguard.

'Sergeant Igor, get on your bicycle, ride to Moscow and report that we have beaten a Nazi battalion!'

'My bicycle is punctured, sir,' replies Igor, helping Wolf to an armchair, in which he immediately falls asleep. He just manages to order Igor to repair the puncture.

The medical orderly puts a dressing on Heide. The top of his left ear has been shot off.

Shortly after, Wolf wakes up and wants to throw us all out. He is about to set the wolf-hounds on us, when the telephone begins to ring angrily and impatiently. One of the guards takes it.

'Herr Stabfeldwebel and Chief Mechanic not here,' he answers brusquely. Then he suddenly seems to shrink, clicks his heels together and stands to attention. Even though he is from the Russian army, he has been a prisoner-of-war for so long that he can recognize vocal nuances and can judge if they are dangerous or not.

'What shit's that?' roars Wolf from the depths of the armchair.

'Inspector of Military Police Zufall,' the Russian says, with doom and disaster in his voice. Anything which smells in the slightest of police is deadly dangerous to his mind, particularly when they turn up between two and four o'clock in the morning. The death hours.

'Ask that bloody copper what he thinks he's doin' ringing at this time of night?' roars Wolf, making the rafters echo. 'The bastard can ring tomorrow between ten and eleven.'

'*Gaspodin*, Inspector Zufall says it is important,' reports the Russian, saluting with the telephone.

Wolf roars with laughter.

'Make that dobermann-pinscher of a cop understand that it may be important to him but it's not to *this* Greater German Chief Mechanic!'

The Russian gabbles Wolf's message off at such a rate that the man at the other end cannot manage to interrupt, bangs the receiver back on the hook and rushes out of the store-room to hide himself until the whole matter has been cleared up.

A little later the telephone rings again.

'Let me take it,' says Porta self-confidently. 'We professional soldiers don't have to take any shit from these half-assed beetles.' He rips up the telephone with the assurance of a Rockefeller about to accept an offer for a dried-up oil well. 'Listen bighead!' he roars into the telephone. 'Ring tomorrow between ten and eleven, if you're so mad keen to talk to us. We're having a christening party, so you can stuff your important business crossways, friend! Sure, come on over if you want to, we'll christen you too if you like. Who you're speaking to? *Me*, you dumb twit! Who else? I couldn't be less interested in getting to know you, so if that's what you're in need of you might as well not come. I don't give a fuck for you or your courtmartial, chum. I've *told* you. Come if you want to. You don't seem able to remember what you say yourself. That's the third time you've told me you're comin'. Well then for Jesus Christ's sake get your finger out an' get over here. If you can sing, so much the better! End of message!' Porta bangs down the telephone decisively. He gives the rest of us a superior nod. 'These nonentities from the police have to be given the rough side of your tongue straight off. Then you've soon got them licking your hand. Now he knows it's us an' the Army who give the orders round here.'

'Hear, hear!' drools Wolf from the armchair. He has a big bouquet of beer-sodden carnations in his lap. 'We hold all power firmly in our hands and when we win the final victory out go the goddam bluebottles. They're an unnecessary drain on the exchequer.'

'New song,' orders Heide, who has collected the choir in a ring around him.

With beer-soaked voices they sing:

Geht auch der Tod uns dauernd zur Seit',
geht es auch drüber und drunter,
braust auch der Wind durch finstere Heid',
uns geht die Sonne nicht unter[5].

5. Even though death walks by our side,
Walks with us up and down.
Even though winds blow through the ride,
For us the sun ne'er goes down.

193

'Caps off! Let us pray!' commands Porta.

We kneel down in spilled beer and remnants of food. Solemnly we press our helmets against our chests.

Porta prays for protection, and that our souls may be allowed to enter the eternal home when the time comes . . .

'But first we'll finish up this war,' thunders Wolf, 'then we'll have a word with God, afterwards.'

'When I'm well be'ind the bleedin' lines in peace an' quiet, an' out o' danger, I don't give a shit for all that God stuff,' Tiny explains to the wolf-hounds and the bear, 'but you understand, mates, soon as I'm out 'ere again where they throw red-'ot bleedin' lumps o' iron at your 'ead an' you run the risk of fallin' out any old time at all, I keeps meself close to God, an' I'm that religious you wouldn't believe. Everythin' 'as its time an' place.'

'We're gonna *do* that cop bastard,' promises Wolf, in a thick voice.

'We'll show him what tough guys really are,' says Gregor, striving to put on a villainous expression.

'Look tough. It's a good thing,' drools Julius, fanning me with the sorry remnants of a bouquet of roses.

Gregor brings his fist down decisively in a large pool of schnapps.

'Drink, that's *something*! You know where you are. Know what's gonna happen to you. Women're much more dangerous. You never know what's goin' to happen next! Did I ever tell you 'bout when I got between the sheets with my general's bint? That wicked bitch near got me shot, she did!'

The door crashes open. A little fat man in a greatcoat much too large for him rolls into the storeroom. His head is round as a cannonball and reminiscent of an aged pig's head. His ears stick out like braking flaps and are all that stop his oversized cap falling down over his face. He marches straight over to Wolf and shines a large torch directly in his face, despite the fact that the room is brightly lit.

'Chief Mechanic Wolf,' he confirms in a piercing voice, snapping the torch off.

'And Stabsfeldwebel,' corrects Wolf, pouring some drops of beer over his guest's head.

'You deal in tea,' states the fat little man.

Porta is suddenly in a hurry. He sees trouble coming over the horizon. Two huge gorillas in slate-grey police uniform stop him at the door.

'Goin' somewhere, obergefreiter?' grins one of them, throwing Porta back so hard he falls across the table. 'Don't. We're gonna see some fun soon! You ain't ever seen nothin' like it, I'd reckon!'

'Who the devil *are* you?' asks Wolf, condescendingly, slapping the little man on the shoulder.

'Zufall, Inspector Zufall.'

'You *look* it,' says Wolf, breaking out into a roar of laughter.

'You are a real comedian,' says the Inspector. 'You're going to need all that wonderful sense of humour soon.' He takes off his enormous cap, passes his hand over his completely hairless skull, and claps the cap on his head again. 'D'you know what the punishment is for those who sabotage the work of the General Staff?'

'They put 'em up against a wall an' shoot 'cm,' declares Wolf without a moment's thought.

'We are completely in agreement,' smiles Inspector Zufall, happily. 'I am here to investigate a case of such a nature.' He points a thick finger at Wolf, in the gesture of a public prosecutor. 'And *you* are the saboteur!'

'I don't understand what you mean,' mumbles Wolf, beginning to see dark clouds coming up over the horizon.

'Of course not,' smiles Zufall, making a heroic effort to appear friendly, and failing completely. He pulls a fat black notebook from his pocket. 'You have sold some tea to QM officer Zümfe of the 4th Panzer Army. You guaranteed it to be Darjeeling tea with an addition of green tea.'

'Is that forbidden?' asks Wolf, cockily, throwing himself down in a chair.

'No, decidedly not,' laughs the Inspector, ominously, 'but you forgot to tell the QM officer that there was a little surprise item added to this tea!'

Wolf throws a sharp questioning look at Porta, who is at that moment taking a swig at a bottle to liven his spirits up.

'Surprise? I don't know about any surprise!'

'The German General Staff knows all about it, though,' roars the Inspector, red as a turkey-cock in the face. 'They are all in process of shitting themselves to death. There aren't shit-houses enough to go round.'

Gregor explodes into a roar of laughter, which infects the whole room. Even the two gorillas at the door break out laughing.

The Inspector is moved to laughter, but more discreetly.

Only Wolf and Porta seem to have lost their sense of humour. Wolf is noted for always being able to see the funny side of a joke, particularly when it's against somebody else.

'Where did you get that tea from?' Zufall throws the question at him, as the laughter dies away.

Wolf points silently at Porta.

'Ah yes! Obergefreiter Joseph Porta,' the fat Inspector murmurs. 'I have heard of you and long wished to meet you.'

'An honour, sir,' says Porta, bowing in a servile manner.

'And from where did Herr Porta obtain the tea?'

'From a parachute,' says Porta, truthfully.

'Don't joke with *me*,' snarls Zufall viciously. 'Tea doesn't grow in the sky. Both of you tea dealers are under arrest. A whole lot of generals want you roasted over a slow fire. You'll curse the day you went into the tea trade.'

'We only know about real tea,' Porta defends himself. 'Maybe the QM put something in it on the way to the General Staff.'

'Perhaps it's affected the gentlemen's stomachs. It might make 'em shit if they're not *used* to proper tea, you know,' suggests Wolf.

Inspector Zufall smiles falsely.

'The tea has been analysed at the laboratories. It contains a strong aperient – a laxative – the working of which our doctors have not been able to stop. Before long, if it continues, these gentlemen will have shit themselves away down the toilets.'

'Did *you* put anythin' in it?' Porta turns to Wolf.

'D'you think I'm crazy? I'm a businessman, not a bloody saboteur.'

'One thing of which we are certain,' sighs the Inspector. 'The tea came from you two. If the enemy were to attack now they

196

would have an easy task. Thanks to your tea, the entire General Staff is out of action. They have been shitting now for sixteen hours and this seems only to be the beginning. A group of specialists are flying from Berlin. If you intended sabotage, you have succeeded beyond all measure. In all my thirty years on the force I have seen nothing like it.'

'We don't know a thing about it,' whispers Wolf, weakly. He feels a dreadful sucking sensation in the region of his stomach. He can almost see the entire General Staff sitting in a row in the latrines with Generalfeldmarschall Model sitting off there on the right flank. Where else would the Generalfeldmarschall be placed in such a situation?

Porta looks at the little, overfed Inspector helplessly.

'You must realize we'd never sell laxative tea. Even a drivel-ling idiot from the padded cells at Giessen'd know better than to do that.'

'So I think, myself,' answers Zufall. 'That is why I want to know where you got the tea from? I do not imagine you to have started a tea plantation here in Russia.'

'I bought the tea from Obergefreiter Porta,' declares Wolf, and obviously feels that this clears him completely.

'And it was wafted down to *me* from the sky attached to a pair of yellow parachutes,' affirms Porta, assisting his explanation with gestures.

'Do you really expect me to believe that story?' asks Zufall, who is in possession of a large degree of healthy distrust. He believes only what he can see and feel. 'Why in the world should anybody drop tea by parachute?'

'Obviously to get the German Army to shit itself out of its mind,' says Porta, without realizing that he has guessed right.

'From what I can see of you two tea traders, you will go to any lengths to ensure your leaving the Army with respectable for-tunes,' says Zufall, with a bitter smile.

'Too true we are,' Wolf emits a forced, noisy laugh. 'It ain't forbidden to try to make your fortune, now is it?'

'Honest people rarely get rich,' considers the Inspector, philosophically.

'Let's say, only the stupid stay poor,' Porta suggests quietly, 'and most people *do* stay poor.'

'Poor people are good people,' says Zufall, and thinks of himself. 'Civil servants do not often get themselves seen in wealthy circles.'

'No, by God!' comes spontaneously from Wolf. 'My old man was both good, poor *and* a civil servant. There wasn't much grey matter under his hair either, but he had a good reputation. Nobody doubted him to be trustworthy. He was at peace with both God and his neighbours. On holy days there he was in church, and at night you could hear him sleeping the quiet peaceful sleep of the just. If the entire police force had come banging on his door between two and four at night he'd have snored comfortably on. Rich he never was. We were nine kids and he had his worries gettin' clothes to put on our backs.'

'Did any of your brothers or sisters follow in your father's footsteps and enter the civil service?' asks Zufall interestedly. He feels for Herr Wolf senior.

'Not on your life,' grins Wolf. 'We all took after our mother's side where brains was concerned. She'd a bit more'n German blood in her veins.'

'Jewish, perhaps!' Zufall lets the question fall innocently.

'Couldn't swear she wasn't. But a drop or two of Jew blood ain't for a man to turn his nose up at. It clears the thinking. An' this Aryan certificate'll soon be out of the way.'

'You don't believe in the final victory, then?' asks Zufall with an odd note in his voice.

'Do you?' grins Wolf.

The gorillas at the door laugh with the rest of us. But they are not aware of what they are laughing at.

'I do not wish to answer your question at this time,' answers the Inspector, turning his head away.

When they arrive at staff HQ, the first person they meet is the QM, Zümfe. He rushes up to Wolf.

'Jackal, hyena!' he howls. 'You'll swing for this. How could you do it to me? I've always treated you well, you dirty bastard!'

'I didn't want to sell you the tea,' Wolf affirms. 'Quite the opposite. You threatened to confiscate it if I wouldn't sell it to you. It's your own headache you've sold it to the General Staff,

Who knows, you may even've mixed that shit-powder in it yourself. You look mean enough to've done it.'

'You are my witness,' shouts Toadface, gripping the police Inspector by the arm. 'This man is making false accusations against me? He is working for the Red Army and uses weapons forbidden by the Geneva Convention.' He doesn't get any farther. He has to make a run for the toilets. He unbuttons his trousers as he runs. All the seats are taken and with a despairing scream he dashes to the reserve toilets. These are all taken too. With both hands pressing the pink cheeks of his bottom tightly together, and with his trousers flapping down round his riding boots he rushes for an open window, where red roses sway in the breeze. Sighing he drops his backside out over the window edge. He sputters like a machine-gun in full swing.

It is a comical sight but nobody feels like laughing. Particularly when two red-tabbed generals come rushing in on one another's heels and practically throw a major and an oberstleutnant off their seats. In the German Army rank has its privileges, even in the toilets.

Porta and Wolf watch the gold-braided generals with interest. They are staring straight ahead with the dead eyes of zombies.

'They look like a pair of drowned cats,' Porta permits himself to remark.

'Pity the bloke who thought of it couldn't be here to see it,' grins Wolf.

The Toad comes panting back. He has a few more things to say to Wolf.

'You're the wickedest man I've ever met,' he sobs, waving a threatening fist under Wolf's nose. 'Do you realize I've been arrested because of your damned tea? No, no, not again!' he howls, hopping away up the corridor. He falls into a seat next to the generals, pushing aside a rittmeister whom he outranks.

'Tell me! Where does Generalfeldmarschall Model do *his* shittin'?' asks Porta with interest.

'He has had a toilet installed express in his office,' explains Zufall, despondently. 'Thank God I didn't taste any of that tea. I came close to it, but that snobbish bastard, the adjutant, refused to allow me even a sip, and chased me out of the casino. He doesn't like civil servants.'

'If he'd only known there was shit-powder in it he'd 've forced you to drink a bucket of it!' grins Wolf.

'He's got something else to think about now, that bastard,' says Zufall, happily. 'He's shit himself unconscious.'

Porta and Wolf are taken to the Army secret police, which is in a state of feverish activity all aimed at finding out where the tea came from originally. After an hour of interrogation they are confined in separate cells. They pump the water out of the toilets and are able to talk to one another.

'We'll show those German shits that at least we know how to die, when they execute us,' shouts Porta gloomily down into the empty w.c. bowl.

'Yes, we got to keep our chins up,' stammers Wolf, nervously. 'Keep smilin' an' take defeat the way we took victory.'

'Yes, it's some consolation that this is the last and biggest defeat and shoot us dead more than once they can't do,' says Porta, with dignity.

After three days they agree to go on hunger strike, but after two days of this the guards come along with steaming bowls of brown beans with a large piece of pork floating in each bowl, and they have to give up.

'My favourite food,' says Porta, regretfully, and the contents of the bowl are inside his shrunken belly in the twinkling of an eye.

They plan an escape. Digging themselves out presents difficulties since they have only a wooden spoon each to do the job with. A crooked obergefreiter amongst the warders gets them a pair of hacksaws but before they even get started the whole affair is over. A thorough investigation has been made and the authorities feel they have found the solution. A British Lancaster MK II had been observed over the lines. There is proof it has dropped containers. The times fit those in Porta's statement. The tea has come from England, or, at any rate, it has been dropped by the English.

'You've been lucky,' sighs Inspector Zufall, openly disappointed. He points to a row of carbines, as they walk down a long corridor. 'Twelve of those are loaded and ready for you two. I'll be keeping an eye on you, and we'll keep them loaded for a bit! I think we're going to have a use for them.'

'Faith can move mountains, they do say,' says Porta virtuously, in a religious tone.

'I consider you both to be my opponents, and I shall do my best to combat you,' says Zufall, darkly.

'Nice to know your enemies,' smiles Porta.

They are taken before Generalfeldmarschall Model who has now recovered sufficiently from the tea to be able to hold his monocle in his eye again. He is a small man with a hard face, slim as a young girl. His personal courage is legendary, but there is a comically schoolmasterish air about him. He walks round them for ten minutes looking at them through his big monocle.

'So that's what you look like, is it?' he begins, in his own special tone. He seems to spit words out as if he hated them.

'Herr Generalfeldmarschall, *sir*!' roar Porta and Wolf as if with one voice. They crack their heels together violently. They know that if they make a bad impression now, it's the scrap-heap for them.

'You've reached the limit!' Model runs his fingers over his Knight's Cross with oak leaves and sword.

'Yes *sir*, Generalfeldmarschall, *sir*!'

'If you have any of that terrible tea left I suggest you send it as a gift parcel to our Russian opponents.'

'Yes *sir*, Herr Generalfeldmarschall, *sir*!'

'I ought to have you hung up by the heels . . .'

'Yes *sir*, Herr Generalfeldmarschall, *sir*!'

'But I intend to be merciful to you, since you are partially free from guilt in this tea party affair.'

'Yes *sir*, Herr Generalfeldmarschall, *sir*!' Porta nudges Wolf.

'But there are some very nice things said about you in *these*!' Model bangs his hand down on a pile of reports lying on the desk in front of him.

'Yes *sir*, Herr Generalfeldmarschall, *sir*!'

'Permission to speak, sir? One shouldn't believe everything one hears, sir,' says Porta hurriedly.

Model polishes his monocle and looks out of the window.

Then he turns round slowly, screws the monocle into his eye, and runs his finger again over his decorations and gold braid.

'Has no one ever told you that the penalties for black market dealing are most severe? That death is one of them, in certain circumstances.'

'Yes *sir*, Herr Generalfeldmarschall, sir, we have been told!' It comes from them with one voice.

Model flexes his knees, walks round them a few times and looks at the adjutant who is standing as stiff as a wax dummy against the wall. He seats himself on the edge of his desk. He is so small that his feet do not reach the floor.

'Your business methods are quite reminiscent of black market dealing.'

'Permission to speak, sir, *no* sir, we do *not* have *anything* to do with the black market, *sir*,' shouts Porta. 'We do *not* touch 'ot things, *sir*, an' we *never* go outside regulations, *sir*, an', *sir*, we do not take big profits, *sir*!'

'Do you consider me to be a fool?'

'No *sir*, Herr Generalfeldmarschall, *sir*!'

'It appears to me that you are trying to pull my leg! What are you laughing at, man!'

'Permission to speak, *sir*, no, *sir*, not *laughing*, sir!' Porta rattles it off. 'Beg to state, *sir*, it's my *nerves*, sir! When I'm scared, *sir*, I look like I'm laughing, *sir*. The MO, *sir*, says it's like gallows 'umour, *sir*!'

'Get out of my sight!' orders the Feldmarschall, pointing to the door.

Safely outside they let out a long breath of relief. Smartly they salute a generalmajor who drags himself, pale and tortured-looking past them.

'Jesus George,' says Wolf, with relief. '*That* was a close 'un! Those English are a dirty lot o' swine!'

'It was a wicked thing to do to us,' Porta admits, 'but maybe we'll get a chance to pay it back one of these days.'

They agree that it would be bad business to throw the remainder of the tea away. Wolf promises to give Porta twenty per cent, if he can get rid of it, but Porta demands fifty, with the guarantee that Wolf's name won't enter into it if things go wrong again.

Porta finds an Italian division, and in record time has sold the tea to a Quartermaster who is organizing transport of illegal goods to Milan in a big way.

'I'd be packing my bags for a trip to Sweden, if I was you,' says Gregor, darkly, when Porta tells them about the deal.

'When them Spag's start shittin'', boy, you'll have the whole goddam Mafia breathin' down your neck. I wouldn't be *you*, son!' says Buffalo.

For a while Porta is packed and ready to move off at the drop of a hat, then without warning the Italian QM turns up with nodding plumes in front of Wolf's stores, where Porta is sitting drinking morning coffee.

Before he can make a move the Italian is by his side. But there is no danger. It isn't the Mafia who have arrived in the cross-country Fiat but a delighted Italian who embraces him and kisses him on both cheeks. He is disappointed when he hears there is no more tea for sale.

'You must get *more* of that so *wonderful* tea, Signor Porta!' begs the befeathered Bersaglieri QM, bobbing his plumes in Porta's face. '*Signor* comrade, I promise you. The Italian military good service order will look well on your chest!'

But Porta cannot supply any more tea. There is none to be had.

When the Italian has gone Wolf and Porta discuss the phenomenon. Porta comes to the conclusion that the English have used a highly refined laxative, so cleverly compounded, in fact, that it only works on Germans.

'*Hitler is true to nobody. In a few years time he will also have betrayed you, Herr Generaloberst!*'

     General Ludendorff to Generaloberst von Fritsch,
                  Spring, 1936.

Himmler looks coldly at 'Gestapo Müller' as he reports to him that SS-Obergruppenführer Heydrich has been seriously wounded in an assassination attempt at Prague and has been admitted to the Bülow Hospital.

'*He is alive?*' *whispers Himmler hoarsely, and clenches his hands until the knuckles become dark blue. 'I will fly to Prague immediately! Make the arrangements! Send Kaltenbrunner to me!*'

'*Very good, Herr Reichsführer!*'

Teleprinters heated up. The telephone services were blocked with calls. A state of emergency was proclaimed in Prague. Hundreds of arrests were made. It is as if a wasps' nest had been stirred with a stick.

In RSHA[1] on Prinz Albrechtstrasse when the news comes through, all hell breaks loose. With screaming sirens and warning lights blinking, Himmler's black Mercedes rushes across Berlin to the Tempelhofer Airport.

'*I must get to Prague first,*' *he thinks, and slaps his gloves impatiently on his long black riding-boots.*

In a short time he lands in Prague. He bounds up the steps of the Bülow Hospital. His face is chalk-white and his eyes staring.

Two doctors and a nurse attempt to stop him entering the operating theatre, but he pushes them brutally aside and kicks open the door.

'*Get out,*' *he hisses to the doctors, who are about to commence the operation.*

1. RSHA: (Reichssicherheitshauptamt): State Security Services HQ.

Open-mouthed they stare at the little man in the mouse-grey uniform.

'Get out!' he repeats.

'But Herr Reichsführer,' stammers the chief surgeon. 'The general is under anaesthesia!'

'Wake him up. I must speak to him immediately.'

'Impossible,' answers the chief surgeon, shaking his head. 'It will be three or four hours before the Reichsführer can speak to the general.'

'He is to be conscious within at most three hours so that I can speak to him. If he is not you will be executed for sabotage,' screams Himmler in a piercing voice and rushes from the operating theatre.

SS-Obergruppenführer Frank comes hastily down the corridor and reports to Himmler.

'Frank, you take over with immediate effect Heydrich's position as Reichsprotektor for Böhmen-Mähren. Surround this hospital with SD-troopers and, mark this carefully Frank, nobody, absolutely nobody, not God or the devil himself, is to enter or leave this hospital without my personal permission, Frank. Your head will answer for it!'

In the course of a few minutes the hospital is sealed off from the outside world.

SS-Gruppenführer Ernst Kaltenbrunner reports to Himmler, who is raging up and down the corridor outside the operating theatre.

'General Professor Sauerbruch is on his way to take over treatment of the case,' says Kaltenbrunner softly.

'By whose orders?' asks Himmler angrily.

'The Führer!'

'Damnation! Is he flying from Berlin?'

'Yes, Reichsführer! He has already landed in Prague.'

Himmler presses his hands together so that the knuckles crack.

'Did you know that the Führer had signed Heydrich's appointment as Minister of the Interior and supreme head of all police units?'

'Wha . . .?' comes in amazement from Kaltenbrunner.

Himmler nods sombrely.

'*And that is not all. I have heard other things. Go straight back to Berlin and assume command at RHSA. Post security guards on all Heydrich's offices. Isolate Heydrich's personal assistants, but cautiously. You are dealing with poisonous snakes!*'

'*Trust me, Reichsführer,*' Kaltenbrunner smiles. '*I know how to handle them.*'

'*I hope you do, for your own sake,*' Himmler smiles coldly back.

Two hours later Himmler bends over Heydrich's bed and stares down into the pale, skull-like face.

'*Heydrich, can you see me?*'

'*Very well, Herr Reichsführer.*'

'*Where is your "explosives box"? Your secret documents?*'

Heydrich smiles with bared teeth. His slanted eyes stare coldly into Himmler's.

'*The papers, damn it!*' snarls Himmler impatiently.

Heydrich closes his eyes without answering.

Himmler shakes him.

'*Heydrich, the papers? Heydrich, listen! You are Minister of the Interior today. You are Germany's Supreme Chief of Police! The papers?*'

After a while Himmler accepts that Heydrich has fallen back into unconsciousness. He sits as if carved in stone by the side of the bed and stares at the long, sharp face with the crooked Mongol eyes.

That evening Professor Sauerbruch operates on Heydrich. Himmler does not move from the patient's side. Every word of his fevered mumblings is taken down by a stenographer. On the morning of the 4th of July Heydrich dies without having regained consciousness.

Himmler flies back to Berlin and himself leads the search for Heydrich's secret files. They are never found.

At Hitler's order a post-mortem examination is made of Heydrich's body. The pathologist's report states that the cause of death was infection of major organs and glandular tissue in the region of the spleen. Grains of explosive had penetrated the chest. It was possible for death to have been caused by toxic substances.

DEMON HEIGHTS

A RISING and falling rumble sounds continuously, broken now and then by the chatter of machine-guns. The earth beneath us seems to shiver like a dying animal.

There is an atmosphere of pressure. Fear catches at our throats. The only one of us who seems unaffected by it is Porta, who is playing away merrily on his piccolo. But as we get closer to the front line a strange don't give a damn feeling takes hold of us. This is something everyone feels when they are continually exposed to death in brutal and violent forms. We march in close column of threes, and carry our weapons as we please.

Tiny rolls along, with the SMG over his shoulder as if it weighed no more than a spade.

'Keep your distance!' the shout comes from up front, but we are frightened and uneasy and clump together for fancied protection. From a military viewpoint it is madness to march so closely together. A single 105mm shell could wipe out the entire company.

An endless column of wounded passes us, going in the opposite direction. Most of them are from the 104th Rifles, who have been hit terribly by an unexpected barrage.

'They've got caught by the new shells they talk so much about,' explains Julius Heide, looking down his nose.

'*What* new shells?' asks Porta, jeeringly but unable to conceal a certain inquisitiveness. It is always nice to know what you might get killed by.

'Jumping Jacks with compressed air,' answers Julius, conceitedly. 'They can finish off a company in a minute.'

Rasputin lumbers along beside Porta without paying any attention to the noise from the front.

Rumour has it that we are to get King Tigers. Heide affirms

that they are on rail already at Kassel. He has got the word from a comrade in the Party. Gregor says that they have only just got on to the drawing-board, and that the Wehrmacht is not going to get tanks any more. The SS are to have them. Porta thinks they will have to cut down on the whole mechanized arm. It is too expensive.

He has heard that they have begun to send people to the Red Army to learn to ride like Cossacks. 'But it is top secret,' he says with a warning wag of the forefinger. 'It must not be talked about. We know nothing!'

We couldn't really care less if we get tanks or not. There are advantages in belonging to the infantry.

The company makes a halt on the outskirts of the forest. Some begin to dig in immediately. They are the nervous types, who take cover at the mere sound of a pebble rolling down a slope.

The forest is a sinister-looking place. Shells have torn terrible holes in it. The waste material of war lies everywhere.

Porta, who has gone on ahead some way to obtain news, comes back filled to bursting with rumours.

'We're to take part in a bloody regatta,' he shouts, while still at a distance. 'Anybody who can't swim, has got half-an-hour to learn. There aren't enough boats to go round!'

'What's all this nonsense?' hisses the Old Man, puffing anxiously at his silver-lidded pipe. 'There's no sea in the middle of Russia!'

'Think again, Feldwebel Beier! There's water in other places than the sea. Wait till you see the river we're going to have to cross. There's more water there than *you'll* fancy and the bridge engineers say it's so deep it goes all the way down to hell!'

'An' me as 'ates water,' shouts Tiny resignedly. 'D'you suppose Rasputin can swim?'

'Bet your sweet life he can,' answers Porta proudly. 'He could take the Soviet swimming badge in gold, if he was human. They let him take the extended free-style tests when he was with the Moscow Officer Training School, *and* he came in first, my son!'

'Is it a *very* big river?' asks Barcelona, shuddering. His experience with rivers formerly has not been of the best.

'Broad as the Atlantic Ocean,' declares Porta delightedly, spreading his arms to show how wide the river is.

'Up shit creek again,' sighs Gregor Martin, despairingly, throwing himself down in the tall grass.

'We must take things as they come,' considers the Old Man, scraping away at his pipe with the point of his bayonet.

'Why do we *stand* for it?' asks Barcelona, shaking his head.

'You should be the last one to moan,' jeers Porta. 'War mad *you've* been since you were seventeen years of age. Volunteer in Spain, where you had no bloody business to be at all!'

'I feel it to be my duty to fight for the weak,' protests Barcelona. 'The dictatorship was forcing them into slavery.'

'Piss and wind! Bullshit!' snarls Porta. 'There's dictatorships all over, but I must admit the Reds are the most honest. They show themselves in their true colours. They *like* to see blood. Our lot do too, but they hide themselves behind their brown camouflage.'

'You ought to go an' get a trick cyclist to 'ave a peep inside your 'ead, Barcelona,' suggests Tiny. 'Maybe 'e'd 'ave a pill as'd 'elp you.'

'Section leaders to the OC,' comes a shout from within the forest.

The Old Man rises, swings his Mpi to his shoulder and trots off, his bowed legs twinkling. He goes straight through mud and water, puffing fiercely on his silver-lidded pipe.

'*Mille diables,*' cries the Legionnaire, 'it will cost lives to get us across that flood. If they are just a *little* bit clever they'll wipe us all out before we can get to the other side.'

'We are German soldiers and will do what the Führer orders us to do,' decides Heide, proudly. 'We owe the Fatherland everything. I am happy to be serving in the Army. Only the best men belong there.'

'I don't give a short, sharp shit for the Fatherland *or* its fucked-up Army,' states Porta, coarsely. 'I don't owe either of 'em a single thing. On the contrary they owe *me* plenty!'

'Those engineer shits can't be bothered to throw a bridge over that bleedin' river, so we can march over it without wettin' a boot!' shouts Tiny disgustedly. He throws a stone at two engineers who come puffing by with a large roll of barbed-wire on a rod.

'Come to that, what's it matter if you kick it dry or wet,' considers Barcelona, sorrowfully.

'It's supposed to be quite a pleasant death, drowning,' remarks Heide, apathetically.

'Jesus Christ, man, we're shit lucky then after all,' shouts Tiny, happily. ' 'Ere we've been thinkin' we were gonna get it in some 'orrible way or other, an' now we suddenly find out we've 'ad nothing' to worry about at all. We're all *right*! The Führer and our good German God 'as seen to it we'll 'ave a pleasant bleedin' death in a Russian bleedin' river!'

'I can tell you something a bit different from drowning,' inserts Gregor Martin. 'Me an' my general came close to it when we were practising invading England. Out we go in these landing craft with the whole division at our backs. The Navy towed us a hell of a way out to sea. To start with my general gets seasick. When that happened the rest of us followed suit. Every good Panzer Division follows its general in everything. *He* gets seasick, *we* get seasick.'

' "Let's get ashore, lads", he ordered, quite green in the face, between two bouts of sea-sickness. "This is no place for a Panzer Division. Let the Navy *keep* their blasted sea!"

'He ordered me to start his Horch staff-car, so that we could get away from that rolling, dancing bath-tub those Navy shits had tempted us into, as soon as we touched land. The second we felt the bottom of the bath-tub scrape on something solid, my general roared:

' "Flaps down, take off, and let's give these Englanders something to remember us by!"

'And *how* we took off. Believe you me, friends, inside one second we were up to top speed with that supercharged Horch. The general's gold-braided dress cap flew off his bald head, and his baton took off through the air like a mini-glider. But, I said to myself, when my head stopped jolting enough for me to be able to see through the windscreen, where the *hell's* France got to? There was nothing but that wicked, wet sea in front of me. Not a sign of land.

' "Where the devil are you taking me, Gregor?" was all my general had time to ask.

'The next moment the Horch was giving a respectable imitation of a submarine. It hadn't been the beach we'd scraped on but a treacherous bloody sand bank. Well here we were on our way down with only surprised French fish to salute us as we sank past them. How long we sat in the sinking Horch enjoying the view, I don't recall. I had heard that it was best to remain in a sinking car until it had filled with water. Then out of it you shot like shit from a cow. This was no problem for us, though, since the car we drove round conquering the world in was a cabriolet. To underline the seriousness of the situation my general put on his field service cap and screwed one of his reserve monocles into his eye. He pointed upwards towards where the normal world should be. He smiled, showing the horsey teeth he'd developed in his time with the cavalry, pleased at Staff HQ Company's obedience. There they were, all the way down after us. P-3's and the entire radio station.

'Well, suddenly we started to rise again. We soon discovered how practical it was to have gills when you live in water. There was a crowd like in a department store on the first day of a sale when we got up to the surface. I reported for duty, saluting as best I could.

'My general thanked me reservedly, as usual, and ordered me to find some form of transport fit for a general officer, in order that the invasion could be continued with according to plan. The worst thing that can happen to a general is for things not to go according to plan, but it was easier said than done to find a suitable means of transport. Our transport was at the bottom of the treacherous English Channel.

'We trod water for a while. During the night along came the abominable Navy again with their horrible fast motorboats and splashed water all over us, which we didn't need at all.

'Now my general really became annoyed. He had never liked the Navy. He considers it unnatural for human beings to move about in the water. If the good German God had intended that sort of thing He could have seen to it that the German people were born with fins on their backs.

' "This will be a court-martial matter", he said seriously,

screwing his fifth spare monocle in his eye. He really exploded when he discovered that they were saving the technical personnel first. He lost his last three monocles during the outburst, and his gold-braided field service cap took off on the water on its own.

'I told a P-4 driver to save the general's cap, and my general never forgot me for it.

' "Unteroffizier Gregor Martin, you are a German hero", he said, solemnly. "You will be awarded the War Service Cross for this. If we had more men of your kind we would long ago have made our brutal enemy sorry they started this war!"

' "Very good, Herr General, sir!" I said, swallowing half the Channel as I saluted.

'We reached the beach at dawn. There we threw an infantry oberst and his adjutant out of a Kübel, and made straight for Army Corps HQ to complain about the Navy.

' "Infantrymen were born to march", said my general as we nodded a condescending goodbye to the two foot-sloggers, who didn't seem too happy about our commandeering their Kübel.

'The invasion exercise was aborted. Me an' my general had to get a bit more used to this drowning business first, but *don't* come telling *me* drowning's a pleasant death. It was an experience you could only call bitter. My general always said it was the Supreme Command's fault that the whole of the division's transport ended on the bottom of the English Channel. Bohemian corporals, he called them.'

'It is to be hoped that your general no longer has a command,' says Heide. 'He seems to reek of Imperial conceit.'

'*Imperial!* You can bet your sweet bloody life we were,' shouts Gregor, proudly. 'I've never met the old Hohenzollern but my general told me so much about him, that I can't do anything but like him. Emperors have to be *born* to the job!'

'Take up arms,' orders the Old Man, back from the company commander. 'No. 2 Section goes over first, and you can thank Tiny for that, because he just *had* to get across that shitehawk von Pader!'

The air shivers and trembles. The explosion is a long way off and must have been very violent.

'Hard luck on the poor sods who were under that lot,' says Barcelona.

'Shit boys, 'ear that!' shouts Tiny, admiringly. ' 'Ear them old neighbours shittin'!'

'So what?' says Gregor.

When we are moving up to relieve the line we always feel anger towards the enemy, but after only a couple of days at the front we begin to develop a friendly feeling for the other side. They are lying in the same muck as we arc, and shells don't know the difference.

A new salvo falls. The tall trees bend to the blast. We duck involuntarily. Some of us begin to put on our steel helmets.

'Make a lovely bang, don't they?' says Tiny. 'It's a surprisin' thing the *power* there is in shells!'

We march up through a murdered forest. There is no bark left on the naked stems of the trees. When we top the heights the Russians will be able to see us. This is where companies of men are turned into mincemeat. Everyone fears this stretch. It has to be passed in short dashes, but as soon as the first party makes a move tracer comes at them from the other side. Men scream for stretchers. They are the ones who didn't move fast enough.

'No. 2 Section forward! Move! *Move!*' shouts the Old Man waving us on with his Mpi. 'Run like hell, if you want to stay alive!'

I spring along, seem almost to fly over the ground. The machine-gun feels heavy and clumsy. Tracer winks past me. Earth and fire cascade upwards. A jump of several yards lands me in a shell-hole.

Now they are shelling the heights with field artillery and mortars. No. 3 Company runs straight into a salvo of shells. Their OC, the well-liked Oberleutnant Soest, is tossed into the air and his body seems to explode on the tip of a burst of flame. No. 3 Company is wiped out of existence in just a few minutes. Most of them are smashed beyond recognition. The enemy field batteries have got a bead on the heights.

Porta and Rasputin come rushing along in a cloud of dust. The bear is running on all fours in long bounds. It seems as if it is trying to protect Porta with its body. Every time he drops down it covers him. When we finally reach safety on the other side of the heights we find that the action has cost No. 5 Company seven dead and eleven wounded. This is light in comparison to the regiment's other companies.

'Poor bloody supplies runners,' I say, looking up at that fiery hell. 'Twice a day through *that* with food containers on their backs!'

It is midnight, and black as the inside of your hat, when we reach the river. Silently we climb into the assault boats. Nobody has any illusions about anything. We've been there before.

'Once round the harbour, boys,' chuckles Porta. 'Free beer after the ride. If you're good you can come along on the next trip for nothing!'

Nobody laughs.

Tiny installs himself in the bow with the LMG. I carry the explosive charges on a long rod.

Julius Heide and I have to get to the enemy emplacements while the section gives covering fire. I curse the day I volunteered for that explosives course. Now I'm paying for it. This is a one-way trip to heaven. Still and all, when I volunteered all hell was loose at the front and when I came back most of the boys I'd known were pushing up daisies.

'Run like the devil as soon as we touch bottom,' whispers Heide nervously to me. 'We've got three and a half minutes to get to them.'

Our fate hangs on what happens in the first minute. Then the enemy are usually still confused, but after that they are on their toes and know it has to be them or us. They have to get us before we can get up to them with our charges.

'Above all keep your heads,' the Old Man exhorts us in a whisper. 'Don't play hero! Life is short and you'll be dead a long time. Do what's needed and not a thing over and above that.' He taps Julius lightly on the shoulder. 'You and Sven have to get to those defensive posts with the charges. Run like the devil was after you. They mustn't get to the lifting gear. If they do we've had it. If you get wounded twenty times on the way you must still somehow drag yourselves up these emplacements. *Hals-und Beinbruch!*'

The slender boat grates on a sandy bottom. In one long spring we are over the side, race through the mist and clamber up the sloping bank.

Our lungs are bursting with effort. I throw myself down behind a large rock. My old lung wound is troubling me[2]. There is only a stretch of ten yards left to make, but every inch of it full of death and danger.

An SMG rattles, but behind us. They are giving us covering fire.

Concrete towers above us. The fortifications are much larger than we had thought at first. I push the charge through an observation slit and pull the release string. In one long jump I am down under cover, open my mouth and stuff my fingers into my ears. The wall falls outwards. The explosion is terrible. A wave of heat washes over me.

There is a blinding flash and human bodies are thrown from the pill-box. I feel as if Satan himself had taken a bite at me and spat me out again.

Two more hollow, rolling explosions and the two other pill-boxes crack apart like eggshells. Automatic weapons rattle noisily.

Tiny comes sprinting with the SMG in his hand.

'Get goin', dope!' he screams, kicking me as he runs. 'If they get straightened out, they'll 'ave our balls for breakfast. Them 'eathens know what they're up to!'

The Old Man storms forward, with the rest of No. 2 Section in spread order. In a twinkling they have cleaned up the enemy position.

Hauptmann von Pader throws himself down heavily beside the Old Man. He is pale as death and on the verge of a nervous breakdown. He is wearing his steel helmet backwards.

'Why don't you let the company spread out?' asks the Old Man disrespectfully, looking wickedly at him. 'Just one direct hit as we are, and half the company's for the scrap-heap.'

'Don't try to teach me my business, feldwebel,' wheezes the Hauptmann. 'I'll have you on report!'

'Good Jesus Christ!' pants the Old Man, in despair. 'Are reports all you've got in your head? You're at the *front*, Herr

2. See *Wheels of Terror*.

Hauptmann, and you're responsible for two hundred German soldiers.' He gets half-way to his feet and points at von Pader with his Mpi. 'I warn you, if you make a mess of this, I'll relieve you of command!'

'Who do you think you are?' screams Hauptmann von Pader, excitedly. 'A lousy peasant like you can't relieve an officer of command!'

'Read your own Führer's orders,' snaps the Old Man. 'Latest orders state that even a private soldier can relieve a regimental commander of command if he thinks that commander has failed in his duty.'

'I've never seen that,' mumbles von Pader, weakly.

'Better take a day off for reading orders, when we get back,' suggests the Old Man, ironically.

A runner throws himself down panting by the side of them. Blood is running down his face from a gash in his forehead.

'Herr Hauptmann, sir! Regimental HQ wants to know if the fortifications here have been taken?'

'No!' the Old Man answers for his OC, 'the attack is held up. No. 5 Company is sitting around in shell-holes scratchin' its collective arse.'

'The oberst'll be glad to hear it,' grins the runner, throwing a sneering glance at the officer lying gripping his steel helmet tightly.

Porta and the bear slide down to them in a shower of dust and dead leaves.

'What the hell're we pissin' about here for?' screams Porta, taking no notice of von Pader. 'Where the devil's the rest of the company? Me an' Rasputin can't win this fuckin' war on our own!'

The Old Man waves to the neighbouring section. The signal is answered. No. 5 Company storms forward. Only Hauptmann von Pader remains behind in his hole. With terror-stricken eyes he looks at the ground in front which is being ploughed up by the field artillery barrage.

The earth seems to rise up like a huge curtain towards the sky. Bodies and equipment spew out to all sides. Flame shoots up from the ground in giant geysers.

A gun with six horses comes sailing through the air and smashes into the ground.

Hauptmann von Pader breaks down, sobbing. His stomach clenches and cramps. He knocks off his helmet and tears at his collar, the cloth ripping under his fingers. He has never imagined the baptism of fire to be like this. For the first time in his life he feels the Fatherland could be asking too much of him.

The hole he is lying in shakes and sways. It is as if all the evil demons of hell have been let loose and are roaring together. One deafening explosion is followed closely by another. The unbelievable noise rises to an infernal crescendo.

A body falls in front of him. Blood, entrails and brain matter splash into his face.

He screams desperately, thinking it is he himself who has been badly wounded. But it is a nineteen-year-old leutnant whose first day at the front has ended.

Shells rain down. Whistling, howling, exploding. Fire, earth, rocks, whole tree trunks, fly through the air. We are in a gigantic, hellish stadium, where blast plays ball uncaringly with everything inside it.

'My company,' gasps von Pader, and creeps still deeper into the hole.

His company is a long way off. It is engaged in fierce fighting for the Russian positions.

I see two heads behind a Maxim and send a stick-grenade whirling at them. I watch carefully to see it doesn't come back again. We are not up against recruits.

The grenade whirls straight down into the MG nest. A khaki-uniformed body is thrown into the air together with an SMG.

I sprint forward with the LMG under my arm. It is one of the Russian models, an excellent weapon for close quarter work. I go down behind the sandbagged wall of the nest. The air cuts at my lungs as I breath. That damned lung wound. I'll never be rid of it.

A Russian sergeant moves close beside me, but before he can fire his pistol I have crushed his head with the LMG butt. Feverishly I ready another grenade.

As if in slow motion I see Gregor come racing out of the bush, spit a Russian captain on his bayonet, tear it out and smash the officer's face with the butt. A kick in the crotch and he disappears into the connecting trench.

Up on the heights an SMG rattles unceasingly. A violent blow almost knocks my legs from under me. A bullet has torn off the whole side of the boot. It burns and smarts, but it is only a crease. If that had been an explosive bullet my whole leg would be gone, I think in horror, as I tear the burning leather away. But then I would have been out of it all. Or would I? They are even sending amputees back into action again now.

With wheezing, painful lungs I spurt to the next piece of cover. In a few minutes I have got my wind back again. I am covered with blood. Terrified, I feel myself all over. Nothing wrong.

We run heavily down the narrow trench, throwing hand-grenades into dugout openings.

Mpi's spit death. Half the trench blows up behind us. The trap was sprung a couple of seconds too late. Otherwise none of us would be alive now. A miracle of war.

I find Porta and the Legionnaire in a deep shell hole which is still smoking from the explosion. We load magazines. Fill our pockets, our boot-tops, our belts, with them.

Gregor and Tiny slide down to us. They have a whole bunch of Russian water bottles with them.

' 'Ere's a drink fit for 'eroes,' says Tiny, sharing out the bottles between us. 'The neighbours must've just got their rations when we come visitin'. Pity, ain't it?'

The bear lies down close to Porta. It has a nasty bullet burn across the shoulders. We clean the wound and bandage it. It gets two Russian beers as solace and almost swallows the bottles as well.

'You should see him fight,' says Porta, proudly. 'Sometimes he takes two at a time, and smashes 'em together. They break up as if they were made of glass.'

'*Pravda*'ll make a good story out of this,' laughs the Legionnaire. 'They will say, no doubt, that we have suffered such great losses that we are having to train animals as soldiers.'

'He must *really* be fed up with the Bolshies,' reckons Gregor, scratching the bear's neck. 'What if we were to send him to a meeting of the Party? Be fun if he felt the same way about our golden pheasants!'

'I'm sure he does,' considers Porta. 'Socialist dictatorships are not his cup of tea!'

'Come on then! Come on!' shouts the Old Man, impatiently. 'Peace isn't going to just lie waiting around until you've got time for her, you know!'

The field artillery lays down a close barrage. We press ourselves down into the shell holes. Earth and stones rain on us. We have to keep hard at work digging ourselves out again. There is a stench of picric acid from the exploding H.E. It tears at our throats like the fumes from an acid vat.

The Russians pull back. They run over ground which has been shaved clean. The earth trembles like a wounded beast.

Our heavy artillery at Elipsy is shelling the Russian backward positions. Where these 380mm shells fall they do unspeakable damage. The blast alone is enough to blow a human being to atoms.

I take cover by the side of Julius. He has one of the new MG-42's and is as proud of it as if he had invented it himself.

'Holy Mother of Kazan! This is a *real* German weapon!' He presses his feet against a rock. It is difficult to lie still with the '42. He laughs with glee. 'With a chopper like this a fellow can really show the Bolshies the way home!'

A long burst kicks up the ground in front of us. Scared, we slide rapidly down to the bottom of the shell hole.

'Those *swine*!' snarls Heide, wickedly.

'Gimme coverin' fire,' roars Tiny, from another shell hole.

'Are you ready?' shouts Julius, releasing the safety catch of the '42.

'You just fire your bleedin' gun off, you brownie twit,' screams Tiny, infuriated. 'But don't you 'it *me*, you sod, or I'll 'ave your bleedin' guts for bootlaces!'

Heide fires short well-directed bursts.

Tiny comes thundering. It is a mystery to us how such a mountain of a man can move so fast. He is past us like a whirlwind. As usual he is talking to himself.

'I'm comin' to get you, you wicked sons o' Stalin! It's your own fault, too!'

I jump to my feet and follow him. We climb up an almost vertical slope. Tiny throws the LMG over the brow and swings himself after it.

'Shoot at Tiny would they, the godless bleedin' 'ell'ounds!' He throws two grenades one after the other. 'We got the *German* God on *our* side!' he roars with the full strength of his lungs. 'I'm comin' over an' blow you Soviet arse'oles straight to 'ell!' He empties the LMG in one long, rattling burst. Then he jumps forward into close combat. Skulls crack. 'You should've stayed in bed, Ivan, then you might've kept your brains inside your head!'

The machine-gun barks viciously. Hand-grenades whirl through the air in both directions.

'Get your bleedin' finger out!' rages Tiny, giving me a push that sends me flying forward.

I throw a stick-grenade and rush forward as it explodes.

Julius Heide is at our heels, with the '42 cradled in his arms.

'Goin' like a bomb, ain't it?' screams Tiny, thrusting his combat knife into the middle of an infantryman, who comes up from a dugout with a large loaf under his arm.

I snatch the bread and push it into my belt. There is a little blood on it, but that can be cut off.

We are into the narrow connecting trench. I turn a sharp corner and a Soviet soldier comes rushing at me. Before I know what is happening I am down. A steel-shod boot is swinging at my face.

I have just time to think, this is yours, you've had it! Then the Russian is lifted into the air, his feet kicking at space. There is a horrible sound of bones snapping and his lifeless body falls across me.

A pair of hairy legs brush by me, and a fierce growling pierces even the noise of battle. Porta's bear has saved me.

Two Soviet soldiers gape at the sight of the bear, with a German helmet strapped to its head, coming lolloping along the narrow communicating trench. It rears up and, catching both of them, smashes them together with supernatural force. Then it gallops off again on all fours. It has learned long ago how to take cover from all the whining and screaming pests which infest the air out here. It throws a Russian body into the air and tramples on it when it comes down.

None of us understand what has given it such a terrible hatred of khaki uniforms.

Porta is at its heels. When he peers over the parapet of the trench, the bear stays down behind him watching with interest, but as soon as he goes over the top it is right behind him. When Porta takes cover it imitates him. It does its work like a veteran infantryman, experienced in trench warfare, who never goes into an enemy dugout unless a hand-grenade has gone in first.

A shell from the heavy artillery lands on a mass grave, throwing remnants of bodies to all sides. The whole terrain is like one huge slaughter-house. Torn-off legs, heads and entrails hang in the trees, as if some madman had attempted to decorate them in preparation for a sadistic Christmas.

A whole transport section's trucks and horses are thrown high into the air and explode like giant sparklers. Telephone poles snap like matchsticks. Wires swish through the air. A house splits from top to bottom and falls into dust. A blinding yellow flash lights up the sky. They are blowing up everything behind them. That several hundreds of their own men go with it is apparently of no consequence. Josef Stalin has never concealed the fact that a million lives more or less are of no importance in the big picture. So what does it matter that several hundreds are blown to bits here in pursuance of his plan?

I take my arm well back, and throw the next hand-grenade. We have reached the outskirts of Jassy now. It looks as if the big offensive is going to succeed. The Russians are on the run everywhere, but we will soon have reached the limit of our strength. Cautiously we sneak through the deserted streets. The 104th Rifle Regiment is in the lead. They have to fight their way from house to house.

In front of us is the 6th Motorcyle Regiment and No. 2 Section is lying on the slope down to the river close by the bridge. We are waiting for the signal to move forward again, and this short break saves our lives.

'See them?' cries the Old Man, pointing up at the sky.

A huge formation of bombers is coming in over the town.

Fearfully we press ourselves even more tightly into the slope. The next moment the air is filled with a dreadful howling noise. The long street with tall houses on each side is lifted into the air as if by a giant hand. For a few seconds everything seems to shimmer like a mirage. Then it falls back to earth again with a shattering roar. It is a fantastic sight. People fly across the nearby fields only to be mown down by roaring Jabo's skimming close to the ground.

The great fleet of bombers turns towards the east. It seems to disappear into the sun. The town no longer exists. It has been converted into a rubbish tip of beams, stone, wood and iron, from which project feet, bodies, heads and arms.

A sweetish odour is carried to us on the wind.

'What the military *can* do!' says Tiny, solemnly. ' 'Alf-an-hour ago a nice neat market town, an' now nothin' but a bleedin' great shit 'eap!'

Breathlessly we jump down into a trench, where young Russians lie in rows, killed by a tank salvo. Some of their faces are pushed in, flat as a piece of cardboard. Strangely enough, although they no longer have profiles, they retain their individuality of appearance, and could be recognized. The dead men are young officer cadets who have remained at their posts and have been steam-rollered over by three hundred tanks.

The attack rolls mercilessly onwards. Death takes its toll amongst the ruins. A khaki-clad soldier falls with his hands pressed against his middle. Blood oozes between his fingers.

The little Legionnaire jumps nimbly over him and a short burst from his Mpi accounts for another who comes rushing at him.

'*Vive la mort!*' he screams, fanatically.

Tiny gives a hollow laugh, and splits open the jaw of a captain.

'That'll per'aps learn you not to aim at Tiny from the bleedin' Reeperbahn again, my son!' He drops just in time to avoid catching a burst from an Mpi. 'Treacherous Soviet sods!' he yells, throwing a hand-grenade.

I dash after Porta down into a cellar. Shots ring out. Bullets fly in all directions. Plaster and whitewash spray from the ceiling. Some water-pipes are hit. Fountains of water spurt out over us.

Something comes whirling down the corridor. I grab it and throw it back where it came from. There is a thunderous explosion and a hot wave of air rolls over us.

The Old Man pats me approvingly on the shoulder. If I had not caught that Russian pineapple and thrown it back the whole party would have been killed.

We clean up the cellar rapidly. Those still alive are neckshot irrespective of whether they are civilians or military. We cannot take prisoners and the hard school of experience has taught us that even the seriously wounded can summon up the strength to throw a hand-grenade after those who have just shown them mercy. Dugouts and shelters are gone through with a fine-toothed comb. We grab whatever is useful to us.

Porta is staggering under the weight of two sacks. An aroma of coffee hangs about him.

Tiny drags three heavy wooden cases after him on a wheeled MG carriage. We are like crazy men. It's as if it were Christmas, and the presents just shared out. We open tins of food and stuff ourselves regardless of what the contents are.

A machine-gun rattles viciously. Siberian infantry counterattack, but we managed to dig ourselves in and they meet death in our concentrated defensive fire. For the rest of the afternoon our section of the front is relatively quiet.

Hauptmann von Pader arrives, and tries to be comradely.

'You've done well, Feldwebel Beier,' he flatters. 'I was sorry not to be able to be with you during the latter part of the attack, but I was put out of action by shell-shock,' he explains, with a forced smile.

The Old Man turns on his heel and walks off without either saluting him or answering. Hauptmann von Pader looks wickedly after him.

Tiny gets up noisily. His face is caked with mud and blood. He draws himself to attention in front of his company commander, smashes his heels together and throws up an immaculate training school salute.

'Request the 'err 'auptmann's permission to report in, *sir*!'

223

Hauptmann von Pader grunts something inaudible. Suddenly he realizes who it is standing in front of him. That dreadful half-human creature whom he has sworn never to speak to again. He turns away in disgust, but Tiny follows him stubbornly, marching to attention and saluting.

'Request permission to speak to the 'err 'auptmann, *sir*!'

Silence.

'Request permission to ask, sir, if it's the 'err 'auptmann as be in command o' No. 5 Company, sir?'

Silence. They are moving faster now, but Tiny still needs only one pace to von Pader's two.

'Request permission to tell the 'err 'auptmann, *sir*, as 'e do *look* like the 'err 'auptmann as 'as command o' No. 5, 'e do, sir! Be I wrong, sir?'

Silence.

'Obergefreiter Wolfgang Creutzfeldt, Class IA, reportin' back from doin' battle with they neighbours, *sir*! Beg to report, sir, as 'ow I 'ave done away with four officers. 'Ave also 'ad the pleasure of rollin' up a enemy position, *sir*! Beg to tell the 'err 'auptmann as 'ow I am still in good 'ealth, mind and body, and ready as can be to give they ol' neighbours a good 'un when ordered, *sir*!'

Hauptmann von Pader turns away from him, but Tiny is over on his left-hand side as Regulations lay down. Von Pader can no longer contain himself.

'Are you mad, man? Where the devil did you come from?'

'Beg to report 'err 'auptmann, sir, as 'ow I were born in Sankt Pauli in 'Amburg. There it were as I see day's first light, so to say! Would not say I were mad, in answer to the 'err 'auptmann's question from before, but 'ave always been what might be called a bit wild, like! There's a lot o' things always 'appenin' in the family, sir! Me ol' dad 'e 'ad 'is 'ead chopped off in Moabitt 'e *did*. Me big brother got 'is the very same way. But 'e were done in Fuhlsbüttel. My two sisters, now, they do 'ave a nice little place each with very nice young girls, if the 'err 'auptmann knows what I means, like. On the Reeperbahn they are. But they 'ave got that big in the 'ead they don't 'ave nothin' to do with the rest on us no more, they don't sir! Then the 'err 'auptmann must know as 'ow I come in the Army when I weren't no more'n sixteen years o' age. The 'oly men as were runnin' the school o' correction I were in, they reckoned as 'ow that were the right place for me, sir, they did. They 'ave surely thought as 'ow it wouldn't be long 'fore I were a dead 'un, I'm thinkin', sir. 'Err 'auptmann, sir, I must confess I 'ave been busted all the way down three times, but am still Class IA, an' they 'ave told me as "I" that's for intelligence, but I disremember what that "A" do be for, sir. Beg to report further, sir, as 'ow they do still be stoppin' from my pay . . .'

'Get to hell away from me!' screams von Pader, fumbling for his pistol.

Tiny stands to attention and salutes idiotically.

'Fall down!' screams von Pader. In his rage he can find nothing else to say.

Tiny falls like a log into a puddle of filthy water and sends a wave of mud over von Pader, who screams like a madman.

Tiny is sitting with us a little later, pulling the machine-gun barrel through.

'The bleedin' shit that twit can spew up,' he says, thoughtfully. 'An' 'e'll 'ave a university degree, I'll bet. Thank Jesus I ain't one o' that lot. I couldn't *stand* it, I couldn't!'

'People like him ought to be glad there's such thing as the Army,' remarks Gregor, quietly. 'They'd have their work cut out finding a job if it didn't exist.'

'Yes, they couldn't be used for much else than prison warders,' considers Porta, pouring water into the coffee-pot.

The Legionnaire comes along carrying a beautiful tart he has baked over an open fire.

'What you cooking, Fritz? Smell good!' comes from the Russian positions, only a hundred yards away.

'We're having afternoon coffee,' Porta roars back. 'You're welcome, but you'll have to supply the cognac yourselves!'

For some unexplained reason we are ordered to withdraw to our old position. Everything wasted. As we see it, those who have died have died for nothing. But we're not strategists, just foot-sloggers.

Horses whinny from the other side. The smell of them carries to us on the breeze.

'Bleedin' arse'oles, lads!' cries Tiny. 'They've sent the cavalry to the bleedin' rescue!'

'*C'est la guerre*,' sighs the Legionnaire. 'In war *anything* can happen.'

'A cavalry attack's not the worst thing that could happen,' considers Porta, optimistically. 'We could soon slaughter those steaks on the hoof, and they'd provide us with food for a good while. Salt down a nag and it'll keep for a twelve-month. You've got to remember to boil it though before you roast it. It tastes soggy if you don't.'

'Tell me. Just *how* would you transport a salted-down horse with you?' asks Barcelona, sceptically. 'Something tells me this shop here'll be moving on pretty soon.'

'You maybe haven't noticed my limousine, here,' grins Porta, pointing to the Russian MG carriage. 'All I need now's a couple of rickshaw boys from over the other side, and Obergefreiter (by the grace of God) Joseph Porta'll be able to see Holy Russia in style. Old Tolstoy says you've not got class in Russia if you haven't got a set of wheels under your old botty. Only the working-classes use their poor ol' feet.' He gets up to go over and talk to the new postings, and to tell them how to look after themselves here at the front. It is important for all of us that they are taught, as soon as possible, all the things they *didn't* teach them in garrison. We need them, and are interested in them staying alive as long as possible, and that they don't dash out straight away into an artillery barrage or tread on a mine or some other kind of wickedness.

We only get half the replacements we need. They have been scraping the bottom of the barrel in Germany for a long time. Even the race-conscious Waffen-SS are taking in Russian volunteers. *Untermensch* – until they volunteer. The other day we ran into a unit of German Negroes. They could not speak a word of German. When we explained to them how stupid they looked, they just grinned back happily at us.

Porta is sitting on an abandoned ant hill. The new recruits have made a circle around him.

'First and foremost you must understand that your object in being here is to knock off the enemy and not, repeat not, to allow the enemy to knock off *you*! There's no profit in *that* for

226

the Fatherland. Forget what they taught you at Sennelager. Heroes we've got no use for here. It's brains, not bollocks, you need to get by in this branch, and *never*, *never* forget that our heathen neighbour knows all the tricks in the book too! The only edge you can get is by bein' faster than the other fellow. Kill anything that's not wearing a German uniform. If in doubt, the slightest *trace* of doubt, then shoot, an' shoot to *kill*! Don't, repeat don't, go rushing forward at the drop of a hat. Those boys load with live rounds, remember, an' they're just aching to snip your life-line over with a well-aimed lead pill. When we go over the top, visitin' Ivan, keep your eyes open for a good hole. Never move before you know where your next piece of cover is, and when you've reached it take good care to find out soonest, repeat *soonest*, where fire's comin' from. Aim, but for the Holy Elizabeth's sake, aim quick. Fire then and get it over with *quick*, or you'll never fire again, my sons! Ivan says Adolf's boys're losin' a man a minute. If it was true the war'd soon be over, so maybe I wish it was, so what's left of us could go home, but unfortunately Ivan's as big a liar as we are. Lies an' war go together, and there's nothin' we can do about *that*! Lying's a Godgiven thing, and as such we've got to use it. *But!* The most important thing out here is to be faster than the neighbours. If you *are*, then you'll stay alive. When you shoot, shoot to kill! A partly dead man – or woman – is still a danger to you. He'll go happy to hell if he can take one of you with him.' Porta holds up his entrenching tool. 'Hang on to this. It's one of the best tools the Army ever gave you. Dig in with it first chance you get. Every spadeful of earth you move lengthens your life. It can split an enemy's skull open for you. It's an excellent frying pan. In a tank you can use it to shit on and keep the deck clean. It'll fry a pretty good egg. Don't use grease on it. Clean it with sand, earth or grass.' He puts down the spade, and holds up a Russian *kalashnikov*. 'When you're out visitin', to see if Ivan's putting on weight, maybe, take care of your Mpi. Don't shoot her off blindly. Looks good in the movies, but it's quite different in reality. The bullets you shoot out of an Mpi fan out, *but fast*, from her muzzle. There's no difficulty at all in shooting ten of your own mates in the back, *at relatively short distance*, with one burst from your Mpi, if you don't *know* what it can do! And don't just stand staring like a bloody cow if Ivan pops up under your nose. Club, shoot or stab him! Think about it afterwards when you've got the time! Out here you haven't.

'Don't take pity on a wounded neighbour. He'll shoot your head off, like as not, while you're helping him up. Don't go into a house without sweepin' it clean first with your Mpi or a grenade, and most important of all: if you're doin' sentry duty at the front don't, *just don't*, even wink an eye for a second. Cats sound like a herd of elephants compared with those boys moving, and if they get their fingers on you then you've *had* it! When they've got what they want out of you – and they will – you get a bullet! Prisoners are a nuisance in a trench war.

'Now we might likely, more'n likely, get attacked by tank units. If we do, then don't, repeat *don't*, leave your hole in the ground. Make yourself flatter'n a flounder. Begin to run and you're sure of gettin' yourself killed. There's a lot of things been invented lately, but they ain't invented the man who can run faster'n a machine-gun bullet, *yet*! Somebody's coming at you and you're in doubt what side he's on then shoot him! If you've made a mistake, and he's one of ours, too bad! Comfort yourself with the thought he wouldn't have lived long anyway! If you see one of the trench-boys on the other side taking a stroll, enjoying nature, don't, *please* don't, pick him off. He's on his own muck-heap. If you kill him it's murder. What's more to the point his mates'll see to it the score gets evened up with one of us!

'Well that's enough of that! Find out the rest of it yourselves. The dummies won't last more'n a fortnight anyway.'

He goes a little way along the communicating trench and then stops. Scratching Rasputin behind the ear, he addresses them again.

'There's one other small thing, though. Always, repeat *always*, keep the part of you that holds your ears apart below the edge of the trench. Ignore this piece of advice and you can stop worryin' about your next leave. Ivan's snipers *never* sleep. Just show your nut and you've got an explosive in it.'

He laughs noisily, and moves away together with the bear. At the angle of the trench he turns again and says: 'Hey you shits, listen here. If you see a body with gold teeth it's mine. Report it immediately!'

'Isn't that forbidden?' asks a seventeen-year-old rooky with the HJ³ emblem in gold on his chest.

'Yes, if *you* pinch 'em, son. *Then* it's strictly forbidden,' laughs Porta loudly.

In the course of the night we take over Demon Heights. We relieve a police-regiment which has been almost wiped out in the course of four days. They look like zombies. You look like that when you've been under artillery fire for several days. They stagger off down the long trench. Old, old men, all of them!

Tiny looks after them and gives Gregor a push.

'Knocked the shit out o' the bleedin' coppers, ain't it? Not as easy as beatin' up drunks.'

'Don't like Schupos do you?' asks Gregor.

'No. I would not say as 'ow there's been much love lost between us ever,' grins Tiny, spitting after them.

Porta has got a piece of shrapnel in the leg. He digs it out with his combat knife and tucks it into his wallet.

'Think if that got a fellow in the head,' he philosophizes. 'Stop your farting in church, wouldn't it?'

'Luck, that's what it's all about,' says Tiny, picking his teeth with his bayonet.

'If you've got luck, even a little bit of it, the shrapnel 'its your leg 'stead o' your napper. A little bit *more* luck, an' it don't do no real damage, even.'

'Think if it'd nipped off your old dingle-dangle,' laughs Gregor, 'and you'd had nothing to tickle the girls up with any more!'

'Holy Vera of Paderborn,' cries Porta, horrified, 'I'd rather take it in the napper. Women and me can't live without one another. We *belong* together, if I may put it that way!'

'Now you're talking about women,' the Old Man joins the conversation. 'The clerk says there's a theatre group coming to visit the Army Corps.'

'*Now* you tell us. And us on Demon Heights,' wails Porta.

The cook's runners roll down into the trench, shaking with

3. HJ (Hitler Jugend): Hitler Youth Organization.

shock. Crossing the open stretch two of them have been hit. Three of the containers have been cut open, and half the rations have been lost.

'You twits've been stuck up one another's arsehole making a lovely target for the bloody heathen, I suppose!' Porta scolds them furiously. *Food* has been wasted.

'Why the bleedin' 'ell couldn't you 'ave stuck your fingers in the 'oles, then we'd at least've got somethin' to eat,' snarls Tiny, throwing a helmet at the nearest runner.

Everybody is angry at the food having been lost. The bear almost takes an arm off one of the cooks. Our section gets by, thanks to Porta who has surrounded some Russian tinned rations. They are half-rotten but still eatable. Only Gregor complains, but he has been used to general officer's rations.

'You'd have to have been in *their* bloody Army a long time to eat *that* shit,' he shouts, disgustedly, throwing a tin far out into no-man's-land.

The bear has the best of it. Porta has got hold of half a pail of honey. Two bone-dry army loaves are broken up and mixed with it. The bear gets outside it in record time.

There must be something big coming up. A stream of replacements are coming in from Germany. Since 1939 the regiment has never been so close to being up to strength, but the replacements are poor stuff. Much too young or much too old and with only sketchy training. There are even invalids amongst them. A stiff leg is no handicap any more. The German Army is mechanized, so what? Who *needs* two legs?

In the first hour three of the replacements blow themselves to bits in our own minefields. They are blown up so effectively that nobody can be bothered to look for the pieces of their bodies. The others sit down in the dugouts paralysed with fright. They want to go home, they say.

'Us too go home!' laughs Porta. 'It's thataway!' he points a thumb to the west. 'But we're not going. We're staying here. Here we *know* who the enemy is. Back there they've got watchdogs ready to string people up on a branch of the nearest tree!'

When the mortar fire begins, as usual at around five o'clock, the rookies go mad and begin to bang their heads into the walls of the dugouts. We have to knock them unconscious. Just at present things are comparatively quiet. The mortars they only put on for the sake of appearances. We reply with grenades merely to hear the noise of them. In our opinion we're having a real holiday. We can sit peacefully in the bottom of the trench enjoying the sunshine. We are having beautiful autumn weather. Yesterday three hares came right to the edge of our trench and looked at us. Tiny ran one of them down. Not even Ivan's snipers shot at him during that fantastic race across no-man's-land. When he holds it up proudly by the ears a cheer goes up from both sides of the line and steel helmets whirl into the air. It's not every foot-slogger who can run down a hare. So we are having roast hare for dinner today. Porta makes the sauce, and potato mash with diced pork, and we feel like millionaires.

Tiny has got hold of some cigars. He went past the office where they had been careless enough to leave a window open, and commandeered a whole box which had been left on the sill. We know that they are the property of Hauptmann von Pader. This makes them taste twice as good.

There is a nasty rumbling in the distance. They're dropping at least fifteen miles away but still the ground trembles where we are.

The good weather continues, but the whole front seems strangely nervous and sniping increases. In one day there have been nine shot through the head in our company alone.

Porta holds up a helmet and immediately there is a hole in it, but Tiny gets the sniper.

When we pass through the open machine-gun posts we have to move like lightning. The Siberian snipers are trained in on these spots, and even though we have warned the rookies they still get two of them in the course of the afternoon. This kind of thing annoys us. It seems so unnecessary. A bayonet in you during an attack we can understand, but this sniping business is damnable.

Hauptmann von Pader is sitting half-dead with fear down in the company deep shelter. Whenever a shell goes off close by he throws himself flat on the ground with his hands over his ears. We regard him with contempt. A tough and ruthless commander we can respect, but not a coward. Oberst Hinka has sent for him twice, but von Pader sends back the excuse that the artillery fire is too heavy for him to be able to get through to Regimental HQ. The orderly who tells us this almost dies laughing. He is Oberst Hinka's personal Obergefreiter Müller, called Little Jesus because he *looks* like Jesus. Together with a battalion orderly he has picked a whole pail of raspberries on the way from Regimental HQ to the front line.

'It's that peaceful you could set up a bloody knocker out there!'

'Isn't the oberst doing his nut about this yellow bastard not comin' runnin' when he sends for him?' asks Barcelona, wonderingly.

'He's hoppin' bloody mad, he is,' laughs Little Jesus, 'but this von Pader shit has got such good connections in Admiral Schröder Strasse that he can shit on obersts both before and after breakfast.'

Tiny loves the early mornings. He is always first up. We live like the best families on the French Riviera, with coffee and toast every morning. We go hunting too, but not often with any luck. The war has taught the game a few things, speeded the animals up, but we do manage to hit a wild boar. We roast it and the aroma wafts along the whole front. Two of the Ivans run over to us. They have cucumbers with them.

All night long we can hear motors roaring over on the other side. They are getting ready for something. If they mount an attack with tanks we'll be finished. Our spotting planes have reported long columns on the move, some with up to 200 tanks. They are the new Josef Stalin tanks.

Panzerfausts[4] are issued, a suicide weapon. They look very effective in the propaganda films, but the reality is quite otherwise. If you ever hit a tank with one you can be dead certain of getting smashed by the next tank. In most cases the rocket glances off, and before you get the chance to load again you're getting mixed up with the tank's tracks. But, by now, we've been so long at the front we don't worry about what's going to happen an hour from now.

Tiny leans up against the assault ladder and sings to the music of Porta's piccolo:

4. Panzerfaust: German bazooka.

232

Der Sieg ging an uns vorbei,
verbrannte uns die Finger.
Zum Todesschmaus der Wodka fliesst,
doch niemand ist betrunken . . . [5]

A machine-gun coughs long and viciously. The trench mortars spit out their bombs.

Porta takes the piccolo from his lips and looks into the periscope.

'Sounds as if they've got something up their sleeves for us,' he says, thoughtfully.

'Let's send 'em a couple o' callin' cards,' suggests Tiny, 'to stop 'em gettin' too bleedin' big in the bonce. They've just got replacements in over there. Pissy bleedin' Guards, from Moscow, sent out to get a whiff o' powder 'fore it's too late. You've all seen 'em. Collar an' tie bleeders, who're frightened they might lose the crease in their trousers and ain't tried shittin' their pants yet.' He screws the grenade cup on his rifle and sends a couple over. The Maxim goes silent.

Tiny laughs hollowly, lies back against the ladder again and continues his song:

Aufs Wohl ist erster Trunk,
und darauf folgt der zweite,
der fünfte und der zehnte, – dann
der bittere, der Abschiedsschluck . . . [6]

The expected attack does not develop. The days go by and the good weather continues. None of us dare think of the winter, the third Russian winter. No one who has not been through a Russian winter in the trenches can know what winter really is. But now the sun is shining and hares and rabbits gambol behind the front line.

5. Victory passed us by;
Burnt our fingers on its way.
At the death-feast vodka flows,
But not a man gets drunk.
6. The first toast is Farewell!
And then the second follows.
The fifth – the tenth – and then
The bitter stirrup cup . . .

233

Porta and Tiny get hold of an electric hailer and amuse themselves with the Russians.

'*Russki tovaritsch!*' roars Porta, so that it echoes along the front. 'We know you have to use gravel to wipe your arseholes dry with! Come over to us, an' we'll show you how to polish 'em with ni-i-i-ce, so-o-o-oft, shit'ouse paper!'

'Fritz! Fritz, your old sausage women are getting sausages stuffed up the other end from the sausage boys at home,' comes back from the other side.

'That's *great!*' Tiny howls back happily. 'They'll be well greased for us lot when we get back to 'em!'

'Ivan you crazy *alik*,[7] what *do* you think the boys at home are doin' while you dummies are fartin' about here?' shouts Porta. 'Why, they're fuckin' your bandy-legged old Tartar mares all to bits. There'll only be bones an' hair left of it when *you* get back!'

An angry burst of machine-gun fire is the answer.

'Ivan, Ivan, 'ow can we *take* you anywhere?' Tiny shouts reproachfully. 'Don't bite the 'and that's feedin' you good advice!'

For hours they continue, tirelessly, without repeating themselves once.

'Hey, neighbour, you old tramp, you! Scrape the shit out of your ears and hear the news,' shouts Porta. 'We're comin' visiting tonight. We've taken the edge off our knives so it'll take longer to saw your throats open!'

'Fritz, bighead! It's us that are coming over to chop off your tiny little pricks and take 'em back to Moscow to give the girls a laugh!'

A few days later these shouted exchanges are forbidden by Regimental HQ. Instead we throw hand-grenades with insults written on them.

The earth shudders as if in an earthquake when a 380mm shell drops on the section of trenches next to ours.

'Holy Mother of God, those things can certainly dig up a potato patch,' cries Gregor admiringly, following with his eyes the course of the bodies thrown high into the air.

Ten minutes later another one drops, this time even closer to

7. Alik: Russian slang for the male sexual organ.

us. The blast wave hits us like a hot wind and throws Barcelona to the floor of the trench.

'God's death,' he mumbles as he gets up. 'Better have a little chat with the sky-pilot, maybe, so's to be ready for a sudden departure!'

'What about strengthening the sentries?' asks the Legionnaire, looking at the Old Man, who is sucking thoughtfully at his silver-lidded pipe.

'It appears that this war, which has been forced upon us, will be conducted with increasing violence,' Gregor imitates the tone of the Wehrmacht communiques.

At eleven o'clock I relieve Porta at the SMG. It is quiet again along the front. We cannot understand what the violent shelling meant.

Far to the south there is an unceasing rumble of shell-fire, and the entire horizon is a bloody red. Perhaps they are trying to make a break-through there. If they succeed we'll be left hanging in the air. Before long they will be behind us.

'Watch out, keep awake,' the Old Man instructs me when I take over sentry duty. 'They captured two men from the boys next to us last night, without so much as a squeak out of them. They've got a depressed gun just over there. They have a go with it now and again, so keep well down behind the parapet.'

'Nice work if you can get it,' I answer, pulling the hood up over my helmet. It is cold at night.

Mist rises from the marshy ground. Fear is a dead weight in the stomach.

The Old Man pats me encouragingly on the shoulder and disappears silently around the elbow of the trench to check the other sentries.

Now I am alone and scared. Through the periscope I can just see the Russian lines. I can feel the presence of the forward posts. Everything seems peaceful, and not at all dangerous, but as a veteran of the trenches I know that there is nothing at the front which is not dangerous. Death never takes a holiday.

The front is dozing with a faint rumbling noise like a heavy snoring. A couple of magnesium flares light up the terrain. In their glare I can clearly see the sunken road behind the Russian position. Death Alley we call it. It is paved with bodies. The position is not called Demon Heights for nothing. It is not really a hill but the brow of a ten-mile-long fold in the ground.

I turn the periscope. Bodies everywhere. Hundreds of skeletons and partly mummified corpses. They lie singly, and in heaps, covered with reddish-yellow filth. Just in front of me a boot projects from the ground. The rest of the body is buried in the earth. It is a German boot. A little farther out, a skull grins at me from beneath the brim of a Russian helmet. Over there an arm, with a rag of grey-green uniform fluttering from it. The fingers of the hand point accusingly at the heavens. A young German Jaeger lies across a torn-off gun wheel. The weight of his pack stretches his body in a bow. The wind plays with his hair, which is longer than regulation length. He screamed for a whole day and died last night. Several of the company tried to bring him in but had to give up and come back with an empty stretcher. The Siberian snipers do not know the meaning of mercy.

Wherever I turn the periscope I see bones, joints, arms stripped of their flesh, hands, vertebrae, grinning skulls, staring, glassy eyes under battered helmets, fresh corpses, corpses half rotted away, corpses, expanded by the gases of degeneration, which burst like balloons if one happens to tread on one of them. The breeze carries a sweet, sickening stench over to me.

I become sleepy, have terrible difficulty in staying awake. My eyelids feel heavy and inflamed, but it is dangerous to doze off. Not only is it punishable by death, but also in the mere wink of an eye they can be on top of you. They can have rolled up a whole trench before I know where I am. It has often happened that two whole enemy companies have sneaked up on a trench company, and once they are down in the trench not many are left alive.

I press my tired eyes against the rubber eyepiece surround of the periscope, wriggle my toes in my boots, bite my lips, do everything I can think of to keep myself awake. I count the bodies again. Are there more than there were? I am wide awake in an instant. Fear trickles like ice-water down my spine. For a moment I think I see dark shapes. I count them again and keep an eye on the bodies. It is an old trick, moving forward pushing a body in front of you.

A couple of shells explode in bursts of flame just behind the line. Lines of tracer come whistling from a hidden MG. A mortar barks with a hollow sound. Then everything goes quiet again. A rabbit, grown accustomed to war, hops down towards the reeds, stopping to sniff at the dead German Jaeger. Its long ears turn, first towards the Russian position, then towards the German.

A shot sounds. The rabbit rolls over and over. I have seen the muzzle-flash. It is enough for me. I sense him, jumping up in the air, over there. I hit him. He won't shoot any more rabbits. God knows who he was? How he lived? Was he young? He was, at any rate, a Guardsman, and belonged to the fanatics.

I examine the MG. Check that all the belts are filled. Our lives depend on this. I look through the periscope. Something is moving. Movement in no-man's-land means enemies. I have the flare pistol in my hand. Should I send a light up for safety's sake? My front-line instinct warns me. Every nerve in my body responds to the alarm.

'Pop! Whi-i-sh!' the signal flare spreads a ghostly white light over the dead, lying out there in the shattered landscape.

Now I am quite sure. There is something not as it should be out in no-man's-land. In one leap I am over at the SMG, tear the canvas cover off and snap the lock. Cautiously I bend down. The snipers have got the new infra-red sighting telescope and a Siberian sniper does not need much time to take a human life.

The MG rattles wickedly. A long pearly row of tracer hastens towards the Russian position. An explosive bullet goes off close to me. I drop, in fear, to the bottom of the trench. I pick up my Mpi and wait a moment before showing the helmet above the parapet.

'Crack!' comes the shot immediately.

Splinters of steel whizz about my ears. The helmet spins from the muzzle of the carbine. There is a sizeable hole in its side. He is observing my area. He knows I am here. Now the question is, is he just an ordinary murderer, or do the shots have a much more dangerous meaning? A patrol out clearing up, or perhaps sent out to take prisoners?

I lie, quiet as a mouse, and wait. I cannot see very far to either side along the connecting trench, but years in the front line have sharpened my hearing. I could hear a cat coming on tip-toe. I have readied my Mpi, and press myself close to the wall of the trench. I screw the caps off two grenades, for safety's sake. Our patrol must also be on the way, but they do not make much noise either. I can hear them now. They are at least four bends away.

'Password!' I dare not make the challenge loud. The chaps across the road must not hear it.

'Shit and shankers!' comes Gregor's soft reply. That is better than any password. I recognize the voice.

Suddenly Tiny is in front of me pushing his Mpi into my stomach. I let out a soft cry of fright. I neither heard nor saw him. He must have floated in.

The patrol has two new recruits along. They are to relieve sentries alongside me. Heide gives them explicit instructions.

'Don't show your heads above the parapet, or your lives'll be bloody short ones!'

The patrol disappears as silently as it came.

'If you catch a woman soldier, give me a shout!' calls Porta. 'We'll all bang her before we send her back.'

'Send 'er *back*?' Tiny shouts in annoyance. 'What do you mean send 'er back? What's Rasputin done, then? Ain't 'ad a fuck in a month o' Sundays *that* poor bleedin' bear ain't!'

The Old Man scolds us softly. He doesn't like filthy talk.

I can hear the rookies talking. They are crazy and it is very, very dangerous. If the kidnap squads are out, the noise of voices is an invitation, and who is to say they are not lying out in no-man's-land waiting their chance?

Over on the enemy side a steel helmet is moving about oddly. I watch it inquisitively through the periscope. It disappears for a moment. Then it comes into view again, alongside the opening where they have placed an SMG. That fellow must be the world's prize chump I think, and feel a burning urge to let go at him. A dangerous hunting fever flames up in me. The sniping rifle is already in my hand, but front line instinct warns me. Suddenly I dare not even move over to the SMG. There is something I don't understand about that bobbing helmet. It draws me like a magnet, yet, at the same time, it shouts a silent warning at me. I have my rifle half up, but lower it cautiously again. The recruits in the section next to me have also seen the helmet. The dangerous hunting lust has also taken hold of them. They have never before fired at a live human target. Shaking with excitement they camouflage a firing slit with twigs and sods of grass. Carefully they rest their carbines in it. They are wildly excited. Silently they agree to fire one after the other.

Calmly the first of them presses the stock of the carbine against his cheek, takes the first pull, restrains his breathing; all exactly as he has been taught on the range at Sennelager.

His comrade waits his turn anxiously. It will be their first Russian. Something to write home about, at least.

'Ping!' sounds the shot.

A long whine, and a rain of sparks explodes before the eyes of the marksman. A violent blow knocks his head back. He is dead before he hits the bottom of the trench.

His comrade gives a frightened shout, and stands up. At the moment he rises he feels a blow on the side of his head, as if from a piece of red-hot iron. His helmet flies far away and the explosive bullet tears off half his face.

I realize what has happened as soon as I hear the scream and sound the alarm.

The whole section arrives at the double, Porta working feverishly at the flame-thrower as he runs.

'What the hell's up?' asks the Old Man, excitedly. 'Where's Ivan?'

'The slit-eyed bastards've knocked off the two new boys,' I answer.

'Fools!' says Heide, annoyed. 'And I *told* them to keep their heads down.'

'*C'est la guerre*,' sighs the Legionnaire, tiredly. 'You can talk till you're speechless, and still they don't – or *won't* – under-stand. They've got to learn the hard way before it sticks and then it's usually too late.'

Stretcher-bearers remove the bodies and the guard goes back to the dugout. Soon the brief intermezzo is forgotten.

I whittle at a walking stick to keep myself awake. Everybody is making walking sticks whilst on sentry duty. Some of them are real works of art. Behind the lines they are willing to pay almost anything you ask for one of these beautiful sticks. *Volchow* sticks they call them. Not because they have been made by that particular river, but because that was where the soldiers first began to make them.

A line of clouds marches across the moon, and everything goes completely dark. A couple of puffs of wind blow in, carrying dirt from no-man's-land with them.

The tin-cans hanging from the barbed wire defences rattle warningly, as if someone was trying to break through. I stare into the periscope and listen intently, but I can neither see nor hear anything. It *must* be the wind, I think, attempting to calm myself.

The marshy ground, south-east of our positions, lies in pitchy darkness. It is said that they have constructed a path through it below ground level. The Russians are good at that kind of devilishness.

There is an hour for me to get through before my relief comes. The watch I have caught is the worst one of all. Two to four. The death watch we call it. If anything at all happens it happens then. Still, if they had been going to pull any tricks tonight they would have been pulled already, I think to myself. I slide a few berries from the grass stalk I have threaded them on. Everybody is plucking berries and threading them on grass stalks. Porta has collected two large pailsful of berries. We are planning to steal a cook-pot from the QM and make schnapps out of them. We have sugar, and yeast is easy to get hold of.

I shoot off a rocket for the sake of appearances. As it floats down the rocket reveals a fantastic sight. The only trouble is you get even more nervous when the magnesium flare goes out, and darkness sweeps down on you again. The rocket also has the effect of bringing the front to life again for a short while.

Nervous trigger fingers contract and send bullets fleeting out over the shell-torn ground. With bad luck it could be the last rocket one's sent up.

The lowered cannon thunders and a series of explosive shells strike behind the maze of entrenchments. Shrapnel whizzes over my head and buries itself in the walls of the trench. Then all is quiet again.

A faint noise further along the connecting trench makes me start. Pebbles rattle down to the floor of the trench. In a second I become a beast of prey, taut and expectant with all my senses wide open, ready to receive impressions. Can it be the patrol on its way back? Or is it some crazy officer who thinks he is still in garrison and is out inspecting the guard? More than a few new officers have lost their lives in this fashion. It is highly dangerous to move around in the trench network at night. It would be just like von Pader to do that very thing. He would love to catch a sentry napping.

I cock my Mpi, safety off, decide to shoot if it does happen to be von Pader. Nobody can prove I recognized him. It would never be murder, merely self-defence. He wouldn't be the first idiot to have been killed by a nervous sentry.

By now I am quite sure there is somebody in the communicating trench. I hear metal clink on metal. I catfoot a little way further along the trench. The night is black as ink. I can see no more than a few yards in front of me. An animal screams from the marshes. There is an answering scream from close at hand.

'Who goes there? The password!' I shout, nervously.

No reply.

I can perceive a large shadow, a little further along the trench. I press the trigger but the gun merely clicks. The lost fraction of a second is enough to bring the world falling down around me.

A broad dark form bounds at me. The barrel of the Mpi is pushed to one side. To struggle to hold on to it would be madness, the end of me.

I let go of the weapon and push the attacker's Mpi to one side, just as he has done mine.

A series of shots explode into the air. A bullet tears the collar from my great-coat. At the same time something hits me hard in the stomach, but I am still mobile and let out a kick which gets him in the crotch. He is an officer. I feel the broad shoulder-straps under my hands. I pull him towards me by them and crash the brim of my helmet into his face. A Danish kiss, they call it. I didn't learn it in Denmark but at the battle school at Senne.

Fear of death gives me superhuman strength. I bite, kick, and tear with my nails. My helmet flies off. My Mpi has gone the same way. I cannot reach the combat knife in my boot.

The Russian officer has a slight edge on me for size and he is as fast as lightning.

'Ssvinja,' he snarls, grinding his teeth and trying to put me out with a swing of his edged hand. I twist to one side and his hand hits a stone. He curses viciously.

I manage to jolt my knee up between his legs. He falls forward and I sink my teeth into his throat. Blood runs down over my face but I don't notice it. I am fighting for my life. He struggles desperately to tear himself loose, but I clamp my teeth together like a mad bulldog. My mouth fills with his blood. He makes a long rattling noise and a terrible shiver goes through his body. I have bitten his throat out. There are whole rows of figures behind him. They push and shove but the trench is too narrow for them to pass one another.

I suddenly realize that they are afraid to shoot as long as we lie entangled with one another in the bottom of the trench.

'Help!' I scream, in horror. 'Ivan's got me! Help!'

An Mpi chatters furiously close by.

'*Job tvojemadj! Khrúpkij djávol!*[8]'

'Help!' I shout with all my might. 'Help! Ivan's in the trench!'

I wriggle underneath the body of the dead Russian and get hold of his Mpi. I turn it towards the others and pull the trigger but the magazine is empty. With all my strength I hammer the muzzle into the face of the foremost of them. With a shrill scream he collapses. His face is a bloody ruin.

'*Job tvojemadj!*' sounds furiously from the others.

They rush towards me. The first of them knocks me head over heels with the butt of his Mpi. They don't want me alive any more. Their kidnap patrol has failed in its object. Now their aim is to get back with whole skins and to kill as many of us as possible whilst doing it.

A spade chops down less than an inch from my face. I avoid

8. Khrúpkij djávol: (Russian): Crazy devil.

242

it by rolling over. A steel-shod boot hits my shoulder. I creep under the SMG and my hands fall on my own Mpi. I am almost crazed with fear. I cock it like lightning. Get it off a few times. A tall thin soldier in a green NKVD cap knocks me off my feet again. He tries to stab me with his combat knife. The others are right behind him. A machete swishes through the air, striking my Mpi and showering sparks up and around us.

'*Job Tvojemadj! Djávol!*'

'Help! Help!'

The soldier in the green cap raises his combat knife. It is one of the long Siberian knives, double-edged and deadly.

'*Finished!*' flies through my brain.

The butt of a weapon crashes down, crushing green cap's shoulder. He falls back into the arms of his comrades.

I smash the Mpi muzzle into his face. The sight slashes it open lengthwise. Flame shoots from the muzzle. The chest of the nearest Russian is torn open. I change magazines, tear back the bolt, and the Mpi rattles again for a moment before going on strike.

'Bloody German shit,' I curse it. A cartridge has jammed. I use it as a club.

'Fire along the trench!' I hear Porta shout.

'I'm in the elbow,' I scream. 'Shoot for Christ's sake! They're murdering me.'

I am bathed in noise. Blue muzzle-flames spit from the darkness.

I rush forward and fall over a Russian lying in the bottom of the trench. At first I think he is dead, but he is fully alive and only taking cover from the desperate fire in the narrow trench. Like a steel spring he shoots up and aims a blow at me with the spade. I manage to kick him in the face. It cracks open like an egg. Madly I kick him until he is dead.

The fighting in the narrow trench is desperate. Every man burns with blind rage. We strike, kick, stab, bite! When our magazines are empty there is no time to change them. We use our weapons as clubs.

Through the din we hear Tiny's murderous battle-cry:

'Slaughter 'em! Slaughter 'em!'

'*Vive la mort!*'

243

Porta comes rushing helter-skelter with the bear at his heels. It catches hold of two Russians and smashes them together. The bodies it throws whirling up into the air. It snarls murderously and shows its terrible teeth. Mpi's bark devastatingly in the close confines of the trench. Any minute hand-grenades may come flying through the air and tear us to pieces. If the Russians once get out of the trench they won't bother about their comrades, alive or dead. They'll use grenades, and grenades have a terrible effect in the confined space of a trench.

I have got hold of a Russian Mpi. One which works.

A man appears down by the long trench.

I shoot immediately friend or foe. He goes down with a sickening death-scream. I smear my boot across his face. It is better than risking a hand-grenade coming after me.

We hear hoarse commands in Russian, and running steps rapidly disappearing.

'Kill 'em, the shits!' screams Porta, from the darkness, and an Mpi spits blue flame.

From the other side comes a whole series of shots.

'I've got me a 'eathen!' roars Tiny. 'Call bleedin' Rasputin off 'im, willya. The bleeder's eatin' me prisoner!'

'*Stoi*, up with your hands!' howls Gregor, excitedly, pointing his Mpi at me.

'Don't shoot, you twit! It's Sven!'

'You were lucky,' he grins, panting. 'I was just getting ready to send you straight to the Russian district of hell!'

'See what I bleedin' found,' shouts Tiny, pleased, as he appears dragging with him a giant of a man in the uniform of a Russian lieutenant.

'Has he got any gold teeth?' asks Porta, with interest, bending over the prisoner. 'I've been told that the ten best at the officer training schools get their traps filled up with gold to show they belong to the elite.'

Tiny grips the cursing officer by the throat.

'Open up, *djádja*[9] so we can see if you're in the top ten or only a bleedin' *durák*[10].'

The Russian officer bites Tiny viciously in the hand.

9. Djádja (Russian): Uncle.
10. Durák (Russian): Dummy.

'I don't know whether 'e's got gold teeth or not, but sharp they bleedin' are,' snarls Tiny, wiping the blood from his hand.

'Where in the world did they come from?' asks the Old Man, examining the terrain through the periscope.

'Obvious! Through the marshes,' answers Heide, in a superior tone.

' 'Struth,' cries Barcelona in amazement. 'They must've had canoes on their feet to get through that lot.'

'How did you discover them?' asks the Old Man, looking at me.

'I just don't know. All of a sudden there they were.' I wipe the sweat from my face with my sleeve. The reaction is coming now.

'Was it you bit the throat out of that NKVD chap?' asked Barcelona, admiringly.

I nod and begin to throw up violently.

'*Pas mal, mon ami*,' the Legionnaire praises me and pats me on the shoulder. 'A man can do much with his teeth when he has to.'

'I bit a bleedin' 'orse once,' announces Tiny, solemnly. 'It was when I was with the bleedin' dragoons. A white bleedin' 'orse, as the band 'ad, fixes 'is choppers in me chest, when we're supposed to be gettin' matey, like. I stopped 'is fartin' in church for 'im I did!'

' "Bite me will you, you bleedin' goat!" I shouts into 'is long 'orse's bleedin' face, an' I sinks me teeth into 'is nose. Up 'e goes on 'is 'ind-legs with me followin' 'im up 'angin' on with me teeth for dear life. It took two bleedin' *wachtmeisters* to get me off the white bleeder. Then the dragoons wouldn't 'ave me no longer an' sent me to the infantry who didn't keep me very long neither. They 'ad 'orses as pulled the machine-guns an' they used to get 'ay-fever whenever I came near 'em. So that's 'ow I wound up in a Panzer bleedin' Regiment.'

Hauptmann von Pader comes trotting up in his squeaky boots. He has even put on his spurs and has a riding whip under his arm. He stops in front of me, spreads his feet, and looks me up and down with a sneer.

'So it was you, you Jonah, on sentry duty? Why the devil didn't you sound the alarm?'

'Beg to report, sir, I had no time to sound the alarm. They were down in the trench before I observed them!'

'Are you insane, man?' he screams, and his little, chinless face puckers into a grimace. 'Do you mean to say that the Russian *untermensch* can surprise a German soldier? Isn't it true that you left your post without permission?'

'No, sir, I have at no time been absent from my post!'

He takes a gold cigarette case from his pocket and taps a perfumed cigarette thoughtfully against the lid. Arrogantly he lights the cigarette and blows smoke into my face.

'If you did not leave your post then you were asleep at it,' he states shortly.

'In no other circumstances could the *untermensch* have got down into the trench. I shall see to it that you go before a court-martial.'

'Herr Hauptmann, sir, I will guarantee that this man has not been asleep at his post!' the Old Man breaks in.

'Have I asked your opinion?' shouts the Company Commander, in a rage. For a moment he looks as if he is going to hit the Old Man with his riding whip.

'Sir, I am i/c this section, and it is my duty to defend my men if they are abused without cause!'

'*So!* That is your duty is it? I am perhaps to ask your permission before addressing one of your swine? It is your duty to keep your mouth shut and speak only when you are spoken to.'

'As long as I'm in charge of this section I shall speak up on behalf of my men,' answers the Old Man, clenching his jaws. 'I will not permit them to be called out without cause!'

'You are relieved from your duties as section commander. You will be charged with mutiny.'

'Oh shut up, you stupid shit,' comes jeeringly from somewhere in the ranks. 'We'll soon pull your arsehole up over your ears!'

'Who said that? One pace forward, that man!' screams von Pader in a shrill voice.

'It was the wicked ol' witch of the swamp,' shouts Porta, cheerily. 'She'll come and rub mud all over your little mary, she will, one of these days!'

'The whole company will be charged with insubordination,'

howls von Pader, and flies off down the communication trench. 'You will all be in front of a firing squad before long!' he shouts from a safe distance.

Porta throws a Russian hand-grenade after him, without removing the pin.

Von Pader screams wildly in terror and throws himself down into the mud so fast that it splatters up above the trench parapets. He crawls off on hands and knees.

'Joke's gone too far,' the Old Man prophesies, ominously. 'He's got pals in Berlin who can make it hot for us!'

'Shit!' says Tiny, optimistically. 'We got bleedin' mates in the Führer's 'eadquarters, ain't we?'

'Who the devil do *you* know at the Führer's HQ?' asks Barcelona in surprise.

'The Führer 'imself as God 'as sent to lead us, o' course,' says Tiny, looking down his nose at him and kicking a skull out of his way.

Hauptmann von Pader goes personally to Oberst Hinka to charge No. 5 Company with mutiny. He has a senior NCO, Unteroffizier Baum, with him as witness.

Oberst Hinka receives them lying on a field cot, and listens, without a word, to the stream of words which pours out. Then he swings his legs off the cot and pushes his feet into a pair of battered old straw slippers. His slate-grey riding breeches are stained and worn. There is a marked contrast between the one-armed oberst and the elegant, scented hauptmann.

'What is that man doing here?' asks Hinka, nodding towards Unteroffizier Baum, standing stiffly, and looking important, at von Pader's back.

'He is my witness,' replies von Pader with a confiding smile.

'Witness? Isn't your own word to be believed? Unteroffizier, get back to your company. *At the double*, man!'

'But he's driving me!' shouts von Pader, fearfully, as his batman and bodyguard is sent about his business.

'Tell me, Herr Hauptmann, are there not certain things to do with this regiment that you have not yet fully understood? Who says you *have* to be driven? Are you not aware that petrol is precious? I cannot imagine it to be vital to the war effort that you should be moved by motor transport wherever you go,

March like the rest of us. That's an order, Herr Hauptmann!'

Hinka tears the long charge sheet from von Pader's hand.

'Tell me now. Are you out of your mind? You come here to me and charge a company of elite troops with mutiny and want the best section commander in the regiment court-martialled!' Hinka shakes his head and slaps the closely-typed sheets against his false arm. 'Your charge is not accepted. It is pure fantasy. Shall we tear it to pieces and forget it? Or shall we continue with this nonsense?'

'Herr Oberst, I request that my charges be sent forward to the Divisional Commander.'

'You mean to say that you consider me to be incompetent?' asks Hinka, in a dangerously soft tone, sitting down on the edge of his desk.

'Very good, Herr Oberst!' answers Hauptmann von Pader, chalk-white in the face. And yet his thin lips draw back in a confident half-smile. He thinks of his friends in Berlin. There an oberst counts for nothing. To be removed as easily as fly-shit from a window-pane.

Hinka snatches up the telephone and orders the adjutant to get over to him on the double.

In a very few moments, the adjutant, Oberleutnant Jenditsch, is in the hut. He looks oddly at Hauptmann von Pader as he enters the room. Oberst Hinka rocks on the balls of his feet and nods to the adjutant.

'Who is No. 5 Company's acting commander, Jenditsch?'

'I haven't heard of any acting commander, sir,' answers the adjutant, smiling. 'Until I entered this room I believed Hauptmann von Pader to be in command of that company.'

Hinka jumps down from his desk and goes over to stand close to von Pader.

'Am I to understand that you have left your company without advising Regimental HQ the name of the acting commander you have appointed in your absence? Am I to understand that No. 5 Company is now in the front line *with nobody in command*?'

'Herr Oberst, I . . .' von Pader stammers.

'Has No. 5 Company a commander? Yes or no?' snarls the oberst, rapping on his artificial arm.

'My Hauptfeldwebel knows I have left the company to prefer charges of mutiny, sir!'

'You must be mad,' shouts Hinka, in a rage. 'Have you left your company to an NCO? What about Leutnant Pötz commanding No. 1 Section?'

The adjutant laughs to himself, picks up the telephone and asks for No. 5 Company.

'Get Leutnant Pötz to the telephone,' he orders, when the connection is made. 'Leutnant Pötz! Where is your commander? At the Command Post, you think? Go and see please!' The adjutant whistles softly through his teeth whilst he is waiting for Leutnant Pötz to return to the telephone. 'Hello, Pötz! The OC is not there? And nobody knows where he is! Yes *we* know!' laughs the adjutant. 'A bad business! The regimental commander orders you to take over as acting commander of No. 5 Company. That's all!' With a quiet smile he replaces the receiver on the hook.

For a moment there is dead silence in the hut.

Hinka is looking out of the window and filling his pipe. The adjutant plays with a riding whip. Hauptmann von Pader shuffles his feet uneasily. He realizes that he has got himself into a dangerous position. A position not even his friends in Berlin can extricate him from. If the CO lets it go to a court-martial he will be more than lucky to get away with being broken to the ranks and posted to a field punishment regiment.

'Get out!' snarls Oberst Hinka. 'Get off back to No. 5, and God help you if you ruin that company. You'll hear from me later!'

'Herr Oberst . . .'

'Shut up and get out,' screams Hinka, furiously. 'Do you *still* not understand that you have been guilty of dereliction of duty of the gravest possible kind?'

Hauptmann von Pader backs out of the door. The adjutant bangs it after him, almost giving him a bloody nose.

He staggers back to the company with the gait of a drunken man. He is a whole hour crawling over the open ground. When a shell crashes above his head he thinks, for a moment, that he has been hit, and that his trousers are filled with blood. They are filled with something quite different. He gets his underpants off and throws them away. He is just pulling his trousers up again when Porta and the bear appear.

'Beg to report, Herr Hauptmann, sir!' roars Porta stupidly. 'Obergefreiter Porta and Bear Rasputin en route to HQ by CO's orders, sir!'

'Get away from me!' whispers Hauptmann von Pader, unhappily.

'Beg to ask, Herr Hauptmann, sir!' crows Porta, clicking his heels. 'Has something happened, sir, to your arse, sir, since you have had to dispose of your pants, sir? Beg to state, Herr Hauptmann, sir, a shot in the arse, sir, can be dangerous thing, sir! Shall I send an orderly, sir, to dress it, sir?'

'Nothing has happened,' his OC brushes him off shortly. 'Be off with you!'

Porta falls out in a tornado of saluting, trouser-slapping and heel-clicking. The bear growls warningly. It does not like von Pader's self-made khaki uniform. They disappear down the narrow path.

'Believe it or not, Rasputin me old brown brother, but he's shit his pants,' Porta confides to the bear in a voice loud enough for von Pader not to be able to avoid hearing it.

*The strongest are the best, and the best will survive. This is
nature's law. We are the strongest. We, the German people.*

Adolf Hitler, 4th August, 1940.

*There is a heavy knocking on SD-Obersturmbannführer
Sojka's office door in the RSHA. Quickly he flicks a por-
nographic magazine under some documents relating to exe-
cutions carried out at Plötzensee.*

'*Come in!*' *he cries, in his musical Viennese dialect.*

'*Heil Hitler, Obersturmbannführer!*' *Hauptsturmführer
Tölle greets him, swinging his arm nonchalantly towards the
ceiling in the approved RSHA style.*

'*Well, Tölle, what brings you here? You haven't come to
tell me the war is finally over and we've won it, have you?
What's new from the great wide world outside?*'

'*Our troops are withdrawing to concentrate for a massive
attack on our enemies. The iron fist of National Socialism will
crush them with one all-destroying blow.*'

Tölle lays a pink folder on the desk in front of Sojka.
'*Urgent,*' *he smiles, and raises his arm in the salute.*

Sojka opens the folder and reads:

GEHEIME STAATSPOLIZEI[1]
From: Staatspolibeistelle Hamburg
        Hamburg 36,
        Stadthousbrücke 8.
        Geheim[2] Sofort[3] 23. Nov. 1943.
To: Reichssicherheitshauptamt,
        Berlin SW 11.
        Prinz-Albert-Strasse 8.

In the Zhitormir battle area, Oberleutnant Albert Wunder-

1. Geheime Staatspolizei: Secret State Police.
2. Geheim: Confidential.
3. Sofort: Urgent.

251

*lich and Feldwebel Kurt Weith have deserted from the 6th
Mounted Rifle Regiment. There is proof that they have volun-
tarily gone over to the 48th Russian Army Corps. In accordance with paragraph 99 and 91b StGB[4], all close relations are
to be arrested, and closely interrogated in order to discover
whether any of them have prior knowledge of this treacherous
act. In the event that any of them have such knowledge, the
person concerned is to be turned over to the Criminal Courts
and punished in accordance with paragraphs 98c and 91a,
StGB.*

*Such relatives as cannot be convicted of guilt are to be
confined as hostages in one of the main concentration camps as
a warning to others.*

Obergruppenführer Dr Müller

Der Chef der Sicherheitspolizei und des SD[5]

*Sojka laughs with pleasure. His finger whirls the telephone
dial happily.*

*'I need all personal papers concerning Oberleutnant Albert
Wunderlich and Feldwebel Kurt Weith of the 6th Mounted
Rifle Regt., Home Garrison: Krefeld. All first degree relatives
to be arrested and escorted here. They are to be imprisoned
under paragraph 91a. Get to it smartly, gentlemen, repeat
smartly!' Sojka bangs down the receiver.*

*Five hours later twelve innocent people are on their way to
Berlin. None of them has any knowledge of the fact that a close
relative has deserted.*

*It is late that night when the heavy doors of the Moabitt
detention house clang shut behind them. None of them knows
what a hell on earth awaits them.*

4. StGB: (Strafgesetzbuch): Penal Code.
5. Chief of Security Police and Security Services.

THE COMMISSAR

A RUSSIAN kidnap patrol picked up three of ours one night. Oberleutnant Strick, the orderly officer, was one of them.

Early one morning the Russians show a white flag. A sergeant leads a man in field-grey out into no-man's-land, and leaves him there. It is a German officer.

A party brings him in. It is Oberleutnant Strick and he has been treated terribly. Where his eyes should be are two swollen, running sores.

Strick tries to speak but can only make weird gulping noises. His mouth is a blood-caked hole from which the tongue has been torn.

'*Mon Dieu, mon Dieu!*' mutters the Legionnaire, and leaves the dugout.

'Do you understand what I am saying? asks Oberst Hinka, laying his hand on Strick's shoulder. 'I must ask you a few questions. Shake your head or nod in reply. Are the other two men alive?'

Strick shakes his head.

'Were they tortured too?' Hinka's hand whitens on his pistol holster. His face is like granite.

Strick nods.

'Was it Russians who tortured you?'

Strick shakes his head.

'Was it a commissar?'

Strick nods tiredly, sways and would have fallen from the stool but the adjutant catches him.

The Medical Officer gives him an injection and a little later Oberst Hinka can continue questioning him.

'Did the commissar speak German?'

Strick nods.

'Did you get the impression that he *was* German?'

253

Strick nods.

'Did you hear his name spoken?' Hinka stops abruptly, realizing that he has asked a question which cannot be answered. Oberleutnant Strick cannot write. The bones of both his hands have been crushed.

Dr Repp stops the questioning and orders the oberleutnant to be taken back for emergency treatment. He commits suicide in hospital shortly after admission. A nurse forgets a knife on his table. He slashes his arteries and the bed is swimming with blood before a doctor can get there.

'We'll get that pig of a commissar even if he's hiding in the Kremlin itself,' says Oberst Hinka in a hard voice. 'We need prisoners *now*, to find out who he is.'

Only two hours later a combat-patrol brings in an elderly Russian captain.

The Divisional Intelligence Officer, who speaks fluent Russian, comes out personally to interrogate the captain. In the beginning the Russian is stubbornly silent, but when he sees the fierce faces around him, and the intelligence officer threatens to turn him over to the men, he becomes a little more co-operative.

'It was the *Vojenkom*[6] from the 89th Division who was responsible for the torturing,' explains the captain, with nervous gestures.

'What is his name?' asks the intelligence officer. 'We believe him to be a German.'

'He is a former German officer, who came to Russia with a military mission,' says the captain. 'He was sent to us a short while ago to tighten up discipline. He started by executing two regimental commanders and putting very many officers and other ranks on court-martial.'

'What is his name?' asks the interrogating officer.

'It used to be Josef Geis, but he does not call himself that any more,' adds the captain, with a smile. 'Now he is *Vojenkom* Josef Oltyn. He has made a standing order that all German officers captured by our division are to be shot immediately after they have been interrogated.'

'Where is he now?'

6. Vojenkom (Russian): Divisional Commissar.

'Hidden away safely,' answers the officer, with a shrug of his shoulders. 'Right back at Beresina in Olszany in a castle together with his special staff.'

'Thank you, that is all,' says his interrogator, closing his file.

'Are you thinking of going after him?' asks the captain in amazement, emptying the glass of vodka the intelligence officer pushes over to him.

'Not *thinking*! We are going to *do* it!'

'Forget it!' says the captain, with a short laugh. 'The good commissar is *very* well protected. After a few miles your commando will run into security units, and *should* they, which isn't to be expected, get past those fellows, they'll never get back again. You've got a distance of over eighty miles to cover and, if you don't follow the roads, you have to go through terrible stretches of swamp and impenetrable forests, which can only be negotiated with special equipment.'

'Will *you* help us?' asks the intelligence officer. 'You won't regret it if you do.' He offers the captain a cigar and lights it for him. 'As soon as our commando has picked up Herr Oltyn, you can return to your unit.'

'What guarantee do I have of that?' asks the captain doubtfully.

'My word as an officer!'

The captain appears to be turning the offer over in his mind. He continues to smoke his cigar in silence. Stubs it out. The regimental clerk brings in coffee. The interrogator signals, and cognac is brought.

'I will help you catch that scoundrel,' the captain says suddenly. 'One of the officers he executed was my best friend.'

He marks out the route on a chart and warns against the dangers of the Jasiolda marshes.

'You *must* go round them, even though it means a detour of forty miles. You must go by Grolow and then in the direction of Ufda and it is absolutely necessary to have a rubber boat with you. Otherwise you will never be able to get over the Sna, not to speak of the Slutsch where you will have to hide the boat. Luckily an inflatable rubber boat is easily concealed,' he adds with a wave of his hand.

'What about the other rivers?' asks the intelligence officer. 'They are quite deep and the current is rapid.'

The captain bends over the map again and marks several positions.

'Here there are fords. They are guarded, but not very strongly. Usually a single sentry. Your commando must wear Russian uniforms and carry Russian weapons and equipment. I would not advise you to send a commando larger than a section. The road back will be the worst. As soon as the *Vojenkom* has been taken the whole area will be put on the alert.'

We stand in the trench ready to crawl over into no-man's-land. The Russian captain is inspecting our equipment together with the intelligence officer. He points to the big French water-bottle Porta has at his belt.

'Get rid of that! That's madness!'

'I'll die of thirst,' protests Porta, angrily. 'Those tiny Russian things don't hold enough to keep a sparrow alive!'

Despite his grumbling the French waterbottle is exchanged for a regulation Russian one.

Our artillery hammers at the Russian lines, to keep them occupied. Engineers pilot us through the minefields. Like lightning we are down into the enemy trenches and finish off the few sentries, who are taking cover under the forward trench wall, in no time.

Porta has trouble holding Rasputin in check. The bear can smell Russians and *Machorka*, and cannot understand why we are not killing them as usual.

The artillery fire follows our advance. It drops in front of us, sweeping a path clear which we can follow.

The first fifteen miles are taken at a blazing speed. The collapsible boat is heavy and unwieldy, and we change bearers continually.

The Old Man gives us only short rests. We must get over the Sna before daylight.

My lungs pump and heave. I feel the stab of my old wound. The only one of us who seems untouched by the pace is the bear. It has time to play games, climb trees and fall out of them, roll itself into a ball and bite its own tail.

We cross the Sna quickly and enter the woods east of

Lutszczak. Suddenly Rasputin stops and stands sniffing the air. He growls and moves carefully forward.

'Heathen about! Close!' warns Porta, in a whisper.

Cautiously we follow the bear, but still without seeing or hearing a sign of the enemy.

With a grunt Rasputin disappears into the woods as if the devil were after him.

Something dark can just be seen between the fir-trees.

'A wolf or a dog,' thinks Porta.

'Bloody foolishness!' scolds the Old Man. 'We haven't time to waste while that bloody bear goes chasing dogs! Aren't you ever going to grow out of keeping pets, you childish sod? Cats, dogs, pigs, and now a bear! What'll it be next? A sodding elephant, I wouldn't wonder!'

'They used to go to war on elephants in the old days, so you oughtn't to moan about one of them,' laughs Porta. 'The ones with the most and biggest elephants were the ones who won!'

'What the 'ell did they *do* with them bleeders?' asks Tiny, surprised. '*Eat* 'em?'

'They were a kind of tank,' explains Heide, and goes into a long, muddled description of the uses of war elephants.

'Must've been somethin' lovely to 'ear a 'erd o' them bleeders come gallopin',' considers Tiny. 'Where'd you learn all that, anyway?'

'Read it,' answers Heide, importantly.

'In the *Völkischer Beobachter*[7], I suppose?' sniggers Tiny. 'If it was there forget it, then. You can't believe a bleedin' word of it.'

There is a sound of cries and growls from amongst the trees. Branches snap loudly.

'What the devil's that?' says the Old Man, startled.

Rasputin has killed a Russian sergeant of signals. He is bloody meat when we break through the brush.

'The question now,' says the Old Man, thoughtfully, 'is whether this signaller met our bear by accident or whether he's been keeping an eye on us all the time and signalling our whereabouts.'

7. *Völkischer Beobachter:* Nazi newspaper.

'Impossible,' answers Porta. 'If he'd been near us Rasputin would have warned us. The smell of a heathen within a mile of him turns his stomach over.'

'Well, we'll find out soon enough, I reckon,' says the Old Man, pessimistically, lighting his silver-lidded pipe.

We reach the Slutsch late in the afternoon, but wait to make the crossing until midnight. We hide the rubber boat on the opposite side and go into hiding in the brush, which is very thick here. We roll ourselves up in our groundsheets and fall quickly into unconsciousness.

Immediately after dawn we continue moving in single file. We make a wide circle around Nowojeinia and come out on a wide plain where the grass is as tall as a man. A company of Russian infantry passes us a short way off. They wave to us and we wave happily back. A mounted officer examines us through his binoculars.

Rasputin lets out a warning growl.

'For God's sake keep a tight hold on that sodding bear!' says the Old Man, nervously.

We turn into the forest again. Just past the top of a hill the bear goes down flat on its belly, its incisors showing, gleaming whitely.

'What the hell's wrong with that big shit?' whispers Gregor, in alarm.

I pull a hand-grenade from my boot and arm it.

'Watch it with that banger, then,' warns Barcelona.

Rasputin creeps slowly forward with Porta just behind him, but suddenly he refuses to continue. Growling softly, he stares up into the leafy canopy of a great tree.

'Bloody neighbours,' whispers Porta.

Three Russians are sitting up in the tree-top with a heavy machine-gun. A first-class position has been built up there and beautifully camouflaged. Thanks to the bear we have seen them first.

'Get them down out of there,' whispers the Old Man to Porta, 'but without noise.'

Porta rises and walks jauntily forward down the narrow path. Tiny holds on to the bear which protests, growling, against Porta leaving it.

'Hi, *tovaritsch*,' yells Porta, pushing the green cap to the back of his head in NKVD lower-rank fashion.

'Who are you?' comes a screaming voice from the tree. 'Give the password!'

'*Job tvojemadj!*' shouts Porta back, pointing his *kalashnikov* playfully up to them. 'Up you's the password, you yellow monkey, you! Know what this is?' He pats the green hat on the back of his head.

A broad Mongolian face comes into view from the thick foliage. 'Up you, too, Moscow peasant,' screams the Mongol. 'Go home and learn good Chita Russian, so proper Russians can understand what you say!'

'Come down here, you woodpecker,' shouts Porta, his voice echoing through the woods. 'I'll pull your liver up through your tonsils, I will!'

'What do you want?' shouts a sergeant, showing his face alongside the Mongol's.

'Come down!' answers Porta, with an air of authority. 'I have an important message for you!'

'Can't you do it from down there?' asks the sergeant, arrogantly.

'*Idisodar*,' roars Porta, harshly, in the tone people use when they feel they have authority behind them. '*Dawai, dawai!* The Sampolit wants to tell you something.'

'What's he want to talk to me about?'

'How the hell do I know, *djadja*[8]? All he said to me was: "Corporal Joseph, get your arse out of here and tell those three *duraks*[9] up in the tree I want them." I think you're going to be given special treatment.' Porta laughs noisily. 'Have you begun to believe in God?'

'Are you alone?' comes doubtfully from the tree.

'*Djadja, djadja,* did you knock your head crawling up in that tree? Can you see anybody besides me? Now I can stay no longer talking to fools. I will go back to the *Sampolit* and tell him you refuse to obey his orders. *Dassvadanja*[10], little *duraks!*'

'Take it easy, comrade,' shouts the sergeant, nervously,

8. Djadja (Russian): Uncle.
9. Durak (Russian): Fool.
10. Dassvadanja (Russian): So long.

259

beginning to climb down the tree, closely followed by the two others.

The sergeant's feet have no sooner touched the ground than the bear has him and kills him with one bite. Frightened, the Mongol loses his grip and falls out of the tree. The third soldier manages to draw his *Tokarew* pistol but the Legionnaire is faster with two well-aimed shots from his Mpi.

The Mongol has broken his back and blood trickles from the corners of his mouth. He is not much longer for this world.

'We are going to visit a Herr Oltyn,' explains Porta, with wide swings of his arms. 'We have an invitation for him. Can you tell us the quickest way?'

The Mongol spits blood.

'Do you mean the *Vojenkom*?' he asks weakly.

'Clever lad. Ten out of ten,' smiles Porta. 'That's the very *gaspodin* we're looking for!'

'When you enter Olszany, it is the third house from the end of the broad street. A red house with blue windows.' The Mongol coughs, and a stream of blood jets from his mouth.

'*Germanski?*' he asks, weakly.

'You must be clairvoyant,' laughs Porta. The Mongol's body jerks convulsively and he dies.

'It must be a bleedin' surprise to a bloke to get eaten by a bear in the middle of a war,' says Tiny, stirring the bodies with the muzzle of his Mpi.

'Lots of funny things happen in wartime,' proclaims Porta, solemnly. 'You go along enjoying life to the full and suddenly there you are, gone!'

'I don't like the sound of that commissar in the red house,' says the Old Man reflectively.

'Why not?' asks Porta. 'If a Soviet commissar isn't to be found in a red house, who the hell *can* be?'

'That's not what I mean, you fool,' growls the Old Man, irritably. 'That captain said he lived in a white château and now we're told he's dossing down in a red house. If you've got a château available it's unlikely you'll move into a house, however red it is.'

'You don't understand politics!' shouts Porta, knocking the dust out of his NKVD cap. 'A communist commissar with any respect for himself can't go farting about in a white bloody château when there's a nice red proletarian hut close by just waiting to be taken over.'

At a narrow bridge two sentries stand leaning over a half-rotten, wooden fence. They take turns spitting into the water out of sheer boredom. They have been so careless as to leave their weapons leaning against a post. They cannot dream of anything unpleasant happening here. Everything breathes quiet and peace. The frogs are the only things making a noise.

'Sacha, I've made up my mind to rape Tanja tonight,' says one of them. 'I'll tell you what it was like tomorrow.'

'It'll cost you your life,' murmurs the other. He gets no further. His throat has been cut. His comrade suffers the same fate. Neither of them saw or heard Barcelona and the Legion-naire behind them.

'Come death, come ...' hums the Legionnaire, sadly, through his nose. 'This is what happens to part-time soldiers who do not realize that every minute of a soldier's life is dangerous.'

'They got a good quick death,' considers Barcelona. 'They never had time to get frightened, even!'

Cautiously we move through Olszany and soon find the red house in which the *Vojenkom* is supposed to be living. There is only one man on guard. A corporal of Jaegers, who is sitting on a stone at the corner of the house, cutting strips from a piece of smoked pork. He stretches himself lazily and yawns audibly. The yawn is cut off abruptly by the Legionnaire's garroting wire.

Porta and Tiny sneak over to the window and peer through a hole where the black-out material has broken away. They see a low-ceilinged room. A man lies asleep on a wooden bench. The commissar. The cloak and cap lying across the table are un-mistakable.

'There 'e is, that bleedin' ex-German, layin' there 'avin' a snooze in a Ivan uniform!' whispers Tiny, angrily, spitting on the window.

'We'll get him easy as the devil gets a nun's maidenhead at Whitsuntide,' says Porta, resolutely, pulling the heavy *Toka-rew* from its yellow holster.

'Don't fuck it up, now!' warns the Old Man. 'He's not to make a sound!'

'Just 'ave a seat 'ere and get quietly on with your knittin',' Tiny calms him. 'One little tap 'tween the eyes with this 'ere Russian job an' 'ell lose any thought 'e may 'ave of singin' out!'

'Jesus Christ, slow *down*, man!' snarls the Old Man. 'Throw a blanket over his head, but don't knock him out or we'll have to carry him!'

'We'll treat him gentle as a young virgin the white slavers are gonna make a packet out of in Hong Kong,' says Porta, grinning.

'Why don't we knock 'im orf?' suggests Tiny. 'Why go to all this trouble with a bleedin' torturer who's in with the 'eathens! They'll do 'im in when we get 'im 'ome, anyroad. Let's just cut 'im in bits and 'ang 'em on the bleedin' walls. 'Is prick'd just fit that bleedin' flower-vase over there with the bluebirds on it. They ain't never seen a flower like *that* before!'

'You'll go in front of a court-martial if anything happens to him,' threatens the Old Man, furiously. 'This picnic's been laid on to bring that bastard back alive. An order's an order! Understood?'

'Couldn't we even scratch 'is bollocks a bit for 'im with our little German knives from Solingen?' asks Tiny disappointedly.

'Do as I order!' the Old Man closes the discussion.

'Why not send him a written invitation, with swastikas and those bloody birds and everything?' suggests Porta.

' 'E'd only wipe 'is arse on it!' decides Tiny.

'Get him!' snarls the Old Man. 'You can undress him and bring him naked if you want, but not a scratch on him, understand!'

'Come on then,' says Porta, 'let's get the introductions over with! The start of a party's always the worst!'

In the doorway Tiny turns his head and looks at the Old Man.

'It ain't *our* fault if 'e dies of a 'eart-attack out of pure 'appiness at the sight of 'is fellow countrymen!'

Gregor has the greatest trouble holding the bear in. It always gets uneasy when Porta is out of sight.

Noiselessly they enter the low-ceilinged room. A half-bottle of vodka catches Tiny's eye. He empties it on the way in two long swallows.

'Bottoms up, *tovaritsch*,' he whispers, putting the bottle down again carefully.

As Porta bends over the sleeping man, he opens his eyes and a half-strangled scream escapes him. His instincts have warned him of danger.

Tiny drops down on him and pushes the green commissar cap into his mouth. In a moment they have him tied up.

'No nonsense, now,' threatens Porta. 'Or off go your bollocks, and you know how little a man and his bollocks are worth apart from one another!'

' 'Ow do, *tovaritsch*,' Tiny greets him, saluting. 'You're goin' on a trip, mate, 'ome to Adolf's Mafia! There's somebody wants to 'ave a little chat with *you*!'

They leave the town at the double. Tiny manages to take a large jar of preserved tomatoes with him.

They stop a good way inside the forest. The cap is removed from the commissar's mouth.

'You are War Commissar Oltyn?' asks the Old Man, in German.

'*Njet, njet, nix panjemajo*[11]!' howls the terror-stricken prisoner.

'Cut out the piss, son,' says Porta, catching him by the front of his uniform jacket. 'When our *tovaritsch* feldwebel says you're Oltyn then you bloody well *are* Oltyn! Think we're nuts, do you?'

'Pull 'is arsehole up over 'is bleedin' ears,' suggests Tiny. 'Make 'im think better, it will!'

'*Nix* Oltyn,' howls the prisoner, stubbornly.

'Who the bloody hell *are* you then?' roars the Old Man, furiously.

'*Politkom*[12] Alexej Viktorowitsch Sinzow. *Nix Vojenkom* Josef Oltyn!'

'Confess, what was your mother's name?' roars Porta.

'Anna Georgijewna Poliwanow!'

11. Njet, njet, nix panjemajo (Russian): No, no, not understood.
12. Politkom (Russian): Political Commissar.

263

'What the 'ell's 'is 'ore of a bleedin' mother to do with us?' growls Tiny. 'Cut 'is bleedin' guts open an' let the bear 'ave what 'e's got in it. It ain't 'ad its breakfast yet.'

'Don't, just don't tell me you've got the wrong man,' shouts the Old Man, despairingly, gripping his head with both hands.

'*Bien sûr que si, mon sergent*,' the little Legionnaire chokes with laughter.

'That Soviet bleedin' miscarriage could at least 'ave introduced 'imself,' says Tiny, sourly. 'Any soldier knows that's what 'e 'as to do when strangers come to inspect 'im.'

'Listen now,' says the Old Man, sitting down resignedly by the side of the frightened prisoner. 'You are *not Vojenkom* Oltyn, then?'

'*Njet, njet,*' howls the prisoner, '*njet Hromoj*[18].'

'Up with you, you Communist beetroot,' orders Porta, 'and God help you if you limp.'

The prisoner runs up and down the road without the slightest trace of a limp. But Porta makes him goosestep, dance with Tango as a lady, do knees-bend and stand on one leg and pirouette.

'*Njet Hromoj,*' howls the prisoner in between the tests. 'Me little *Politkom*! *Vojenkom* Oltyn, he *big* swine!'

'He's telling the truth,' says Porta, shrugging and holding his hands out to both sides. 'I sincerely regret it, old 'un, but we've nabbed the wrong piece of Soviet shit. Just goes to show it's right what they say. Those Russians are twisters all along the line!'

'Let's do 'is knee for 'im so 'e *will* be bleedin' lame then,' suggests Tiny, 'then we can take 'im back an' swear 'e's the *real* shit, only lyin'. The bleedin' Gestapo'll make 'im confess 'e's *Hromoj*! They've fixed bigger blokes'n 'im!'

'Nonsense,' snarls the Old Man. '*What* a shower to get saddled with!'

'Let's go back to town and ask 'em where big, bad Mr. Oltyn hangs out, then,' grins Porta.

'We can just say we're some of 'is *tovaritsch* pals come to town to look 'im up,' suggests Tiny.

'I wish the devil had you two shits,' the Old Man scolds

13. Hromoj (Russian): The limping devil.

264

them. 'That *I* should have the bad luck to have to command the craziest section in the whole bloody Army!'

'Well, you can't say you've 'ad many dull moments with us lot,' considers Tiny. 'If they give you a new lot you'd soon be longin' for us. There ain't many sections *like* us.'

'Listen here, *tovaritsch*,' says Porta, patting the *Politkom's* cheek, 'you've got yourself mixed up in a very annoying mistake.'

'Two,' Tango breaks in, 'the first 'e made was getting himself born in Stalinland!'

'Yes,' smiles Porta, 'but now it is the last one for him. We're going to have to *squeeze* you, *tovaritsch*, or you'll be sending all your Communist pals after our arses. *You* understand we owe it to ourselves not to let you go!'

'I will give word of honour, say nothing,' shouts the prisoner, despairingly.

'Ain't he a nice feller,' says Buffalo. 'Lower your sabres, boys!'

The Old Man sits down on a stone and shakes his head violently. He is trying to think things out

'There's nothing else for it,' he says finally. 'That damned War Commissar has got to go back with us.' He looks over at Julius Heide. 'You must find out from him where his big colleague is hiding. We'll pick him up tonight!'

'Reckon there's a good 'otel around 'ere where we could get a rest an' a bit of a snack while we're waitin' for night to sneak up on us?' asks Tiny.

'No, I'm afraid not,' says Porta. 'There are *no* good hotels in this area. The cooks've all joined the Army.'

'Stop that childish nonsense,' shouts the Old Man, angrily. 'It's hard to believe that you are grown men, and *soldiers* to boot!'

'Do you 'ave to be grown-up to be a soldier?' asks Tiny. 'The most of them *I've* met don't look more'n twelve years old.'

'Shut up, you great dope!' snarls the Old Man. 'This is dangerous business we've got into here.'

'Count me out, then,' shouts Porta, dancing away down the path singing, 'I'm going home . . .'

'Heimat, deine Sterne . . .'

'What'll we do with the prisoner?' asks Barcelona, practically.

'Liquidate him, as soon as we have obtained the information we need,' says Heide, coldly.

'*You'll* shoot him perhaps?' asks the Old Man sarcastically.

'Why not?' answers Heide, murderously, drawing his *Tokarew*. 'The Führer's orders of August, 1941, state that all commissars and Jews are to be neckshot.'

'The poor chap's shaking like a jelly from fear and terror,' says Porta, patting the prisoner on the shoulder in kindly fashion. 'He's no worse than anybody else, even if he has got himself a green hat. He's just smart, that's all, and has found out being a commissar's a good thing!'

The whole section looks at the prisoner, who is chalk-white in the face with fear. He knows we cannot let him go and he knows what we want with his colleague. Feverishly he begins to tell us about the *Vojenkom*, whom he paints as black as possible in an attempt to soften us up.

'Communism, and all Jews, are pests,' he cries, throwing out his arm convincingly.

'You can't mean that,' laughs Porta, heartily. 'Think of all the pretty little Yiddisher bints there are in the world. Give me a dozen of 'em here and now and see what'd happen!'

'It's obvious enough. He's an anti-Communist and has been our Adolf's pen pal all his life,' grins Buffalo.

' 'E's a shit of a traitor to 'is Fatherland,' shouts Tiny contemptuously. 'It's bleedin' 'orrible to 'ear for a real 'onest idealist, 'ow 'e, who is a *Politkom*, can turn 'is wicked tongue on old Uncle Joe.' Tiny collects all his pretended contempt into one enormous gob of spittle.

'Let's hang him up by the feet, and let the sense run back into his head,' suggests Tango.

'Tie him to a tree,' orders the Old Man, 'then he's at least got a chance of being found. If they don't find him that's *his* bad luck.'

The Legionnaire and Barcelona tie the unhappy prisoner to a tree. Tiny says we could have tied him to an anthill, then at least he'd have had some company if he didn't get found.

'Shall I send a message to the regiment?' asks Heide, ready at the little short-wave sender.

The Old Man thinks about it.

'It's a bit risky. They could get a bearing on us.'

'Impossible,' says Heide, pulling up the antenna. 'I'll send it short and sharp. It's Oberfunkmeister Müller on the other end, and nobody can send too fast for him.'

The Old Man nods his agreement.

The short wave bands are thickly populated and very lively. There is in particular one very powerful Russian Army station.

'You can give *that* up,' sighs the Old Man, when he hears the confused howling and buzzing. 'You'll never get through to our lot.'

'Leave that for radio people to judge,' answers Heide, sourly, going right out to the edge of our sending-range. He is one of the best telegraphists in the Army.

Suddenly our identification signal is on. The powerful Russian Army station breaks in continuously, asking us irritably for identification.

'*Job tvojemadj*, you Red shit,' Heide morses back, furiously.

Suddenly the identification signal comes loud and clear.

'P.4–F.6.A–R. KARLA–4, come in!'

'WERNER,' repeats Heide five times, with short pauses, and then at a demoniacal speed 90 he sends the report.

Oberfunkmeister Müller is just as fast. Only the very best telegraphists can make anything of a message sent at that speed.

Gregor, who is assistant telegraphist, loses his way early in the signal and never catches up again. Resignedly he lowers his message book.

Heide closes the set and hands the Old Man the clean copied message:

CONTINUE ACTION. PLUCK WHEN RIPE.
REPORT AT AGREED TIME. END OF MESSAGE.

'It is unbelievable that the *untermensch* have designed so good a transmitter,' says Heide, admiringly, stroking the little set lovingly. 'These small Soviet sets are fantastically good.'

'Yes, there ain't no limit to what the *untermensch* can do

267

when they try,' says Tiny, patting his *kalashnikov* with a shake of his head in acknowledgement. 'Who else 'as a balalaika like this 'un, ready to reel off a bleedin' tune at the drop of a 'at?'

We lie in the forest, dozing, for the whole of the day. The prisoner has told us that Oltyn leaves the officers' mess every night in high spirits. The club is in a small château a short way out of town. He has drawn us a map and given us all the details. We simply cannot go wrong.

Late in the afternoon the Old Man and Barcelona go over to feed the prisoner and find him slumped against the ropes. Strangled!

The Old Man goes berserk and threatens to shoot the lot of us.

'I want that murderer, and I want him *now*,' he roars. 'I've had enough! I won't take any more of this!'

'Murderers?' answers Porta, smilingly. 'Do you intend to insult us?'

'We could 'ave you *pinched* for sayin' things like that,' shouts Tiny.

'Murderers, I said!' screams the Old Man furiously. 'Oh what a lot of wonderful bloody ornaments you are for the new Germany! Kill a poor defenceless prisoner, you cowardly bastards! But I'll find the shits who did it! There's not more'n three of you who'd use a wire!'

'Eh, eh! Ain't you the bleedin' tec?' shouts Tiny, admiringly. 'If I'd got that much in me 'ead I'd 'ave 'ad a go at gettin' into the Kripo's. You're better'n Pretty Paul[14] any bleedin' day. If 'e drops 'is Party badge on the bleedin' floor 'e 'as to get the 'ole bleedin' section *an'* Customs and Excise to 'elp 'im find it again!'

'Life is ugly and hard,' sighs Porta, moodily. 'That poor little heathen boy is no more.' He wipes his eyes falsely on a filthy handkerchief.

'Wicked shower!' shouts the Old Man, angrily. He pushes a large chew of tobacco into his jaw and spits fiercely.

'He was a commissar. A tool of international Jewry,' snarls Heide, coldly. 'He deserved to be liquidated!'

'Shut your filthy mouth,' shouts the Old Man, red as a

14. See *Assignment Gestapo*.

turkey-cock in the face. 'If *your* Führer ordered commissars to be liquidated a thousand times over, I'll see you in front of a court if it was *you* did it!'

'*My* Führer?' asks Heide, threateningly, and with slitted eyes. 'Your Führer too I hope, Herr Feldwebel?'

The Old Man looks at him wickedly.

'*You* voted him to power. *I* didn't!'

'It will be interesting to hear what the NSFO has to say to this,' answers Heide, and begins to whittle viciously at a twig.

Porta cuts thick slices from a long Russian loaf. We toast it at a small fire and cover it with preserved tomatoes and garlic. It tastes wonderful.

'This was Red Spain's secret weapon during the civil war,' says Barcelona, taking a huge mouthful.

'That's why they bloody lost,' laughs Porta.

The moon is high when we leave. Its light shimmers like silk through the leaves.

A dog barks in the distance and the fur rises on Rasputin's neck. He is, as usual, in the lead, together with Porta.

Strangely there are no blockades at all outside the town. Perhaps they cannot imagine the possibility of an attack. There are not even police patrols in the streets. All breathes peace and quiet.

In a side-street a party of soldiers sit singing with their girl-friends.

We march to attention and give the eyes right to a passing major. It is not difficult for us to imitate Russian soldiers. Their service regulations and drill are a true copy of our own. The same kicking goose-step, the same swing of the arm up and across the belt buckle.

Porta notices two personnel trucks standing parked in a yard.

'Let's commandeer those waggons,' he suggests in a whisper, 'they'll give us a quicker getaway when we've picked up the meat course!'

Tiny tiptoes closer and takes a look into the yard.

'There's only two 'alf-asleep bleeders in there,' he whispers, 'We can '*ave* them in two shakes of a lamb's tail!'

'Right then,' nods the Old Man, 'take 'em, but no noise!'

Two seconds later the two Supply Corps men are dead,

strangled. We throw the bodies into a well. We push the lorries out of the yard and only start them when they are out on the street.

At breakneck speed we flash through the narrow street. Nobody takes any notice of us. That is the way Russians drive. Suddenly we find ourselves inside a large barracks. Some sentries scream at us as we roar back out through the gates.

'*Job tvojemadj!*' Porta screams back at them.

We turn into a narrow cul-de-sac in which there is a prison.

An NKVD man looks pleased. He thinks we are bringing prisoners, but we have to disappoint him.

'What's your destination?' he asks, sourly.

'*Vojenkom* Oltyn,' answers Porta. 'Could you tell us how to get there, mate?'

The green-capped NKVD man comes right up to the leading truck.

'That's a hell of a dialect you've got there. Where are you from? Not Tiflis at any rate.'

'Karelia,' laughs Porta, cheekily. 'Me mother was a Finnish whore and me dad a Russian elk!'

'You *look* it, mate,' laughs the NKVD guard and tells us the way to the château.

'What the 'ell was it, now, that bloody password was for tonight?' asks Porta, taking a chance. 'Us Karelian sons of 'ores don't remember so good.'

'*Tarakan*[15] and you answer *Papojka*[16].'

'Yes, that's it,' chuckles Porta. 'Sounds good don't it? Are there a lot of cockroaches here since you use 'em for a password?'

'No,' answers the NKVD man, 'nor parties neither!' He offers a packet of Papyros.

Porta hands him his water bottle. He takes a healthy swig of the vodka it contains.

We back out of the blind alley and soon afterwards we have parked the trucks under cover of some large lilacs in the park surrounding the castle.

Porta swings his *kalashnikov* over his shoulder, pulls the

15. Tarakan (Russian): Cockroach.
16. Papojka (Russian): Party.

270

round Russian steel helmet down over his eyes, and saunters aimlessly towards a soldier who is standing close to the steps up to the castle. Heide and the Legionnaire sneak along the wall to get behind the sentry. He has the whole of his attention fixed on Porta, who comes dancing towards him over the open ground singing softly:

> Sonce nysenko[17]
> spischu do tebe,
> wetschir blysenko,
> letschu do tebe . . .

He kicks at a fir cone, dribbles it like a footballer, and shoots it at the sentry who traps it smartly and passes it back. Then he is dead. A few flustered jerks of arms and legs. The Legionnaire tightens the wire a little more. They drag the body into the rhododendrons, empty the pockets, and take whatever they have a use for.

'Idiots,' sighs the Legionnaire. 'As soon as they are out of earshot of the front line they think there is no danger any more, and wander about like so much poultry in a wired-in yard. *C'est la guerre!*'

Porta takes the place of the dead sentry, but keeps in the shadows, in case somebody should come by who knows the Russian.

A clock chimes the hour, sonorously, from its tower, and plays a little tune.

A group of officers comes noisily laughing from the château. One of them trips and tumbles down the steps.

'Oh, oh, Nikolajewitsch, can't you take *tovaritsch* Oltyn's champagne?'

Porta shoulders his Mpi and brings his heels together.

A fat officer with a green pelisse over his shoulder snaps a finger carelessly at the peak of his cap. A cloud of schnapps and garlic surrounds the group, as they disappear, singing drunkenly, over towards a long building.

'Drunk pigs, *untermensch*,' mutters Heide, contemptuously.

17. The sun is sinking,
   Evening is near,
   I hurry to you,
   I fly home to you . . .

He is lying under one of the trucks with his LMG ready.

Porta pulls an apple from a tree and crunches it noisily.

'He's crazy,' whispers the Old Man, 'makes as much noise as a horse eating a frozen turnip.'

Four women in Red Army uniform come giggling out of the club. One of them pulls up her skirt and there is a merry splashing.

' 'Oly Mother of Kazan, Jesus Christ Almighty,' cries Tiny in a whisper. 'Guncunt! Let's take 'em along with the bleedin' *Hromoj*!'

The girls stop by Porta and dance teasingly around him. They promise him all sorts of good things if he will come over to them when the guard is changed.

'He'd better not try,' mutters the Old Man, fearfully.

'Jesus,' groans Tiny, as one of the girls slips her hand between Porta's legs and lets out a scream of delight, 'shell'ole 'ores!'

'They could do with a car in the garage,' mumbles Barcelona.

Some officers come out of the club, and the girls leave hurriedly. They have a dog with them. It stops and looks in our direction, sniffing the air, and begins to growl.

Rasputin, who is sitting in the cabin of one of the trucks, begins to hop up and down. The springs creak. He shows his teeth at the dog, which runs a little way towards us.

A sharp voice calls it back.

One of the officers looks closely at Porta as he passes him, and orders him to get a haircut. Russian soldiers are clipped close to the head.

We release our safety catches, but the officer goes on without further comment.

'Hell,' groans the Old Man. 'I can't take much more of this!'

'Excitin', ain't it?' says Tiny taking a deep breath. 'Amazin' to think, ain't it, 'ere we are lying right in the bleedin' middle of ol' Ivan's lair. Close enough to spit in 'is bleedin' eye, if we wanted!'

'They'd shit bricks if they knew we were here,' grins Gregor, unworriedly.

' 'Ow long we gonna 'ang around 'ere, anyway?' asks Tiny, impatiently.

'If it was *me* as 'ad the section I'd be in there an' 'ave the bleedin' meat out an' off.'

'Yes, try that kind o' shit and *you'd* be off, with an entire division hanging on to your arse,' hisses the Old man, pressing tobacco viciously into his silver-lidded pipe.

The wind gets stronger. Clouds cover the moon and the darkness becomes complete.

'The German God is with us,' whispers Barcelona, cheeringly.

'Too right He is. It says so on our belt-buckles,' laughs Buffalo.

Another noisy group of officers comes clattering down the steps. A little, thin lieutenant berates Porta for dirty boots and long hair.

'Report to me in the morning for two hours punishment drill,' sings out the lieutenant. 'What's your name?'

'Private Serpelin, sir!' Porta replies quickly, crashing his heels together.

'I'll remember you,' promises the lieutenant, as he turns away.

'You *bet* he will,' grins Gregor, convincingly.

'My *feet* are going to sleep,' complains Barcelona.

'I'm lying on a stone,' I say.

'Move it,' suggests Gregor, yawning widely.

'Or move yourself,' comes in an irritable tone from the Old Man.

I roll away from the large stone I am lying on and drop my Mpi, which goes rattling away down the slope.

A bird screams piercingly from a tree. The others curse viciously and call me names. Only Tiny laughs. He does not care what happens as long as *something* does. A Sunday child, who believes nothing can go wrong for him.

Rasputin is nervous. He presses against the windscreen, which bulges outwards. Gregor has to go over and quieten him.

There is silence for some time. From the château comes the sound of music and song. A dog howls long and mournfully. A guard party marches past down on the road. We hear sharp commands and the rattle of weapons.

'Hell,' cries Barcelona, '*now* we're up shit creek all right!

Porta can't change! Even if they do wipe their arses with gravel and don't believe in God they'll soon see he ain't one of theirs!'

' 'E'll be well away before they get to 'im,' Tiny is optimistic. 'Nobody what ain't got pure shit under 'is bleedin' 'at'd stand there waitin' to tell the neighbours 'e's over from the other bleedin' FPO!'

The Old Man pushes his Mpi up in front of him.

'D'you think it's the relief?' asks Heide nervously.

'Might be,' answers the Old Man, 'and it might also be a patrol. We'll find out!'

Porta marches to and fro, kicking his feet out in the Russian manner. He calls to a cat, which comes walking over the open ground with its tail in the air. It comes slowly over to him. He picks it up and begins to stroke it.

'I'll choke that sod, I will, if he drags a Soviet cat back with him,' snarls the Old Man.

'We'll brainwash the bleeder, an' make 'im a good Nazi,' grins Tiny, happily. 'We'll soon get them Commie ideologies out of 'im. We've broke worse cases'n a bleedin' Commie country cat. We'll make the bleeder learn *Mein Kampf* by 'eart!'

Several tanks start warming up. The air trembles with the noise of their heavy Otto motors.

'T-34's,' says Heide, knowledgeably.

Heavy trucks roar at the other end of the town. Running feet and loud commands can be heard.

We strain our ears, listening, but it cannot be anything serious or they would not still be sitting at their party in the club.

Windows are opened wide and light splashes the grounds around the château. Nobody seems to be worrying about the blackout. They probably do not consider the German Air Force dangerous any longer.

Women's voices scream excitedly. We hear laughter and song. An accordion is being worked hard. There is the stamping of Russian dances. The women scream again.

'They're takin' their clothes off, now,' says Tiny, licking his lips lustfully. 'There ain't nothin' as much fun as when they're all goin' at it in a 'eap in the middle o' the floor, an' all the bare arses bobbin' up an' down in time like a shoal of 'errin' winkin' in the sun in August.'

'Filthy pig,' the Old Man scolds him. 'Haven't you anything else in your head?'

'Let's go over an' find out, shall we,' says Tiny. 'I like bein' what they call a *voyeur*!'

'That might be fun!' laughs Buffalo, pleased with the thought. 'Then when the heathens've done their job we could take over!'

'I 'ave 'eard that Russian wenches like to get on top of a man,' says Tiny. 'If we was to stick our old tomatoes inside there we could decide that question once and for all!'

We glare enviously at Porta who is standing quietly looking through the open window. He turns round, looks over at us and clicks his tongue.

'Don't you think we ought to cut 'im, just a *little* bit, this wicked Russian-German commissar feller, when we *do* get 'old of 'im?' asks Tiny, expectantly.

'Watch yourself,' answers the Old Man sharply.

It seems to me we have been lying here for hours. My whole body itches and tingles.

Several owls flap around between the trees. A horned owl screams ominously.

Suddenly a tall, broad figure appears at the head of the castle steps. A long cape flaps about him. He wipes at his completely bald head. A soldier runs, bowing and scraping, to bring him his cap and pistol belt.

'*C'est lui*[18],' whispers the Legionnaire, hoarsely. 'No more mistakes now!'

> Nach der Tür zur Hintertreppe,
> auch als Hintertür bekannt,
> lebt im Haus ein schwarzer Kater,
> der dort seine Wohnstatt fand . . .[19]

sings the commissar loudly in German.

18. French: It is him!
19. (Freely translated) By the door to the back stairway,
    Also called the backstairs door,
    Lives a dirty great black tomcat,
    And it sleeps upon the floor.

'We'll give him tomcats,' growls Gregor, sucking at a dry cigarette butt.

The commissar takes a few dance steps. He is drunk and goes three steps down and two up, then suddenly roars with laughter.

Porta breaks out of the bushes, marches noisily up the gravel path, and throws his helmet clownishly up in the air.

'What the hell, you dog, you,' roars the commissar, in amazement, 'are you drunk then, you son of a bitch?'

'*Job tvojemadj*, dad,' shouts Porta, laughing foolishly.

'*Stoi*, you bastard, you,' screams the commissar.

'*Job tvojemadj*,' Porta repeats the insult.

'*Stoi*,' roars the commissar, raging, and rushes down the steps. '*Stoi*, you son of all the stinking Mongols from the steppes. I'll have you in the cage at Vladimir for this!'

Porta stops in front of the lilacs where the section is hiding. The commissar rushes over to him.

'You damned Kalmuk hyena, what do you think you're up to?'

'Easy now, dad, easy now,' hisses Porta, pressing the muzzle of his Mpi against the commissar's stomach.

'What the . . .' The rest is smothered in the heavy cloak which is thrown over his head. A pair of mighty arms press the breath from his lungs.

' 'Ome to the family you're goin', me old troll o' the German forest!' grins Tiny. ' 'Ome to the dear ol' Fatherland!'

The commissar kicks and struggles desperately. Gregor and Barcelona catch his legs and pull him to the ground. Tiny hugs him in a crushing grip and falls heavily on top of him.

'Careful, now,' warns the Old Man. 'Don't hug the beggar to death!'

Porta lifts his *Tokarew* and brings the butt down on the commissar's neck.

With a grunt the big man collapses. Quickly we tie his arms behind his back. A loop goes round his neck which will tighten at the slightest movement. Like a sack of potatoes the bound commissar is thrown into the back of the lorry.

Tiny sits on him. Porta starts the truck, with a noise which makes the air tremble. A nearby rookery is awakened and protests harshly at the noise.

'If we get out of this I'll *run* to Mass every Sunday from now on,' promises the Old Man, solemnly, wrapping his fists tightly around his Mpi.

' 'E *is* the right Commie, *this* time, isn't 'e?' asks Tiny, nervously. 'There's that many of 'em around 'ere it's easy enough to make a mistake!'

'Wrong 'un or right 'un, he's the last I'm fetching out,' says Gregor, with decision.

'It's OK,' says Buffalo. 'He limped like a goat with three legs. He's gotta be this *Hromoj* guy!'

'He'll get a surprise all right, when he meets his fellow countrymen again,' laughs Barcelona.

'*Then* the bleedin' starlin's gonna be let 'ave a crack at the tomato, son,' says Tiny, drily.

'He'll hang,' confirms Heide, brusquely.

'He ought to be hanged five times over,' adds Gregor.

'Yea-a-a-h, an' with thin violin strings, the way they do in Plötzensee,' suggests Tiny, radiantly.

The second truck is following close behind us with the Legionnaire at the wheel. Porta drives like the devil himself. We have to hang on to the sides of the truck to avoid being thrown out.

Soon we have left Juraciszki behind us. Shortly after, Porta swings away from the main road and on to an uneven, broken, side-road, but without reducing his speed.

'He'll smash the sodding axles,' shouts the Old Man, banging on the wall of the cabin with the butt of his Mpi. Porta pretends not to have heard him, and increases his speed even more.

Rasputin has one paw round Porta's shoulders and growls lovingly as he licks the back of his neck. The bear is happy to see him back again.

The Old Man smashes the tiny window with his Mpi muzzle.

'Reduce speed, you bloody madman, you're nearly killing us in the back here!'

'So what? If you're killed one way or the other, what's the difference?' As he speaks he tramps on the brake and we are all thrown violently forward against the cabin wall.

Three Russian MP's, each with an Mpi at the ready, have

made a cordon across the road and are swinging a red lamp in circles.

'Drive over them!' orders the Old Man, sharply.

Porta tears at the gears and switches on the headlights. The Russians are completely blinded.

The heavy personnel truck jumps forward.

'Come death, come . . .' hums the Legionnaire.

The three guards are thrown up in the air. One of them lands with a bang on the shield, but slides straight down to the road. We feel the bumps as all three sets of wheels go over him.

The two others lie stretched out on the road behind us.

At breakneck speed Porta races on down the narrow forest road and wrenches the wheel round suddenly. The heavy half-armoured vehicle bounces up and over a hill and across a half-rotten bridge which sways threateningly. Without hesitation the other truck follows us at the same breakneck speed.

With a cracking rumble the bridge collapses behind us, and disappears into the river.

'All you need's just a *little* bit of all the luck there is in the world, to get by with,' grins Tiny, in satisfaction.

Soon after we are out on a wide main road again, and Porta draws to a halt.

'Where the devil *are* we?' he asks, looking about him.

'We have, of course, gone wrong,' answers the Old Man, grumpily, studying the map. 'Why the devil do you have to drive so damn fast? You've been driving towards Rakow. We'll have to turn back!'

'Back?' cries Gregor, fearfully. 'Not me!'

'Back at least fifteen miles,' says the Old Man. 'We've got to get to Gawja, but there's no danger till we get to the Lida crossroads. They've got a special checkpoint there, by what the captain said. We go through at top speed! It's an ordinary green-cap point with no heavy weapons. They shoot at us, we shoot back! Down behind the sideboards and MG's in position! Any questions?'

'Will we be home in time for coffee?' asks Porta.

'Shut *up*,' growls the Old Man, and crawls up into the truck.

In Wolozyn Porta turns off and drives straight towards Iwje without our seeing a living soul.

278

It is growing light when we near the Lida crossroads.

'They'll get a balalaika turn as'll take their breath away,' says Tiny, lifting his *kalashnikov*.

'Don't count your chickens before they're hatched,' the Old Man warns him. As the words leave his mouth Porta brakes violently, locking the wheels. Like lightning he is out of the cabin and has the motor cover open. He pretends to be making repairs.

'What's up?' whispers the Old Man.

'Stay inside,' warns Porta. 'Half the neighbours' bloody Army's up at the crossroads looking through their Commie glasses. They're certain sure out looking for the wicked men who've pinched their *Hromoj*!'

Carefully the Old Man positions his binoculars behind one of the truck's narrow firing-slits.

'They've sent out an alarm! No doubt about it,' he says. 'There's four tanks behind the house. Now they're turning their turrets this way. We've got to get out of this place. Can you turn here?'

'Leave that to me,' snarls Porta. 'Hold on tight in there! We'll be movin' but *fast*!'

'Where the devil are the others?' asks Barcelona, and looks back down the road.

'They've stopped round the bend,' says Tango. 'They must have seen the heathen before we did.'

'You Fascist swine aren't going to get away with this,' growls the Commissar, who has regained consciousness.

'*Hromoj*, keep your bleedin' mouth shut, an' speak when you're spoken to!' says Tiny, treading heavily on his stomach. 'Otherwise we just might serve you up for breakfast to Rasputin!'

'We can't get away with it,' mumbles Barcelona as Porta begins to move slowly forward. 'Soon as we start to turn they'll do us with their bloody tank guns!'

'Nothin' bad can 'appen to me,' says Tiny, with assurance. 'I'm goin' to 'ave an 'appy death with no pain. Far as I'm concerned they can shoot as much as they bleedin' like!'

'Turn, for Christ's sake!' snarls the Old Man, impatiently.

'Not yet,' says Porta. 'Further on. Then I can get round in one go without having to back.'

Tiny peers over the sideboard of the truck.

'Swarmin' with bleedin' green-caps. They'll make mince-meat of us, if they ever get 'old of us!'

'They'll gouge out your eyes,' promises the commissar, spitefully.

'We'll 'ave cut your bleedin' belly open first, though,' Tiny assures him, wiping his long, pointed combat knife along the man's upper lip. '*An*' we'll've cut you up a bit longways an' crossways, just to make your mates laugh, an' your Commie bleedin' arms we'll 'ave 'angin' round your neck, so you won't need a tie no more, even if you 'ad arms to tie it with!'

A tank rolls out from behind the house and stops across the road.

'Those dopes must think we're coming straight through,' grins Porta. 'Take a lame-brained Russian to think that one out!'

'They'll shoot you to pieces,' laughs the commissar, tauntingly.

' 'Ere now, me old Commie bell-weather,' Tiny pricks his chest with his knife. 'When we've 'ad our fun with you we'll take a trip to your 'ome town an' 'ave your ol' mum's eyeballs for breakfast, we will!'

'I'll take care of you personally,' the commissar promises, taut with rage.

'You're full o' shit,' replies Tiny. 'You ain't got more'n five days left! By then you'll be danglin' from a piece of good German rope an' the crows'll be sittin' on your shoulders 'avin' a good time with *you*!'

Porta moves forward slowly in first gear. I bite my lips with excitement and press the machine-gun into my shoulder.

'Hold on!' shouts Porta, tearing the wheel round. The engine whines at maximum revolutions.

We roar out into a field. The truck rocks, and is close to turning over, but we make it back onto the road.

'Fire!' screams the Old Man, and all three MG's rattle away at the astonished NKVD troops by the road-block.

Several of them fall, but then there comes a short sharp report close behind us and a shell drops on the road in front of us.

Another tank gun fires and the shell explodes a little closer. Then we are round the curve. The truck is on two wheels and comes close to turning over.

Seven miles further on we meet the other truck. We wave to them without lessening speed.

Porta swings into the forest along a road which is no more than two wheel tracks, and stops under some trees. In the distance we can hear the drone of the tanks. Shortly after they roar past along the road leading to Oszmiana.

'Go on,' orders the Old Man and waves a signal to the other truck.

After a few miles a deep roaring makes us look up. Low down over the road a 'Crow'[20] comes rushing. It swings off into a steep climb, then comes down at us in a howling dive. It is so low that we can see the pilot clearly.

Two bombs fall right behind us but do no more damage than to throw a great deal of stones and dust up into the air.

'That sad sack's in contact with the green-caps,' shouts Porta. 'There'll be a shower of tanks trying to work it up our arses before long!'

'I'll fix him,' boasts Heide, swinging his MG round.

'You couldn't *touch* him with that ant-piss syringe!' says Gregor, contemptuously. 'Don't you know Crows're armoured against MG fire?'

'The *untermensch* in the cockpit isn't, though,' snarls Heide, wickedly.

The Crow comes at us again, this time swooping down from the opposite side.

Heide opens fire immediately. Bullets splatter and rattle off the Crow's armoured sides.

Bombs go off in front of and behind us.

Heide fires like a madman, but without hitting the pilot.

'Another of these mad bastards who shoot at people without hitting 'em,' shouts Porta, raging. 'That's the kind of idiots who bring all the troubles of a war down on us!'

20. 'Crow' (Slang): Polikaspow Po–2 reconnaissance plane.

The Crow disappears with an earshattering roar. We see nothing of the tanks.

When the Crow is out of earshot we continue, skirting the edge of the forest. The road disappears in the end in tall grass but the earth is so firm that we are able to keep moving.

Suddenly a huge shadow falls across us. It is the Crow, gliding along with motors cut off.

The pilot sees us and begins to drop bombs. Shrapnel tears great holes in both trucks.

We fly helter-skelter into the shelter of the trees. Tiny has the MG at his shoulder ready to fire at the Crow when it returns.

'We'll stop *his* farting in church for him,' hisses the Old Man, tight-lipped.

'There he is!' shouts Porta, pointing.

'I've got him!' roars Tiny, pressing the butt into his shoulder.

All three MG's fire simultaneously. A long row of smoke-tracks bore themselves into the pilot, who falls forward. The machine wobbles and puts its nose straight up into the air. The pilot is thrown back.

Joyfully we watch his death flight. There is not a soldier in the Army who doesn't hate the Crows.

The plane flies straight into the tall tree-tops and seconds later the silence is torn by a gigantic explosion. Bombs, petrol, everything on board the Crow, goes up in one blinding sheet of flame. A yellowy-red finger of fire shoots up over the forest and changes to a great black mushroom of smoke.

'One Communist less,' says Heide, folding the MG supporting legs together.

'Climb aboard!' orders the Old Man. 'Let's get on. It won't be long before those tanks are after us.'

A little later we turn in to the forest. The grass comes half-way up the sides of the trucks.

'Let's hope there's not a tree trunk across the road,' mumbles Porta, nervously.

'If there *is* we'll turn a somersault that'd sure be worth big money in a circus,' considers Buffalo.

We drive along the Sehtschara, circle Selwa and disappear

into the Bialowiejer forest. Now the road becomes impossible. Brambles have grown together to make tunnels down which we drive, despite the strong autumn sun, in a sinister green twilight. Even Rasputin does not like it. He becomes hard to handle when a herd of wild pigs crosses our path at the gallop and disappears into the forest.

Tiny is going to shoot at them but the Old Man forbids it.

'You silly sods,' he rates us, when we agree with Tiny. 'Start shooting and we'll bring the whole of the Red Army down on us. Not forgetting that there are large partisan units in these forests!'

We can only move at all now by using the booster gear. We are continually having to navigate round large holes and up over steep inclines. The engines are boiling.

We stop for a moment. In the distance we can hear the roar of heavy motors. The tanks are on our track.

'So the Crow *was* in touch with those four bastards,' says Tango, scratching his thin chest nervously.

'Bad shit,' says Tiny, looking back in the direction of the deep rumbling.

'Now they've got you!' says the commissar, triumphantly. 'As soon as you took to the forest you'd had it!'

'Shut your trap, you dirty bleedin' traitor,' hisses Tiny, pricking him with his combat knife, 'or just maybe the bear'd like your liver for bleedin' hors d'oeuvres!'

'Cut his ears off,' suggests Porta. 'He won't listen to what we tell him, anyway, so what does he need ears for?'

'You'll find out soon,' jeers the commissar, 'soon you'll be finding out what it's like being dragged behind those tanks!'

'Old 'un, let me turn this shit off,' shouts Porta, angrily.

The Old Man does not reply.

Now we can hear the noise of the tanks even above our own engine noise. They are gaining on us steadily and we are easy to track. Our broad tyre marks show clearly in the damp ground.

'Can't you go faster?' shouts Buffalo, nervously.

'Sure, son,' grins Porta, 'but you'd fall off!'

''Ow much bleedin' further to 'ome?' asks Tiny, impatiently.

'A damn long way yet,' answers the Old Man, moodily.

Porta brakes the truck so sharply that the Old Man flies forward over the bonnet. If the windshield had not been down he would surely have broken his neck.

Porta has stopped the truck at the last moment, on the very brink of a cliff. We sit semi-paralysed, gaping down into the depths below us.

'So far and no farther,' sighs the Old Man, quite worn out.

He is right. It is impossible to turn the truck and even more impossible to go round this enormous gap. Behind us the sinister rumble of the motors has become louder. Every moment the tanks are closing on us.

'Empty the trucks,' orders the Old Man, 'at the double now, lads!'

We snatch up hand-grenades and ammunition, load all magazines. Luckily there are two automatic loaders in the truck and we get it done fast.

'Into the woods,' orders the Old Man, 'spread out!'

Porta and Tango pour petrol over both the personnel waggons, throw the empty cans into the cabin and dash to cover amongst the brambles just as the first of the tanks noses it's way round the bend. It is an old Landsverk 30.

'Where the devil did they get *that* from?' whispers the Old Man, wonderingly. 'Far as I know they haven't been to war with Sweden long as tanks've existed?'

'No, but with Finland,' answers Heide, who knows everything. 'The Nyeland Dragoon Regiment had them on trial.'

The Landsverk sends a long MG burst above the trucks in the belief that we have taken cover on the other side of the ravine. Bullets smoke their way with a thud into the trees.

Two BA-64's round the curve. They are close together, a proof that they are inexperienced. A little behind them comes the most dangerous of them, a Humber Mk II. The turret flies up and an officer examines the ground cautiously.

'A *Starschi Leitenant*[21],' says Porta. 'He must be tired of living, the way he opens his turret before he knows where we are.'

'He's probably been brainwashed that much by the Commie buddies, he doesn't know what day it is,' reckons Buffalo.

21. First lieutenant.

'They shouldn't use such strong soap for washin' brains with,' says Tiny, seriously, pushing off the safety catch of the MG.

'Shut it,' whispers the Old Man.

The Russian platoon leader has trained his glasses straight on us.

The trapdoors of the other tanks clang open. A fat sergeant crawls, with difficulty, from the Landsverk.

'They've got away,' he shouts, annoyedly. 'They'll have cut the *Hromoj*'s throat by now!'

'Good luck to 'em then,' shouts a warrant officer from the leading BA-64.

Tiny nudges the commissar, who has again been gagged with a cap.

'Your bleedin' comrades don't seem to like you. Thats 'ow it goes with all wicked men! You get pissed on, an' you don't even know it!'

The commissar sends him a killing look.

The lieutenant lifts his arm and the motors stop. All four tank commanders jump down and saunter over to the deserted personnel lorries.

'The German dogs have poured petrol over them but haven't had time to set them on fire,' says the lieutenant and laughs aloud.

'Here's *Hromoj*'s cap,' shouts a corporal, holding up the commissar's green cap. 'Let's hope they manage to liquidate the bastard, before we get our hands on them!'

Tiny nudges the commissar again, and nods encouragingly.

'Real comrades o'yours, ain't they?'

The Old Man holds up a magnetic mine. The Legionnaire nods his understanding and sneaks over to the nearest tank. Porta and I are to take care of the two which arrived last. I am afraid of the Humber and Porta takes it. Heide crawls towards the Landsverk.

The Old Man disappears into the thick brambles with the rest of the section.

I am only two yards away from the rearmost BA-64. All the doors are wide open. As long as I get to it unseen there will be no problem in putting the mine through one of the open doors.

The Legionnaire is over by the tracks of his tank. In two jumps I get to mine and throw the charge through the trap.

The explosion is terrible. Blast throws me through the air and bangs me up against a large tree. A torn-off tank turret buries itself in the ground beside me.

Half a man is smeared across it. For a few seconds I lose consciousness.

Machine-guns chatter all around me. The section opens fire at the four amazed commanders standing by the trucks. They disappear in a sea of flame. It was a good idea of Porta's to soak the trucks in petrol.

'See,' says Tiny exultingly to the commissar, as we stand by the glowing wrecks. 'Our German God looks after *us* all right, don't 'e?'

'You'll never make it,' snarls the commissar, stubbornly. 'You've still got to cross the Pripjet Marshes!'

'We'll manage,' boasts Porta. 'We got our training with the special swamp trolls commando.'

'Idiot,' sneers the commissar. His Saxon dialect irritates us enormously.

Gregor advises him to learn proper German before he is dragged in front of a court-martial.

'All Saxons are traitors,' considers Heide, striking out at the commissar, who ducks the blow.

'Leave him be,' orders the Old Man. 'You can volunteer for the execution squad when the court-martial has sentenced him.

'And you call that justice?' jeers the commissar. 'Sentence a man before his case has even begun!'

'Yes, and that kind of justice we learnt from you Soviet pigs,' shouts Buffalo, making an easily-understood sign with his finger across his throat.

We slide down the steep slopes and cross the bottom of the ravine.

The Old Man chases us hard. He wants us as far away from the smashed armour as possible. He feels sure they have kept in continual radio contact with their parent unit.

We make camp when darkness falls, and sleep through the night and most of the next day. In the distance we can hear security units combing the woods.

The commissar listens, his eyes wide. He is like everyone else and clutches at the slightest hope. He will not accept the fact that we will kill him before we are captured, even though Tiny constantly lets him sniff at his long, pointed combat knife.

Everything superfluous is jettisoned so that we can move faster. The darkness is so thick that we can only see a few inches in front of us. The moss we walk on absorbs every sound. Where we are marching all is silence. Not even the call of a bird, nor the croak of a frog.

I am afraid of having lost the others and stop for a moment. Buffalo runs into me, and the machine-gun mounting.

'What the hell are you standin' here for, boy?' he whispers angrily, rubbing himself. 'Throw that goddam thing away!'

'The Old Man ordered me to bring it along,' I whisper back.

'He's a goddam sadist,' says Buffalo.

We move along silently over the thick moss. We feel as if we are walking on heavy rubber. Suddenly I run into the back of a man.

'*Mushyk sstarashyt borof*[22]!' he shouts, irritably.

Without a word I push my combat knife up into his back. He makes a rattling noise and collapses. I stab him again. He must not, above all, be allowed to alarm the other sentries who must be posted all about us.

'Ivan!' I whisper in horror to Gregor, who is just behind me.

There is no doubt that the Russian sentry thought I was a comrade stationed close by.

We lie, still as mice, beside the body. Warm blood runs across my hands. 'Alex, what's the matter?' comes a nervous voice from the darkness.

Gregor disappears in under the leaves. There is a short frightened cry. Then everything is quiet again.

Gregor has cut his throat.

'Filthy job,' he whispers, wiping the combat knife on his trousers. 'Must've had *hundreds* of gallons of blood in him!'

'Alex, Pjotr, keep your cursed mouths shut!' roars a hoarse voice from the brush. 'You know damn well those German swine are coming this way! When we've caught 'em you two stupid bastards can shout all you want!'

22. Yokel, look out, boar!

287

'Get him!' orders the Old Man.

Porta and the Legionnaire are swallowed up by the darkness.

Shortly after a horrified scream rings through the forest. Another one. It dies away in a long gurgle.

The section drops flat and holds its breath.

'Those two have sodded it up,' snarls the Old Man, viciously.

'Probably cut 'is prick off first,' Tiny grins, hollowly.

'He saw us before we could finish him,' explains Porta, emerging from the brush. 'Let's get moving! They'll have heard that howl back in Moscow!'

'People ought to learn 'ow to control themselves when they're bein' killed,' declares Tiny aloud.

'You'll never get through,' states the commissar, maliciously.

'If you don't keep your mouth shut, I'll personally tear the fucking tongue out of it,' says Porta, clenching his teeth.

'Get your fingers out and get going!' commands the Old Man. 'The whole forest must've been alarmed by that scream!'

We balance our way across a narrow bridge. Buffalo, of course, falls in with an enormous splash, and when Tiny goes to help him out *he* falls in too. The current in the river is very strong and we have a lot of trouble pulling them out again. Tiny gets away from us twice. He rushes at Buffalo when we finally haul him on to dry land.

'You did that on bleedin' purpose,' he roars in a voice that could be heard a mile away.

The Legionnaire has to put him out with a chop from the side of his hand. When Tiny is in that mood it is the only thing to do with him. Buffalo would be wise to keep his distance for some time. Tiny could easily get the idea of slipping a knife into his back.

At last we are over on the other side. The ground in the forest is easier to walk on. Suddenly a light flames in front of us. The Old Man stops as if he had run into a wall. The flame shows again and we catch a glimpse of a pale face under a Russian helmet.

There is a heavy thud and a faint groan. The Russian has been cured of the smoking habit for ever.

The section joins up again in a dip close to the road.

The Old Man is obviously excited. He keeps opening the lid

of his pipe and smacking it shut again, a habit he has when nervous.

'*Sergei, idisodar*[23]!' a guttural voice comes suddenly from the other side. 'Those German dogs aren't coming this way anyway!'

'Don't you be too sure,' comes from further down the road. 'Those grey-green chaps are devils! You can't be sure of anything with them. I wish the Holy Mother of Kazan'd give 'em all a dose of the plague!'

'Tin bleedin' soldiers! Bags o' shit tied up in the middle!' growls Tiny, contemptuously. 'Asleep on bleedin' duty, eh! Ought to be bleedin' court-martialled. Poor bleedin' Stalin, 'avin' to make do with shit like that!'

'Damnation!' The Old Man curses. 'If we go back they'll open up on us, and yet we can't stay *here*.' He strokes his chin thoughtfully. 'Let's go forward as if we were their own lot. We've got to surprise 'em and take 'em without noise.'

'There can't be many of them,' whispers Heide, 'or we'd've heard them.'

Heide is right. When soldiers sit waiting for something it is impossible to avoid a certain amount of noise. A couple of them whispering, weapons knocking against one another, somebody coughing. Ordinary people would not call these things noise, but they are more than enough to give warning to an experienced fighting group.

Cautiously we sneak across the road one at a time with Mpi's at the ready. An Mpi goes off close behind me. It is as if my head explodes. Porta is firing only a few inches from my ear.

A scream of horror cuts through the noise.

From the darkness Mpi's spit blue flame. The angry burst of firing lasts only a few minutes, then a paralysing silence sinks down on the forest. It is as if the night were listening at full stretch after the roar of the shots. We hear Tiny's powerful voice:

'All clear! Four 'eathens despatched onwards!'

Tango is dead. The first burst from the Mpi's tore his chest apart. It saved the Old Man, who was right behind him.

We stand for a moment in silence by his bloody form.

23. Come here!

289

'He's had his last tango, now,' says Porta, closing the corpse's eyes.

'An' 'e promised to learn me the tango. It's the best cunt dance there is, I've 'eard,' says Tiny, laying Tango's arms across his bullet-torn chest.

Heide empties Tango's pockets and removes his identity discs. Personal belongings go to the family. There is not much. Line soldiers are almost always poor: their only harvest the fruits of sorrow and death.

To the east, in the direction of Rozany, a flare goes up, colouring the sky a bloody red. It is so far away we cannot hear the noise of the burst.

Along the dirt road two half-tracks come rattling. Their searchlights are directed towards the edges of the road.

Silently we drop down and wait until they have passed us. We can see the infantrymen clearly, standing up with their guns at the ready.

'This kind of job makes me nervous,' sighs Porta, stuffing a handful of berries into his mouth. A picnic like this and you know what a wolf feels like with a party of humans with guns pissing up its backside!'

'Nerves can drive you round the bend,' explains Tiny, seriously. 'I 'ad it from a psychopath doctor I 'elped to execute at Torgau. 'E said it was somethin' called insulin an' diabetics as go flyin' up in a bloke's bonce when 'e gets frightened.'

'If that's right then we've all had diabetes for years without knowing it,' considers Gregor, 'I couldn't count the number of times I've been close to dying of fright.'

Late in the morning we reach the bend of the Horyn but we have to wait until it gets dark before we can risk making the crossing. The river is very broad. It takes us at least twenty minutes to row across, putting our backs into it.

The rubber boat is where we left it. We spread it out and make it ready for inflation. We lie down under the thick bushes and doze. In between we throw dice and consume a few tins of preserves.

Porta wants to brew up coffee but the Old Man forbids it. Time goes slowly when you have to lie around waiting for darkness. We dare not move about much for fear of hidden sentries along the river. The terrain looks bare and deserted but an entire battalion could hide in it. A commando behind the enemy lines cannot permit itself to become careless for a second.

Tiny lifts his head suddenly, listening.

'What's up?' asks the Old Man, uneasily, raising himself on to his elbows.

'There's a 'ole bleedin' flock of 'eathens comin' this way,' mumbles Tiny, staring down the road. 'At least a bleedin' company of 'em, an' comin' as if Jesus was whippin' 'em out o' the bleedin' Temple!'

'Are you sure?' asks Heide, doubtfully, taking a grip on the LMG.

'Course I'm bleedin' sure,' answers Tiny sullenly. 'Ever know me an' my bleedin' ears to be wrong?'

The rest of us can hear it now. A good-sized column is on its way, heading straight for us.

'Scatter!' orders the Old Man, sharply. 'Camouflage yourselves with leaves and boughs and nobody lets off a shot till I give the signal!'

We can hear the rattle of weapons clearly now. Water-bottles bang against gas-mask containers. The sounds which identify a column on the march.

Sweat pours down my face. My teeth chatter like castanets. We have no chance at all if they find us.

'Kamppanjija, pjenje!'[24]

Just opposite us they begin to sing:

Ty obiciala,
mene u wik lubyty,
ni s kim ne znatys,
y iosich curatys
Idla mene syty[25]

When the singing company has passed us, the Old Man

24. Company, sing!
25. You have promised me
Ever to love me;
Never to love another;
To turn from any other;
To live for me alone!

291

orders the Legionnaire to find out whether the sentries along the river bank have been strengthened.

Quickly he shrugs his greatcoat off, lays aside all weapons, pushes his combat knife into his boot and disappears silently into the reeds. The better part of two hours passes, and we have begun to wonder whether the Russians have caught him when he arrives back, breathlessly.

'Thirty yards down the bank there is a fool snoring away in a hole,' he tells us, spitting into the river. 'A little further along another one like him. Also snoring! I made a detour into the forest and almost fell over a third one, with an LMG. He deserved to have it stolen from him. He was snoring so hard you could hear him at a great distance. *Merde, alors*, I was so close to him that even a deaf Swede could have heard me!'

'*Soldiers*, they call 'em,' Tiny scolds contemptuously. 'Snorin' on bleedin' guard! They *deserve* to 'ave their bleedin' throats cut, they do!'

'Finish 'em off,' orders the Old Man.

Twenty minutes later the sentries are dead. Strangling-wires are quick and quiet!

Cautiously we push the boat out. The current is so strong that it carries us a good way down with it.

A hoarse shout comes from the opposite bank.

'*Stoi kto!*'[26]

An Mpi cracks sharply. The marksman shows up clearly against the sandy bank.

Porta kills him with a short burst. We are on our way out of the boat when shouts come from the bank we have left.

'*Germanski, idisodar!*' A dull thump sounds immediately afterwards, and a flare swishes up into the night sky. The river and both banks turn blood-red.

We take cover behind the boat until the flare goes out, but soon after a signal rocket spreads green and red stars across the heavens.

Further over behind the woods a whole series of flares go up.

'What the hell are they up to?' mumbles Porta, scared, gazing at the rain of light from a signal rocket.

We deflate the boat quickly and pack it up. We have to take

26. Halt immediately!

292

it with us to get over the Slutsch. Without a boat we could never make it.

The commissar tries to make a run for it, but Porta catches up with him and throws him to the ground. The noose is tightened again round his neck. We had loosened it a little, but here is proof again that one must never slacken one's watchfulness in battle.

'If I was him I'd sooner get knocked off here,' says Buffalo. 'When the SD get hold of him they'll boil him alive in his own goddam grease!'

'We've got our orders,' says the Old Man, shortly. 'And we're going to carry them out. Afterwards they can do what they like with him. He had no mercy on Oberleutnant Strick and the two others!'

We cross the Slutsch without trouble, and continue rapidly on through the forest after destroying the boat.

During the night we reach the edge of the marshes. The Old Man orders a message sent to Regimental HQ.

Heide makes the transmitter ready. The call signal gets through quickly. They expect us back in the course of the next twenty-four hours.

'They must have security guards out here, *bien sûr que si*,' says the Legionnaire, looking searchingly at the thick forest of reeds.

'No doubt about it,' answers the Old Man, curtly. 'Keep your distance, damn you! How many times do I have to tell you?'

Porta is in the lead as usual, together with the bear. Suddenly he lifts his hand, signalling us to stop.

Without a word the section drops to the marshy ground. Frogs croak deafeningly. Fish leap in the muddy-green water. In the distance a machine-gun chatters. We are getting closer to the front-line.

'*Stoi kto*, who goes there?' comes a harsh shout in front of us.

'Where the devil *is* he?' whispers Porta, holding on tightly to the bear, which shows its teeth, the fur on its neck lifting.

'Give the word! Who goes?!'

'Pal with the pox from Leningrad,' shouts Porta, merrily, in Russian.

'Password!' comes stubbornly from the heavy brush.

'I forget, mate, what about *Job tvojemadj*?' Porta laughs loudly.

'What's your unit, you bent twatt?'

'Tanks, lover,' shouts Porta so that it rings through the forest.

'Regiment?'

'87th Guards,' Porta laughs, unworriedly.

'Commander's name?'

'Colonel Bollockbrain,' Porta shouts back. 'He's never had the politeness, *dadja*, to introduce himself to *me*!'

'Get up you Leningrad miscarriage, you talk like a Finnish Fascist! Scratch at the fucking sky or I'll put one through you!'

Porta gets up, leaning his Mpi on the ground. To fire from where he is standing would be certain suicide.

'Quiet!' he whispers to Rasputin. 'Still! Down, down!'

The bear understands him and presses itself flat to the ground behind the stone.

'Come forward, you crazy bastard,' shouts the invisible sentry.

Porta goes two paces forward, slowly.

'Alexis, get your arse down here,' yells the sentry. 'Here's a twitt of a tankman from your regiment doesn't even know what his CO's name is. You must know him!'

Porta stays where he is with his hands above his head.

An Mpi chatters. Who fired the Old Man never finds out.

Porta drops, like lightning, where he stands.

'*Germanski, Germanski*,' come hysterical screams from all around us, and a storm of firing breaks loose.

The Legionnaire gives a shrill scream and goes down. His right shoulder has been ripped open. He is hit in the throat and blood spouts like a fountain.

It takes both my field dressing and his own to stop the blood.

Tiny and Buffalo storm forward like avalanches with their MGs at the hip.

A sentry, sitting in a hole, is killed by a kick in the face.

Rasputin thinks something has happened to Porta. With a hollow roar of rage he rolls forward on all fours and literally smashes a Russian sentry.

The forest is alive with Russians. We withdraw towards the marsh, shooting as fast as we can.

Night falls. Flares swish up, exploding with a heavy thump above the three-tops. The forest is as light as day.

I throw a hand-grenade past Porta who is lying in a cross-fire from two MG's. It goes straight into one of the nests and the gun whirls into the air. Ammunition explodes in one long rolling roar.

We rush forward. Rasputin is like a mad thing. His head and chest are covered in blood. He strikes and bites at mutilated bodies.

At last we are through.

We drag the Legionnaire after us on a ground sheet. He has lost so much blood that he can no longer stand. Most of the time he is unconscious. When he comes out of it he moans heartbreakingly. He thinks his arm has been torn off. It does not help to show him it is still there. But he is lucky. The explosive bullet hit his weapon. If it had hit the shoulder direct it would have taken his whole arm off.

Once inside the marshes we are able to rest for a while. A threatening silence presses down on us. We cannot understand where the Russians have got to but they cannot be far away. We hear nothing but the croaking of frogs.

'There must be *millions* of those boys,' says Porta, in an undertone.

'Noisy buggers,' mutters Gregor back.

A flare whistles up. Quickly we go down in the reeds and stay quiet as mice. The smallest movement can be seen in that glare. But the bear becomes nervous and stands up on its hind-legs.

An Mpi chatters. Rasputin roars wildly and falls forward.

Porta rushes forward, ignoring the bullets. The bear whines like a child. The whole side of its head has been blown away. Lovingly it licks Porta's face, rolls itself into a ball and dies.

Two more flares wobble up, but the noise dies slowly away.

'Ivan's going to pay for this,' hisses Porta. 'I'll cut the throat of every one of those godless bastards I meet from now on!'

None of us say anything. We understand him. The section

had come to love that bear. We pull it after us on a ground-sheet. It is heavy but we manage it. We will not suffer it to be left behind like so much battlefield rubbish.

Some way behind us harsh commands ring out, and auto-matic weapons crack. They are apparently keeping up their courage by shouting and firing off their weapons. It is stupid of them. All they are achieving is to let us know where they are.

'We *must* soon be at the path through the marshes,' says the Old Man, tired and discouraged.

'Hope we haven't passed it,' comes worriedly from Gregor.

Porta is completely cast down by the death of Rasputin. His usual flow of talk is cut off. He will not even answer questions. He keeps going over and running his hand lovingly over the bear's fur.

'We'll have to snap him out of it before he goes round the bend,' says the Old Man.

'Piece o' the other'd soon put *'im* right,' says Tiny, who never thinks of anything else.

At last we find the path through the marshes. It moves under our feet like a ship under weigh. You have to be careful here. Slip and fall into the marsh and you're finished. In a few seconds the green, bubbling ooze has closed over you. Forever!

'Cease fire! Close up!' a guttural voice comes from behind us. 'Those German swine can't have got far!'

Flares fly, like tiny comets, over the forest and marshes. A machine-gun hammers out a long burst close behind us.

The Legionnaire comes to himself and screams piercingly.

Gregor claps a hand over his mouth, but too late. They must have heard him.

'There! Forward! Take them alive!'

I screw the cap off a couple of grenades and examine my *Tokarew*. I shall need it for myself. None of us want to fall into the hands of the Russians alive. We know what to expect behind the lines in enemy uniform.

Tiny lifts the Legionnaire up on to his back. It's quicker than pulling him after us. We have to take care not to knock him against obstacles.

We double down the shaky path.

'They can only go through the marsh,' comes a shout from

our rear. 'Dobroschin Section, make a rifle chain! Forward march, you lazy sods!'

The Old Man lifts the signal pistol high above his head and fires off two flares immediately after one another. In the sky blaze six orange stars which can be seen miles away.

'Down!' he orders us. But already there is a rushing sound like that of a long goods train roaring through a tunnel.

An SMG barks viciously, but its rattle is drowned in the terrible explosion of the first shells. Forest and marsh are ploughed up in a wall of fire. Iron and earth roil upwards in front of us. Whole trees fly like javelins through the air.

The Old Man has sent up his signal exactly as planned. He is a master at that.

'For once in a while they were on the ball,' Gregor commends the artillery.

The section crawls on. We have to keep in front of the creeping barrage of shells if it is to help us get back.

'Soon be 'ome now, mate,' grins Tiny, wickedly, digging the commissar in the ribs with his Mpi. 'They'll cut your balls off! Adolf don't like bastards like you gettin' girls in the family way!'

'Adolf doesn't know what it's all about,' says Gregor, disrespectfully. 'His prick stopped growing when he was seven years old!'

'I 'ave 'eard as 'e tosses 'imself off while lookin' at dirty pictures a Party mate of 'is sends 'im from Scandinavia in Red Cross parcels,' shouts Tiny, joyfully.

'Shut it!' snarls the Old Man, sourly. 'We're not back yet!'

'Shoot me,' begs the Legionnaire. 'I cannot stand it any more!'

'You 'ave your 'ead examined, when we get back, mate,' says Tiny. 'You're goin' into 'ospital anyroad. They'll soon get you in a good 'umour again. When you're lyin' there 'avin' your arse powdered by them randy bleedin' BDM[27] 'ores in the white overalls.'

A battery of Stalin Organs spurts out rockets. It feels as if the very core of the world is exploding under us. An area of the forest is literally shaved clean.

The German artillery continues scattered firing over the

27. Bund deutscher Mädels: German Girls Association.

Russian positions to keep the infantry down in the trenches, and help us to cross the front. The Russians have the answer to that one. They let go not only with mortars and Stalin Organs but also with their heavy field artillery.

Thick sulphur fumes tear and eat at our throats and lungs. The stink of TNT makes us retch. We throw up. It is as if we were strangling in the pestilential stench of high-explosive.

A shell comes rushing and earth fountains upwards. Thousands of glowing scraps of steel whistle through the air.

I go head over heels down into a hot, steaming shell-hole. My throat burns, my nose feels like one running sore. It is as if all the demons of hell have been let loose at once and are trying to turn the earth inside out. Trees, earth, stone, huts are thrown upwards, fall, and are thrown upwards again.

Tiny grabs a leather water-bottle from a body as he rushes past on his way to find cover. In a shower of mud he slides to the bottom of the shell-hole. He sniffs suspiciously at the contents of the water-bottle.

'Ah! Extract o' Turkish 'ore piss!' he declares, knowledgeably. 'Still, anythin's better'n nothin'.' With a long belch he passes the bottle over. ' 'Eavens above, 'ow that did put a poker up the back o' me old patriotic pride,' he declares. 'There ain't no God but Germany an' Adolf is 'er prophet!'

'I've got that down,' shouts Heide, indignantly. 'The National Socialist gallows will tremble with pleasure when you swing on 'em!'

Red balls of light are going up along the whole of the front, sending out stars under the darkened sky. Shells are coming over in a close-knit, shielding barrage, like a wall of flame and steel rising from the earth. The world is exploding. Thousands of volcanoes are being born continuously.

Bending low we run forward, crash through the enemy defence blocks, throw hand-grenades behind us. Machine-guns chatter. A long row of trip-mines goes up. Then we are at the final stretch of marshes.

An umbrella of parachute-borne rockets sinks towards the ground, lighting up the night as if it were a clear summer day.

'*Idisodar charoscho, germanski*,'[28] comes from behind us.

28. Come here quickly, Germans.

They know the marshes and are right on our heels. This is the way they come when they are out picking up prisoners.

The Old Man stops, blowing hard, and holds his hand to his heart. He is nearly all in. But then he is also much older than the rest of us.

'Grenades! In their faces! Soon as – they show – their bloody faces – through the reeds . . .' he pants the order.

I throw the first grenade, but it explodes in the marsh and does no damage.

Porta drops down behind the bear's dead body. The MG-42 rattles wickedly. Short well-aimed bursts smash into the leading pursuers, throwing them out into the ooze.

I throw another grenade. It explodes in the midst of an enemy group.

Screams of anguish rend the air.

Porta sends a mowing burst at the soldiers huddled together in the reeds.

We retreat in short spurts. Run – turn and fire – run – turn and fire!

A shell-splinter has torn open the commissar's arm. Blood runs down over his hand. Nobody attends to him. It is not worthwhile. They will hang him anyway.

We ready ourselves for the last stretch.

I am half over the low earthwork when the Old Man gives a sharp shrill cry and slides back. Terrified, I dash over to him.

It looks bad. His back is one bloody wound. Shredded flesh, clothing, bones, leather and blood. He looks up at me with a faint smile on his lips.

I light a cigarette, and put it in his mouth.

Heide jumps down to us, tearing open a field dressing as he moves. Then Porta. We dress the wound as well as we can and carry him along between us. We hardly notice the concentrated infantry fire.

'I'll cut that bleedin' commissar bastard in strips, I will,' roars Tiny, raging. 'It's all 'is bleedin' fault, the dirty, rotten traitor!'

'Take him back alive,' groans the Old Man, painfully. 'Heide, you're responsible!'

The Old Man knows what he is doing. Heide is a slave to

regulations. He would let himself be shot to ribbons rather than not obey an order to the letter.

Suddenly there are familiar helmets and yellow-green camouflage dress around us. Hands reach up to help us down into the positions.

'Holy Mother of Kazan, we *made* it!' groans Porta, and lets himself drop to the floor of the trench.

Water-bottles are offered us. Lighted cigarettes pushed between cracked lips. Like lightning the word goes down the lines.

'They're back and they've got him with 'em!'

The regimental MO looks after the Old Man and the legionnaire personally. They are taken back, immediately. They are sent off so quickly we hardly have time to say goodbye to them.

Barcelona takes over the section, and No. 2 is satisfied with the choice. He can never replace the Old Man but he has the experience which is necessary for a good section-leader.

The commissar is taken straight back to Regimental HQ, where two SD officers await him impatiently. One of them, Sturmbannführer Walz, lets loose a cascade of foul language at him and strikes him in the face with his fist.

Oberst Hinka moves between them.

'*I* give the orders here, Sturmbannführer!' he says sharply, pushing the SD officer back.

'*Do* you?' snarls Walz. 'If I have not been misinformed about this case, the prisoner is a political commissar and a deserter from the Reichswehr[29]. In other words this is a political matter and of no particular military importance.'

'It could perhaps be looked at in that light,' comes hesitatingly from Hinka.

'Then we are in agreement?' smiles the Sturmbannführer, coldly. 'The prisoner is the responsibility of RSHA and I will accept that responsibility and return with him to Berlin.'

'My regrets! The prisoner stays here, until I receive a written order, with regard to his disposal, from my superiors.'

'I have such an order here, Herr Oberst, and I expect you to obey it,' shouts Walz, triumphantly.

'I accept only the orders of my Commanding General or of

29. German Army before Hitler.

300

the Commander of the 5th Panzer army,' states Oberst Hinka, brusquely.'

'Am I to understand then that you *refuse* to hand over this prisoner to us?' asks the SD officer threateningly and taking a step towards Hinka.

'You have understood me correctly, Sturmbannführer,' smiles Hinka, sitting down easily on the edge of the table.

'Do you realize, Herr Oberst, that this business can cost you dear?' snarls Walz, red as a turkey-cock in the face.

'I think you can leave that to me,' answers Hinka, lighting a cigar quietly.

The SD officer bites his lip. He has obviously great difficulty in controlling himself, but he knows that he cannot, for the moment, overrule Hinka.

He makes himself a quiet personal promise to look after this puffed-up *Wehrmacht* officer before too long. The day is not far distant when all power will be in the hands of the SS-Reichsführer.

'Will you permit me to question the prisoner?'

'No!'

'Do you realize what you are saying?' asks Walz, in amazement. 'Do you intend to sabotage the work of the Security Services?'

'When you bring me a properly signed order from the Commanding General I shall immediately place myself at your service!'

'You can be damned sure I shall bring you a properly signed order,' smiles the SD officer, dangerously, pulling his gloves on slowly. 'You'll hear from us, Herr Oberst, and it is not beyond the bounds of possibility that you will accompany your prisoner when he leaves! At present you can only be regarded as an officer who has attempted to obstruct the work of the Security Services.'

He jerks round at the prisoner, who is standing between two Military Police guards.

'We shall hang you twenty times over before you die! We shall make you beg for death!' He spits viciously in the commissar's face.

The next second the commissar's fist lands in the middle of

the SD officer's refined features. Blood spurts from a broken nose.

Three shots ring out one after the other. The commissar falls gurgling to the floor. A great pool of blood spreads from under his body.

For a moment there is wild confusion. The MP's have drawn their pistols but cannot decide who to shoot.

Oberst Hinka has remained seated, swinging one leg carelessly. The adjutant lights a cigarette and commences to blow smoke rings towards the ceiling.

'Lohse, you're the biggest idiot in *boots*,' screams Sturmbannführer Walz at his companion, 'why the *hell* did you have to shoot that Communist? What am I to tell Berlin?'

'Perhaps that SD Hauptsturmführer Lohse has liquidated a valuable prisoner!' smiles Oberst Hinka pleasantly, rearranging the empty arm of his uniform.

'This will have to go on report, Lohse,' screams Walz, raging. 'You have been with the SD a long time! You'll be allowed to shoot all right, I can assure you of that! But it'll be in the Dirlewanger Brigade[30] and you'll start at the *bottom*!'

They leave without saying goodbye.

An hour later the commissar is buried, a little way inside the forest. A board with his name is stuck into the ground.

30. Dirlewanger Brigade: Notorious SS Penal Brigade.

The people will always attempt to find the positive aspects of all circumstances, which, in themselves, are not susceptible to change.

Josef Stalin to Molotov, July, 1937

The transit prison of Osmita, which lies almost three miles outside the town of Chita, is stated to be the 'safest' prison in the world. It is, at any rate, the most sinister and ugliest, built of large dirty-grey ashlars. It is not a prison in the true sense, in which the prisoners serve out their sentences, but a caravanserai, for that enormous freightage of human beings which streams through here from all the prisons in Russia, on the way to Siberia.

At Osmita the prisoner meets, for the first time, the world's greatest hunter of men, the smiling little Siberian convoy soldier with the feared nagajka hanging over his shoulder. He is most often dressed in a grey greatcoat reaching down to his ankles, and a tall white cossack cap with a scarlet top and emblazoned on it a green cross. Despite his small size there is something terrifying about him. A Kalashnikov, with its round drum of bullets, hangs across his chest. By his side swings a cossack sabre in a black leather sheath. In front, on his stomach, is a black open holster from which the butt of a Nagan pistol projects. The pistol is attached to a white cord which goes through both shoulder straps and down over the chest.

When the prisoners arrive at Chita they are given into the custody of these small men with the green cross on their caps. It is a shocking experience for most of them. On the prison trains to Chita soldiers were only allowed to strike them on the orders of an officer, but the tiny men with the green cross are allowed to use the dreaded nagajka on their own responsibility. As soon as they have signed for the prisoners the nagajka begins to whistle through the air, spreading terror where it falls. Before the convoy has reached Osmita the weakest have been lashed to death.

What goes on inside the walls of the transit prison nobody really knows.

The prisoners are, however it is achieved, trained to an animal-like obedience. When they leave, three weeks later, transported off on hundreds of sleighs, all life has gone from their faces.

These small policemen-soldiers have become notorious, since the great Siberian desert has become the world's largest liquidation centre.

At least four million German prisoners of war passed through Chita, and were 'educated' at Osmita under the biting lash of the nagajka, before being sent to the mines along the Kolyma river in Siberia or to the camps which lie spread around Novaja Zemla. Only a very small percentage of them returned to Germany after the war.

WAS IT MURDER?

HAUPTFELDWEBEL BLATZ has ventured into the front line to check our ammunition consumption, which he thinks is too large. He is not, on the whole, satisfied with the state of discipline amongst the men in the line. He has complained to the NSFO who, to his horror, has ordered him to make an inspection of the trench commando.

The day Blatz arrives the front is completely quiet. He stumbles first over some of the lightly wounded who are lying down in a dugout.

'Bloody malingerers,' he roars. 'I'll make your arses that hot you could fry eggs on 'em! Outside, march, march, you sons of vultures!' He chases them through the trenches, makes them hop forward with bent knees and carbine at stretch, and crawl across the dangerous open stretch. Strangely there are no snipers on this particular morning.

'Where's all those Siberian snipers?' screams Blatz, triumphantly. 'Lies, that's what *they* are! Made-up, lying reports, but they don't fool *me*! You'll get to know me better! It's time we had a few courts going here!'

Blood seeps through the wounded men's bandages. When some section leaders complain, they are rebuked sharply.

'To me a wounded man is a man who can't move! Anything less is malingering! Blood, you say? They bled the sick in the old days. It was healthy. So it is today! Too much blood makes a man lazy!'

A little later he decides to inspect the forward MG-posts. He might be lucky enough to drop on a crime which carries the death penalty.

Finally he gets to the forward SMG. Even at a distance he can hear a thunderous snoring. He shakes with excitement, and rejoices at the thought of arresting the sleeping sentry.

Cautiously he crawls over the earthwork and rolls down into the narrow communicating trench. At the bottom of the trench lies the sentry rolled up in a ball like a wet dog. He is not only asleep but has had the effrontery to roll himself into a lambskin robe and place a little blue feather pillow under his head.

Hanging above the SMG is a sheet of cardboard on which, in large, ill-formed letters is written:

DEAR MISTER HAUPTFELDWEBEL,
      PLEASE PASS BY QUIETLY!
DO NOT DISTURB BEFORE
          13.00 HRS!
THANK YOU KINDLY SIR!
          YOUR OBDT. SERVT.
OBERGEFREITER WOLFGANG CREUTZFELDT.

Blatz does not know whether to shout or to cry. He chooses the former, every NCO's tried and true weapon when up a blind alley. Just keep on shouting long enough and *something* will occur to you.

Tiny opens one eye and places a finger to his lips.

'Ee! Stop that shoutin', man. Can't you see as 'ow I do be tryin' to get a little shuteye, like?'

'You are sleeping at your post!' roars Blatz in a voice which cracks several times from rage.

'*Course* I be sleepin'! What's wrong with *sleepin'* now?' Tiny smiles broadly.

'You admit to my face that you were asleep on sentry duty?'

'An' why shouldn't I be? I *were* sleepin'! An' I was 'avin' a lovely dream, I was. There the 'auptfeldwebel was, 'angin' out on the wire, like, an' we was all 'avin' a bang at 'im, with rifles, like. Everytime we got a bullseye 'ow you did 'op about, you did! Just like one o' they jumpin'-jacks as they make in Saxony! *You* know!'

'Sleeping at your post'll cost you your head, man!' shouts Blatz in triumph. 'Up on your feet! You're under arrest! We don't make a lot of fuss about pigs like you, Creutzfeldt, you're getting a summary when we get back to the company and two

306

of the three judges'll be me and the OC! You'll get shot, Creutzfeldt, *we* can guarantee you that!'

'Why do the 'auptfeldwebel keep sayin' "*we*". More'n one of you, like, perhaps? Got the crabs 'as the 'auptfeldwebel?'

'You wait, pig!' shouts Blatz, sure of himself.

'If the 'auptfeldwebel's tired of livin' any longer, I'd advise 'e keeps stickin' 'is 'ead up like that, now,' smiles Tiny. 'They Siberian snipers'd be 'appy to put a bullet in a 'ead like that. Minds me of a dog I once 'ad,' he says, reflectively.

'Up on your feet,' roars Blatz, beside himself. 'You are speaking to a superior! You're under arrest, man! If you attempt to escape, I shall use my weapon, and it will be a pleasure to do it to *you*!'

'You 'it your bleedin' 'ead on somethin' on the way out 'ere?' asks Tiny, suddenly dropping his country cousin act. 'You sound like a Norwegian bleedin' cod-fish as 'as got lost on the road to bleedin' Sweden. Arrest, summary, firin' squad, shot while escapin'. *All* suit *your* bleedin' book, wouldn't they? Listen 'ere you clapped-out excuse for a NCO! You come out 'ere to kick us bleedin' trench pigs in the arse an' think you can get away with it, do you? We know what *you* were 'fore you joined the club, son! Fuckin' shit-remover for a load o' bleedin' giraffes in the Berlin Zoo *you* were!'

'How'd you know—?' comes from Blatz in amazement.

'What the fuck's it to you? I know it an' that's enough, fatguts! An' another thing I know, too! You ain't goin' to ever *see* them giraffes ever again!'

Tiny's smile has become thin-lipped and dangerous.

'You're under arrest,' repeats Blatz nervously, fumbling at his holster.

'Get your fingers off that pea-shooter!' Tiny lifts his Mpi threateningly. 'Don't try it! There's explosives in this thing. 'Ow'd you *like* to get your bollocks pushed up in your bleedin' throat, Blatz?'

'You are threatening a superior? This is mutiny! Get up on your feet!'

Tiny gets up slowly and Blatz suddenly realizes how big he is.

'Suit you all right wouldn't it?' grins Tiny, wickedly. 'Court with you on it and your velvet-pricked Hauptmann as President! Death sentence! Bang! An' you'd like to tie me to the bleedin' post with your own 'ands, wouldn't you, you worn-out bag o' shit!'

'Yes, and bloody well *will*!' shrills Blatz. 'And I'll put the mercy bullet into your filthy body myself, too!'

'You're round the fuckin' bend,' Tiny laughs, noisily. 'Amok pig, that's what you are! Look now! There ain't nobody, not you nor nobody else in this man's bleedin' army, as is goin' to tie Obergefreiter Wolfgang Creutzfeldt to no bleedin' post, but *'e's* goin' to turn off you an' a few more little bags o' shit in uniform like you. You ain't arrested *me*, Blatz! I've arrested *you*! *Did* you know I was a secret Commie?'

'You're mad, man,' screams Blatz, with fear crawling up his spine. Is he face to face with a psychopathic murderer? Are those stories of murders committed in the field really true? No, no well-disciplined German soldier would do such a thing. 'Let me pass,' he screams, hysterically, trying to push Tiny to one side.

'What's your 'urry, mate?' smiles Tiny, coldly. 'Let's clear up a few points first. You arrested me, and that's been voted down. You wanted a court-martial, we'll 'ave that 'ere. Now we've 'ad it, an' I've 'ad to sorrowfully sentence you to death. So in five minutes from now you'll be flyin' away from the front all dressed up like one o' God's little bleedin' angels!'

'You are threatening an NCO and refusing to obey an order. I demand to be allowed to pass! I am your Hauptfeldwebel and your direct superior,' splutters Blatz, with panic fear in his eyes.

'Shut up, giraffe shit shoveller! You ain't nothin' but a babblin' bleedin' corpse! Come on! Be a man! It ain't the first time you've taken part in an execution. You said yourself you'd often been on the Morellenschlucht, but I suppose it ain't such a 'appy affair when it's your own execution you're takin' part in!'

'You wouldn't dare,' whines Blatz, terrorstricken and seeming to shrink into himself.

'*Listen*, giraffe afterbirth, *you* ain't left me a choice in the matter, 'ave you? *You* started all this. It was *you* started screamin' about bleedin' courts an' firin'-squads, an' all that war-mad bleedin' piss, an' all because I was 'avin' forty winks! I'm *against* the bleedin' death penalty!'

'Help, help, murder!' howls Blatz, desperately.

Tiny looks at him with cold interest.

'They know that voice of yours on both sides of the front. Think any bleeder's comin' to 'elp *you*? When you went over that parapet, mate, everybody knew where you was goin' to end up!'

'Then this is a plot!' screams Blatz, in despair.

' 'Ow you do talk, man. Porta says we're all sentenced to death from the second we're born. God decides it an' a big black angel with a flamin' great sword come to me while I was 'avin me snooze there an' said: " 'Auptfeldwebel Blatz's number 'as come *up*!" '

Blatz crawls sobbing along the muddy floor of the trench.

'Comrade Creutzfeldt, don't kill me!'

'Comrade Blatz I've bleedin' *got* to! Stand up an' be a good boy, now, so we can get it over with quick an' easy!'

'Comrade, let me live! I've two children at home!'

' 'Ave you 'ell, Comrade Blatz! You ain't even married. I *told* you we know all about you! You never fucked anything' but a female giraffe at the Berlin Zoo an' nothin' ever came o' that effort!'

'Comrade Creutzfeldt, don't make yourself a common murderer! I've always liked you! You're a *good* soldier!'

'Yes, an' I've appreciated it,' laughs Tiny, heartily, and pulls the shivering Blatz close up against him. 'To 'ell with all that shit! I'll see you get an 'ero's burial, so the Fatherland and all your family'll be proud of you!'

'It's murder,' cries the doomed man, struggling desperately. Tiny holds him firmly, and when they are right behind the SMG, Tiny butts him into unconsciousness.

' 'Ere's your papers comin' through!' growls Tiny to himself as he lifts the unconscious man's head up above the parapet. The Siberian snipers are back on the job and put four bullets into Blatz's fleshy face.

Soon the relief comes along.

'What's this?' asks Barcelona, astonished, pointing at the body. 'You haven't bloody well shot him?'

309

'Think I'm barmy?' answers Tiny. 'Why do the neighbour's boys out of a job? Members of the same union, ain't they?'

Heide sends Tiny a suspicious look, as he bends over the body.

'What you lookin' for?' asks Tiny, threateningly.

'Marks from the edge of a hand,' smiles Heide, poisonously.

'D'you know what 'appens to informers, Julius?' asks Tiny, playing with his *Kalashnikov*.

'I know,' answers Heide, looking at the four bullet holes with interest. 'I know what happens to murderers, too!'

'Me too,' smiles Tiny. ' 'Ad it in the family. Guillotine at Plötzensee! Snick, an' off goes your old turnip!'

'Four holes,' Heide thinks aloud. 'He must have been standing up there all day! I'd find a hell of a good explanation for that if I was you, Tiny. I know what happened without even being here!'

'What happened then?'

Heide picks up the body and lifts it slowly above the parapet. A shot smashes into the dead man's head. This time it is an explosive bullet which destroys the entire face.

He drops the body in shock, and wipes brains from his face.

Porta laughs like a hyena.

'You gave Tiny a bit more of a helping hand there than you meant to! The evidence is gone!'

Heide looks fearfully at the body's smashed features.

'You are my witness,' he shouts, in a rage. 'You all saw those four holes!'

'No, Julius, no!' grins Porta. 'He was still alive when you lifted him up! I'd watch it if I was you, Julius my son!'

'What a bunch of crooks,' snarls Heide, obviously nervous.

Tiny swings the body nonchalantly up on to one shoulder. At the dressing station he drops it at the feet of the orderly feldwebel who takes off the identity discs roughly and goes through the pockets for private effects.

'Throw that shit over with the rest,' he orders his assistants.

Tiny saunters, whistling happily, back to No. 2 Section's dugout, where he runs into Buffalo.

'Smart work, son! They're all talkin' about it. Can't prove anything, I hope?'

'Nobody can,' laughs Tiny, confidently. 'Not when you're from the Reeperbahn an' 'ave 'ad Chief Nass for a teacher!'

That afternoon Tiny is called to the OC's office, where a legal officer is also present.

'You were alone with Hauptfeldwebel Blatz in the SMG post? What happened?'

'The 'err 'auptfeldwebel swarmed all over me 'cause I was keepin' under cover up by the trench wall.'

'Was there firing?'

'No, sir, only if you was barmy enough to stick your nut up. That was why I was takin' cover, sir. I tried to explain that to the 'err 'auptfeldwebel. 'E didn't seem to believe me'n said I was a cowardly bastard as was scared o' the *untermensch*. 'E said I was to come to attention an' I did. An order's an order, sir!'

'And you were not hit?' the legal officer looks at him doubtfully.

'No, sir! I stood to attention with me knees bent you see, sir. The 'err 'auptfeldwebel wouldn't believe there *was* any snipers like I was tellin' 'im, sir, an' wants to see 'em for 'imself. I pointed out to 'im where the slit-eyed devils usually sit with their pea-shooters an', well, the 'err 'auptfeldwebel stuck 'is 'ead up to 'ave a look at 'em. If 'e saw 'em or not we'll never know, will we, sir? Anyway suddenly there's a bang and the 'err 'auptfeldwebel's face is gone, sir!'

'You didn't hold him above the parapet, did you?' asks the legal officer, threateningly.

'*Sir*!' says Tiny, deeply offended.

'Well now! You and Hauptfeldwebel Blatz were not exactly good friends, were you? At least from what I have heard.'

' 'Ad the 'auptfeldwebel somethin' against me?' asks Tiny, wonderingly. 'I liked 'im. We often cracked a joke together.'

The legal officer shrugs his shoulders, shakes his head resignedly, and looks uncertainly at Hauptmann von Pader.

'Be off! God help you if I ever get evidence against you.'

When Tiny has gone van Pader bangs his fist down on the table.

'Everything tells me it is murder! Can't we get any evi-

311

dence? It will be the happiest day of my life, the day I see that horrible man tied to an execution post in front of a firing squad.'

'Murderers are beheaded,' said the legal officer, coldly.

'Still better,' shouts von Pader. 'I'd have the pleasure of being a witness.'

'Herr Hauptmann, in the first place we *have* no murderers . . .'

'Obergefreiter Creutzfeldt is a murderer,' screams von Pader, with a wild glint in his eyes.

'No more than you or I. It is wishful thinking on your part. There is no proof. Quite the opposite. I believe Creutzfeldt is telling the truth. Hauptfeldwebel Blatz *would* have acted in just that foolish way.'

Von Pader pours cognac and empties two glasses quickly. He does not notice that the legal officer has not touched his.

'My friend,' says von Pader, confidentially, bending forward across the table. 'I have connections in Berlin. Would you like to come to serve with me in Berlin soon? I have merely to inspect the front when there is a little action. I have then had front-line experience and can leave.'

'I don't know quite what you mean, Herr Hauptmann?'

'Could not you and I together produce evidence of murder?'

The legal officer gets up quickly and puts on his greatcoat.

'Herr von Pader, I think you are the most infamous swine I have ever met! I am ashamed to wear the same uniform as you. For your information, every word of this conversation will be reported to Oberst Hinka. I believe you will have need of your connections in Berlin!'

'You have no witnesses,' shouts von Pader, red as a turkey in the face.

'We shall see whom Oberst Hinka believes. You have not gained friends in your time with the 27th Panzer Regiment!'

The legal officer slams the door with force enough to make the white-wash flake down from the ceiling.

Hauptmann von Pader jumps into his Kübel and races to Signals at Kowel, where he puts through an express call to Bendlerstrasse.

His friend, SS-Brigadeführer Ahlendorf, chief of SD Inland,

promises him an immediate recall to Berlin and a posting to the SS.

On top of the world, von Pader returns to his company, and decides to have a look at the front line for the last time. Who knows? Maybe he just might get the chance to settle matters with Creutzfeldt.

'Where to, sir?' asks his driver, Obergefreiter Bluhme.

'To the front!'

'*Where?*' jerks Bluhme in astonishment. He can hardly believe his own ears.

'Got dirt in your ears, man? I said the front!'

'No sweat for me, sir,' grins Bluhme, and starts off at a speed which makes it seem as if he cannot get von Pader out there quickly enough.

'Keep your stupid remarks to yourself!'

There is a general stir along the trench when we discover von Pader has come out to us.

Cockily he struts down the connecting trench, inspects the advanced posts, observes through the periscope.

This then was the bulwark holding back the Mongol wave. Suddenly he feels himself to be a bigger man. He straightens his new steel helmet.

'Where is the enemy?' he asks Barcelona.

'300 yards that way, sir,' grins Barcelona.

'Keeping well out of sight, the cowardly pigs. *Untermensch*, that's what they are.'

'Don't suppose they're tired of life yet, sir,' smiles Barcelona. 'If the Herr Hauptmann was to stand over on the other side and look through *their* periscopes, he wouldn't see anything over here either. 'Less it was some damn fool like Hauptfeldwebel Blatz.'

'Keep your mouth shut,' snarls von Pader, viciously. He feels his heart beating strongly in his chest. Here he stands. An officer in the army of the Führer. A German crusader fighting the heathen hordes of Asia. Softly he hums 'Wacht am Rhein'.

Barcelona observes him wonderingly. They continue on through the communicating trench where von Pader stumbles on Tiny, who is sitting in the bottom of the trench with a bucket of hot potatoes in front of him.

313

'You've lived most of your life, Creutzfeldt,' von Pader makes a demonstrative gesture, one finger cutting across his throat.

'The 'err 'auptmann can tell fortunes, maybe, then?' Tiny clicks his heels in the sitting position.

Suddenly the hammering of a gong fills the trench with sound.

'Alarm! Panzer alarm!'

'What's going on?' von Pader asks nervously, looking at Tiny, who continues to stuff potatoes into his mouth.

'It's the yellow monkey's comin' with some bleedin' armour, I reckon,' answers Tiny, carelessly, offering von Pader a hot potato. Angrily he knocks it to one side.

Tiny gets up slowly and takes the cover from his SMG. In a moment the trench is full of men.

The air shakes to the threatening rumble of motors. A wall of fire rises up some way behind the positions. A barrage. Shells howl and thunder. But this is nothing special to the veterans of the front line. An ordinary drum-fire barrage such as the Russians usually set up before a local armoured attack. To Hauptmann von Pader it seems as if the gates of hell have opened wide. Teeth chattering, he throws himself down by the side of Porta and Tiny, who regard him with pleasure.

'Now 'e's shittin' 'imself again, the bleedin' peacock,' says Tiny exultantly.

Von Pader grips his steel helmet desperately.

' 'E's holding on to his tin hat and look at him shaking like a jelly,' laughs Porta.

A series of mortar bombs drop, showering earth over them.

Von Pader gives a scream of terror, convinced that his last moment has come. He does not realize that this is only the beginning. He has always known that many people die in war. It was a way of dying he has always regarded as something fine and noble and not particularly painful. That wonderful hero's death which he has so often described to officer cadets. What is happening here is quite different. There is nothing beautiful here. Mud! Screaming splinters of steel! Remains of bodies! Torn-off arms and legs! His mouth fills with bile. It runs down his nose and over his chin. His trousers are full long ago. The beautiful mouse-grey tailor-made riding breeches,

314

Blast throws him a little way down the trench. Porta drags him back and pushes him down in the SMG pit.

'Jesus, how he pongs,' he says, holding his nose delicately. 'That's how it goes with all these dressed-up dummies. They come walking tall, and they crawl off the size of a louse!'

'Don't leave me in the lurch, comrades,' sobs von Pader.

'We'll drop you in front of the T-34's when they get 'ere,' promises Tiny.

'Comrades, we are comrades!'

'Sure, sure, Comrade Herbert,' smiles Porta, 'don't forget it now when the noise stops, will you?'

Von Pader cries and screams his misery into the thunder of the shelling.

The SMG chatters at the khaki attack wave, which is approaching slowly with hoarse shouts.

'*Uhræh Stalino! Uhræh Stalino!*'

'Come on up and take a look,' suggests Porta, nudging the sobbing Hauptmann with his foot. 'The neighbours are coming to visit us! It's you they want to have a word with!'

But the Führer's brave officer stays down in the mud of the trench bottom begging two lousy trench pigs to help him.

A new khaki wave of Russians storms across the barbed wire. Spades and bayonets sparkle. Hand-grenades fly through the air. T-34's rock forward like a herd of wild buffalo over the deep shell furrows. With a deafening thump the heavy vehicles land in front of the wire.

They stop to fire. A blinding flash and shells blast field-grey figures to tatters.

The *Panzerfausts*[1] bark wickedly. Steel giants splinter. Turrets whirl into the air, together with torn human bodies.

The darkness grows thicker. Suddenly the whole scene is bathed in a blinding white sea of light. The T-34's have turned on their searchlights. Something only the Russians do. It has a sinister psychological effect.

Machine-guns bark. Soldiers in field-grey are knocked backwards, mashed under the broad tracks of the tanks.

'*Servus*, 'err 'auptmann,' grins Tiny, whipping the SMG from its mounting.

1. Panzerfaust: Bazooka.

315

Porta throws a couple of hand-grenades, salutes his company commander nonchalantly and follows Tiny over the lip of the trench.

'Don't go! Don't leave me, comrades!' screams the Führer's officer, who for five years has preached the honour and glory of dying for Führer and Fatherland. He gets up and stares towards the roaring monsters of steel which are coming, rocking and bouncing, towards him.

Searchlight beams pick him up.

'Comrades, help me! I don't want to die!'

A searchlight beam transfixes him. He presses his hands to his ears, screams madly.

A tank turrent turns slowly. A shell explodes and covers the terrified officer with earth. He scratches and claws his way out, and crawls, howling like a wounded animal, across the battlefield.

A T-34 comes roaring at full speed but passes close to him. without crushing him.

He gets to his feet and runs forward through the blinding light of the searchlights with both hands pressed to his ears. He has lost his helmet. The noise is terrible. Wherever he turns there is nothing but T-34's shells bursting, machine-guns chattering.

He jumps down into a trench, runs screaming through the communicating trenches without knowing where he is going. He does not see a T-34 which comes flying over an earthwork and lands with a crash a few yards behind him.

The next moment he is on the ground. The broad tracks catch him, whirl him round and round, crushing his legs and arms. He no longer calls on the Führer or any of the people and things he has idolized. He screams, sobbingly, for his mother, whose tears, when he joined the Army, he scoffed at.

The T-34's roll the German front-line up, and return in the course of the night to their bases. The sun comes up and colours the sky red above a quiet front.

No. 2 Section sits enjoying the weak rays of the autumn sun. Soon it will be winter, the terrible winter of Russia.

Porta deals out the cards. We are playing nap. Every now and then we take a look through the periscope. There are more bodies out there today. There are some who are not quite dead yet, but we cannot go out to bring them in. The Siberian snipers see to that.

Just in front of the SMG post is a blood-drenched heap. A silver shoulder strap with two gold stars gleams from the greyish-red mass. This is all that is left of the Führer's proud officer, Hauptmann von Pader.

THE END